WARRIORS OF THE HEART

*The Journey of Shell and Heart
Saga One*

Maurice Grant

Raider Publishing International

New York   London   Cape Town

© 2009 Maurice Grant

All rights reserved. No part of this book may be reproduced stored in a retrieval system or transmitted in any form by any means with out the prior written permission of the publisher, except by a reviewer who may quote brief passages in a review to be printed in a newspaper, magazine or journal.

Second Printing

The views, content and descriptions in this book do not represent the views of Raider Publishing International. Some of the content may be offensive to some readers and they are to be advised. Objections to the content in this book should be directed towards the author and owner of the intellectual property rights as registered with their local government.

All characters portrayed in this book are fictitious and any resemblance to persons living or dead is purely coincidental.

Cover images courtesy of istockphoto.com

ISBN: 978-1935383901

Published By Raider Publishing International
www.RaiderPublishing.com
New York London Cape Town
Printed in the United States of America and the United Kingdom

For my father Grantlet, who gave me the freedom to explore and have many adventures.

Introduction

The following documents were collected and put together as part of a manuscript titled the Prophesy of the Empty Beat, written by the well-known spiritual Nodrog Niarlum. Only ten pages have ever been found.

The time will come when man will lose control of the earth, new and old creatures will come to take what will be left of the rock floating through the vast endlessness of space. Mystical creatures that man only thought existed in fairy tales will come back from lands long forgotten to become involved in mans affairs once again. Look out for those whose skins are grey for the White eyed cannot be trusted.
PAGE 44 FROM THE SECRET SCROLL OF MICHEL DE NOSTRADAMUS

October 29th 1950, the Greys proclaim they come in peace. We have allowed them to reclaim two of the bodies that had died in a crash in Roswell New Mexico 1947. They have offered to trade technology with us for large quantities of water. It has been decided that first contact must be kept from the public for their own safety. I have now become a full member of Majestic.
PAGE 3 OF THE PRIVATE JOURNALS OF F.B.I. AGENT
RONALD J HOWELL.

January 22nd 2005
  I am 73 years of age and the last original member of Majestic. First Contact has been kept from the public for over 50 years while the deal between governments and the Greys have become deeper and deeper, technology for man had become quick and fast, we began to learn more about nuclear

i

power and weaponry. Microwaves and propaganda digital tell-lie-visions and other technology are sold to the public to keep their minds away from the alien contact that we are receiving.

I was part of the team of special agents that were sent from the FBI to communicate with the aliens and cover up any discovery that may have leaked out into the public. Everything we did, and everything we learned about the Greys was written down in secret documents. The whole affair became a top secret project known as Project Blue Book and the agents involved became known as the Majestic Twelve. As years went by the aliens no longer wanted water or animals such as Cows and Monkeys, they had demanded a new deal or no more technology would be passed on, they had threaten to pull out the Greys they had working with our men at a top secret military research centre called Area 51 in the Nevada desert. They had told government officials that their species were dying and they wanted to find a way of combining their DNA with human DNA in order to preserve their life. So, in fear of losing our technology, in 1969 a deal was made allowing the Greys to abduct humans. A document was drawn up stating the agreement and the rules the Aliens must abide by during these abductions. The first four laws stated this:

1: Alien contact with human life other than that of government agents or leaders already involved in alien projects. Must first of all be covered up by any means necessary.

2: It is the responsibility of Alien agents to erase any memory of events that took place between Alien life and any abductee.

3: Under no circumstances must any human life be lost, taken, or injured by any alien life form.

4: A List naming all the Abducted must be written and given to agents involved with Project Blue Book.

The last one read:

34: Alien life must abide by these rules; if any one or more rules are broken it will be received as an act of war. And any technology/ element or live tissue trade between The U.S Government and other Governments Involved will cease.

Now after thirty-six years it is believed that this deal is not *being kept and an investigation is being issued. I hope in the event of my death that this journal will become public for it is time the people should know.*

MAJOR PAUL MARTIN FITZGERALD, RETIRED HEAD OF ALIEN TECHNOLOGY AND RESEARCH. LAST ENTRY IN HIS PERSONAL JOURNALS BEFORE DISAPPEARING WITHOUT A TRACE ON JANUARY 23RD 2005.

WARRIORS OF THE HEART

*The Journey of Shell and Heart
Saga One*

Maurice Grant

Prologue

It had been discovered that for many years the Greys had only been giving a partial list of abductees to the world governments. Human bodies were found dissected and drained of blood, new agents from Project Blue Book received letters from C.S.I offices all over, America stating that:

The Instruments used to cut and drain these bodies are unknown to any technology C.S.I Headquarters has seen before. We have sent our report to 10 top scientific research centres and all have come up with the same conclusion—that the technology used is of an unknown origin.

People were also becoming aware of their ordeals during their abductions and publicly announcing them. The FBI tried at every turn to make these people look unstable to the public. Many of the abducted were implanted with foreign objects believed to be a location device, and these were also being discovered. Not just a few, but many. People became aware of their abductions. Although it was covered up or ridiculed by the people involved with Project Blue Book, the new majestic twelve became aware that the Greys' motives were not good. Their investigation revealed that the Greys were making human replacements through cloning and accelerated growth processes in a plan to expand their population and to dominate the earth.

In 2010 the president of the United States of America and presidents from many other countries made a speech that shocked the world. Telling the public of world government involvement with the Greys, and calling every man, women and child to take up arms to fight against them.

The war began, with many human lives being lost. But the aliens had disturbed hidden places, belonging to the hidden creatures of the earth. Elves came out from hiding, and made a union with man for the first time in 1000 years; dwarves came to join the cause— eager to fight for justice, and so earth forces became strong. Great battles were won and lost; Over America flew the US Air Force, while in England the British Air force flew beside dragons to fight against the Greys and their flying ships. On the ground, beside Elves and Dwarves with machine guns, fought man.

Elves used arrows that flew like bullets; and magic that caused tornadoes— that ripped through the Grey's androids and Orcus armies that seemed to be produce by the thousands. In the sea, submarines and battleships fought beside magical and powerful Mermaids. They fought Krakens and Leviathans who had joined with Alien forces. Earth fought hard but the war was at equal balance— neither side giving length or quarter, there were many losses on both sides until the death of the Elfin king.

King Liththor was murdered in his bedchamber during the battle of Laguna. It was said that while they fought back the thousands of humanoid drones that had passed over the boarders of Italy into Switzerland, the king was hit by a laser shot to his shoulder, a minor wound for an Elfin king but his men insisted he went back up into the mountains to heal and rest. Whilst his men fought bravely beside humans and dwarves to gain their place in history as the victors of the greatest battle known to man, Elves or any creature from this planet, King Liththor was being stabbed seventy times in his back by an assassin that had somehow sneaked past a hundred Elfin guards.

Maxius Millidor, the nephew of Liththor was heir to the throne and became king and ruler of his people. He believed the war had gone on far too long and for his people's sake he tipped the balance of the war by making a treaty with the Greys so in the event of winning the war he would govern the earth. The Elves had switched sides and the effects were devastating. The Greys brought mankind to their knees and entered the Elves onto the path of darkness.

The legendary Elves over time had become evil, and were one of the most powerful forces on the earth. Mermaids fought continuous wars against the Krakens and Leviathans to gain domination over the sea and the clean waters. Dwarves had retreated underground to caves unknown to any manling in order to hide from their mystical cousins the Elves who had vowed to destroy the entire Dwarf nation. But the most powerful force that governed the whole of the earth was, those that came from above, orbiting the earth for the past hundred and forty years in a ship the size of earth's moon. Those that fought a war with its occupiers for over fifty years taking away what power man once had, annihilating over half mans population leaving them to live as peasants. Rebellions had started against the Greys but all of them are believed to have been crushed. The Greys mined the earth for what riches it had left and mermaids protected its waters. For men technology had become scarce, while the Greys ruled, the Elves became their law enforcement using ancient mystic magic to keep power over those that refused to abide by their law.

Although Fairies had never officially taken part in the war, a few individuals went at it alone and left the forest and wandered the earth helping man. But the Greys or the Elves never bothered the fairy places or could not, and Fairies were hardly ever seen. Dragons were thought of extinct because for the past 50 years none had been seen or reported. The year is now 2210 AD and my name is Nodrog and this is the true story of the bravest men I know.

> INTRODUCTION TO THE *CHRONICLES OF XELA SIRROM*,
> PROPHECY OF THE EMPTY BEAT,
> NODROG NIARLUM,
> 2210 AD

1
The Dwarf

It was Monday morning, and the heat outside was unbearable. Though Katie never minded the heat, it was still too hot for nearly every human being that would venture outside that day.

Katie's mother had told her to stay in the Shallows; the sheltered community building built into the cliff side where almost everyone lived and those that did not retreated to when the weather became too hot. It was cooler in the shallows, not just because it was dark and no natural sunlight could penetrate beyond its great doors, but because it was the only place the villagers had air-conditioning.

Air-conditioning was a rare thing to find in any human colony, but within the village lived a technician who had been trained by his father in the old ways and knew more than anyone about technology and other things from the old times, It was this technician the young girl planed to sneak out to meet, she enjoyed spending time with Navi because he told her stories and adventures from the past, he also taught her about cars and the way they once worked.

Navi would fill her mind with information about human made air machines similar to the flying machines that the Greys flew through the skies in, and how men once flew them and fought great air battles against them.

Such talk was outlawed and punishable by death, but Navi was not afraid to speak his mind— and their conversations were secret, conversations that would never be repeated to anyone.

Navi had taught her about air conditioning and how electricity could be created and harness for mans personal use. The whole thing was fascinating and made her eager to learn more about technology.

Navi had no children of his own so Katie consider herself his apprentice, although he would never say such a thing. Half the time he pretended he did not like her much but she knew he did. Sneaking out of her room that day and heading for the front door of their living space Katie knew her mother was in the cooking room. She moved ever so quietly and as she reached the cooking room, the door was half opened and she could see her mother cooking what smelt like some kind of fish. Her mother was humming a beautiful tune to herself; it was from a song she had sung to her when she was a little younger.

Her mother had told her that it was a fairy song and not many people could understand it, this always made Katie feel special because she understood it clearly. She could not help but admire how pretty her mother was still after so much time. Lydia was one of the most beautiful women in the village, some people had said that she had aged very little compared to the rest of the people that she had grown up with, and though her mother Lydia had reached her fifties she looked no older than a women of thirty five, her age only reflected in her crystal blue eyes and her words of wisdom.

Katie stood listening to her mothers' song admiring her slim figure and graceful movements as she danced to the rhythm of her own tune. Her long light brown hair floated from one side of her neck and around her back to her bottom. Katie pulled her shoulder length brown hair over her own shoulder turning her head to look at it. "I wish my hair would get that long." Letting the thought run through her mind she continued towards the front door.

Katie stepped into the hallways of the shallows closing the door to her home behind her. The hallways were dark and every few yards a dim lantern would be alight so people could find their way. The walls of the shallows were made from tin but there was never a shine to it as it was always very dirty. The tin came from trading with neighbouring villages. Navi was the leader of the trading party because he always knew the best things to trade for and it was another hope of Katie's that one day she would be picked to go and visit other villages.

She walked noiselessly down the hall wearing no shoes, as she often did; "One day you'll cut your feet" she heard her mother's voice in her head. Right and left and left again she turned before she came to the star ways, the star ways were a cross road of hallways that went in five different directions, but only two paths lead to an exit, there were no signs or clues to which path lead where so if you did not know the shallows it would be very easy to get lost in the vast maze of hallways that lead deeper and deeper into the cliff side and down into the earth. It was made this way so intruders would find it hard to find the centre hall where all the villagers' food and water supply are stored for the burning month which was due to begin within two to three days.

Katie like most of the villagers had explored every path of the shallows but one, and had found herself lost a total of seven times, once she was lost for a whole day before her mother came and found her, but now she knew the place so well there was no chance of her ever getting lost again. As she walked she began to wonder about the path she had not explored, the path that was restricted to everyone except the members of the council and of course Navi.

"Maybe I could get Navi to take me there" She mumbled to herself wondering if he really would.

"Allo Lass." Katie squeaked a little in fright, during her wondering she never heard or noticed the Captain coming towards her.

"Oh it you Captain" she said with a sigh of relief.

"Yes it be me, and what might a young good looking lass like you be doin sneaking around the shallows." said the captain.

The Captain and his crew were the only men permitted to sail the seas beyond Neptune's point to fish and to travel to faraway lands, they were the only men the maids would talk to and trade with. Navi had told Katie many tales of the Captains adventures and even claimed to be part of one of them.

"I'm not sneaking around, I am just going to the gathering hall to see if any of the girls want to play hide and seek." Katie replied.

"Well then be making sure you don't be wandering off outside, it be too hot out there for a young pretty thing like you, you'll be passing out before you know it."

"No way Captain I would never go out in that heat besides mother has already forbidden me, and you know how I love to obey." She said with a hint of sarcasm.

"Good good, I must be off then so run along, and don't be bothering none of us grown folks, I will be hearing if you do, and be sure I'll be straight telling your mother."

"I won't bye Captain." She said as she continued down the hallway.

Katie had no intention of even stopping at the Gathering hall for two reasons. One it was a place where everyone gathered to watch old movies on the big screen, movies that had been seen by all the villagers at least twenty times each, and it was due time that Navi and his trading party brought back some new ones that no one in the village had seen.

Katie had few little friends in the village, and she never really liked the kids that met at the Gathering hall. Nasty, spoiled little brats was all that came to mind when she thought of them. Katie seemed more concerned with other things than how she should wear her hair or what kind of dress she should get her mother to make so she could impress the teenage boys that ran around the village playing soldiers of old, because that was what most of the girls in the village were interested in, it was like they could not see beyond their own village.

She just wanted to get out, see more of what was left of the world, maybe visit a fairy forest if they truly really did exist. There were so many places she had heard about that she wanted to see with her own eyes, she had asked her mother once if they could journey to the great silver city London when Navi's party next decided to go.

"Oh no dear it is much too dangerous, there are bandits, some men some not, and creatures out there that would destroy you in an instant, the journey to the city London is a dangerous one and I have heard that the people and creatures that live there are not too friendly to strangers. Maybe we could get the Captain to take you along the coast in his Gunship."

Katie knew her mother was just trying to protect her but a boat ride along the coast "oh please." She said aloud, if her mother thought a boat trip would be enough adventure for her she was seriously wrong, she had plans to leave the village one day when she was old enough to take care of herself.

She noticed that the hallway had become brighter; this meant that she was nearing the great door and further more that it had been left open. On reaching the door she found Billy, the young lad who had just reached his nineteenth birthday and had been given commission to guard the door that day as a reward to reaching manhood. He was asleep in the guard chair, with his shirt off exposing his thin gangly body. Katie paused for a moment and looked at Billy snoring his head off with his hat pulled over his face and his long blond hair flowing over his shoulders.

"He should really cut his hair; someone might mistake him as a girl." She thought as she giggled to herself tip toeing past him and out of the door.

As soon as Katie stepped out into the burning sunlight she felt the very warm almost hot sand between her toes, she squinted her hazel brown eyes for a moment giving them time to adjust to the brightness of the outside world. The heat outside was lovely to Katie, in fact she found it strange that most people would pass out or die from this heat, because it never effected her, she had snuck out many times in a so called heat wave and not once had she been effected, it made her wonder if burning month was really as hot as she had been told, but she was too smart to ever risk her life to find out.

Katie gazed out at the wide wonderful ocean and admired the small fishing boats tied to the pier; she turned right at the great door and headed down the sand hill to her village by the sea.

Vladlin moved quietly through the bushes, he had been tracking a stag for two days now and the hunt for the animal had become personal, twice now it had been within his reach and twice it had escaped his arrows. He was beginning to think he was losing his wits, never before had it been so hard to kill his prey, but this Stag was different, it was smarter than most animal, it had sensed his presence whenever he had come close and bolted.

"It is strange." He thought to himself, "This deer should have been exhausted by now."

It seemed to run relentlessly with no rest and now it was Vladlin that had become tired, but he pushed on and made himself go that little bit further than most would or could. He felt that he could not return without a good catch being the master hunter for his people as it was expected of him to return with the biggest and best prey, and this stag would be the best catch to offer his king and council at the return celebration. Deer was a rare find even in the Thetford's the only forest left known to dwarves or man in the whole of England, but now he knew his time was growing short for he only had two days left to meet with the rest of his hunting party.

"This will be my last chance." He thought.

He knew if the stag outsmarted him this time, he would have no choice but to return empty handed. He continued to move silently through the bushes until he was at the edge of a clearing, and there it was resting in front of a big rock.

"At last he is tired," he thought.

He slowly began to draw an arrow, from his quiver that he wore around his back. The stag's ears perked up as if it was scanning for unusual sounds, Vlad paused.

"Surly he did not hear that, his ears couldn't be that sharp could it?" his mind was questioning the abilities the creature seem to possess.

The stag lifted his head and began to sniff the air Vlad froze and did not move an inch, the deer's head turned to his direction and stared. Vlad stared back wondering if he really could see him hiding away in the bushes, and as if in answer to his question before Vlad could hardly believe it the stag was on his feet running, but not running away but straight towards him in a mad frenzy in what seemed like the deer's final last stand. Quickly Vlad drew his arrow and placed it in his bow, but his shock and moment's hesitation at the animals speed to run him down had been his downfall.

Before he could draw the hair on his bow the stag was upon him catching him full with his antlers throwing his small dwarf body high into the air, his back slammed into a tree and then he landed in a bush. Vlad was hurt but he was a Dwarf and dwarves were strong and this battle was far from over.

He forced himself to his feet and stumbled from the bush, just then the stag came charging at him again, he looked around for his bow but could not see it, he turned and began to run back towards the trees, but just before he reached the trees the stag had dipped his head hitting him from behind and tossing him over its back. Vlad's backpack became caught in the deer's antlers and he could not get free. The deer tossed him around with his antlers like a dwarf on a string. Vlad started to lose hope as he could feel the life draining from his body, he knew while he was attached to his pack he would surly die, he then remembered the knife in his boot and by reaching for his leg he found the hunting knife, using it to cut one of the leather bands that held him to his pack.

Vlad immediately became free and fell to the ground, the stag turned about and came at him again ready for its next assault, as the animal approached once more, Vlad rolled across the ground avoiding being hit by the deer slicing at the stags face with his knife as it dipped its head. The stag yelled in anger and in pain, Vlad somehow replaced his knife in his boot and got to his feet while the Stag charged at him again, on reaching Vlad the stag bowed his head once more, all Vlad could do was grab the Antlers and swing himself around onto the Stags back. The deer became frantic, kicking and bolting and slamming itself into trees trying to hurt Vlad so he would fall from its back, but Vlad was strong and held on tight, he knew if he was to fall he would never get back up.

The stag did everything he could but the dwarf would

not release him, it bolted for what seemed like an hour though it was not and soon the stag became exhausted and collapsed on the forest ground breathing very heavily. Both Vlad and the stag were tired though Vlad was clearly the most injured. He knew he had won this battle and after a short rest he pushed himself up onto his feet and retrieved his bow and a few arrows, placing two of them to the hair of the bow he drew back the string pointing the arrows at the Stag.

"You were a worthy Adversary it is a shame I must do this."

Just then a deer with an over sized belly stepped out from behind the rock where Vlad had found the stag resting before it had attacked him, the deer walked over towards Vlad and stood over the exhausted stag, she looked down at her companion and then she looked up to stare straight at Vladlin. She was pregnant, and Vlad now knew the stag was trying to protect his family; the look the deer gave him was if she was pleading with him to spare her unborn baby fathers life.

"You know, I would also fight as hard as you did to protect the people I love." He said to the stag.

He put his bow down and walked over to the exhausted male deer pushing it on its side until it rolled on to its knees and then found its legs.

"Go" he waved his arms at both deer's in a shooing motion. "Go with your family and protect them today is not your day to die."

The stag stumbled towards the trees with its partner pausing only for a moment to look back at the dwarf in what seemed to be a thank you for my life gesture before disappearing into the vast collage of trees and deep into the forest. Vlad turned and retrieved his arrows, Quiver and back pack that had all been scattered during the fight, battered and bruised he too stumbled deep into the forest the same way he had come, hoping to make it back in time to meet his hunting party.

Vladlin had been walking most of the day, though seriously injured he concentrated on putting one foot in front of the other, forcing himself to keep moving even though he knew with every step he was risking his life. He had been injured almost to the brink of death and yet he kept moving on.

"I have to reach the hunting party." He kept telling himself.

Trained in the art of healing he knew he needed to rest and tend to his wounds, but his pride overwhelmed him, it was a shame to return without a catch but it would be even more of a shame if he did not return as the head of the party, to return late could cost him his position as head hunter and he would lose all respect from his people.

He finally made it to the edge of the forest, if it were not for his injuries he would have made better time, but now he knew he would be late for the meeting though he knew his men would wait an extra day. Dusk had arrived and now it had become necessary to rest. He began to make a fire to protect him from the amazing drop in temperature that came with nightfall the cold would do no good for his wounds.

The forest did not become as hot in the day or as cold at night as it would be being out of the forest, it had been said that it was protected by fairy magic. Though Vlad had his doubts that the Magic was fairrien. It was obvious some kind of magic protected it, for no place else that he had seen could grow such beautiful greenery in the unpredictable weather of England. The dwarves themselves have only just begun to find good soil below the ground and started growing their own plantation harnessing sunlight with mirrors to reach inside their cave to provide just the right amount of sunlight to enable the plants to grow.

The English weather had now become hot all year round, with the odd thunderstorms that came at least five times a year, but even the raindrops were warm. It also rained sometimes during the burning month but it rained drops of fire. Gas and water clouds where formed over the toxic lands across the sea in France, and like clockwork every year these clouds would be carried on the northern winds straight over England. When the toxic clouds reached England for an unknown reason, a chemical imbalance occurred causing the clouds to rain fire and explode. Vlad's father had told him it was because of the immense heat that came from the sun in that month, but those who did not have proper shelter and cooling were sure to die, but every year the forest remains untouched, not a flame or a burning tree could be found, no one could say that it was not magic.

Vlad had gathered wood for his fire and while he attempted to light it he began to curse himself aloud. "Vladlin Bowen, son of Korin," he moaned "Tallest of his people,"

It was true he stood four feet tall while most dwarves only ever reached three feet. "Master hunter, a respected councillor, hero of dwarves, look at him now." He spoke of himself as a second person.

"Wounded bleeding and bruised from a fight with a deer, two days away from my men and I'm to return with nothing but the scars of my dignity. Some master hunter I am, I deserve to lose my seat on the council."

He pulled some leaves from a strange looking bush and put them over a branch he had broken from a tree and placed them in the fire that he had finally lit. After a short while when the leaves were heated he removed them from the fire and the branch, he then placed them on his cuts and bruises, winching a little from the pain as the leaves burned into his skin.

"What shall I say when I am asked, where is your

prey?" His head began to thud, he now realised his prey was the least of his worries, he put his hand to his head and when he looked at his hand it was covered in blood, he had cut his head open during the fight and in his hurry to get back he had not even realised it. He stood up to find the bush that could stop the bleeding with his type of head injury, but as he stood up he became very faint, the forest seem to spin round and round very fast, he no longer could focus on anything. His vision had become blurred and he felt like he was falling, his body hit what seem to be the ground and then all was black.

Vladlin was awoken by the sound of a big crash that caused the earth to shake, he sat up straight to find himself still in the forest, but there was a difference to the place it was daylight but the forest seemed dull and gloomy, he stood up and noticed a tree that seemed out of place, it bared no leaves and its trunk had rotted, in a flash he found himself standing next to it, staring at a crack that ran down the centre of the tree he slowly reached out and touched it making a piece of bark fall away, in that instant blood wept from the trunk.

Again Vlad heard the big crash but this time it was closer he looked around and found that the fire he had made the night before was gone, it had disappeared like it was never there, he turn back to the tree and found it covered and infested with maggots, he jumped in shock it was an awful sight he knew something bad was happening,

"Nothing ever rotted in this forest." He thought. The crash came again and the earth shook violently, his heart began to pound, something was coming and it was not good. He turned and began to run away from the sound, he ran through bushes and passed trees but did not come clear of the forest. He could of sworn he had reached the edge the night before, now he could hear the swift sound of running feet gaining on him, he was defiantly being chased, the forest was filled with a sweet aroma that filled his lungs and made him light headed, he ran as fast as he could but his pursuers were closer and he would soon be caught.

He heard the crash again but it was in front of him now he changed direction, but the crashing sound seemed to be all around him, he stop running, he was panicking, he felt like a cornered rat and pulled his knife out ready to fight whatever might come at him. The sound of the feet were close and they were all around, but just as they should have been in view the forest went silent, not a sound could be heard, Vlad stood still knife in hand ready, the forest was still silent not a sound could be heard no birds or animal, not even the leaves from the trees rustling in the wind could be heard. He wondered for a moment if he had gone deaf, and just when he was entertaining the idea along came the biggest crash of all.

As trees fell down, out stepped an Ogre of immense size. Vlad took a step back in astonishment, he had never seen or believed an ogre could get that big, just then Vlad found himself falling to the ground and surrounded by at least twenty Orcus, all looking the same with twisted ugly faces. These were the reject clones, the ones that did not take to the human form and were used by the Elves to do their dirty work, they each wore black shell typed armour with the insignia of the scorpion on their chests. They were from the house of Maxius Millidor; he himself had sent these Orcus.

A tall shadowy figure stepped into view, he was wearing a black hooded cloak and his face could not be seen but when he spoke it sent shivers down the centre of Vlad's spine.

"Bring them; Millidor or our masters has ways to make them talk." It hissed in the most horrific voice, then turned and walked away. "Them who's them, there is only one of me." Vlad shouted. He was confused. At that moment the Orcus began to beat him, they were like a pack of animals jumping on him and kicking him, shouting;

"Where are the others, where are you from, where are the others, where are you from" it became almost like a chant. "I don't know" Vlad shouted, "I don't know".

Vlad sat up straight, the forest was dark it was night time and his fire was still burning there were no Orcus or Ogre's around him it had just been a dream. He felt his head and found that it had been bandaged, the forest air was filled with a sweet aroma and he realised it was coming from his pot that was hanging over the fire, someone had been through his things, he moved to get to his feet.

"It is not wise for you to be moving around so soon." Vlad turned to look over his shoulder to find a slender short dark haired young looking man dressed all in grey sitting cross legged behind him, he couldn't help to noticing his pointed ears, but knew instantly that he was not elfish as Elves were only born white haired and white eyed, it was clear this man had neither of the two.

"I suppose I have you to thank for the bandaging of my head and going through my things." he said to the stranger.

"It was necessary, I needed to get cooking equipment so that we could make soup for you to be better by the morning, I sense that you are in a hurry." He replied.

"You are right but I have never smelt a soup that smelt so sweet." The stranger stood up and walked over to the fire producing a bowl that had come from Vlad's back pack he tilted the pot pouring some soup into it.

"It is called Swhyswine, a remedy soup to ail most injuries and give energy", he moved over to where Vlad was sitting and held the bowl out to him. Vlad looked at him questioningly for a moment before receiving the bowl.

"It is made from special herbs and spices that are probably not known to you, my people drink this often especially for long journeys this is all we have." The stranger said as he walked back towards the fire producing a cup of his own and pouring soup into it.

He turned to face the dwarf then sat cross-legged on a flat toped rock that looked almost like it was moulded for him to sit that way. He held the cup to his mouth but did not drink instead he stared at Vlad. The small man thought this odd, "maybe it is poisoned" the thought came to mind but realised instantly that if this man wanted him dead he would have done so while he was unconscious, not nurse him back to health and then poison him, it was a test a test of trust. Vlad put the bowl to his own mouth and drank the soup, it was a taste from heaven, the soup was both savoury and sweet at the same time, and immediately he felt a revival of energy in his body, he looked to the stranger, who then in turn drank the soup.

"This is extraordinary I feel good to go already." Vlad thought. "Settle down Vladlin, it is the first time you have had the soup and it will make you feel like you have energy that you really have not got. It will take till the morning to produce the energy you need inside your body."

"How is it that you know my name?" Vlad demanded

"We heard you say before you fell."

"You were watching me?" questioned Vlad.

"We see all that happens in this forest."

"Who is we?" Vlad became annoyed and agitated, and his head became light and fussy.

"I say we for I am Fairrien, and I am many." Replied the stranger.

"Speak English boy you make no sense," Vlad came to his feet but as he stood up he collapsed once again.

When Vlad woke up it was morning, he felt rested and energised he was amazed to find that his cuts and bruises had disappeared he also realised that his bandage had been removed he felt the side of his head and felt the massive scar that had been a great gash the day before, the stranger was still with him packing things away and putting out the fire.

Vlad watched him for a while before standing up and approaching him.

"Vladlin is my name, as you know already," he extended his arm to shake hands, the stranger accepted. "I am known as Leron, please consider me a friend."

"Well Leron I owe you and your magic soup my life and if we shall meet again I will gladly return the favour."

"You may return the favour to me now."

"How so?" Vlad asked curiously.

"By letting me travel with you, I have rarely been beyond this forest and I must travel east bound, I would appreciate the company." Explained Leron

"I am travelling east to meet my brethren not more than two days away, but from there I go to a secret place where you may not follow."

"I do not mind." replied Leron.

"So when I meet my men we shall go our separate ways, agreed?"

"Agreed" the tall slender man concurred.

They both gathered their things together; Vlad holding his bow swung his backpack and quiver of arrows over his shoulder, whilst Leron wore a little brown sack that crossed over his back and carrying a long staff they both headed off towards the sunrise leaving behind the forest, and entering the waste lands.

They had been walking most of the day with no rest. Vlad had been sipping water from his canteen but needed little rest, Leron's soup had done the trick, it had given him energy far beyond his normal level, on a good day he would have rested at least two times by now, but not once had he felt the need to stop. Leron walked beside him neither of them said a word, they travelled in silence. Vlad could not help but feel that there may be other reasons why Leron was travelling with him. He began to remember conversations with Leron the previous night. "Did he say he was Fairrien?" Vlad thought to himself. He had never seen a fairy before, he had heard stories but never came into contact with them, it was said that the rare few joined the cause in the war against the Greys, but Fairies in this day and age were rarely seen.

"Are you really a fairy?" Vlad needed to break the silence, after all Leron wanted to travel with him because he needed the company, but the silence made him feel like he was no company at all.

"That I am." Vlad had not notice before but Leron's voice was calm and gentle with no roughness to it, almost childlike.

"I almost started to believe you folks did not exist, I have been in that forest many of times and I have never once come across any of you." The dwarf inquired.

"That is because we choose not to reveal ourselves." Leron replied.

"Oh" was all Vlad replied.

They continued their Journey until nightfall, the night had become chilly and Leron removed some small logs from his pack.

"Light them they will burn and the flame will not go out." Leron asked. Vlad did as he was asked; the flames took to the logs and gave back amazing warmth.

"Special logs right." Asked Vlad.

"You are right Vladlin, these logs will produce fire for three nights as they burn very slow."

"Magic?" implied the dwarf.

"No they are from a special tree that permits us to take from it." Explained Leron.

Vlad chucked to himself. "I have never heard of asking

permission from a tree before, I guess you people are a little bit loopy."

"You may laugh and jest but your people once knew the earth the way we do, your people once harness its essence to make weapons of strength."

"There are those at my home that still practice that art, but I am sure they would tell you that they use magic."

"Are they not the same thing" Was the last thing Leron said on the matter?

Vlad pulled a dead rat from his pack and began to skin it. "You look Horrified Leron, do you not eat rat?" he said as he ripped away at the creatures skin, When he had finished he sliced open the belly and began clearing out its guts.

"No my people eat no meat." Leron watched as Vlad poured water from his canteen to clean his food before placing a sharp pointed stick through the rat's mouth and right out of its rear. "Nor do you forgive those that do?" said Vlad

"On the contrary we respect the natural way of life, as the fox hunts the rabbit to live, manlings also choose to do the same, we respect this but eating plants and vegetables has lead us to a higher level of understanding."

"Understanding of what?" he asked as he held the rat on a stick above the fire.

"Of spirit and nature" replied Leron

"You speak in riddles at times; I am a simple dwarf with simple understandings."

"You move to fool me Vladlin Bowen; I have already determined that there is nothing simple about you or your mind."

"You seem to know a lot about a person you just met." Vlad twisted the stick around to make sure the fire cooked the Rat thoroughly.

Leron did not answer, he just watched as Vlad cooked

and ate his rat not saying a word. When Vlad had finished they both sat by the fire in silence for a long while before Vlad eventually spoke.

"Well as much I find this conversation with you so interesting, I must retire so I may wake nice and early." He said sarcastically.

Leron said nothing he sat crossed legged watching Vlad as he laid back wrapping his green jacket tight around him and turning over to go to sleep.

"Good night oh talkative one" Were Vlad's last words before he slept.

The next morning brought intense heat for Vlad, dwarves were known to have very tough skin and were rarely effected by the heat, but this day was far too hot, and Vlad had drank most of his water supply to keep him going in the intense weather, he watched Leron as they travelled and noticed that he was not affected at all by the weather, he drank little from his canteen and did not sweat at all. By midday they had reached some old ruins which was half way buried beneath the sand, Vlad was familiar with the place and knew of an entrance that would lead them under the roof of the old building.

They had both decided to rest for an hour before continuing the journey, so Vlad lead the way through an opening in what seemed to be the side of the building. They found that they had to climb down into the place and upon entering they found before them a great set of stairs. Though sunlight crept into the building from different cracks from the roof, the inside was still very dark. Leron tapped his staff on the ground and immediately the top half of the staff became alight. Not like a flame but a bright pale white light just loomed from it. Vlad looked at it in amazement. "You truly are magic?"

"It is just nature that guilds this light" Replied Leron.

Vlad looked at him a bit puzzled and then lead the way

up the stone stairs and into a hall of some kind, they found a space on the floor and sat down. Vlad chewed on some dried rat meet he had saved for his trip, and asked to sip a little of his companions water. Leron gave him some while he himself sipped cold soup. He knew that being out of the sun for a while would be good for Vlad as he had noticed the dwarfs uncontrollable sweating that morning.

"I came to this place before it was destroyed around two hundred years ago, I past myself of as a man dwarf, humans never knew there were any other kind."

"So humans built this place." Leron was interested?

"Yes this was once a human village, known as Wingfield. This building was one of their learning places, I think they once called them coal ages, this is the only building that survived the war in this village."

Leron looked around the massive hall they were in, it was covered in dust and dirt with boulders of rock that had fell from the building with age.

"What was that?"

"What was what?" asked Vlad.

"I saw something move across the hall, just over there." He pointed towards a dark corner just over Vlad's left shoulder, Vlad turned to look. They both stared silently.

"Arh you must be seeing... "

"Shhh" Leron stopped Vlad from finishing his sentence. They both heard the scurrying sound that brought to mind a small creature with many tin legs.

"O ohh." Vlad whispered.

"What is it" Leron asked?

"It sounds like something I hope it is not." Vlad said.

"Well that gives me a full explanation does it not?" Leron said.

"Sarcasm is not you forte." Vlad replied worriedly.

Just then out from the dark scuttled a creature with hundreds of tiny little legs; it had two sharp pointed antlers on what appeared to be the head of the creature. It opened it mouth and hissed a sound that was both dreadful and chilling showing its many razor sharp metal looking teeth.

"I think we should run." Vlad said backing away slowly.

"Run why?" questioned Leron.

In that instant the creature moved with incredible speed leaping into the air towards Leron gnashing its teeth. Leron produced a blade from his waist belt at such a speed it would seem as though it was magic, striking downwards with precise accuracy he sliced the creature in half it then flopped to the ground in two pieces.

"How cowardly that you would run from a creature as small as a rabbit" Leron said looking Vlad.

"It wasn't just that one I was worried about, look" Vlad shouted pointing behind Leron.

Leron turned to look and out from the dark came thousands of the creatures, tapping their feet and hissing.

"Now I think I understand, Run" Shouted Leron.

They both took of at a pace rarely known by any human but Vlad was finding it hard to keep up with the Fairrien. The creatures chased them through the dark, down the steps and straight up out of the building into the burning hot sun. The desert became filled with them, as they ran, more and more appeared from under the sand hissing and spitting.

"Don't get hit by their spit." shouted Vlad.

"Why, or should I not ask?" replied Leron.

"Its acid it would burn through you instantly." Vlad puffed.

Leron could see that Vlad was losing pace, and the creatures were gaining on them.

"Quick run towards the gap between those hills to right." Leron lead the way and Vlad followed.

When they reached the Gap Leron stopped running.

"Now what" asked Vlad?

"We fight." They both stood side by side before the gap, Vlad with his bow and Leron with his staff.

"Some would say this was suicide but if I died at least I went down fighting." Vlad said before unleashing many arrows into the oncoming creatures.

Leron dived forward with immense speed, swinging his staff with a unique technique; he was fast— every creature that his staff made impact with was splattered like water hitting the ground, it was amazing that he was keeping them at bay.

"Stop them from getting behind me." Shouted Leron

Vlad fired his arrows at both sides of Leron killing the creatures before they had the chance to get behind him. He was proud of his marksmanship, at the rate he was unleashing his arrows he felt his skill was almost Elfish, but his many arrows were quickly becoming very few.

"Pull back," he shouted, "my arrows are nearly gone." Vlad stepped back into the gap as Leron walked back also, fighting the creatures relentlessly. Vlad drop his bow and unsheathed his knife. Leron had reached the gap throwing his staff behind him and in one motion he produce two knives and continued fighting. Both men fought with intensity dodging the spit of the creatures, using their blades to slice as many of them as they could. They stood shoulder to shoulder holding their ground in the gap like they were protecting their homes.

They killed creature after creature and, though Vlad began to feel the strain of the battle, he was amazed to find that Leron seem unaffected by the length of their fight. The way he used his knives seemed effortless, stabbing and slicing and squashing. But the creatures did not become wary of him and rather than to slow their attack they became more fierce as if angered by the bodies of their kin that both Leron and Vlad had laid at their feet. They became wild with no fear of death, attacking ferociously they seek to over come the two, teeth gnashing and spitting acid. A little dropped on Leron's legging's and though it smoked it did not seem to penetrate and reach his skin.

Vlad had noticed how wild the creatures had become, and knew they could not fight them forever, there were way too many of them, the more they killed the more creatures seemed to appear. He was tiring and knew they needed time to get away. It was while they were fighting that he noticed the bolder to the side of them almost on top of the hill. So, as he sliced at the creatures he threw the weight of his body against the rock, trying to make vibrations. Leron had noticed and realised what he was trying to do, so both fought, and alternated slamming their bodies against the rock, the bolder began to move, slowly, but then it came to a stop,

"Now, with all your strength," Leron shouted, as he heightened his speed to another level that Vlad did not think was possible. The speed of Leron was unbelievable as he forced his way towards the creatures pushing them back only a little, giving Vlad the opportunity to stop fighting and throw his full weight against the side of the rock of the hill. Vlad did not hesitate, and when he made contact with the rock the vibrations sent from the mere strength of the dwarf was enough to have the boulder rolling down the hill. Vlad stepped back further into the gap and shouted. "Quick Leron now"

Then within a second Leron had left the creatures and rushed into the gap, the creatures tried to follow but as they entered the gap the rock boulder rolled down and landed in its entrance crushing the Creatures that were attempting to enter.

"It will not take them long to work around or under that" said Vlad "Then let's not waste time." replied Leron.

They quickly picked up their things, Leron sheathed his

knives and picked up his staff and they both began to run once again. As they ran Vlad looked back and could see that some of the creatures had already dug under the rock and were already in pursuit. They continued to run, Vlad using what energy he had left, he was tired, and it seem they had run for a mile. The creatures had now gathered and was gaining on them, Vlad was exhausted but somehow he kept moving. Leron had noticed that Vlad's pace had slowed and shouted at him encouraging him to keep moving. It was just at the point when Vlad felt he could run no more that he had looked back and found that the creatures had stop chasing them. They both ran a little further before they stopped running, making sure they kept a good distance between them and the creatures.

"Why have they stopped?" Leron asked "Because... Huh because they will not leave too far... huuh... from their home" Vlad puffed heavily,

"Why is that?" Leron seemed unaffected by the battle or the run he did not seem out of breath at all.

"The earth below the sand here must be very warm" Vlad still breathed hard when he spoke "they cannot survive without heat,"

"Well let's get as far away from them as we can,"

They began to walk at a fast pace making distance between them and the creatures; it was a while before they slowed back into a casual walking pace and Vlad gobbled down most of what was left of Leron's water. "What were those things?" Leron was curious he had never seen anything like them before.

"They are called Scrivages. They only come out in very extreme heat, that is why they did not follow, if they left too far from their land and the weather changed they would not make it back to their safe heated home and would die."

"Where are they from, I have never ever known such creatures." Leron continued to ask.

"Who know maybe that's a question for a human when you see one?"

They continued walking with very little conversation, Vlad concentrating on putting one foot in front of the other, not willing to rest and wanting to get back to his men as soon as he could. By evening they had reached a little village called Halesworth. Vlad insisted that they kept on the outskirt of the village, as Dwarves were on the top wanted list of the Elves. Some people hunted them to gain money that they could spend in the great city of London. He also explained that the meeting place was in a valley over a hill not far from the village and he was very pleased that they had made it back in good time.

"I know my men have waited for me, I will be pleased to introduce them to you," Vlad said looking at Leron.

"I would like that, any being that fights as well as you must have honourable brethren." Leron replied.

"They are good people; I hope you will stay the night with us before we part."

"I would be glad to" accepted Leron.

They walked up the hill and looked down into the Valley. It was dusk and Vlad could see the silhouette of his men as they appeared to be resting.

"I am here." He shouted as he ran down to greet them.

"Wait" Shouted Leron.

But Vlad ignored him and ran down the hill as fast as his legs could carry him. Leron followed but felt uneasy something was not right. He had sensed it and there was a foul smell in the air. Vlad paid little mind to the stench and ran to the nearest of his men and upon reaching him he began to shake him to wake him up,

"Albe wake up its me Vlad."

The dwarf had said nothing neither did he wake. It had taken a moment for Vlad to notice the blood weeping from the dwarfs back.

"What's this," he was confused for only a moment "wake up dwarf injured?"

He shouted hoping to wake the rest of them but not one of them moved. He stood up and the sudden realisation that something was not right dawned on him, as he walked slowly through the camp he realised that they were dead all of them. Some were beaten badly until their faces had caved in, while others were hacked to pieces. Heads and arms laid everywhere. The letter M from the human alphabet was clearly marked in blood on a boulder that seemed to have been pushed to the centre of the camp. It was a warning, a message to the dwarf nation to let them know that they will be found and this was their fate, Vlad fell to his knees.

"They are all dead Leron." He whispered "They are all dead"

Leron stood beside him placing his hand on his shoulder.

"I know Vlad, I Know." He said calmly as he watched a tear roll gently down the tanned rough skin of Vlad's face.

2
The Shallows

Navi was a dark-skinned man around the age of thirty-five; he was about six feet tall with short woolly black hair and took every opportunity he could find to moan about something. It was not that he was a miserable man, it was more the fact that he had very little patience when it came to people, so he preferred to give them the impression that he was always pissed off so people would leave him alone or think twice before asking him a favour. He did not really like to do things for people unless there was some way he could profit from it, but he was a wheeler and a tradesman so he was always polite and charmed those who he did business with, he found that this was a more effective way of receiving what he wanted.

Navi did not live in the shallows. He chose to live in the village because when it became too hot most people retreated to the shallows leaving him with peace and quiet, as he did not need to hide from the sun unless it was burning month. Since he was a child he had trained his body to tolerate extensive heat, besides black folk could always tolerate more heat than pale humans, it was something to do with the melanin in their skins.

Day in and day out Navi would always be seen wearing what appeared to be the same dirty blue pair of overalls, but as a matter of fact is was not, Navi had two pairs of blue overalls and though he washed them frequently the stains never really came out.

"What the hell." He said to himself while he was trying to wash the grease and oil stains out of his second pair of overalls that he had in a bowl of water as he sat at his table.

"I work too hard for these people, no one expects me to be clean." He liked to spend time alone so he frequently spoke to himself. "What I need is a damn woman."

A smile came to his face as he began to like the line of thought his mind was taking.

"Yes a damn good women, who would cook for me and do my washing and have sex with me whenever I damn well pleased, and most of all not speak back to me, yes that's the type of women I need."

He was so lost in his thoughts that he did not notice the small pretty brown haired freckled face young girl sneaking up on him, she sneaked though the door of his Iron made hut and crept across the main room right up to the table where he was sitting with his back to the main door. She slowly moved her head towards his ear and then shouted "What you doin?"

Navi jumped up out of his chair knocking the bowl with his clothes over onto himself and onto the floor. "Bloody hell women, what the hell do you think you're doing?"

Katie looked bashful. "Sorry Nav, I was just having some fun." She said almost tearful looking to the ground and rolled her eyes up to meet his giving of the sweet innocent look that she had practised time and time again to get herself out of sticky situations.

"You younglings are nothing but a pain in the rear end, look at me it looks like I pissed myself."

"Your right" Katie smirked.

"It's not funny, now I'm going to have to wear shorts." Navi walked off towards his sleeping quarters stopping at the door he turned to face Katie looking none too pleased.

"You can finish washing those overalls now while I get changed; I need them for the council meeting tonight."

"Okay." Katie began to pick up the bowl and the overalls. Navi watched for a moment and then turned into the room with a smirk on his face, he did like her company but he would never tell her that.

Katie began to wash the overalls using the bar of soap that Navi had been using.

"I heard somewhere that in London you can buy a special plant that is said to have come from a fairy forest that has a remarkable soap substance that could wash out any stain." She raised her voice so she could be heard in the next room.

"Yes you are right" came Navi's voice hollering back, he entered the room wearing the raggediest pair of dark green shorts Katie had ever seen. "And I do believe it was me that told you so."

"Yea you know, I think your right." She jested.

"Stop playing games Katie, I have told you time and time again stop coming here in a heat wave." Navi said shaking his head.

"Why?" asked Katie

"Oh my word, must I explain everything?" Navi sounded very annoyed, but Katie knew him, this was his way, he always sounded annoyed and she took no offence to it.

"Okay. Reason number one, it is not good for you pale skins to be out in this heat with no protection from the sun, if you passed out on the way here who would know, you would just lay there and die." Explained Navi

"Really, well you know as well as I that I have never once been affected by this so called heat wave, after all I have been out in them so many times I can't remember." Katie raised her voice to match Navi's annoyance; she was just playing his game.

"Lame excuse try number two" She finished sarcastically.

"Okay number two, if your mother knew you came out in this heat you would be in big trouble she would tan your arse." Navi said waggling his finger.

"But she doesn't doe's she, and if she did so would you for not telling her in the first place" Replied Katie.

Navi realised there was no beating Katie in an argument, so he reverted to bribery. "Okay. You win." He said calmly "What would it take for you to go home, so I can sort myself out for this meeting tonight."

"Take me through the passage way that is forbidden?"

"No, try something sensible?" Navi responded

"Alright tell me the story of why the Captain has good favour with the maids."

"Well that I can tell you." Navi had known she would go for a story. She loved to listen to his tales almost as much as he liked to tell them. He sat down at his table and Katie stopped washing the overalls and sat down opposite to him.

"Many believe the captain has maids blood," he began "some even say that he married a maid and though there maybe some truth to these tales, very few know the true reason why the maids protect him. You see it all goes back to the war. Way before the captain was born, his father father's name was Sir Alfred Niloc Gill, knighted by the queen of Great England herself, and given the position as admiral for a great strategic battle that helped stop some war or something between humans. Well his grandfather was given a ship and a whole fleet to command in the sea battle known to this day as the battle of the Titans. You see Maids had just joined the cause back then, because the Leviathans had started to invade their waters and destroying their undersea cities."

"The maids had cities?" Katie said excitedly.

"Oh yes, though I have never seen one myself it is said they had and still have great cities of light that are built so deep in the ocean that they could never be found without a mermaid guide." Navi explained.

"So how did the Leviathans find them" asked Katie?

"I don't know maybe they had a mermaid guide." Navi said annoyingly. "Can I get on with the story or what?"

"Okay. sorry keep you're head on." Katie had a big grin on her face she loved to wind Navi up especially if there were discrepancy in his stories.

"Where was I," he paused for a moment.

"The Leviathans were destroying the cities of the maids" Reminded Katie.

"Oh yea so the Leviathans were invading their waters clearing a path so the Krakens could attack above and land on the beach of Dover to destroy the port and any living thing that was there. Without the ships at Dover it would be a long time before the maids could get help from other England fleets."

"So Krakens can leave the seas? Katie interrupted again.

"Yes they can, though I don't think they do it much in our days— I don't think they can stay away from the sea too long without dying. So the battle began and the Admiral and his fleet fought valiantly. Big guns from the ships fired big exploding things into the Krakens as they came up to the top of the water, spitting huge gushes of water at the ships, sinking many of them. Under the sea, maids used staffs that shot laser bolts along the water, killing the leviathans. The long, silky black creatures in turn unleashed poison dart type things from their gills, killing the maids and turning the sea into blood— making it hard to find the enemy underwater."

"Admiral Gill had done as he hoped, he held out long enough for the submarines to arrive, firing their… . Um… .

What did captain call them? Torbedoes I think, or something like that. The submarines were man-made underwater ships, and they turned Leviathans swimming back to where ever they came from, but the Krakens fought on never knowing when to leave a battle grabbing at ships and tearing them in half killing hundreds of humans. The battle was now topside and the maids came up to help and leading the maids was the Princess herself fighting as brave as anyone that fought that day. It was by chance that she happened to be in view of the H.M.S Daring, the admiral's ship when a Kraken picked her up in his great wet dirty brown claws.

The admiral, not knowing who she was, ordered his men to turn the big cannon guns and fire at the thing, which they did. Injured, she fell from the creature's hands and into the sea, and with no thought for his own safety, or that the other Krakens were there about in the waters, the admiral jumped into the sea and swam toward the sinking maid. He dived under and managed to retrieve her. Bringing her back to his ship he tended to the cuts she had received from the creature. It is said that when she returned to her kingdom her father learned of the princess mis-adventures, and the hero that had saved her life and promised that his people would protect Admiral Gills life and any generation of gills that shall be born for as long as mermaids swam the seas. The Mermaid King also offered the admiral two requests, but the admiral asked only one, that for as long as mermaids swam the waters and no matter how destroyed she is that they would always try their best to protect and restore the Daring, for the admiral loved that ship. And that my dear and pain in my rear is why the captains ship always look like new and why the maids only speak with and take care of the Captain, that and the fact he is one of the only people I know that can speak their crazy language."

"But..."

"No buts we had a deal I must get ready now go," Navi said ushering Katie towards the door.

"But..." persisted Katie.

"If you go now without saying a word" Navi interrupted Katie once again. "You can come back tomorrow and I will teach you some more about engines."

Katie gave him a look of dismay. She stood up bowed to him jokingly keeping her mouth shut she turned and left his iron made hut and entered outside into the lovely hot sun. She walked along the beach staring out into the sea wondering on what laid beyond, she had never seen a maid before nor a Kraken or a Leviathan. She wondered about these creatures and wonder what life was like under the sea, apart from the few forests, the seas were the only place the Greys desperately wanted control of and could not gain, that is why the krakens and leviathans still battled for all these years. The captain had once told her that they would fight to the last maid before they gave up an inch of their waters. Katie continued down the beach and then sat and watched the sea for a while before she decided to go back to the shallows.

To her surprise when she returned she found Billy still asleep. "Billy" she shouted.

He jumped up. "Yes"

"You're not a very good guard anyone could have sneaked in here by now." She said smiling as she continued to walk down the halls of the shallows. Billy looked confused and stayed on his feet as if to attention realising the truth of Katie's words.

Passing many people lingering and walking around through the shallows, Katie returned to her home and opened the door slowly and quietly before peeking her head around the corner of the door, to her surprise stood her mother cross-faced staring directly at her.

"Been somewhere interesting?" Her mother raised her eyebrows.

"No not really." Katie tried to play it cool, she walked in closing the door behind her walking casually she went and seated herself at the table where her mother had already served her dinner. Her mother still stared at her hard not looking convinced.

"Emm this looks lovely, what is it?" Katie tried to change the subject.

"Fish, bread and gravy, what does it look like? Where have you been?" she said in one sentence staying with the conversation Katie so obviously tried to avoid.

"Err I went to the gathering hall with Claire I did not want to disturb you so I just went." Katie replied looking down at her plate.

"Really was it nice and hot in the gathering room because you look really brown, if I didn't know any better I would say you were outside." Katie's mum said with crossed arms.

Katie was not very good at lying when it came to her mother, her mum always could read her like she was reading a book.

"Come on mother I have always been this brown." Katie replied.

Her mother looked under the table down at her feet. "I see you went out with no shoes on again, and I'm sure if you look closely you will also see the sand from the beach still between your toes."

Katie immediately looked down at her feet, her mother was right and she had been caught out. "I am sorry mum but the heat outside don't affect me why must I always stay in when you know it's the truth." She pleaded.

Her mother walked over to the table and sat beside her, and spoke to her softly, her voice became almost dream like, it was like she was singing but she was not, when her mother told her important things her words always had this affect on Katie, it was like she was speaking another language but she was not because Katie could clearly understood her.

"How old are you now my sweet?" Her words echoed all around the room and gently in Katie's mind.

"Fifteen mother you know." Katie replied.

"I guess you're old enough to know by now that you are special."

"What do you mean?" asked Katie.

"You are different from all the others that live in this place." Katie's mum started to look concerned.

"I don't understand" Katie voice sounded confused.

"Have you not noticed you're... ?" A knocking on the door interrupted Katie's mother.

"I'll get it." Katie skipped to the door and opened it to reveal her closest friend Claire.

"Hey you" said Katie

"Hey" Claire answered, "I just wondered if you were coming out, we could go down to the net room and play tennis ball or something."

"Hmm" Katie thought for a moment, "I am speaking with my mum at the moment but if you come back in half an hour or so I think I have something more interesting that we could do."

"Okay, I had one of those becoming a lady talks with my mother the other day I feel sorry for you" She giggled "I'll see you soon" Claire said then walked away.

Katie watched her walk of wondering what she meant, she close the door and returned to her mother sitting at the table. "Sorry about that mum, please continue."

"No we will talk another time eat up your dinner before it gets cold." All the music from her voice was gone, for Katie it was like waking up from a dream.

"No go on mum you were going to tell me something

important I could tell" She pleaded.

"Look it is not normal for a pale skin human to withstand this heat, and if you keep going out in heat waves someone might notice and then they will think you're a freak and start spreading rumours and rumours can be very vicious, and that is all I will say on the matter for now so eat up." She said abruptly before walking away to her sleeping room.

Katie felt as if she had done something wrong to upset her mother, "maybe it's because I disobeyed her" she thought to herself, she had been wrong to sneak out of the house and when she was caught out she lied, and she knew it had hurt her mother's feelings knowing that her only daughter had lied to her, she thought about ways of making it up to her while she was eating her dinner.

Katie did not finish all her food, she couldn't she felt too upset about what her mother had said, "Freak was the word. Why would people call me a freak" she thought, though she still felt that she had upset her mother she could not help but feel that her mother had not told her what she had intended to before Claire had knocked at the door. She left the table scraping the rest of the food in the recycle bag; her mother would mix all the leftover's up tomorrow and put it to some good use at the farm or something. Then she took her plate over to the washbowl in the cooking room and began to wash the plates and pots that her mother had used to make dinner. She often washed up when her mother cooked, when Katie cooked her mother washed up for her, her mother called it sharing the chores, this way all the chores in their home was done quickly and efficiently. She washed and dried the cooking utensils and put them away in the cupboard under the table, then she poured the water down the funnel. The funnel was a remarkable thing, again this was one of Navi's inventions, the funnel was made up of lots of pipes that ran along the walls and under the floors of the shallows and back into the well room. In this room was two huge wells filled with water, there Navi had made up a filter that cleaned the water and removed any salt and made it a hundred percent pure water again. When the water was clean it passed through another pipe into the second well, and from there all the villagers would go and get their barrels and buckets of water for using in their homes. Navi had once discussed with Katie the idea of making a second pipe line that went to everyone's living space so they could pump the water from the clean well straight to their homes rather than having to walk and carry it. But he had said it took them years to finish the first pipe line and he simply did not have the time to work on the second one right now. Katie was thinking on the miracle of the pipeline when she heard someone at the door. She rushed to open it, and as she suspected it was her friend.

Claire was a pretty blond haired girl, around five foot three inches only a little shorter than Katie, and every young teen in the community liked her, she always made herself look pretty and did her hair nice and almost every boy fancied her. Claire could be best friends with any one she wanted but yet she chose to be best friends with Katie and Katie could never understand why. Katie did not liked to hang around or play out with any of Claire's other friends, so when Claire came to hang out with her she always came alone.

Katie liked hanging out with Claire because she told her all the gossip and what all the other teens were up to who was going out with who and who hated who. It was interesting the way the other acted and as she kept herself out of the loop Claire was her only link to that part of their world. Claire had once asked Katie why she did not like the people her age; Katie's answer was that they were all too superficial.

"But do you not find me superficial" Claire had asked.

"Truthfully yes but you don't try and force me to be a part of that and that's why I like you."

It was true Katie was not superficial herself she never cared about wearing the best necklace or having the best made dress though she wished her hair was longer she never really cared how she wore it. She never really liked to impress anybody with superficial things, she had always told Claire that these things did not matter to her and that one day they would all learn how little these things meant to anyone, and this was the real reason why Claire liked being around Katie. She was different and saw things in a different way from most people, and she always had wise things to say, and also the fact that every time they were together Katie always came up with an idea that would either get them both in trouble or get them both dirty, and Claire always like trouble rather than dirty, but she always let Katie decide what they would do with their day as her ideas were always much more interesting.

"I see you came dressed appropriately." Claire wore a pair of brown baggy trousers and a grey shirt and had tied her hair back into a ponytail. "Well I had a feeling that whatever idea you had today it would get me dirty and I didn't want to get any of my nice clothes in a mess like I did last time."

It was true, the last time they were together Katie had taken Claire cliff climbing and they had both found themselves covered in the white chalk from the Dover cliffs.

"Well you thought right today. We shall play spy and I think we may get a little dusty"

Katie knew the shallows like the back of her hand she had explored every part where she had been permitted to go. She knew every nook and cranny and even had found ways to get in places that she really should not be in, and one of her most favourite place for her to go was where she planned to take Claire that evening. Katie made Claire wait while she went to her room and changed her clothes. She wore black tight leggings and a black long sleeved shirt. Tying her hair back, she led Claire away from her home and down the hallways of the shallows. The shallows was busy that evening as the sun was going down in the western horizon. The people of Dover village were mingling around the halls, going to the homes, or getting ready to go down to the beach for the evening beach gathering. When the sun was too hot in the day most of the villagers went down to the beach in the evening when the weather was cool, to escape from being in the shallows all day, they always lit a fire on the beach while someone would play the guitar and they would all sing songs of old and drink alcohol and be merry. Sometimes they would roast a few pigs on a spit as the farm was becoming bigger and could provide more than enough for the whole village and thank God for the wealth of their homes.

But this evening while everyone was preparing for the evening event, Claire and Katie were heading towards the passageway that was Forbidden. The passageway was obstructed by a huge metal door and there was no passing beyond that point, but there also was a small entrance that went straight into the air-conditioning vents, and in the evening the air-conditioning was turned off.

"What are we doing here?" Claire said curiously.

"There is a meeting in the council room this evening that should have started by now, they always talk about things we should not know, I think we should spy on them" Explained Katie.

"But how?" asked Claire.

"I know a way. Follow me, but be as quiet as you can. Ok?" Whispered Katie.

Claire nodded in agreement and watched as Katie stood on a wooden box that was beside the metal door and opened the hatch that was above their heads. Katie put her hands inside and lifted herself up and dragged herself into the vent, once inside she turned around and popped her head down the opening.

"Come on then," She said to Claire.

"I'm coming" Claire stood on the box. "You look like you have done this before?"

"Maybe a few times" Katie responded as she helped lift Claire into the vent.

Once inside Claire was surprised at the width of the maze of air vents. They were wide enough for both of them to crawl side by side through them but she stayed behind Katie as she had no idea where they were going and found it hard to believe that Katie knew her destination as there were so many passages ways and different directions that the vents led off into, that she believed it would be easier for a stranger to navigate the passage of the shallows than these air-conditioning vents. But Katie knew her way she had explored these vents a few times, and had always had a good sense of direction. She even knew the way to some of the homes of the villagers like the Captain, but he was hardly ever there so it was not interesting to spy on him. She had actually started to explore the vents in hope that it would lead her to the forbidden passageway; she had expected it to lead straight over the iron door. But Navi had been to smart in making the vents. He had anticipated the possibility of someone getting in them and had made the way to the forbidden place part of the vent maze in order to keep any intruders looking. However, Katie was determined and hoped one day she would find it, but in her exploring of the vents she had found her way to the council room and had sat quietly and listened to the private meeting a few times.

Mostly they talked about the farm, was there enough food and preparations for burning month, and when the next trading party would go away trading. Just the normal run of the village, but Katie always liked to be updated about the going on and the running of the place, she felt it was her duty to herself to be nosey.

They both crawled through the maze of vents this way and that, they climbed up into vents above and turned left and right many times. If Claire had to go back by herself she knew she would be lost for a long time, and she hoped that Katie really knew where she was going.

Katie stopped. "Okay" she whispered "The council room is just up ahead so we have to crawl ever so quietly and when we get there just listen and make no sounds, because these vents echo and they will know we are here."

"Okay. let's do it." Claire whispered back, and the two girls began their quiet crawl to the vent hatch that lead down into the council room.

Navi Stood up from the table in his almost clean looking blue overalls He looked around and faced the people that sat at the huge long rectangle table.

"And what do you say Captain if what Mrs Last says is true." Navi stood proud and talked ever so formal when he was in the presence of the council. Here people listened and respected his opinion, but he was not the leader of the village, all decisions came down and on the head of Miss Julie Yenned. The council members helped to produce the ideas and it was Miss Yenned's job to decide which ones were the best for the people.

The captain stood up also, removing his white and blue hat he prepared himself to address the council, and most of all Miss Yenned who sat stern faced at the head of the table in a almost throne like seat.

The captain had tanned skin, some said it was because he spent so much time in the sun others said he had dark skin blood in him as his hair was straight and black. He rarely talked seriously to anyone, but when he did speak serious it was always wise to listen and take note. Everyone knew the captain had been places that even Navi knew little of and had extensive knowledge that he rarely shared with others. Though the Captain was an active part of the council he rarely spoke or made suggestions he always came to the meetings just to listen. So, for the Captain to address the Council everyone became more aware of the seriousness of the matter.

"Me fellow comrades and council members, and of course the lady Yenned our respected ruler of this here wonderful Dover Village. I take pride in greeting such fine Gentlemen and ladies, who have all done so well in preserving a good way of life for all that lives here in this human colony." Navi seated himself fully interested in what the Captain was about to say.

"We've all done our forefathers proud," he continued struggling to cover up his unique accent.

"I know you all may expect me to give some advice that may have great insight and meaning to this matter, but my opinion is a simple one and one course of action that only I and me men might be taking."

"What is it you suggest?" Mr Graham also known as the butcher asked. Mr Graham was a small thin ginger haired man who was in charge of the meat. He controlled how much meat was needed for the day and trained the new butchers how to kill the animals and cut them ready for cooking. He was fifty five years of age and was one of the oldest members of the council.

"I suggest leaving" the captain replied bluntly.

There was a gasp of breaths from the ten council members that sat at the table; the idea of leaving all they have worked for was ridiculous.

"That's preposterous." Graham stood to his feet outraged. "Why would we leave the village there is no threat to us, they are only looking for the three outlaws."

"As I said your ladyship," The Captain continued to address Miss Yenned. "I fear only me men and I would be leaving until the arr coast is clear if you be getting me drift," The captain slipped back into his natural accent. "And for the rest of ya it be your choice what ye will do wid yourself, because no good can come of those things being up in this place mark my words." The Captain pushed his chair under the table and walked across the room to the exit he turned and faced the council. "A good day to ya all I be having preparation to be making, I believe I am still welcome to take whatever stock me crew and I be needing from the farm and storage rooms."

"You are always welcome to whatever stock you need Captain without your help we would not have as much as we do" Yenned nodded slightly to the captain.

"I thank you me lady." The captain nodded back then turned and left the room closing the door behind him.

Katie and Claire huddled beside each other listening to every word curious and frightened. Katie's mind was working over time trying to understand what it was exactly that the council was discussing. "What would make the captain leave like that? Until the coast is clear he had said, No good would come of those things being here was his exact words. What things?" Katie and Claire had both realised that they had stumbled into a discussion of great importance.

"I think we should leave. I don't want to know anymore" Claire whispered frightened.

"Shhh we can't leave now we know too much at least let us learn of what they really are talking about." Katie whispered in her ear then turned her head to observe Navi rising to his feet again.

"Sit down" Navi almost ordered Mr Graham. The man seated himself looking a bit bemused. "How dare you shout

out at the captain like he was some kind of fool have you no respect man?"

"Erbber errrber." The man did not know what to say.

"Stop stuttering man," Many feared Navi when he spoke so abruptly. Mr Graham felt like a child being chastised.

"So" Navi continued to address the council. "Ladies and gentlemen of the council as the Captain takes this matter serious I find I do also. I do not plan on leaving the Village any more than any of you but, there are certain things we must all do tonight, to make sure we are not punished in anyway."

"What do you mean" Mrs Last spoke up?

"Well for instance Mrs Last." Navi begun to explain.

"No need for formalities now Navi just call me Hayley" she replied.

"Oh well Hayley then. For instance, you are in control of communications. If it was not for you we would not know the Orcus were on their way here but it is well known that the Greys allows limited technology for humans; radios and other technologies that we have will not swing in our favour. If they knew we had air conditioning and a generator they would know there was an engineer here and we have all heard of the rumours about engineers found out by the Greys. They are taken away and when they are returned they are never the same all spending the rest of their lives in the great silver city London, working technology for the Elves and having no voice to speak. With a daze look on their faces, I have seen them they are like the walking dead and I do not intend to become one of them.

"What would you have us do?" Yenned seemed unsure of what he was proposing.

"I propose that we get as many hands as we can find and cover up our technology."Navi replied

"How can you cover up the air conditioning unit? The

vents run all over the shallows" Mr Lopez spoke for the first time.

"We block up every vent and make it look like part of the wall system. We must also make a fake wall to cover up the iron door in the outer bounds passage way. Anything that runs of power must be shut down. That means we must hide the well rooms also."

"And I will make sure the people know of this tonight." Yenned informed him.

"No I must object your Ladyship, I feel it would be better if we only told a few so we can have this all done by the morning. Then we can make an announcement to the whole village tomorrow, why spoil all there fun tonight?"

"Who agrees" Yenned looked around the table acknowledging the heads of the council members nodding in agreement with Navi.

"Okay. it shall be done. Council meeting is adjourned. Everyone, we have work to do, let's get it done straight away" Yenned ordered in her most authoritative voice.

The council members all rose up from their seats and tipped their heads slightly in respect to Lady Yenned she in turn tipped her head and turned and left the council room. The others soon followed after. Claire and Katie were stunned at what they had just heard.

"Orcus, the reject clones coming here to Dover village" Katie said.

"I am scared Katie what are we going to do?" asked Claire.

"I'm scared too but excited. I have never seen an Orcus, something exciting is at last going to happen in our village." Katie replied with an enthusiastic tone.

"But what if they kill us all," asked Claire.

"Don't be silly Claire, humans are no threat to them no more, there not coming to kill us, did you not hear what Graham said, they are looking for three outlaws and we have none here so it will be Okay."

"I am still scared," Claire insisted

"It will be ok, come on we better get back but you must promise not to say a word to anyone they can't find out that we spied on them." Katie reassured Claire.

"OK, I promise." Claire replied.

Katie and Claire began to crawl back through the vents to return to their homes. Frightened, scared and excited, all at the same time they were both dirty from the dust that had formed in the air vents and they both wondered if they would get any sleep that night.

Julie was a stern faced blond haired woman, and at the age of forty she had began to wonder if her leadership had now become obsolete. She silently walked the passageways of the Shallows with her closest friend and adviser nicked named Knarf. It had been a long time since he had used his real name, so long that it was possible that he himself may have forgotten it. He was a dark-skinned, short man of 39 years and they had known each other since childhood but now Julie was wondering if their friendship had become distant. Yes, he was always there if she needed him, and he still walked her to her home every night and protected her and made sure she was always safe, but it was the fact that they really did not talk much anymore.

It was as if Knarf had taken his roll beside her as a job, and now felt it was his duty to continue doing what he had done ever since she had been made leader and protector of Dover twelve years ago. To protect and serve her and nothing else. She had missed the closeness they used to have, and wondered if it had been her that had changed. Did her role as leader consume the natural essence that was herself and made her someone different? People for many years treated her with respect but that was all she felt she received from the people. Respect not love, maybe she had changed she wondered.

Maybe she let herself be overwhelmed by the power, but now it seem as though her power did not matter, it had been a long time since she had suggested an idea that would benefit the people. All the ideas came from the other council members, she just enforced the good ones, but she knew the council was capable to run the village without her, and any one of them could easily run the village as good or even better than she did.

Now the Orcus were on their way to her village, it was a good thing that there were no flying crafts for them in England or they would be here a lot sooner. Was it really safe just to hide the technology? Was Graham right, that they pose no threat? If it was true why was the captain preparing to leave? Or was he just fearful that they would find his ship? She hoped so and she hoped it was his only reason, because if he feared more that he let on, the whole village could be in danger. All these things ran through her mind until she finally reached the front door of her home.

"Thank you Knarf for your company."

"You are welcome my Lady." Knarf bowed his head to her as though she was a Queen then turned to walk away.

"Knarf"

"Yes my lady." He said stopping and turning to face her.

She wanted to say how much she had missed him, and she longed for their closeness once again. She wanted to tell him how vulnerable she was feeling and how she believed no one had faith in her anymore, and most of all she wanted him to tell her it would all be alright and hug her like he once used to. But she couldn't, the new her took over, the strong powerful her or the image she wanted everyone to believe and she felt she couldn't show Knarf that she was still really the old Julie on the inside. She couldn't let anyone know because she felt that she would be seen as weak and her position as leader would defiantly become pointless.

The people need a strong emotionless leader someone to make the tough decisions.

"There is no need for you to call me Lady all the time after all we are really good friends are we not." She said looking for a little assurance for the Julie that she still was.

"Yes you are right m... I mean Julie we are good friends." Replied Knarf.

"Good" She half smiled "Have a good night."

"Sleep well." He tipped his head then turned and walked away.

She watched as he walked away and when he turned the corner she listened to his footsteps against the stone floor of the shallows. There had been a time when he would wait and watch her enter her home to make sure she was safe, it had been a long time since he did such a thing. The passage ways were empty, the villagers were still out on the beach, and now she would go in and sleep while the rest of the council stay up all night preparing the village for the coming of the Orcus.

"Am I being selfish sleeping while the rest work?" she thought to herself. "No as the leader of the village I need my rest," she opened the door to her home and went in.

Knarf put his head around the corner making sure Julie had gone into her home safely. He had not gone, he just did not want her to know that he still cared too much about her safety; he knew things had changed between them but he could not help how he felt about her. He turned and really walked away to help make the preparations for the village.

Katie wandered through the forest, she had wondered how she had got there, she had never seen so many full grown trees close up in her life, she had seen a few on the big screen in the gathering hall but never this many and they were never this beautiful. She walked up to a tree and felt the roughness of the trunk, she had no idea what type of tree it was but it was not important to her. She was alone and she could see the sunlight shining down from amongst the top of the trees. She smelt the air and it was fresh, and she heard the creatures of the forest whistling and chirping, a cool breeze brushed against the smooth skin of her body and it was then that she realised that she was naked.

At first she was shocked but then she realised it did not matter, no one could see her and she liked the fresh air on her naked body it made her feel free, being there had made her realise the potential of no restriction, doing whatever she wanted and yes that included being naked in a forest, and she did not care she felt like she was a part of nature, she did not even think too long on the fact of how she came to be in such a place.

She turned away from the tree. The breeze blew something in her eye, she squinted and rubbed her eye to remove the dirt, when she finally gained her focus again she was not surprised to find six other young woman standing around her also unclothed. It was like she had expected them, it was as if they were a part of the forest or that they were the forest themselves. Their skins had a hint of green to them and their hair were long and like gold all except one, her hair was short. Their features were sharp and their ears were pointed like what Katie had expected an elf to look like, but they were not Elves as their eyes were bright green and hair colour was all wrong, every one of them were beautiful.

Katie felt no threat, the breeze turned into to a whistle, and the girl with the short hair stepped forward.

"I am Luceria, you may call me Lucy." Her voice was musical like her mother's when she spoke to her seriously.

"I am." Katie begun.

"Katie," She was interrupted "we know, you must be very special to be able to come here from so far. Listen. Can you hear that?"

Katie listened. It was the wind, it had become musical almost flute like, and the trees began to sway as if dancing to the rhythm.

"Yes I hear" Katie answered.

"Then come, young one. Dance with us."

They began to sway with the rhythm and the world became as though it was in slow motion. The wind became strong but smooth, the leaves from the ground flew up in the air and danced around them. Katie began to dance also, it was heavenly, dreamy, the breeze lifted the hair on their heads and their hair flowed in the wind while they all dance in a circle. As Katie danced she realised each girl was disappearing one by one. Leaving each a beautiful tree standing where the girls had last danced. All eventually vanished; all but Lucy, Katie and the strange girl stopped dancing and faced each other.

"I must go," Lucy said "it is not good for you to stay here long because the wind is changing, But when he comes go with him. You will be safe with him, bring him to us and we can help."

Just then the forest became dark. Katie looked up and saw black clouds above. When she looked back, all she could see was a tree where Lucy had been standing. She heard footsteps coming up behind her. She turned and saw a dark-skinned man of the like she had never seen before. He was different; she could tell, it was not just his hair that reminded her of long twisted black worm like things, it was the way he carried himself. Remembering she was naked, she felt bashful, but by the time she had decided to run he had picked her up in his arms, carrying her as though she was a small child. She felt his strength in his arms and was fearful of what he might do to her, so she decided to scream. Her heart began to beat wildly and she hoped that maybe the girls would return and help her, but, looking over the shoulders of the stranger, she saw something even more frightening than the strange man that was carrying her.

Three dark figures in hooded cloaks were running after them; it was as though they were floating on air chasing them she looked into the hood of one of them and all she could see were bright red eyes peering back. There was something frightening about them, something desperate and something evil that she sensed and made her skin crawl. Now she urged the stranger to run faster, but she realised the stranger was running faster than any man she had ever known. Her heart began to beat frantically, she felt there was something wrong with her. She looked down at her chest, and was shocked at what she saw. A light was pulsating through her skin where her heart was, and she wondered if she was going to die. As if in answer to her wondering, straight ahead of them were more of those things, nine of them stood waiting. And the stranger stopped.

One of the dark things spoke with a voice that echoed though her mind and sent shivers down her spine, it hissed the words "Giiive us the giiiirl and you may pass."

"No!" She screamed horrified "don't leave me with them."

And it was then the man spoke; he put her down and faced her. He had a beard that only went around his mouth and not along the cheeks of his face; with a sad half smile that showed a dimple on his face he said.

"I will never leave you."

Then he turned and rushed at the dark hooded creatures. His speed was amazing but the creatures moved just as fast. A pale white almost human hand grabbed her around the waist; it was one of them dragging her away from the stranger who was being overwhelmed by the creatures. She screamed, but no sound came out of her mouth. The creature covered up her eyes. She screamed again and this time it came out and it was so loud it echoed through the whole forest. Her heart was beating like mad, and she felt a pain in the centre of her forehead, she sat up screaming.

"It's Okay. It's Okay." She heard her mother's voice. She opened her eyes. Her mother had her arms around her hugging her. "It's just a dream dear; dreams can't hurt you unless you let them."

She was right it was a dream, but a dream that seemed too real. She had felt the trunk of a tree and had smelt the forest air, it was something she had never done in a dream before.

"Mum I am scared; please can I sleep with you tonight." Katie asked.

"Of course you can dear, come on."

Katie climbed out of bed feeling her nightdress making sure she was still fully clothed; she followed her mother into her sleeping room and into her bed. She laid there most of the night still frighten to fall asleep wondering about her dream, and about the Orcus and the conversations she had overheard at the meeting.

"Stupid girl" She finally thought, "You're making your own self scared with my own wild imagination about Orcus" She convinced herself.

And not thinking about the meaning of the girls in the forest or the strange man she had encountered in the dream, she turned over and drifted off to sleep once again.

The next day Katie had been awoken by her mother nice and early. The dream from the night before had already become distant in her mind, but she was eager to know more about the Orcus. They had both eaten the breakfast prepared by her mother, they washed and dried the dishes and headed down to the farm to work and meet the other families that was due on the roster to work the farm that day.

The Farm was built at the far end of the shallows right next to the garden that had begun to grow through the sheer ingenuity of Navi and his idea of using mirrors to bring in the sunlight to help grow the vegetables, plants and the little baby apple trees. He had obtained the seeds from a market salesman in the city London, who claimed to have collected many seeds from the Fairy Forest, Thetford. But the farm had begun years before Katie was ever born. She had been told that Navi's farther before he died had helped to make the farm what it was today, and now nothing was ever wasted or allowed to be wasted in the community. Everything was recycled, wasted food would be mixed up and put into the cattle feed for the cows or chickens that were also kept in the villages own personal farm. Everyone helped out because the whole village shared the farms riches. There was a roster for which week which family would tend to the farm and the farm animals, making sure they were taken top side to walk and to receive fresh air. The council's motto was healthy animal produced healthy food. So it was every family's job in the village to make sure they were clean and fed and healthy enough to breed and to be eaten or produce milk and eggs for the necessities of each household.

The farm was a lot of work and at least three or four families tended to it at a time, over the years the farm had become bigger and was becoming more crowded. The captain or Navi had brought back many more animals to produce for the village. This had made the Dover village the most riches human colony in England, so Navi and the council had discussed mining the walls at the back of the farm to create more space. Work was due to begin after the next fall of burning month.

Katie never minded working on the farm because her mother always let her tend to the horses, and she had a passion for the Captains horse. He had named it distant. Navi had told her that the captain took pride in that horse.

He told her a story of how the captain had once been lost in the Arctic ocean for two weeks. The ships compass and all other electronic equipment on board had failed, the equipment had gone crazy and they had no idea why, the sky was misty and cloudy so it was not even possible to navigate by the stars. Towards the end of the two weeks the engines began to fail and his men started to lose hope that they would ever see land again. But just then they sighted land; it was a place he was familiar with, it had been Russia. Somehow the ship had drifted through the Barents Sea along the northern passage and they docked at Chernaya. His ship needed repairs and was going nowhere without help. He had pleaded with the Russian people for help, but many had nothing and were afraid. It was obvious that the ship the captain had was one with extraordinary technology and if the Elves found out that the people helped they would all be punished. The captain was worried he knew that there was an Elfin camp no more than four miles away from where they had docked.

In Chernaya he came across a tradesman who offered the captain in return for food and supplies from his ship, a horse. The trade man had told the captain that the horse was a direct descendant of the Akhal-Teke breed and was one of the very few that was left in the world. He continued to say that the Akhal Teke was one of the most ancient and unique breeds of the world; it was created in Southern Turkmenia by a tribe called the Teke on the Akhal oasis. It was the most distinctive strain of the ancient race of horses known as the Turk Oman or Turkmene. Directly descended from the wild steppe horse, the Turk Oman was legendary he had said. It was also known as the Bactrian and was used by the great leaders Darius and Alexander. The cavalry of Darius was mounted on this horse of quality and very successful because of it.

The captain had heard of the Bactrian, his father had told him an ancient Chinese tale about a battle and a Chinese leader who attacked Bactria thousands of years ago in order to obtain these horses. In Chinese legends it was known as the heavenly horse or the horse that sweats blood. He continued to explain that the horse could cross an amazing distant with very little food and water. The captain was convinced and purchased the horse; he left his men to guard the ship and raced across the lands as fast as the horse could carry him, fearful that there would be little time before the ship was discovered by the Elves. He was amazed at the horse's stamina, the horse had needed little rest because of this they had cleared the whole country of Russia in four days and it was then they stopped and the horse received its first supplement of water. The tradesman had told the captain to feed the horse boiled eggs and dough cake, so the captain did.

They continued their journey and passed through Poland straight into Germany and did not rest until they reached Amsterdam. It had taken them only three weeks to reach Amsterdam, exhausted and starved the captain went out to the sea and made his secret calling. The new horse and the captain spent only one night on the coastline of Amsterdam. He fed the horse what little food they had left forgetting about himself for the horse had done him well. Soon the maids heard the call of the captain and arrived to meet him. The captain had told them what had happened and the maids carried both the captain and the horse across the sea at a great speed in a bubble of magic straight to Dover. They left him there as they set of to Russia to bring the captain his ship and crew, so Navi had told Katie.

When they returned the ship they explained to the captain never to go into the arctic again as it was known to be full of bad magic; the maids themselves did not like to go anywhere near that ocean. The captain realised how fortunate he was; he decided he was now in debt to the maids and to the horse. He named her Distant, because of the remarkable distance she had travelled. He promised that one-day he would return the favour to the maids.

Katie had loved this story and thought about it every time she tended to Distant; she believed the horse was remarkable to travel at such speed for that many miles on so little food and water. She had found herself at the stables where all the other young people from the other families were tending to the horses getting ready to take them top side for a ride along the beach. Each week the teens and some younger would tend to whatever horse they could find, but none of them would go near Distant. They knew Katie tended to this horse and though she communicated very little with them they all had some fear of her. They believed her to be weird, ever since she had snapped at one of the boys for trying to take Distant topside. Besides the captain had made it official that only Katie may tend to his horse, he had realised the love and respect she had for Distant, and felt she was the only one that could best take care of her when she was on land at Dover. Katie groomed distant and mucked out the stable, then lead Distant out through the farm and along the hallways of the shallows to the exit that was near the farm.

The weather topside was cooler than the day before and there were no restrictions on going out in the sun, she stroked Distance's mane, she loved this horse it had been places she could only dream of and knew more about the world beyond Dover than she could possibly imagine. She ran her hands down the side of distant wondering what stories the horse could tell if she could talk.

"Let's go" She dug her heals into the side of Distant and off they went at a gallop. She loved feeling the breeze on her face as she rode down the beach her hair fluttered behind her as distant picked up more speed. There were other youngsters on the beach riding the horses giving them the exercise they needed.

"Katie" She heard the call on the wind, it was Claire. She slowed Distant to a canter as she approached Claire who was running towards her across the white sands of the beach. Distant began to trot as she came to a stop when Claire and Katie reached each other.

"Have you heard anything," Claire said looking worried. Katie knew immediately what she was referring to.

"No not one person has mentioned a thing."

"Why haven't they told us yet, do you think they are not coming anymore?" Claire asked.

"No I think they may make an announcement this evening, the council probably have a few more things to do first, anyway I am trying not to think about it, it drives me crazy when I do, I wonder what they look like and last night I had the most scariest dream, so it's best to put it out of our minds until it happens." Katie replied.

"Your right I could not sleep last night I was worried the Orcus would get me while I slept and I could hardly eat my breakfast."

"Come on climb on, we will go for a ride and forget about it for awhile." Katie put her hand out and took Claire's arm as Claire put her foot in the stirrup and climbed up onto the back of Distant right behind Katie.

"Hold on tight" shouted Katie.

Claire put her hands around Katie's waist and held her tight, as she knew Katie was going to push Distant to her maximum speed. It was what Katie did when she had things on her mind, she believed that the speed, the wind and the mere strength of Distant could wash all her worries away for a short time, and she was right. Claire had been on the back of Distant before with Katie, when Claire had found her boyfriend kissing Anita Baxter, the local teen tart of the village. All she did was cry but Katie had snuck Distant out of the stables and took Claire on the back of her like she was now. Katie had said to her "When we ride all that matters are our dreams and how one day we will fly there."

That was all she said and they galloped off at such a speed into the night with nothing but the stars and the moon and the great sky ship lights to guide them. At first she had been scared and then her mind had drifted with the breeze from the ride and in that moment all was right with the world.

"Let's go" Katie shouted.

Claire snapped out of her reminiscing and Distant bolted and off they went Distant kicking up the sand leaving a cloud of dust behind them. Claire closed her eyes and enjoyed the ride. Katie had become like a big sister to her over the past year or two and though she had never told her, she still always knew what to do to make her feel better about herself no matter what the situation.

They rode all the way up to the peak and they stopped to water the horse. Claire decided that she wanted to sunbathe; she had always thought she was too pale compared to everyone else. So Katie joined her and they both laid on their backs on the peak looking up into the sky wearing tinted glasses and dreaming of better times. It was mid afternoon by the time they had arrived back to the stables. Katie groomed Distant once again and platted her tail, just as she was putting the blanket over her the Captain arrived.

"Arrr I see you've done her tail, how'd you know she'd be taken a voyage?" asked the Captain.

"Just a guess, I thought it's been a while since you have been at the sea in your well hidden ship that we hardly get to see, so I thought today would be a good day to prepare her to leave" Replied Katie.

"You are too smart for your own good young lady" The Captain winked at her not believing a word she said. "I'd be right in thinking that you exercised her well then."

"You'd be thinking right captain." Katie smirked.

"You're a wonderful girl young Katie, I did right letting only you take care of distant."

"Did I do so good that you would show me where you hide your ship and give me a tour?" Katie asked cheekily.

"I would like to but were she is hid aint no place for a child." Replied the Captain.

Child? Katie thought she hated that word, she was not a child she was a young lady, how dare the captain call her a child and after all that she had done for him. She felt like she was going to explode but instead she turned and walked away, without saying a word.

"Katie" The captain called after her.

But she ignored him and walked away all fired up. The captain was an elder and she dared not shout at him though she was so very close to doing it. She walked, or more like stormed along the corridors of the shallows, all hot and angry. As she walked she heard voices coming from the generator room, she had thought they would of sealed the room up already knowing that the Orcus were on their way. She stopped at the door way and peaked a look through the crack of the door, it was Navi and Mrs Last.

"I feel lonely Navi" Hayley was saying. "Ever since my husband died I have had no one, I don't like to sleep alone."

The whole village had known that Hayley had lost her husband three years ago; he was trying to tie his fishing boat up in burning month under one of the cliffs archways, so it would not get burned up, and while running back to the shallows a fire storm had started and he was burnt alive.

"I'm a widow with a child; no one wants to take care of me and my little boy." Hayley said.

"Look Hayley you are an attractive lady and you have a wonderful child, any man would be crazy not to have you." Navi replied.

"Would you have me?" asked Hayley bluntly.

There was a silence before Navi spoke. "There's something I have been meaning to tell you, I have liked you for a long while but thought there was no chance of a beautiful woman such as yourself liking a dirty engineer like me."

"You're wrong Navi I have noticed you for a long while." She placed her hand on his arm and stepped closer to him. "I spend my nights dreaming about you holding me in your arms."

Yuk! Katie was thinking the idea of Navi and Mrs Last smooching or anything, made romance to her seem unwanting.

"Have you… " Navi begun.

"Shhush" Hayley cut him short placing her finger on his lips, and then she leaned forwards and kissed him. Katie felt like she was going to be sick.

"Come to my home this evening and I will make you dinner." Hayley said when she had removed herself from Navi's lips. "Oh and bring your overnight bag you can stay the night," she said as she began to walk towards the door.

Katie tiptoed away as fast as she could, her mind was racing now, this was not a good day for her and things seem to be getting worse, what did this mean? Hayley and Navi together. Would Navi then turn her away and stop teaching her things? He would have too many responsibilities taking care of Mrs Lasts child. He may even teach him to become his apprentice, and Katie would mean nothing to him. How could he do this to her? She had been his friend and apprentice for a long time. How could he just cast her aside just like that for a child he hardly knew?

"Calm down" She told herself "Don't let your mind run away now, like I have not got enough to deal with." She carried on storming the corridors until she reached her home.

3

Monsters in the Night

Knarf walked along the outer regions of the village along the iron wall, straight up to the great gate that had been created to keep unwanted guests and bandits away. He had come to check the guard tower to make sure the four guards on the gate did not fire any weapons at anything that looked suspicious. He was worried that the Orcus would turn up and the guards would shoot not knowing whom they were. Guard duty was a restless job and shooting at anything that moved, was what kept the guards entertained.

"You there" Knarf shouted up at one of the two guards that were up in the tower at the gate.

"Yes sir." They had immediately recognised Knarf as Yenned's right hand man and all respected him. He was seen as some kind of strategist or military commander of the village. It was said that his grandfather had been a great general and had taught his father all about military conduct and strategies just like his father had taught him. All the young boys of the village who only dreamed of what it was like being a soldier, dreamt of growing up and becoming a village guard so they could learn soldiering from Knarf.

"Where are the other two whose suppose to be on duty?" Knarf asked.

"They are patrolling the topside of the wall they should

be back in an Hour sir." Came the reply.

"Well make sure that no one shoots at anything today without reporting to me first." Knarf ordered.

"May I ask why sir?" The young guard shouted back down to Knarf.

"No you may not. All you should know is that it is the orders of your lady Yenned and that should be enough, make sure the others know." Knarf began to walk back towards the outside homes of the Village. It was on his mind that the guns should be taken away from the guards until the threat of the Orcus had past; It would not be good if they arrived and found them standing with weapons they may perceive this as an immediate threat. But what did they expect they were a popular village the riches this far south, not even the other two Dover villages had accomplished what they had achieved, and with human and Golin bandits roaming the desert they need their guns to protect themselves.

It had actually been a whole year since there village was last attacked, it seemed as though the bandits had given up and kept attacking the other two villages and stealing from them. Navi had travelled the seven miles to the nearest village and helped them with repairs only a month ago, next week he is to travel to the silver city to buy more weapons for them and also for their own village. More and more young boys who were ready and willing to learn had approached Knarf to become guards. Knarf already had fifty young men under his command, and to have another fifty trained in the art of weaponry and defence would make the village seem a lot safer, that's if they survive the Orcus visit. Knarf was worried, he was concerned that the captain was leaving, and really the captain had the only real means of escape if anything were to go wrong.

"Mr Knarf sir, Mr Knarf." Came a voice from behind him. He turned to recognise the guard he had just spoken with who was up in the tower. And he was running towards him

"What is it man." Knarf asked when the young lad finally reached him.

"There is..." the boy took a breath "there is something coming our way. It's about five minutes from us and I think there is more than one."

"Sound the alarm" Knarf barked as he ran towards the gate.

Katie was already at home when the siren began ringing, the sound of it echoed through the whole of the shallows. Her mother raced across the room and locked the door.

"Mum lets go and see what's going on?"

"Don't be silly Katie you know the rules, all women and children are to lock themselves in the shallows until told otherwise."

She was right it was the rules and a stupid one at that. Katie had wondered before that if bandits attacked and got through the gates everyone would be trapped in their homes waiting to die one by one when they could be trying to escape. But Katie had thought about this many times and had already made her escape route through the vent.

Outside everyone was running, women and children were running to the shallows while all the men were going to the armoury and getting guns and then running to the iron gate of the village. The village consisted of eight hundred people, of whom two hundred and fifty were women, two hundred were men and three hundred were children ranging from the age of one month to the age of sixteen. Boys at the age of seventeen were considered a man and were expected to defend the village with their lives. But this did not include the fifty men that manned the captain's ship, who followed his orders and his orders only. A hundred women were also selected and trained in using weaponry and were also selected as the shallow defence to protect it if worse ever came to the worse, they were known as the home guard.

Knarf saw the villagers running towards the gates with gun in hand, and he prayed that the visitors were not Orcus. Knarf was not a tall man but he stood on the iron wall, head lifted high wearing his father's uniform that belonged to his father before him. A uniform of a general, as the men of the village and himself watched the dust of the desert swirl up behind the oncoming visitors.

"Is it Orcus." Navi said, he had just arrived and stood behind Knarf.

"No I don't think so, it is only two vehicles, and by the speed they are travelling I would say they were horse and cart." Knarf answered.

"Good." The captain said, "I did not want to be stuck here as I plan to leave early tomorrow, and if it was them my ship would be seen leaving and this village would be in serious danger for harbouring my ship and my crew."

They all watched silently as two horses pulling two carts came closer until they reached the great Iron Gate of the village. In one cart sat a bearded man with a young boy beside him, and in the back of the cart were three young girls and one woman. The other cart had three men two boys and one young girl.

"What is it you want here Stranger," Knarf shouted down from on top of the wall.

"Just a place to stay, and maybe a ride on a ship"

"Fool there be no ships here and if there be a ship there be not one man there abouts brave enough to travel the seas, much far from land." The captain shouted down.

"We heard different, my people have heard of the famous captain Gill, who travels the sea's protected by maids his stories travel far, and very few people know where this man can be found," the bearded man from the cart shouted back.

"And where are your people," Knarf asked.

"They are back at home in the village Dover, seven miles north of here."

"So why are you running. I hear the village there is a good place." Knarf asked.

"Have you not heard?" the man replied.

"Heard what?" Knarf asked.

"The Orcus has arrived at my village."

There was a murmur amongst the men on top of the wall, none of them had heard about the Orcus, as they had not yet been informed.

"Let them in." Knarf shouted quickly.

Yenned had told him not to mention anything to the people as yet, as she was preparing the announcement, but time was running short and Knarf knew it was time that she let the villagers know of the danger they may be facing.

The great Iron shaft was lifted and then it took ten men to push the gate open enough to let the Visitors in with the carts. Rope was then attached to the hooks that was built into the gate so all the men could pull on the ropes until the gates were closed once again.

"Every man must return his weapons to the armoury including guards; no more weapons will be used until further notice." Knarf shouted at the villagers.

There was more chatting amongst the people. They knew something was being kept from them, but they all began to walk away to return their weapons and giving the all clear to the home guard.

"Where do you think you're going?" Knarf said to the four guards that were walking away from him.

"To return our weapons sir" One replied.

"Don't be silly, there are strangers in our mist though they seem honourable they must be guarded, follow us" Then he turned to the bearded stranger.

"I mean no offence but we must be careful we have

heard that bandits have become clever in our days and use all sorts of trickery to get into well guarded villages."

"No offence taken, my name is Kir and I would do the same if the situation were reversed." Replied the man.

"Kir is that really you." Navi stepped closer.

"Navi my old friend it has been a while." Both men greeted each other with a Hug.

"You look different the beard hides your face well that is why I did not recognise you."

"So you know this man then Navi?" Knarf asked.

"Yes and I can vouch for him he is a good man." Navi replied.

"Well I will still need to bring them before the council, so they must stay under guard until we can arrange for a meeting, but this one and this one only may stay with you if you agree to be responsible for him." Knarf explained.

"I agree he may stay at my place."

"No if it is all the same to you I would prefer to stay with my friends." Kir intervened.

"Okay. but I will come to the holding cell and make sure you have all you need and are taken care of until the meeting." Navi said agreeing with his friends wishes.

They all headed towards the shallows under the escort of two armed guards.

In the distant high up on a desert mound, a slender figure stood watching with hawk like vision as the villagers opened the gates and let in some new arrivals. There was someone there they needed to see, and getting into to the village would be simple enough for him but getting in undetected in daylight would be a risk full challenge. He turned to the other two and let them know it would be better to wait until night fall hoping that they had that much time left to wait.

Knarf and Navi had seen their new guests to the holding

cells. Navi had promised Kir that they would have the matter resolved as soon as possible, and that the first thing in the morning they would be brought before the council. The two guards were left to guard the cells for the night while Navi went to make his appointment with Hayley.

Knarf began to walk the shallows towards Yenned's home, it was dusk and the sun was going down in the west it was at this time that Yenned liked to be alone and to focus on the events of the next day. She rarely liked to be disturbed at this time, but Knarf understood the seriousness of the unforeseen circumstance that the council has been put in. The new visitors must be dealt with soon, and if they were allowed to mingle with the population the rumours of the Orcus arrival would spread panic through the whole village. He arrived at her door, he paused for a moment wondering if he should wait till morning to tell her, but just then her door swung open.

"Knarf I was just coming to find you." Yenned said

"Me" Knarf was surprised only for a moment

"Yes I heard the sirens stop so I figured that it was a false alarm."

Of course Knarf thought forgetting that Yenned would be waiting for a report on what had occurred,

"We have a problem my lady." Knarf began to explain.

"Knarf how many times have I told you not to be so formal with me am I not your friend first before I am lady Yenned."

Knarf looked to the ground sheepishly, reluctant to answer the question. Yenned noticed how uncomfortable he was and not pushing the question any further she continued.

"So what is the problem?"

He explain the situation to Yenned. "It is important now that we call a village meeting and let everyone know about the Orcus I fear we have delayed too long."

"You worry too much," Yenned said in an offhand way

"And you don't?" Knarf questioned wondering if Yenned really had lost hope or even cared in being the leader of the people.

"Okay Just make sure that everyone tonight know there is a meeting early first thing in the morning. I will announce to the village the situation and then we will have the council meeting to decide what is to be done with these villagers from across the way. I need my sleep." She said as she turned and closed the door on Knarf.

She leaned against the door wondering if Knarf was still out there. She had been offended by his reaction to answering if they were friends first, and she wanted to hurt him for the way he was to her. She had tried to mend their friendship, but it was hard not knowing what it was exactly that she had done to ruin their friendship. A tear came to her eye, the feeling she had for Knarf was strong, so strong that she did not realise how deep her heart went out to him. Knarf stood on the other side of the door, shocked at Yenned's behaviour, he started to believe her soul had gone dark and care really for nothing. He turned and walked away deep in thought. He had been set a task, now he must get the guards to knock at every door in the village to make sure they all attend the meeting in the great hall the following morning.

Night time had fallen, and the strangers crept closer to the village and made their stop behind a rock not far from the village entrance. The slender figure of the three scanned the desert to make sure they had been undetected, putting his hand on the slender figures shoulder the small man whispered.

"Go quick. If there is trouble we will come."

Knowing the importance of the mission the slender figure stood up closing his eyes in concentration, meditating for only a short time until a glow began to appear around his body, it grew to a bright yellowish light covering his whole shape before the light shrunk to a small ball of energy taking with it the body of the figure. It buzzed around the head of the small stranger like a firefly and then sped off towards the village and over its walls.

"What was that?" A guard on the walls said to one of the others.

"What?" Replied his comrade

"I saw a big bright light out there."

"I think you're tired. Your shift is over soon, get some rest, all I see is that fire fly." The guards all laughed as the smallest firefly flew past their heads and down towards the shallows.

The captain had wandered back to his room after being on his ship and making sure his men were prepared to leave first thing in the morning, His horse had been put in the ship stables which was at the hull of the ship and so had seven other horses. The captain had learned it was necessary to take horses with him whenever he travelled, because when they reach land, food and supplies were never always close. The men had stocked up on food supplies and fuel, it was a good thing that his ship ran on gas fuel because after the war there were plenty of places to find the gases needed. Abandoned barrels of the stuff could be found anywhere on any continent and many markets sold this stuff cheaply people always had a use for it, but there were places also contaminated with gases so bad that most species would die passing through those dangerous lands. Still there were those who went to harness the gasses and contain them for sale, over the years.

The captain had brought and found more than enough fuel and he had been given his own stock room in the shallows where he stored thousand of containers that kept his fuel. He had around fifty years of fuel supply stored in the shallows and he also had more stored in secret places on other continents so he was sure never run out of fuel at sea. The captain also began to wonder about the new strangers from across the way, they had heard of him and they have come to seek a ride on his ship, if they are genuine he wondered if he should take them.

He entered his room and found his clothes case on his bed where he had left it, he began to pack his things away thinking on how much he was going to miss this place, believing that it would be a long time before they came back to the shallows hoping that it would still be there after the Clones visit. But it was for his friends and neighbours he cared the most, sadness fell on him because he had to leave them, but his first priority was to his ship and crew, and as long as they stayed they were both in danger. So it was down to the villagers to take care of their own and he would take care of his. He was so deep in thought that he never noticed the flash of light behind him, or the figure that sneaked up on him. The figure grabbed him from behind and placed his hand over his mouth.

"At last" the captain thought. "They have sent an assassin for me" and he prayed it would be over quick and painless.

Navi laid in bed deep in thought, he tilted his head down to look at Hayley who was deep asleep with her head on his chest, he noticed every curve of her body, he ran his finger down her spine and felt the softness of her skin, how beautiful she was he thought. He would have never believed that he could be here right now in an apartment with a woman so beautiful. He found it amazing that she wanted him just as bad as he wanted her. He never knew the feeling he was feeling right now and he wondered if it was love. Hayley stirred and made a quite moan, he felt every minute he laid there he was falling deeper and deeper in love with her. He began to wonder about her child, he was only a baby nearly reaching the age of four.

He would be a good stepfather to the child, he did not plan to replace the boy's father but he planned to be there for him. Noel was the boys' name, and an intelligent boy he was, he would teach him his trade, and the boy would become his apprentice. For a moment his mind went to young Katie who always longed for this title and believed in her heart that she was his apprentice. Before Hayley he had planned to make Katie his apprentice but now he will have a stepson he would have to make this child his first priority, and maybe he would find time to continue teaching Katie, she was a bright child and he was sure she would not stop pestering him until she learned all she wanted to know. He ran his fingers through Hayley's long brown hair, and then leaned over to kiss her. It was in this moment a loud rumble went through out the shallows echoing down the hallways like a wave of big explosions, something had happened, Hayley woke immediately.

"What was that?"

"I don't know," Replied Navi "Stay here and I will go and check." he got up and started to put on his clothes.

Hayley too began to get dressed

"What are you doing?" Navi asked

"I am coming with you"

"No you're not stay here I will be back" Navi headed towards the door

But just then the sirens began screeching through the shallows and the commotion of the villagers could be heard running around in the hallways.

"I am coming with you now I am not staying here wait for me."

Hayley ran into her child room and pulled him from his bed and carried him in her arms, she returned to her front door where Navi was waiting.

"You should have stayed here something bad has

happened and I don't want you to get hurt,"

"I rather be with you were you can protect me."

They opened the door and headed into the hallways of the shallows, smoke streamed along the hallways and gunfire could be heard further down the halls.

"Quick, this way" Navi took them away from the gunfire, he was heading towards the captains ship.

Katie laid her head on her mother's chest shaking silently with tears streaming from her eyes, she could not find the strength to move, nor did she want too, her night dress was all stained now but she cared little about it, this night had been the worst night Katie had ever imagined, and she believed nothing could get worse. She could hear the commotion going on in the hallways of the shallows and only a moment ago this had made her scared, but now she feared nothing, she was here in her mother's arms and nothing could break this bond between mother and daughter.

Katie wiped the tears from her eyes. She looked to her hand and found blood instead of water. The past moments events were playing through her mind, leaving her in a state of shock— like an old movie playing over and over again in her mind. Only moments ago her mother had come rushing into her room, after the loud bang. She grabbed Katie from her bed, whispering "there is no time" and ushering her to hide under the bed. Her mother started to get under the bed too, but in that moment the door behind came crashing in, and Katie watched her mother being pulled away from her screaming. Katie could see two pairs of enormous feet in her room one of the things had its foot on her mother holding her to the ground.

She heard a chilling laugh; one of the creatures knelt down and Katie saw its face. It was the most hideous creature she had ever seen, its shape proclaimed to be human but it was obviously not. Its face was twisted and deformed in the ugliest way— it was as though someone had taken a hammer to the creature repeatedly to the back of the head. A gigantic lump could be seen protruding from the creatures skull, Katie watched as her mother began to struggle, and the creature took its clawed hand and placed it up her mother's night dress, her mother screamed, this made the creature laugh even more. The other creature knelt down too and held her mother's arms, this one wore a helmet with horns, he held her mother arms tight and Katie could not understand what they were doing to her, but she knew they were hurting her, just as she decided to crawl out from under the bed her mother went silent and turned her head towards her, perking her lips together indicating to Katie to be silent. Just then the creature ripped her mother's night dress exposing her body to them, the one holding her hands put his sharp teeth to her mother's breast, just then the other seemed to climb on to her mother rubbing his self against her in a strange way, she knew it was hurting her mother because her mother screamed violently.

Katie became even more scared these creatures were evil and they had come to do harm. Where is the home guard she thought to herself, why did someone not come to stop this? Katie cried franticly now she could not bear to look anymore she closed her eyes and covered her ears but this did not stop Katie from hearing her mother's screams, moments passed and Katie's mothers screams had stopped. Katie opened her eyes hoping to find the home guard had come to save her mother, But she was wrong her mother had passed out and the creature had slowed it's rubbing and moved itself from being on top of her mother.

It was then the other creature lifted its head from her mother's breast that Katie saw that the creature had tore away at her mother's breast with its teeth and was eating part of it. It was a dread full sight blood oozed out of her mother, Katie feared that her mother was dead, but she was not because she stirred and opened her eyes, the creatures both laughed, and a third entered the room, they spoke with a strange tongue but somehow Katie understood the words. The one who entered had told the other they had problems further along the hallway. And the one that had rubbed her mother said he would now come there. The one holding her mother's hands got up and left the room with the other, and just at the moment Katie thought they would all leave so she could tend to her mother. The creature pulled out the longest of knives, forcing her mother legs apart he stabbed her repeatedly between the legs blood was everywhere, the creature stood and spat on her mother's forehead.

"Ecar mortar" The creature said.

Katie understood this he had called her mother human bitch, and then turned and walked out of the room laughing and joining the rest of his men as they all walked down the hallways of the shallows.

Katie crawled from her hiding place barley finding the strength to reach her mother. She was trying to scream out "why" but only a whisper came from her mouth as tears streamed down her face and her throat became dry, she pulled herself on to her mother and laid her face on her chest, with her gown now bloodied Katie had thought her mother dead, but to her surprise her mother raised her hand and reached for a necklace she had always worn. She took it from her neck and grabbed Katie's arm and placed it in the palm of Katie's hand.

"Mother we will get help, you will be Okay." Katie cried

Her mother was struggling to say something

"No shush it Okay. Don't speak mother please please" Katie cried,

"Listen" her mother whispered, "Take this your father... father" her mother began to cough.

"Mother don't speak" But she continued anyway
"Your father will know this and help you, now you must… . Must Go"
"No I won't leave you,"
"Promise you will … … coo cooo" her mother coughed up blood that spat out of her mouth everywhere then her body went still and motionless and her eyes stayed wide open gazing up towards the ceiling.

"No" Katie screamed "No" she screamed until she could not scream no more. She never found the strength to leave her mother and neither did she plan to. She laid there in her mother's blood hoping they would come and kill her next because without her mother she had nothing nor did she want anything. They had taken her mother's life and no one came to help now she wished to die too. The images of what the creatures had done still played in her mind, and the more she thought about it the more it seemed she drifted away from reality deeper and deeper into a state of mind not many people ever recovered from.

Blood in her hair and on her gown and on her hands Katie began to hum the ancient song her mother had taught her, laying on her mothers' chest Katie curled up rocking back and forth humming.

Billy stood strong with his weapon and what was left of the villagers and the home guard. The creatures had backed off for a while but he knew the oncoming attack was going to begin again soon, he had held the position he had been told to hold by Knarf longer than anyone could expect, and if Knarf did not return soon they would have to retreat deeper into the shallows opening up to wider spaces and he knew that this would be the end of them, but there could be nothing else he could do the ammunition was running low and they would be lucky if they could out last the next attack.

It had only been a few moments ago when Billy who was on guard duty at the gate of the shallows heard the gun fire and explosion, but no alarm had gone off outside at the gate. He wondered then if he should sound the alarm but first decided to look. As he opened the iron door he saw hundreds of creatures running towards the doorway, he quickly bolted the doors and ran, he barley reached the second doors when a great explosion smashed through the first set of doors knocking them off their hinges and flying over his head. Billy fell to the floor, he turned to see the creatures passing through the first doors and was quick to his feet to lock the second doors. These doors were stronger and not so easy to get through. They were made out of a metal that was rare. Navi had once told him that this metal was alien and very strong and he had paid a great price for it. Billy could hear the creatures on the other side trying to get in. He raced to the alarm and pressed the button, the sirens screeched throughout the shallows, and men and the home guard rushed to the armoury and joined him at the doors.

"What is it?" Knarf had asked reaching the doors.

"Creatures lots of them have entered the village", Billy blabbered

Just then there was banging at the door,

"Help"

There were guards out there still alive.

"Quick men take up your arms and fight" Shouted Knarf

Billy readied his weapon,

"Not you," Knarf told him "you are to stay here with the home guard and be our last line of defence if we fail OK?." Billy nodded indicating he understood "close the doors if it seems we won't make it."

Knarf then open the doors and joining the few guards that had fought their way through and together they headed out into the darkness to fight an enemy more dangerous than they could imagine.

The battle raged Billy watched as the guards and most of the men of the village stormed out and down the slope of the shallows pathway, guns blazing killing monsters along the way. The night was lit up with gunfire and laser bolt weapons. They were Orcus Billy had never seen an Orcus before but he recognised the symbol on the uniform of the dead creature before him. The symbol of the house of Maxius Millidor, These were the reject clones the ones that never turned out right, the ones given to the Elves to do their dirty bidding. They were believed to have super human strength, and carried alien weaponry. But why would they attack the village for no reason Billy questioned as he watched the battle.

Knarf was a warrior, a true soldier like his father before him. He went out there fighting and shooting every Orcus he could see, continuing to communicate with his men by hand signals as the battle was too loud to be heard shouting. He signalled for a flare and up it went high in the sky lighting up the whole village. Knarf and his men froze in shock for a moment, they never realised how many men they were fighting but now they could see. There was no way they could win this battle. There were at least 800 fully armed clones standing in the light, and Knarf and his men were no more than two hundred strong.

Knarf shouted and signalled the retreat, but somehow the enemy had closed off the path behind them making the retreat almost impossible. Billy watched as the men fought and died bravely in the battle and how hard they fought trying to make it back to the slope that lead up into the shallows. Men shot and killed Orcus while others ran out of ammo or were over run. The Orcus were beasts, they hacked of arms and heads, limbs were spread out over the village everywhere. Billy noticed the hatred they had towards the humans because they took the time to stop and shoot repeatedly into the heads of already dead humans making it almost impossible to ever tell who the man was. He realised the battle was hopeless for his people and started to believe none of them would make it back alive.

For a moment he lost track of Knarf, but then he came into view again at the bottom of the slope. He had made it. Knarf and three other men stood bravely firing their bullets into the wave of Orcus. Knarf ran out of ammo for his machine gun, throwing down the gun he pulled out his side arm and emptied the chamber into more Orcus. Somehow they made it on to the slope and work their way towards the top. The Orcus began firing laser bolts at them. They flew through the night time air like beautiful beams of light but missing Knarf and the men they crashed into the side of the rock and cause considerable damage to the hill that the shallows was built into. Knarf and the others dodged laser bolt after laser bolt. The Orcus were following up the pathway so Knarf threw a grenade onto the path and blew many of them off and into pieces. They finally reached the top and Knarf stood for a moment to see if anyone else was going to make it. Billy watched the stoned look on Knarf's face as he watched his men die in the battle. He saw men he had trained and men who were closed to him. He watched farmers, fisherman and fathers die. Each man had a family and those who did not, planned to some day and now they would never get the chance. If they make it through this night he would be the one to tell the wives and the children that they had lost their husband and father. Knarf turned and signalled to the other three men to come inside with him, they stopped shooting and ran inside. Billy quickly followed and closed the big doors behind them; it was a sad night for the Dover Village for most of its men had been lost.

Knarf shouted for a weapon and someone handed him a

fully loaded AK- 47, it was an old weapon but most of the villager's weapons were old.

"We must hold this doorway" Knarf had said "It is strong it will take them time to break... " he paused

Just then a drilling sound could be heard in the corners of the great door from the other side, everyone went silent and waited.

Billy knew Knarf had sensed something.

"Ready yourselves men and women" Knarf shouted boldly

At that moment every man and women reloaded their weapons, the cacophony of weapons reloading echoed all around. Then there was silence. Every one waited, guns aimed towards the door, moments passed, and then finally the drilling stopped. Every man and women seemed to have held their breath, because not a sound could be heard, no sound from beyond the door, or even on Billy's side, not a whisper or a breath, a minute passed and nothing happened. It seemed that whatever the enemy tried had not worked on the door. Billy finally heard a few sighs of relief, Knarf to seem to relax.

"OK. The moment has past" Knarf addressed the guards "Know we must prepare. Argh!..." He screamed, as he and many others flew down the hallway from the overwhelming explosion that had took place at the door. It seemed as if everything became slow motion. Billy had ducked almost straight away as the heavy doors flew past him and crashed into many of the women home guard crushing them to death as blood spewed from their heads and bodies. The doors continued their roll forced by the explosion cutting into many as they passed before they came to a stop. Billy was scared as he watched Orcus pour in through the doorway, stabbing and shooting at anything that was in their path. But there was another reason that made him fear, he could not hear, the explosion had been so loud that his ear lobes were damaged, it was like a silent movie.

An Orcus headed towards him and Billy could not find the courage to point his weapon and shoot, he had never killed anything before, and he was now faced with the dilemma that maybe he couldn't ever kill anything. Billy tried to get to his feet, but the creature knocked him back down with a mighty hit, which almost knocked him unconscious. The creature did not want to waste his laser bolt on a puny human such as himself and raised his blade to end it all for him, but out of nowhere came Knarf unloading his weapon into the creatures neck. The creature dropped dead and Knarf was shouting something at Billy, but he could not make out what he was saying. Knarf came close to Billy moving his lips. He slapped Billy in the head and almost instantly sound came rushing in all around him.

"… You boy" Knarf had said. " Huh? I say what's wrong with you? Take up your weapon and fight. We must give the others time to retreat to the star ways"

Knarf was shouting, yet Billy barely heard him over the gun fire and all the commotion. Bullet and lasers whizzed past their heads, and Billy found himself in the thick of the battle, Knarf helped him to his feet and then left him, signalling for the three men that survived the battle outside. But instead of running away from the doorway, they walked bold and fast towards the oncoming Orcus. Like mad men, firing their weapons walking side by side, they were all of one mind, Knarf and his men. They read each other like a book and worked as a unit, something Knarf had always talked about in training. Two of the men stopped and laid down behind the rubble of the explosion still firing while Knarf and the others stood firing either side of them using larger pieces of rubble as cover.

"Empty" One man shouted and another man threw him a Clip and he reloaded.

It seemed that for a moment the creatures backed off, as many of their own men died at their feet. It appeared that these creatures had never come across men such as these; just then Billy noticed a wounded Orcus near Knarf's feet going for his weapon. Without thinking Billy shot the creature, not once but repeatedly he moved forward and shot it in anger and in rage. The thought that these creatures had entered his home and killed his friends and his people raced through his mind, and now they were trying to kill his mentor. Billy could not let go of the trigger as tears rolled down his face from anger and fear, he then felt Knarf's hand on his shoulder.

"Now shoot at the ones that are alive." Knarf shouted over the weapons fire.

And both Billy and Knarf and the other three stood together firing and holding back the Orcus while the others retreated to the star ways.

They held the position as long as they could, but the mighty numbers of the Orcus soon became overwhelming. Knarf took what looked like dough from a pouch he was wearing and stuck it to the wall beside him. "Retreat Quick" he shouted. Billy, Knarf and the other three men stopped firing and ran as fast as they could towards the star ways, Orcus poured in after them running behind them. Up ahead Billy could see that the home guard had built a barricade across the star way blocking off the major passageway that lead towards the council hall and the area where most of the council members were housed. As they crossed the star ways, Billy's mind went out to those who lived down the other paths, hoping that they had all left and had made it to the barricade. But on passing beyond the barricade he could see that not even half of the village women and children were on the other side. All the home guard was fully loaded and ready, some villagers held guns too and their children. They all began firing when Knarf, Billy and his men were safely on the other side of the barricade shooting the Orcus as they charged towards them.

"Fire in the hole" Knarf screamed as he ducked down behind the stone tables and metal chairs and tin cupboards that the home guard had used for a barricade. Pressing a hand held trigger in his hand Billy now knew it was a trigger for some kind of bomb that Knarf had placed on the wall. In the instant, another explosion occurred caving in the path they had just left and sending fire all the way down the hall and into the star ways passing just a little over their heads, everyone felt the heat, and heard the screams of the Orcus that made it to the star ways as their bodies were set on fire, but still alive as if in a last act of honour they charged blazing on fire and screaming towards the barricade hoping to kill some humans before they themselves died, but death for them came to quick Billy thought as he watch the home guard shoot into the burning Orcus putting the attempts and their screams to silence.

It was then that Knarf had left him, putting him in charge and telling Billy that they must hold this position as long as they can until he returned; He had told him he had to find lady Yenned and he was to send his men to find the captain and any surviving members of the council, there was no way any of them could expect to escape without the captain or Navi.

That was a long while ago Billy was thinking as he was preparing for the next attack. The Orcus had broken through the walls of the other hallways to get around the caved in path and had attacked them from the other passage ways that lead to the star ways. The next attack would be the enemies' fourth attack since Knarf had left, and since then Billy had lost most of the home guard only maybe three trained women survived. Those that took up their weapons to carry on the fight were the women and children of the village that had never used a weapon in their life, but they understood that they had to fight, and for them to learn to kill may lead to their or their children's own survival. Billy readied himself as he could see over the barricade the next wave of Orcus preparing to attack,

"Take aim." He shouted, in these past few moments Billy had passed from a young boy into a man, a man with responsibilities to his people and now he and what was left of the villages were the last line of defence.

"Damn I hope someone survives to tell our story." He thought as the next wave of Orcus attacked full force and firing laser bolt, Billy and the Villagers returned fire.

Knarf was running now running as fast as his legs could take him, his real concern was for lady Yenned. He hoped he had done the right thing by leaving the home guard to protect the way. He knew that they all had little time left and he planned to find Yenned and get her to the captain and go back with some help to get what was left of the Dover villagers and help them to make their way to the captain's ship. He had sent his men to look for the other members of the council and hopefully find Navi too. He hoped with all his heart that the captain had not heard the commotion and ran to his ship and departed leaving the rest of the village to their own fate. "No" he shook the thought of, the captain was an honourable man and would not leave people who were in distress, these were his people and it was his village too.

"Let us out." The voices came from the cellblock just up ahead. Knarf had forgotten about the visitors that had only arrived earlier that day. They were locked in the cells waiting to meet with the council.

"Council, it was our fault that we were not more prepared for this," He grumbled at his distant thought. He reached the cells and as he suspected there were no guards, they had joined the battle and were probably dead or amongst the home guard.

"Get us out" Navi's friend Kir shouted. "We know there is trouble here, we heard the weapons fire."

Knarf looked around for the keys to the cell but could not find them and time was running short.

"Stand back" He barked at Kir and the others in the cell. They all moved to the side anticipating Knarf intentions when he raised his machine gun and aimed it at the lock.

"Cover your ears" Kir told the others. And they did. Just as Knarf pulled the trigger and the sound of the bullets hitting metal rang throughout the cell and down the already noisy hallways of the shallows, the metal barred doors swung open and Kir gathered his people together.

"What's going on?" He asked Navi

" We are being attacked by Orcus, and there is only one way out of here alive, so follow my advice. Follow the path to the left of here straight up and then take a right you will then come to an Iron gate, that will be locked wait there."

"And do what" a lady in the group cried out at him.

"Look that door is the only way out, and only two people has a key to it, one is the captain the other is your friend Navi. Wait there for them to arrive if they do not then we all die."

"Why can't we just shoot the door? Kir asked.

"You can't it is some type of special metal not even explosives would knock that door down."

"And where do you go," Kir showed some concern.

"I go to find our Lady." And with that Knarf turned away and continued to run along the corridor.

Two strangers stood upon a mound, as they witness hundreds of Orcus entering the Village and the onslaught of the villagers. Gun fire and laser cannons lit up the village and the night time sky like candle light on a Christmas eve. No warning had the Orcus given of their attack. They were not provoked in anyway, they just stormed the village with no cause, just pure hatred of what they could never really be, Human. The two men solemnly watched the devastation the Orcus were doing, but there was too many and there was nothing they could do. Besides they had their own mission. They had come here for a reason, and now they could not wait for the other to return. They too would have to enter the village, both looked at each other without saying a word they understood what needed to be done, and at a great speed while the commotion of the battle raged, they sped through the village undetected and around the other side of the hill smashing into the iron door and into the shallows through the only other entrance they had noticed while watching the village. It still amazed the little man how much strength his partner had to knock down doors such as these with no effort. It was also luck that the Orcus had not found this entrance, but the small man knew it was only a matter of time.

The inside of these tunnels were like a maze. Almost a different hallway every hundred yards. There was no marking or anyway they could know which way to turn, but the sound of gunfire rang along these tin walls and the only hope of finding what they wanted was to find someone who knew the way and at that moment it seemed a good idea to find the fight.

Navi now ran down the passageways of the shallow clutching a small child in his arms. Tears raced down his face at the remembrance of the gruesome death he had just witness of the women he loved. They had left Hayley's home after hearing the explosion. Navi could hear gunfire up ahead and for Hayley's own safety he told her to wait for him there and he grabbed himself a Rifle from the armoury and headed towards the firing, but before he had even reached his destination, five deformed Orcus had appeared from one of the passageways to the right of him. How they had got there he could not fathom, but it was more than likely they had became lost in the maze of the shallows. Almost immediately they open fire upon him, he dived to the side avoiding there laser bolts and then peeped around the corner and return fire hitting one of them clearly through the centre of its head. Navi had always been a crack shot when it came to shooting a weapon, his father had taught him how to shoot, and this was a skill Knarf had always said was needed in his unit. He called Navi the sniper engineer, but now Navi really had to put his skills to the test, he reloaded his weapon as more laser bolts came thundering down the passage way hitting the corner he was hiding behind with a crackling noise as they hit the walls. Navi rolled in to the centre of the passage way and fired two shots again he hit two more dead centre of their heads. Blood oozed from their skulls as they collapsed to the ground the other two continued their fire as Navi continued his roll to the other side of the passageway barely escaping the laser fire. Navi readied himself for his next attack hoping to get the last two, when he heard screams coming from the passageway where he had left Hayley and her child.

"No." The thought rushed through his head as he turned and ran up the hallway forgetting the two Orcus that were now in pursuit of him, he ran as fast as his legs could carry him, and on turning the corner he saw what was the most hideous of sights. Three Orcus had gathered around Hayley with some kind of blade and were slowly torturing her, they had cut off her arm and leg and one was slowly cutting her fingers off her other arm one by one while another had a Blade ready to slice her throat. Without thinking Navi stormed at the super human creatures shooting two with his rifle clear through the side of their skulls, the other stood turned and knocked him flying against the wall. The creatures were strong and another hit like that could possibly kill him as blood wept from his nose. The Orcus held its blade and swung at him, he ducked out of the way, when the creature swung again he rolled towards it grabbing its side weapon and standing to his feet he aimed the weapon at the creature, and shouted "Why did you not just shoot me you dumb Fuck" And he fired the creatures own weapon at it and the laser bolt burned a clear whole right through the creatures chest as it dropped to its knees and fell flat on its face.

Just then the two that were pursuing him had raced around the corner, Navi turned and shot the laser bolts at both their heads and watched as the bolts burned their heads clean off their shoulders. He dropped the weapon and turned to Hayley who was barely alive, tears rolled down his face, and blood poured from her body.

"The pain," she whispered "Look after Noel. I dropped him but he will be ok. Won't he?"

"Yes he will," Navi cried

"The pain it has stopped. Huh it must mean I am going to make it." She tried to giggle but blood poured from her mouth.

"Yes you are going to make it," Navi lied as he held her in his arms as her body became lifeless. Tears continued to roll down his face the irony of it all was to overwhelming. Why had God brought them together for only a night just for him to lose her. He heard heavy footsteps coming along the passageways. Her last request was for him to take care of her son who had been knocked unconscious by the drop. He picked up the child and ran. And now he found himself still running, at first he did not know where to go or how to get the child to safety, but then it dawned on him, he headed towards the Iron doors and the only way to the captains ship. In the distance behind him he could still hear the footsteps following.

4
Journey Begins

Halesworth was a small dusty village made up of tin huts and a few stone buildings, the biggest building stood wide in the centre of the village. The dusty roads were deserted and the village inn was recognizable as the big building with the sign saying 'Bar' written in human words and illuminated by an oil wick lamp. As Vlad and Leron approached they could hear the sound of many people from within.

Vlad and his companion entered the bar; it was still night and the faces of the villagers which sat in the bar clearly showed their shock and surprise that a dwarf had boldly walked in knowing that there was a price on every dwarf's head. Vlad had no feeling or care for what the people thought he was here for a reason and one reason only. He walked up to the bar and lifted himself up onto one of the very tall bar stalls that were clearly not made for people of his size. Silence fell as everyone stared and watched the two strangers, more interested in the dwarf than they were with Leron. The bar tender approached;

"It's not good for your kind to be around these parts at the moment." He whispered

"I just want a drink." Vlad asked "and then I will be on my way".

"Well a drink I can do you if you are only staying for

one, so what will you have?" The barman said.

"Two mugs of whatever ale you got." Vlad replied.

The barman went and returned with their drinks and Vlad threw a piece of silver on the bar. He seemed surprised and pleased at his payment.

"You're welcome to have anything you like with this currency."

"Well there is one other thing I will pay for." Vlad said aloud so anyone in his vicinity could hear.

"And what is that." The barmen greedily asked.

"Information about Dwarves" Vlad shouted loudly and continued.

"There was a massacre of my friends not far from here. I buried them all this very night." He took a swig of his ale.

Leron stood quietly scanning the room for danger while Vlad continued.

"The thing is when I buried them I soon realized there were less graves then there should have been five graves were missing." He took another swig of his drink and looked around the bar.

"Now I came to the conclusion that the five was not killed but taken and I would give good silver to anyone who could give me information about my companions. Anyone?"

No one spoke but three men stood up holding rifles. Leron could tell these were hunters by the way they dressed and the type of weapon they carried, he had seen enough of them pass through his forest. With a grim look on their faces the tall muscular middle hunter in a coolant long brown Mac spoke.

"And what if I choose to kill you and take your silver and sell your body to the nearest drone post, I think this way I would make more silver." He laughed and the two that stood with him laughed too.

Vlad turned his back on the strangers and took another

swig of his ale.

"That would not be a good idea" said Leron as he step in front of Vlad.

"And why is that skinny man." The middle hunter shouted.

"Because I know my partner here would tear you to pieces even before you pulled your rifles. He had a bad day and I am sure he is really looking for a fight. Normally I would let him kill three arrogant fools like you but I fear he will kill you before he gets the information we need, and this would upset him further. So I propose this"

"Propose what" The Hunter to the right shouted feeling insulted and placing his hands on the trigger of his gun. Vlad turned his back even more away from the hunters with no concern about what was happening. He downed his ale Leron's too and called for the bar tender to make him another. The hunters were slightly puzzled by his behaviour as the people in the bar all moved to one side anticipating a fight.

"I propose that you give us the information we need and I won't kill you for speaking so rudely to my friend when he has had such a bad day." Leron said sternly.

The hunters all burst out into laughter, they laughed for all of a minute until the middle hunter became serious and shouted "Kill this", as he and his men raised their guns and pulled the trigger, each of their guns exploded and one back fired causing a severe injury to the chest of one of the hunters as he fell to the ground. The two still standing staggered back all bloodied from the explosion of their own weapons, the main hunter looked at his weapon and found it had been jammed with bits of rock. Vlad began to laugh.

"You know it is very hard to see when a fairy moves, they move so fast no normal human can see. Ha he he, but I saw when he threw those rocks in your weapons, you stupid." Vlad had become tipsy as he continued to pour more ale down his throat.

The hunters and the people in the bar were surprised at the dwarf's words, Fairy was it possible they wondered. And in a blink of an eye Leron moved from the bar and across the room at such speed it was only seen as a shimmer pinning the main hunter up against the wall by his throat.

All doubts were vanquished about the dwarfs claim that this being was Fairrien; people watched in amazement none had ever seen a fairy let alone one in action.

"Now are you going to tell me what we need to know?"

"Yes anything, anything," the man screeched as Leron loosened the grip he had on the hunter's throat.

They had left the bar over an hour ago, and Leron found it hard to travel with a drunken dwarf. So he found a place out of sight where Vlad could sleep for the night and then he hoped they would discuss their plans in the morning. After receiving the new information from the hunter, Leron was certain they would be heading south. He laid down his cloak and made a comfortable spot. Vlad giggled and laughed and cried all night talking about how funny it was when the villager realised Leron was Fairrien, and then he would cry at the thought of his fallen comrades, this went on until Vlad passed out. Leron sat on a rock that seemed like the one he always sat on and crossed his legs and closed his eyes in meditation, resting his mind but aware of any movements that took place in his vicinity, he sat like a guard protecting his new friend while he slept.

Morning came and Vlad awoke with a thundering headache and the sun burning down on his brow, he had drank so much ale at that bar that he was surprised he did not feel sick. Leron had boiled a mug of something made from herbs he had brought with him and took it from the fire and passed the mug to Vlad.

"Are you crazy it's burning hot this morning, I need something cold?" Vlad shouted.

"Drink it, it will help with your headache and keep you cool through our travels." Leron said whilst pushing the mug in front of Vlad's mouth.

"A hot drink will keep me cool, you carry strange magic Fairrien." Vlad took the cup from him and began to drink, he never noticed much change he had expected the drink to work instantly but yet his head still thudded.

"So what are your plans now?" said Leron

"Well I can't go back without knowing for sure if my men are still alive. I will try and track them. If I remember correctly that hunter from last night gave you some useful piece of information."

"You remember right Vladlin, he kindly explained to me the event of the night before we arrived. He said that a squadron of armed Orcus had entered the village, and came to the bar for food and drink. The hunter looked out of the window and could see there were more outside, he had said in all there could have been around fifty of them."

"And what said he about my men?" Vlad asked.

"He said he could see that five dwarves were locked up in a cage on the back of a Grey made desert vehicle, he said they did not look too good and they were badly beaten."

"I know he told you where they headed right?"

"Yes, he said that while some Orcus were drinking, a slender figure entered the bar in a dark hooded cloak, he seemed like he controlled them because the Orcus feared him. He too feared him for some reason the presence of this being sent chills down his spi... ." Leron explained.

"Okay. Okay. I don't want his whole life story where did he say they were headed." Vlad was impatient.

"He said he heard one of the Orcus say to the strange being that they were ready to head to the dome city Ipswich."

"Well then that is where I go." Vlad said standing up.
"You forget one thing Vlad" Leron replied.
"And what is that?" Vlad asked confusingly.
"You're a dwarf".
"My friend this is one thing I could never forget." Vlad said

"I have heard many things of this place Dome city and one thing I know everyone that goes in and out of that place is questioned and checked. One of the ways they keep people from starting rebellions, learn who everyone is. So I think they will notice you are a dwarf how would you get in?".

"I will think of that when I get there." Vlad replied as he began to walk off.

"As you wish" Leron agreed.

"And what will you do now, Fairrien." Vlad asked.

"I will head south with you."

"I thought you had something to do eastbound?".

"No. I said I needed to travel east, but if you asked me I would have told you that from there I travel south" Leron smiled.

"You are a strange one Fairrien." Vlad laughed letting the matter drop feeling grateful he had a friend to travel with but not quite believing the story Leron was telling him.

They packed up and destroyed all traces of the fire that Leron had made. They had not made friends in these parts and now there were a few men that knew that there was a dwarf walking around this area. Vlad almost expected those hunters to get more men and try and track them. Leron wanted to know why Vlad and he just did not head south, and Vlad explained to him that by heading southeast they would come across the long cargo road that led straight into Ipswich. Leron was a little worried about being spotted by others travelling this road, but Vlad assured him that if anyone came they could hide off the road until they had passed. It was the quickest way to Ipswich, and he continued to give Leron the history of this road that was once called the A12 and made by humans. He told him as they travelled how a lot of this road was destroyed during the war and the Elves had the Orcus rebuild it as a quick way for them to get cargo and send troops from London to any station they have eastside.

"So this Road you speak of goes all the way to the great silver city London" Leron was a little surprised.

"Yes it does and you know what else?" Vlad said

"No tell me?" replied Leron

"That drink of yours is damn good my headache is gone and the sun seems hot but I am cool."

They both laughed and continued the journey southeast talking and joking trying to keep in good cheer, as they knew the path they travelled was a dangerous one.

They had walked only a few hours before they came to the cargo road Vlad had spoke of, and their journey turned south. They walked the road for hours without seeing a soul and it seemed to Leron that this road would never end for as far as he could see there was nothing. The cheerful talk had come to a stop as they both felt wary and exposed walking this path out in the open. They both remained alert and constantly looked all around them as they walked.

"I hear something." Leron whispered.

"What is it?" Vlad asked.

"It's a humming sound coming from behind us."

"I hear nothing how close would you say it is." Vlad tried to listen.

"Close and it is travelling fast because its sound is getting louder as it approaches." Leron whispered.

"Well let's get off the road then" Vlad said as he scurried of to one side of the road and laid in the dirt on the dusty road side. Leron followed him and they both waited but nothing came.

"Are you sure you heard something?" Vlad was not too sure of his friend after they had been waiting for at least five minutes and nothing had showed.

"Shush it is almost here." Leron whispered back.

Then Vlad heard the buzzing too and within a second a hover vehicle carrying one Orcus and three other beings came speeding past them at such speed making a thundering buzzing sound as they past and almost as soon as Vlad had heard the sound it faded away rather rapid as the Vehicle faded of into the distance. They got up and dusted themselves off and began walking the road again.

"A Grey hover Vehicle, damn you Fairriens have great hearing you must have heard that thing miles away"

"It was mainly the vibrations it made along the ground that my ears picked up, but it is our nature to listen to all things." Leron explained.

Vlad gave Leron a strange look he had thought Leron had stopped all his strange talk but he guessed he was wrong.

"Whatever you say oh great one" He said sarcastically "But it would be great if we could get ourselves one of those things it would make our travel much quicker or maybe a horse or something."

"Yes you are right Vladlin." Leron agreed.

Vlad did not speak for awhile and they walked together silently, he thought it was better to let his friend keep his ears alert just in case another vehicle came along. The sun burned bright and Vlad still maintained to be cool, as they walked they came across more and more old ruined buildings, hundreds of them. Leron had ask Vlad about these, so Vlad explained that to either side of this road there were once many villagers and homes for humans, and that either side of the road was filled with forests and fields and farms and that it was all green once, but the war had ended all that and now all what was left was wasteland and old ruin buildings, not a plant to be found.

"Plus the suns intense heat would make it hard for plants to grow here anyway." Vlad said.

The sun began its descent into the west creating a wonderful horizon. Night time would soon fall and they would have to find a place to camp. Vlad began to think how night time weather in England was very unpredictable, many nights could be warm and many nights could be very cold reaching temperatures below freezing. He had been told by his father that it had something to do with the earth's atmosphere and a layer that protected the earth from the sun. Vlad had never understood it but his father had said something to him like the earth had less atmosphere than it once had and this caused the rapid change in temperatures between night and day. Or something like this, it was always a puzzle to him when his father had talked of the stars and the planet; it was a skill his father practiced in his spare time he also wrote books about it. The dwarfs' father was a war fighting general and a scientific genius in his spare time. His heart went out to the man that taught him honour and wondered if it was the right thing to go after his men on his own. Would his father have done the same? He remembered his father had said "Never leave a man in the battle field if he is still alive, never." His father's words rang through his ears and he knew he was doing what was right.

They continued the journey with Vlad deep in thought finding his memories of his father in the old ruins of the buildings they past as they represented to him another time. A past era, an era when his father was still alive. They decided to leave the road and head into one of the abandon villages to find a place they could rest for the night. It was dusk and the low level of the sun cast shadows over the buildings making the desolate village they walked in very dark. Leron was very silent and whispered to Vlad that he sensed something here. They walk quietly and cautiously through the village both very alert, but they saw nothing. They continued to walk around the area they had planned to spend the night in, to make sure it was secure so they would not have any unexpected surprise in the night, all seemed clear. They went back to a building they had spotted on their walk which still had its roof intact, though it had half of its front wall missing they felt it was the best place for them as they could clearly see down the path of the village from the building if anyone was to approach. They set up camp and made a fire with one of Leron's logs he carried. Leron felt uneasy staying in the village and suggested they slept in shifts, so one would always keep watch. Vlad agreed but thought that Leron was overreacting. The village was deserted many years ago and there was not a soul here, but he did not mind that his companion was cautious, and suggested that he slept first as Leron seem to need less sleep than him. They sat by the fire and drank some sort of soup the Fairrien had made,

"I am becoming accustomed to these recipes you have. I may ask you one day to show me how to make this soup, it is very nice." Vlad said.

"Maybe Vladlin, one day I may show you." Leron gave a half smile.

Vlad went quiet and Leron noticed sadness in his eyes. "What is it?"

"It's nothing" the dwarf answered.

"I see."

"What do you see?" Vlad seemed slightly defensive.

"You think of your fallen comrades, it is understandable that you have this sadness."

"What would you know about loss Fairrien tell me?" he raised his voice showing his slight annoyance that Leron would pretend to be an expert at loss.

"We know loss." Leron replied

"We, there you go again with this we stuff I thought you had grown past that. What loss do you know because I never saw a fairy in the wars and never saw your people die like mine. Murdered and hunted down like animals ever since. I have never seen this happen to your kind, I never saw your kind do anything to stop what happened here to our world. So tell me, Fairrien, tell me, tell me your loss." He said aggressively.

"If I told you our loss, would this make your loss seem much better, or would your loss stay the same?" Leron spoke calmly with no malice or anger. Vlad was silent for a minute and the words of Leron sank in to his heart and he realised his anger and what had happened to his people had taken over him and he was directing it at a person who had only ever shown him kindness and respect. Leron was right; Leron's loss, if he had any, would make no difference to Vlad's loss and now a tear rolled down his face, noticing this he quickly wiped it away, and dropped his head.

"I am sorry my friend you are right. I am sad because those men were more than just my hunting party. They were like my brothers, and when I first realised that they were dead, I felt I was alone, and that I would be forever. Back home we all laughed and drank and did everything together, they were my only friends."

"And what of the five that may still be alive?" Leron asked.

"Out of all this they are my hope, my second hunter and second in command of the hunting party is my cousin Mada, He is also one of the five that is missing and he is the closest to me of all my men. I had taught him all he knows and had great hopes for him of one day becoming the best hunter of us all. I miss him, and his mother. They are the only family I feel I still have left. How could I go back and say to her I have lost your son." Vlad's sadness was deep he could never remember shedding tears since his father had died, but since the loss of his men he had often felt there was no hope. Now he felt like an emotional fool as another tear rolled down his cheek. He fought down the urge to cry and lifted his head high. "So this is why I will return with her son and if not - die trying" He said like a true warrior.

"Then I will join your cause, or die trying too." Leron said.

Vlad was shocked. "Why would you do this?"

"Because I see honour in your words Vladlin Bowen, and your cause is a good one and you are a friend to us now. My people never let a friend face danger on his own. So I will go with you, to hell and back or to our deaths." He smiled boldly

Vlad smiled too and expressed how he appreciated all Leron had done for him, and that no man could ask for a better travelling companion. They both laughed and conversed some more until Vlad grew tired and slept. Leron took his first shift and watched over Vlad while he slept. He found some bricks and made them into a place where he could sit and sat crossed legged and alert as he scanned the night with his hawk eye vision as Vlad's snoring rang though his ears. He looked to his brave new friend and smiled as he knew that it was more than likely that neither of them would ever return to their homes.

It had been many hours into the night and Leron had woken Vlad and took his time to sleep. Vlad stayed awake looking into the darkness for a few hours while Leron slept noiselessly. He thought of his father, and then his comrades and then he thought of the place that had become home for the dwarves for many years. He was trying to find ways of keeping his eyes open but he knew he was still tired and as his mind drifted to other places his eyes became heavy and he found it difficult to keep them open. He began to question why he was still awake, after all he knew the village was deserted and also he could not see very far beyond the fire place. The night had stayed warm so Vlad did not even have the chill of the weather to keep him awake, his eyes began to close slowly and soon he found comfort in the wonders of his dreams. The dream of places long forgotten, of an England filled with green, and a place where species of old and new joined together in union to try and defeat a common enemy. He dreamed of a time when there was hope, and he remembered a mystical place where his people once lived. A place protected with the magic of Elves, a world within a world hidden from the prying eyes of humans. A place where the Elves and the dwarves lived side by side, and then his dream turned into a nightmare. As he dreamed of the creatures the Elves had become. How most of their features had changed and they had become dark and twisted, seeking to destroy their own flesh and blood. Their distant cousins. Vlad's people.

In his dreams they were monsters killing and maiming his people, tall being now tall and slender, his nightmare was interrupted by a sharp blow to his abdomens and he began to cough as the pain sunk deep within him. He opened his eyes to find what first appeared to be a group of humans surrounding him. He looked around and found that Leron was nowhere to be seen as four pairs of strong arms picked him up with no effort at all and began pounding him in his face and stomach. It was the symbol on their clothing that made him realise who they were. They were clothed all in the same black overalls the symbol of the grey hand that was on all of their uniforms put fear into the heart of Vlad.

These being was not human neither where they alive. They were humanoids; dangerous killing machines put on the earth to make sure order was kept, and to watch that the Elves governed the earth as was expected of them. They had amazing strength, and no human could withstand more than one blow from these things, It was in Vlad's favour that dwarfs were strong. Vlad began to wiggle furiously making it hard for the four to hold him, two let go but the other two held him firm. They never spoke— they never made a sound. It was said they communicated by radio waves instructing each other what to do. Vlad kicked with his legs hitting one in his knee.

The humanoids loosened their grip for only a second, but this was enough for Vlad to break loose. He dropped to the ground and quickly found his feet he looked for a way to run, but there was none. He could now see through the flickering of the burning log that there were about ten of them and they had the main exit covered. Vlad half prayed in his mind to his God hoping he would listen, and as if in answer, Leron came speeding through the entrance staff in hand, hitting the first one fully on his skull. The human robot stumbled back. Vlad grabbed his pack of the ground and picking up his bow quickly unleashed the few remaining arrows into three of them, the arrows showed little effect on the beings as they surged towards him. Leron dived onto the back of them and shouted to Vlad to run.

Vlad did not think twice he headed for the exit as quick as he could running as fast as his legs could carry him. He ran into the dark having no idea which way he was headed. Not long after, Leron was running besides him shouting at Vlad to hide. Vlad Knew he was right and they both ran towards an old wired rusty fence knocking it down and running into a clearing in the darkness. It was well known that the humanoids were fast, possibly as fast as Leron and if this was so Vlad had no chance of escape so the only thing left was to hide. But it was the hiding place that found them, running in the dark was not bad when you had a Fairrien with you, but when a Fairrien was distracted by his pursers, it then became not the Fairriens fault that there was no warning when they found themselves falling down a big hole. At first Vlad saw Leron fall with him and then he saw a little light and then he could not see him at all. Vlad hit the bottom of the pit with a great thud almost knocking him unconscious, blood wept from his nose from the beating but the blood that came from his mouth was from the fall. He was bleeding internally and was seriously injured; he looked around but could see nothing it was pitch black in the hole.

"Leron" Vlad whispered painfully.

"I am here beside you, shuush they are up above and have good vision we must move further down this tunnel."

"Tunnel, we are in a tunnel," Vlad asked.

"Yes I can see come." Leron whispered.

Leron helped Vlad to his feet and put his arm around Vlad's shoulder and helped him to walk further into the tunnel. They walked only a short way and rested when they seemed that they had come to the end of the tunnel and they leaned against what seem to be a smooth tunnel wall, and waited. Minutes past and they both sat in silence making no sound apart from the slight heavy breathing coming from the injured dwarf.

"It will not be long before they find us, we know of these being's they have come to our forest as if in search of something," Leron whispered.

"I know.... I know of them they are not human." Vlad found it hard to speak through the pain he was now feeling.

"They are good trackers and they will find us soon. We must find a way out of here. If it was not for this iron wall I am sure the tunnel would have gone on further."

"Iron wall?" Vlad asked.

"Yes." Replied Leron.

"Light your staff Leron. Let me see it" Vlad requested.

"But the beings may notice it."

"Only for a second quick let me see." Vlad insisted

Leron could sense a bit of hope in Vlad so he did as he was told and tapped his staff on the ground and the wonderful pale light loomed from it.

Vlad was amazed at what he was seeing; it was not a wall it was a great door made of some kind of metal. It had a box attached to it with square buttons and human numeral imprinted on them and attached beside it was what appeared to be a human finger print imprint. As if to confirm what Vlad had half expected when he heard they were at an iron wall, above the door was written in large human letters.

R.A.F BENTWATERS SCIENCE DIVISION
AURTHORISED PERSONAL ONLY

"I knew it" Vlad giggled, "My father was right they were doing something here"

"What is it?" Leron was confused by Vlad's excitement and noticed that the more he giggled the more pain he was in.

"It's a door Leron it's a do coo co... " Vlad coughed half excited.

Leron became worried for his friend when more blood came up from his mouth.

"Okay. it is good news, we must open this door and then I will tend to your injury, If I don't I fear you will not last much longer."

Vlad then laughed, "By the time we work out how to open this door they would have found us, killed us and gone back to wherever they came from. It's a key pad combination my father taught me of these. There are over a million different combinations and if we were lucky enough to guess it, we would still need to have the right finger print. Face it Leron there is no hope for us," he sighed and slumped down in the corner.

"So you are telling me all I need to do is tap the right numbers on this key pad and put the right finger in here and the door will open?"

"Yes" he whispered finding it hard to breathe now. Vlad

sat motionless.

He watched as Leron approached the door, he placed his hand on the door and put his ear against it, as if he was listening to what was on the other side. Vlad opened his mouth as if to ask what he was doing but Leron shushed him, and continued doing whatever he was doing. Vlad was aware Leron had still left his staff light on and he knew time was running very short for both of them. He then became very dizzy and light headed, he felt that his life was slipping away from him, and he smiled to himself thinking that by the time they find him he would already be dead and they could not torture him for information about his people. He began to wonder why everything had gone wrong for him ever since he left his home for the hunt. It was like Narobus the Goddess of fate for his people was playing a mean game with him and this was how she was going to end it. He continued to smile as his head began to spin and he felt the overwhelming peace of what he was sure happened right before you die.

"I am free now he whispered" Knowing Leron had heard him and then all became black.

Vlad was drifting now, floating through a tunnel, he could see that at the end of it was a bright light. He was overwhelmed with the feeling of peace and rest at last, he heard music, a sweet melody played on a wind pipe that surrounded him drawing him nearer and nearer towards the white light. This is it the place all his people hope to go to when they died. He knew it was the entrance to Valdarrior the place where all true hearted dwarfs went when they passed on, a place where all dreams could be fulfilled. He had often wondered if his heart was true enough to make it here when he passed, and now he knew the answer.

As he drew closer he saw tall beautiful spirits float out towards him as if to greet him. They flew around him humming and singing in the old tongue of his people, the tongue of the ancients most of them were women of such beauty none of them could be compared to any creature that was on earth. They floated as if dancing around him making themselves seen to him and vanishing before his eyes and then reappearing. The women wore long white thin see through dresses and the men wore only what appeared to be a long floating skirt of some kind, though he could see through their clothing. he found it strange that he could see through them also. It was like they were in two dimensions, not certain of which to stay in so they stayed between the two. One of the beautiful maidens came close to his face and smiled a smile that could make the sun shine on a cloudy day. She caressed his face gently and then beckoned him to come forward and follow her. He was floating now faster than before towards the light, faster towards the entrance smiling, pleased that it was not pain that awaited him in death but beauty. He drew closer and closer but then he heard a voice.

"VLADLIN BOWEN" it boomed in his ears.

Immediately he stopped floating towards the light, he knew the voice and it was a voice he always heeded to.

"Father" he tried to say but it was like he had no mouth to speak and his words came from his mind and echoed through the tunnel.

"YOU CAN NOT ENTER HERE MY SON"

"But father I wish to be with you" his words went out again from his mind.

He looked towards the tunnel and he saw a spirit float from the entrance and towards him, it was his father looking better and much taller than he last remembered him. He looked vibrant and youthful; he wore a long white gown with a gold chain around his neck with an axe shaped pendent that represented the house of Bowin. The clan of Dwarves that once were leaders amongst his people when his father was alive.

"MY SON" his father's voice still echoed. "I HAVE SEEN THE FUTURE OF WHAT WILL HAPPEN IF YOU PASS THROUGH THIS DOOR NOW, AND I HAVE BEEN GIVEN PERMISSION TO SHOW YOU, COME CLOSE."

Vlad floated to his father's spirit, and Korin placed his spirit hand on what seemed to be Vlad's face, but then something happened, it was as if his father's hand had slipped into his head into his mind.

"NOW OPEN YOUR MIND AND SEE SON. OPEN YOUR MIND"

And almost instantly Vlad was back on earth, at the foot of a tall hill, he looked around and then he soon recognized the area he was in. It was the place the humans once called Shaddingfield and at the foot of this hill was a secret entrance which was now wide open for all to find. It was the entrance of Ainamor his peoples new home for over a century. He was back home, he smiled for half of a second before he wondered why the entrance was wide opened, and it was then that he heard the screams and the cries echoing from the entrance that lead deep down into the earth. Within a third of a second he was in the cave in his city, the underground city lights burned bright everywhere, so bright that he could clearly see the horror that was occurring amongst his people.

Orcus of all kinds were everywhere killing and raping and maiming his people, His people were trying to fight back but they were overwhelmed by the immense force that had entered their city, and to make sure that no dwarves escaped, a small army of Elves had joined them unleashing arrows into the dwarves so fast that there was little hope of escape for his people. Vlad stormed towards the nearest Elf he could find, filled with hatred to what they had done. The elf looked straight at him but did not release an arrow towards him. Instead he turn and fired it into Vlad's mother who had appeared from nowhere, "Noooooo" Vlad screamed as he stormed towards the elf but as he reached him and dive he floated right through him.

"It is a time that has not yet happened" Vlad father had appeared beside him his voice not so loud but calm.

"Why father, why will this happen?" Vlad asked

"Because your cousin and his men could not withstand the forces of the Greys"

"Explain to me" Vlad asked.

"They will be taken to Millidor and tortured and when Maxius cannot retrieve any information from such brave men. Humanoids will come and take them to the big moon in the sky, there the Greys will enter their minds and find the location of the city, they have ways that are not known to the fully living" his father explained.

"And this will happen if I enter Valdarrior?" Vlad asked.

"Son it may happen if you don't enter too, we cannot be certain that you will find them before this happens."

"You have seen the future you should know father" The sound of the killing around them had become silent, and Vlad soon found that he was back in the tunnel at the entrance of his heaven.

"The future has many paths and many possibilities my son, what I have shown you is only one path, but what I do know if you do not go back our kind amongst the living will no longer exist on the worldly plain,"

Vlad was silent deep in thought for a moment. "How do I get back?"

Korin smiled. "I had always known you had great heart son, take this it will help you when you are most in need"

Korin then took the golden chain he wore around his neck and placed it around Vlad's neck.

"But how will I get back?" again he questioned.

"JOURNEY SAFE MY CHILD" Korins voice echoed loudly once again as he slowly vanished before Vlad's eyes.

Vlad was in the tunnel alone now, no spirits around him but the entrance to Valdarrior before him. Just as he thought to go in to ask how to get back, he felt a surge in his chest, a slight pain, he began to think how strange it was for the already dead to feel pain as he started to float backwards away from the light. Before he could think anything more another surge went through him and he flew backwards at an incredible speed so fast that within an instant the light at the tunnel became like a very small pin hole in the darkness and instantly Vlad sat up with a pain surging through the centre of his forehead. He coughed and all the aches and pains that he was feeling before he passed on were back and blood came up and out from his mouth as he continued to cough.

"I had thought I had lost you." Leron spoke.

The Dwarf found he did not have the energy to speak, he looked around and wondered where they were. There was a small light looming from the corner of the room where he sat and lots of unfamiliar objects all around them, he had only a minute to see his environment before he passed out.

^
—

Maxius stood looking dismayed staring out from the wide window of his throne room watching Nairda and Lrac parry with each other playfully as they both fought skillfully with the snipe blade. It was a weapon, that was half the size of an Elvin sword but too large to be called a dagger. Its purpose was not just as a blade but also while fighting it could also harness sunlight or moon light if held at the right angle to release a fire bolt at an enemy. Both Nairda and Lrac were masters with this weapon and used this trick in their training sessions, knowing that the other was skilled enough to deflect the blow, besides they only aimed to cause flesh wounds to each other, it was a game to them, and Maxius found himself a little jealous.

They had all grown up as best friends before the wars, and they played, learned and did everything together, always playful, until the war came and threatened their home and their families. But now things were different; there was a distance between Maxius and them. He was the king now and this made a difference. At first Maxius wanted to keep the friendship and by doing so he made Lrac the general of the Elfin army, as in times of war Lrac had proven himself to be a dangerous strategic adversary to any that threaten him. Lrac had trained hard in every single Elfin fighting technique, and when he had mastered them he went on to master many human fighting techniques as well. Maxius had also made Nairda the head of the royal guards. Nairda was very loyal; he always had been to both him and Lrac. But now Maxius wondered If Lrac wanted his throne and feared him a little, and because of this he kept him close and always kept an eye on what he was doing. Times had changed now and the Elves were no longer a peaceful race. Fifty years ago many were still complaining of how the Elfin race were once a nation of peace but had become ruthless under the rule of Maxius, and now was a feared warrior race. Those that had complained had either died or vanished without a trace. Maxius smiled a half smile at the thought of what he knew he had done to stop the complaining amongst his people.

Now no one dared speak out against him. Their mystical lands were also changing, there was no longer a continuous summer of forever blooming flowers. In some parts of the land there was rain and thunderstorms and the seasons changed erratically. They had lost some parts of their kingdom to weathers way below freezing but this change had not yet reached the heart of Laysenia the world in which all Elves lived. Their world was protected by a magic which covered them from the vision and weathers of the world they once left behind to the vast growing numbers of humans thousands of years ago, and now this magic was failing.

Elves over time had become tall slender being, but Maxius himself had sustained the everlasting rumours that had befallen Elves for hundreds of years. For he was small in height, he had not grown no taller than five foot throughout the whole four hundred years that he had lived, but still he was young for an Elfin king. Elves expected life span was around nine hundred years if not more, and now it was the young that ruled, and very few aged Elves still lived. This was due to the war and Maxius knew he played a part in this.

Lrac used the fire bolt trick to put Nairda off guard. Nairda hit the bolt to one side defensively with his snipe, but as he did this Lrac gave him a quick kick to his back leg making Nairda fall to the ground and standing on his arm while kicking Nairda's Blade away from his hand. He leaned over with his snipe blade to Nairda's throat, they both stayed motionless in this position for a moment, and then they both laughed as Lrac sheaved his blade and extended his arm to help Nairda to his feet.

"Huh" Maxius turned his nose up to their display as he walked away from the window, as always Lrac had won. He had hoped that he would lose, so he would know that there was weakness in Lrac, but so far this had not been shown or proved and this made him respected amongst his men, the kings army Maxius's army. Maxius had started to believe that his men and the people of his Kingdom respected Lrac more than him, and Maxius was a very jealous king. If he had not grown up with Lrac then he would have put an end to it years ago, but there was also the fact that to turn on Lrac now would cause division in the kingdom, and this was a time where they must all stand strong together. This was a time where the Elves would claim all back and become all powerful amongst all and Maxius would lead them to this and he would have more respect from all and Lrac would fear him. He grinned once again as he sat in his throne, which was in front of the original Elfin throne that was a seat made from a base of an Ash bush Tree. It had carved itself in the shape of a mighty throne with the most wonderful shapes of fairies and Nymphs.

At the head of the seat was the carving of every Elfin king that ever ruled. The chair still had roots from the tree and they went deep down under the castle and under the ground into the earth rooted and nurtured by nature. The chair made the carvings itself but now the chair had become rotten and its roots were dying. It was because it was dying that the chair had never carved Maxius at the head of it, so Maxius believed, but it never bothered him as he had his own throne made and placed in front of the old so it was not to be seen. His new throne was velvet red, and gold outlined it and gold was also the chairs arms and legs. It was soft and comfortable with a gold carving of his own head with rubies for eyes on top of the head of the throne. He was pleased with the chair in which he ruled from and had wished the Ash bush throne removed, but it would cause a stir amongst the people, as the tree represented Mother Nature and the greatness of Laysenia's previous kings. Some Elves still believed their cause was a cause for the peace and unity of nature and not ready to except that they were slowly drifting away from the old ways. His mother had reminded him of this and stopped him from doing such a foolish thing, so now he could only hope that the Ashe Bush throne would die quicker. Maxius thoughts were disturbed by a knock on the throne room door.

"Come" he bellowed and his voice echoed all around the

empty massive throne room.

The door opened and entered Tsomelpoep his new chamber guard.

"Your Mother is… " He never finished his sentence.

"I need no introduction to my own son," She barked as she stormed into the throne room

"Leave us," she said looking back at Elpoep as he was named for short.

Elpoep looked to Maxius and Maxius nodded. He then turned and closed the throne room door.

Maxius's Mother was named Deerg Dnah Sifles, but was known as Deerg amongst the people. She was beautiful for an elf of the age of seven hundred and fifty. There were no wrinkles of any kind upon her brow, and the length of her bright white hair went down her back and almost touched the ground as she walked towards the throne that her son had seated himself upon. The look in her squinted red eyes and the stern look upon her pale sharp Elfin features made Maxius know that she was not pleased by something, and this intrigued him. She wore a long black thin see through dress wearing what only could be described as gold short nightdress underneath. She was pale as most Elves were, but Maxius himself had very tanned skin as his father was a dark skinned elf, and there was those such as Nairda who was very dark in colour as dark as the black humans. There had also been a change in his people. Not all Elves had white eyes anymore, his mothers eye colour had changed to red many years ago and so had many others, including Maxius himself, while others such as Nairda and Lrac had maintained the whiteness of their eyes. It was a phenomenon that no one could explain, but it had did no harm to the people and if anything it had increased their vision so no one thought much about it.

"More and more these days you act like human kings of old." Deerg said as she climbed the few steps that lead up to the throne.

"How do you mean mother?" Maxius said calmly knowing full well what his mother was implying.

"First this gold throne and now you have a servant to tell you who knocks, and what makes it worse is he is one of those things."

Elpoep was a reject clone and wore a white pale mask to cover his ugliness when in the presence of Elves. It was not commonplace for an Orcus to be permanently inside the castle walls, for though they were allies they were rarely trusted amongst Elves.

"Mother I must find something for these creatures to do, why have them if I make no use of them." Maxius explained.

"Why did you not send him with the others to govern the world outside?" asked his mother.

"Elpoep is different." Maxius replied

"Elpoep, you even name them" She spat bitterly.

"Like I said he is different, I have taught him the human language, and I was thinking about teaching him the Elfin tongue that we use so little in these days"

"Have you ever thought that he already knew English and our tongue and that he is sent here as a spy." Maxius mother said sternly.

"Mother you are to suspicious, not everyone thinks like you."

Deerg sat beside Maxius in the throne he had made for his future Queen and faced him.

"Forget him I have more important news." She said.

"Pray tell Mother," Maxius over the years had become very arrogant with his power and his mother was slowly beginning to despise him.

"An Orcus messenger has reached the communication point in Sweden." She began to explain.

Since the war, communication through electronical

devices using radio waves had become very difficult over large distances. The Greys had used some kind of magnetic weapon to disrupt all earths' communication during the war to make it difficult for any units calling for back up. The weapon was more powerful then it was intended and disrupted communication even for the Greys to communicate with their own subjects on earth. It had taken many years before the magnetic disruption in the earth's atmosphere began to dissipate, but now it only left room for short distant communication some places could communicate at greater distances than others but for anyone making communication to the Laysenia they had to be at one of three Elfin stations and one of them was North Sweden.

"And what did he say?" Maxius asked.

"He claimed he was sent by the dark one who went out with an Orcus Squadron"

"And?" Maxius was becoming impatient

"And he says that they have captured five Dwarves and killed many also,"

"Did they find it?" A great smile rose upon his face at the hope that the dwarf city would be found. It had been many years since anyone had caught a dwarf, and none had ever brought one back to him alive.

"No they are bringing them back to you. So they head to Paris where there is a flying ship due to arrive they will take command of the ship and fly them here to you, and then the dark one will return to his moon"

"Good, you serve me well Mother." Maxius seemed pleased

"Serve" Deerg shouted as she stood to her feet. "I serve no one, do you forget who put you on the throne"

Maxius face became sheepish almost boyish as he faced a scolding from his mother. "I never forget..." he tried to speak

"You shall never forget my son. In future I would watch how you speak to me, it was easy for me to place you were you are and it would be as easy for me to have you removed"

She stared at him with only anger and evil in her eyes and Maxius knew that she had meant every word of it. He felt stupid that he still feared his mother, but he knew there were good reasons for anyone to fear her.

"I am sorry mother I did not mean to offend. I have spoken wrongly I only meant you have served our cause well, both our cause," he tilted his head slightly as in to show her respect.

"Well just watch what you say in future my son or you will find your future would be a short one" She turned and walked proudly along the strip of red carpet that led from the throne to the throne room door. It took her a few moments before reaching the door of the massive hall of the throne room, and when she reached it and open the door to find Elpoep standing at the door she turned and barked back towards the throne,

"And do something about this" pointing at the Orcus and she left closing the door behind her.

Maxius sat in his throne angry at the way his mother had made him feel, and alone having no one to confide in but an Orcus. Though he never told Elpoep everything he was beginning to think of this creature as a companion, his only companion. His mother had wanted him to get rid of him, so he shouted for Elpoep and the Orcus entered the room.

"Now" Maxius said with a great smile on his face.

"I think today we will teach you the Elfin Tongue." He had no intention of getting rid of Elpoep, in the days to come he will make this Orcus his greatest allie. He smiled at the thought as he beckoned the creature to come sit with him.

5
Shell of a Man

Vlad had been awake now for some hours. Leron had taken good care of him while he slept, and woke him during nights to feed him soup and medicines to stop his internal bleeding and help build his strength. The dwarf could not understand how two days had past while he was unconscious, and to him it seemed he had been under only a short while. He was grateful also that Leron's medicines were helping him to make a speedy recovery. He had expected no less from the Fairriens amazing medicine, he too was a healer and these new potions would do well for his people in times of sickness.

When he had realised that they had past beyond the entrance in the tunnel he asked what had happened to the things that were pursuing them. Leron told to him that he had heard the Humanoids on the other side of the big iron door the night he had opened it and carried Vlad through. But they could not open the door and was not certain that Vlad and he were in here. They waited there for one day and he believes that they have now left to look elsewhere. Vlad questioned him about how he had opened the door, but all Leron would say is that he asked it.

"Asked what" Vlad had pursued the question

"Fairrien ways are not like your ways." And Leron

would say no more.

Vlad had thought maybe he meant he asked the door, but the idea of that was ridiculous, so he did not pursue the matter. He soon found that he could get on his feet and walk around the place slowly. He took time to look at all the strange objects in this new strange environment and realised that they were in a big huge laboratory.

There was dust on many things and bottles of see through and coloured liquids with dead creatures or animals inside them. Some of which Vlad had never seen before. At the end of the Laboratory there was a big chamber of some kind with wires leading from it into one of the computer desk nearby that did not seem to be working. When he placed his hand on the chamber, his hand immediately became cold, it was some kind of refrigerator and the silent humming indicated it was still receiving power and was in full working order, but the glass was icy and he could not see what was inside. Above it was written the words Cryo-Chamber 1.

Vlad had never heard of this word and he asked Leron and Leron new less than him when it came to human things. They wondered about it for only a short time and then continued to look at other things. In their exploration of the facility they came across a locked cabinet and it did not take too long before they found a way to open it. Inside were many documents and notes that Vlad believed was about what had happen here, he took them and put some in his back pack.

"Why do you take these?" Leron wanted to know.

"I realised when we were at the door that we were in Woodbridge At an airbase that was closed down many years before the war called Bentwaters. There had been many rumours about things that happened here, experiments and all sorts, but the greatest rumour that sustained the place was an alien ship sighting in

Rendlesham forest. It was rumoured that they had Greys down here and did experiments on them. My father always believed there was a secret laboratory underground here and many had looked for it." Vlad explained.

"And it was never found in all these years" Leron asked.

"Well before anyone had much time to search the base properly, the war broke out and the base was reopened, but it was destroyed like most of the human bases after the war. My father had said that at this base they were doing something that might have helped them win the war."

"How would he know?" Leron quizzed.

"You forget my father was a general and fought with the humans, he had heard rumours of these things during his days with the human Military." Vlad explained.

"The war is over now what will you do with these papers?"

"I might be able to find a way to protect my people if the day comes when they are discovered. All I need to know is what it was they were doing here."

Leron said no more and let Vlad take the time to look through as many documents as he could while he went off to explore. Vlad began to read and learn about human genetics and D.N.A processes. A lot of the documents spoke of grafting different genes from different species on a subject, and how the subjected needed to have a blood type which was rare to find in a human subject. He finished reading the document understanding what he could but not fully comprehending the whole concept of what the scientists here were trying to do. He then picked up the next folder to read and it was titled:

PROJECT SIRROM,

And marked in big red letter across the front page was.

TOP SECRET, Need to Know basis only.

Just as Vlad was about to open it Leron called him from somewhere in the dark. Leron had left his staff for Vlad so he could read. He placed the folder down and took up the staff that was producing light and went to look for him. He had found the Fairrien at the bottom of some steps at the right side of the lab that lead upwards above the metal entrance and exit of the science department. Both of them had thought there would be stairs or something leading up and out of the facility but neither of them had expected another level to the lab and both became very interested into where the stairs led.

They began to climb the stairs and followed them upwards until they came to the end of the steps. To the right of them was a door, on turning the handle they were both surprised to find that the door was not locked like everything else had been in this facility. They stepped in and Leron could see a switch on the wall. Vlad had told Leron that these switches were light switches when they had found some downstairs in the lab but when they tried them they did not work. So Leron took the opportunity to see if this one too did not work, but when he flicked the switch the light of the room came straight on and they both marvelled at the display of the room.

The room was filled with lots of computer desk and buttons and switches and screens but it was Vlad that noticed the switch that read power, and found himself pressing it instantly like an excited child pressing buttons on a toy. Immediately they both heard the power surge through the underground building while all the desks and computer systems came on creating a wonderful light show in the room, the humming of the facilities generator had startled Leron.

"What have you done" Leron seemed a little worried.

"I think I have put the generator on full power, I bet if

we turned the lights on in the lab now it will work" Vlad seemed excited and Leron was intrigued by his infusionism in this.

"If you wish we could go and see?"

"Yes we should. I have had enough of darkness; let's get some light in this place" Vlad answered smiling. But as they were about to leave the words written above two switches caught Vlad's eye. One had the words written OBSERVATION WINDOW and the other had the words CRYO-CHAMBER.

"Wait" Vlad called to Leron

And Leron stopped in his tracks, as Vlad had become like a giddy child, giggling and saying how great and fascinating this all was to him. Without worrying about any consequences he first pressed the switch that said 'Observation Window', and what seemed like a metal wall to the right of the room, began to lift up slowly revealing what only could be described as a large window which went along the whole right side of the room. The window looked out into the Laboratory which was still dark. Vlad felt like he had found some new toys, still excited he eagerly reached out to press the switch that said Cryo-Chamber

, but Leron was concerned about pressing things they knew nothing about and put his hand on Vlad's arm and stopped him.

"Do you think it is wise?"

"Why it is only a freezer, what could be in it that is not frozen." Vlad voiced no concern.

"As you wish" Leron said and let go of Vlad's arm.

Vlad went ahead and pressed the switch and though the lab was still dark they could see a blue light turn on within the Cryo-Chamber.

at the back of the laboratory, and steam seemed to be released from it, at first it was only a little steam and then it became plentiful covering almost half of the lab. Vlad moved as quick as he could still feeling slight pains from his injuries and holding Leron's staff to navigate through the darkness as both him and Leron went down into the lab and made their way to the back. When they had finally arrived at the chamber they were disappointed to find that the chamber was opened and nothing was inside, Leron noticed concern on the dwarfs face.

"What is it?" Leron asked.

"There was something in this, look it has a shape inside made for a body."

He was right, inside the chamber was what seemed to be a glass table standing upwards but slightly tilted back and it was as if someone had moulded the glass for the shape of a body with two arms and legs to fit perfectly inside. The wires they had noticed earlier on the outside of the camber leading from a computer desk which had now become operational were also on the inside but they hanged loosely like they were once attached to something inside that was no longer there. However, the biggest clue was the puddle of blue water that had obviously came from the refrigerator, and from the puddle were foot prints that went off in the direction behind them along the other side of the lab. Leron could clearly see the prints without the aid of his staff and was sure Vlad had noticed them too as Vlad seem to point the light from the staff downwards towards them.

"You are right Vlad, be on guard as it is alive and could be dangerous"

Just as Leron spoke they both heard the sound of something whizzing past behind them. They spun around to look.

"Did you see it?" Vlad whispered.

"No I did not it was too fast."

This did not make Vlad feel comfortable, something that was as fast as Leron or even faster was a big problem and made Vlad slightly on edge. Vlad took out his dagger and prepared himself while Leron took his staff from Vlad and held it firmly. They circled around back-to-back scanning the darkness for any movement. Leron felt worried for Vlad, he had not fully recovered and he feared any further injury could result in his death. But just as he was about to whisper his concern to his companion to tell him that maybe he should hide, out of the darkness at Fairrien speed came a shimmering shape of human form casting a blow with immense power. So powerful that at the last moment when Leron had realised what was happening and raised his hand blocking the blow from connecting with his face, the force of the strong attack still knocked him backwards making him drop his staff and fall into one of the computer desks breaking it into pieces causing sparks to fly up in the dark.

Leron was quick to his feet needing no light to see his assailant, standing before him was what appeared to be a young naked human man. But Leron was not fooled, he had felt the blow and knew no human possessed this strength, he watched as the colour of the strangers eyes changed, they became a bright yellow and the iris of his eyes stayed black but changed shape making his eyes almost cat like. A half smirk came to Leron's face realising that now the stranger could also see in the dark.

"Vlad stay away from this, this is my fight." He shouted as he darted towards the attacker with such speed. It had surprised the stranger that someone else could move this fast, but he reacted quickly and was not caught off guard. Even Leron's speed was not enough to inflict a blow upon the stranger. Every blow Leron made the stranger blocked and countered, but Leron was just as good. They fought moving around in the dark and held position when finally they found themselves standing in the blue light of the Cryo-Chamber.

. Whirling and kicking and punching at a speed that sent

vibrations throughout the whole of the laboratory. Vlad could see them now and could keep up with the fight while they were in the light. The boy or man or whatever it was had amazing skills, and used fighting techniques that was worthy of the Chinese masters of old. Vlad could not help but to admire the both of them as he had never seen such a display of fighting skills at this speed ever. It was like there was a rhythm to their movement and though each blow could be deadly they seem to dance around each other's attacks in such an acrobatic way with such ease, they seemed evenly matched. But then everything seemed in Vlad's mind like it was slow motion, as Leron moved near him and flicked his head back to avoid a blow, a small glimmer flickered from Leron through the light of the Cryo-Chamber.

and hit Vlad on his hand. He felt it and it was wet and then he tasted it, and it was salty. He was amazed it was sweat, the first he had ever known the Fairrien to sweat. He knew then that Leron was tiring and he snapped out of his daze that had held him in awe at the skill of their fighting. He rushed as quick as he could to pick up Leron's staff, But as he did Leron threw a right handed punch towards the stranger, the stranger then block the punch with his own right hand, pushing Leron's punching hand down with his left. The stranger than countered with his right hand using the back of his fist. Leron was fast and blocked the punch with his only free hand whilst raising his foot to kick, but the stranger raised his right foot and placed it firmly on Leron's knee preventing him from making the kick. Before Leron could think of his next move the stranger used a move that surprised him.

The mysterious man then leaned in towards Leron placing his right foot back firmly forwards on the ground swinging powerfully the elbow of his right hand into Leron's chest sending him flying backwards into the dark smashing computers and experiment bottles along the way causing mini explosions as he hit powered electrical equipment breaking them with the power and the speed of his fall. He finally made contact with the wall near the metal door at the far end of the Lab hitting a button with his back that was on the wall. He slumped to the floor. Vlad made his way to where Leron had landed. As he came close he heard a screeching sound and a creaking. It was the metal doors they were beginning to open. Vlad found Leron getting back to his feet slightly bruised and blood dripping from his nose. The objects he had hit flying backwards had caused him to bleed before hitting the wall, he had always wondered if Fairriens bled now he knew the answer.

"You are Injured" Vlad was seriously concerned.

"It's nothing," replied Leron

Leron stood taking his staff from Vlad ready for the next attack. Leron felt strong with his staff, he was undefeated with it, no Fairrien or even any other being had matched his skill with the staff. He felt now that it was his turn to strike the stranger, but before he could get the chance, the metals doors opened wide and standing in a now burning torch lit tunnel was the ten humanoids.

They stood there in a line, eyes shut as if they had been sleeping— waiting for the door to be opened. In a fraction of a second their eyes all opened in unison and they sped into the laboratory, now making things from bad to worse.

Leron rushed at them hitting two and stood to fight two more, Vlad now was swinging his blade at the first one that reached him, but the creature had circled around him with his speed and picked him up in two hands. Vlad used all the strength he had to grab the creatures head placing one of his hand at the side of its jaw and in one upwards motion he twisted, cracking the mechanical works of the Humanoids neck. His head twisted upwards and immediately released Vlad. Vlad began stabbing at it cutting into it, it bled a green liquid before Vlad found his way to wires and cut at them.

The creature was now on the floor, with Vlad on top slicing at it, kicking its legs it still made no sound as it shook violently, but before Vlad could get a chance to get up after he had successfully terminated one of them, he was grabbed by another two. He looked to Leron but he was now surrounded by the rest of them fighting the best he could, he was tired before the humanoids had come and Vlad felt that Leron would not win this battle. It was over for the both of them and Vlad felt he had come back from the dead for nothing. But just then unexpectedly out of the dark walked the stranger. Still naked Vlad could now see him fully, he was a young dark skin man and Vlad would have said he was human, but he saw that as the young man stepped into the light his yellow eyes changed to a dark colour, as if adjusting to the light of whatever environment he was in. He was not tall but neither small for a human and he had a muscular build, and what was most striking about the being was his hair.

Vlad had seen knotted or dreaded hair before, but this beings style was different he had long locked hair but it only came from the top of his head, as the man approached at walking pace he used a piece of his own hair to tie back his locks in to a tail. He then walked boldly towards Vlad and the humanoids; they had stopped what they were about to do to Vlad and began to focus their attention on the young man. At first Vlad had thought he was with them, but as soon as he approached they released Vlad and went towards him in full attack mode. Speeding at the stranger, but the stranger stayed calm and continued his walk towards them, and when they all met on that short journey towards each other the stranger blocked there blows effortlessly and countered using one strike to each of them and they froze.

The stranger changed his direction now and walked

towards where Leron was fighting and as he did passing between the two Humanoids that seemed frozen, a crackling sound began to stir and it became obvious to Vlad that the sound was coming from the motionless humanoids. And then the creatures exploded sending bits of their body parts everywhere as the stranger continued walking at a steady calm pace undeterred by the explosion and the bits of humanoid that was flying all around him.

The Humanoids that were fighting with Leron turned at the sound of the explosion and as if in recognition of the approaching figure they left Leron and rushed straight for him in a mad frenzy. As they approached they attacked in unison at different angles, but in seven swift fast strikes it was all over, the creatures broke down and five of them exploded, and standing in the fire light from the burning humanoids behind him stood the stranger being untouched and naked. Leron was shocked, and readied himself to continue the fight with the strange being. Staff in hand he stepped closer, he now knew this stranger was dangerous and a fierce warrior, but Leron believed now that he was the only thing standing between the creature and Vlad's life and he would die first before he let a being such as this attack his companion.

"Wait" Shouted Vlad.

Just getting to grips with the amazing sight he had just witnessed, Leron stopped his movement and Vlad entered between the two of them. He turned to the stranger.

"We did not bring you here; we have nothing to do with this place." He spoke slowly

"Do you understand?"

The being stood motionless, staring at them both.

"What are you doing" Leron asked.

Vlad walked closer to Leron, "I don't think he means to hurt us."

"What?" Leron seemed annoyed

"Look at my face Vladlin and tell me again how you believe he does not mean to hurt us?"

Vlad could see that blood was still dripping from Leron's nose. "I understand why he attacked us, he thinks we were part of this place and we had something to do with him being here"

Leron was silent for a moment and considered the logic of his companions' words. Considering the being had just save them he thought he would let Vlad have a go at peace making. Vlad then turned back to the stranger, and began to try and talk to him explaining everything and how they came across the facility. Leron watch silently and wondered if this being would turn out to be friend or foe.

The Stranger sat silently understanding everything he had been told, he was confused and did not understand how he had come to be here in this place. This laboratory with such strange looking beings, he listened to the small man, as he explained that they had found him in the Cryo-Chamber.

He was familiar with the word it was a cryogenic cell that preserved life for long periods of time, he could not understand how he came to be in this cell and found he could not utter a word to the small man. So he nodded to express that he understood what he had been told. He was also amazed at his own skill that he had used to fight the slender one and the humanoids.

Though he had no recollection of who he really was, he had remembered those creatures, with the hand on the clothing, he was not sure if it was a dream or a real part of his memory, but the creatures had once came after him, they had did something to him. He had flashes in his head of him struggling as they carried him, they did something terrible to him he was almost sure and if not they took him against his will, and when he had seen them he had felt hatred towards them and knew then that the little man and the tall man were fighting his enemies, and something the little man had said rang through his mind when he had stopped him and the tall one from fighting again. "My enemies' enemy is my friend" and he was right, he knew that he did not belong in this place and the only hope of getting to grips with anything was to make friends.

He sat quietly listening to the small man while the slender one stared at him. He felt that the tall one did not like him, and he could not blame the man. He noticed how pointed the man ears were and thought it was strange, he half smiled, this had reminded him of Spock from the star ship. Yes he remembered this, a program he watched once on television to do with space travel he liked this show. So why could he remember this and not who he was and how he came to be here. He was confused, but found himself even more confused when the small man had told him the date, he was not sure he had heard right, 2210 he was stunned.

He knew or believed the date was 2010 or this was the date he last remembered in his head. He could not have been in a chamber for that long it was not possible, "Was it?" his mind questioned. He wondered if he had family or friends, and if it was really 2210 they would all be dead now, and no one would know him. Who could help him remember? Remember what had happened and who he was, a tear left his right eye and rolled down his cheek. He was empty, he had nothing and knew no one and he felt alone.

The small man had noticed his sadness, and tried his best to comfort him and be friendly. He offered him something in a mug that the slender one had made using a pot and a tripod over a Bunsen burner, so it was obvious the gas taps still worked in the place after so many years. At first he was a little suspicious of what was in the mug, a few moments early the slender one was ready to kill him and he wondered if they had poisoned the drink, but the little man had a mug too and both the little man and the slender one drank it so he tried some. It tasted like lentil soup, another thing he remembered. Lentil soup that came in a red can.

He hated the fact that he remembered such trivial things and could not remember more important things. He drank the soup and gave them both a small smile to show his appreciation and express thank you. They sat and drank soup together. The stranger had covered himself up with white overalls that were hanging up in the now fully lit facility. The tall one finished his soup and then left, but soon after he returned with some clothes and some weapons. He told the little one that he had found a door up in the power room that led to other places and rooms, he explain that the underground facility was much larger than they thought and that he had found an armoury, and that they had also coolant hooded cloaks and baggy coolant trouser. He had thought that the stranger would like them.

The tall one never talked directly to him. Whenever he had something to say that concerned him he would tell the dwarf and the dwarf would repeat to him. It was as if the slender man had no time to speak with him, but this did not bother the stranger. He understood that the slender man was just as unsure of him as he was about them both. It was while the stranger was putting on these so called coolant trousers that the small man told him both their names.

"I am Vlad" he had said, "and my companion is Leron". He then explained that the trousers and hooded cloak were designed to keep a person cool in extreme heat. He had wondered why they would need to keep cool from extreme heat, and then he wondered if he was no longer in England. Maybe he was somewhere else, but he had remembered that Vlad had said earlier that they were in R.A.F Bentwaters, and he remembered this base, it was in Woodbridge. He could still remember places and destinations. Vlad continue to explain that these clothes were rare and he would take some with him on his journey, because they were very expensive to buy and they could use them to barter with.

The stranger was puzzled by a lot of things that the small man had told him, but continued to listen to everything he said trying to make sense of what had happen in the years he had been in a cryogenics chamber. The slender man walked over to him and offered him two weapons, he immediately recognised them both. The M4, the light weight version of the M16 capable of firing seven hundred to a thousand rounds per minute standard navy seal issue. The words rushed through his mind, it was as if the knowledge of these weapons where programmed into his head,

"Tell him he will need these weapons if he travels with us." Leron looked at Vlad

"I think he heard you."

Leron still refused to speak with the stranger and ignored what Vlad had said. But the stranger took the weapon anyway and he felt comfortable holding it. He placed the strap over his neck and took the second weapon. It was a berretta semi automatic 92f handgun. It was a silver barrelled black handled weapon and on taking the weapon, he immediately took out the clip, removed the barrel, brought out the coil and separated the frame, in under two seconds. He was slightly shocked at how quick he had done this, but took up the overalls he had used earlier and ripped them making a cloth, and began to clean the parts; he resided to the fact that this was all possibly a dream.

"It is obvious to me that he know these weapons well" Leron smirked

Vlad was stunned, but the stranger just looked up and nodded in answer to Leron and continued to clean the weapon.

After another day of rest, Vlad had decided it was time they all left and found a way out of the facility. They packed up their things and went up to where Leron had said he found the weapons. The stranger on reaching the armoury found a rucksack and took it and placed ammunition in it for him and Vlad as the dwarf too had taken a berretta hand gun. He noticed there was grenades and decided on taking along a sound suppresser that was designed for the berretta. He had no idea why he would need these weapons but Leron had clearly stated that trouble seems to find them, and he did not want to be caught unprepared. They took what they could and continued the exploration of what seemed like the never ending facility.

They walked until they found some more flights of stairs that went upwards and they took them. When they reached the next level they entered a door at the end of the next corridor, and this had lead them into a hanger, that was filled with as many as fifty dusty human flying crafts. The stranger recognised the planes, and they all knew they must be near the top level for these planes could not be too far underground if they once flew.

They walked through the hanger and marvelled at the machines as they passed through another door that took them to what looked like an empty caged storage cupboard. The stranger walked in and beckoned them to enter; when they did he slid the wire cage door down shut and pressed a button. The ground began to move. It startled Leron a little, but Vlad now knew they were in a lift he had been in one a long time ago when he walked along side humans, but none had ever looked like this. The lift went up for a short time and then it appeared as if the roof above them opened up and they found themselves in the cage in what looked like a small rotten derelict building. There was no windows and half of the room had fallen in. They all squinted their eyes at the overwhelming sunlight that was above them. The building had no roof and they had finally made it topside. They left the lift and the building and ventured outside, they stopped outside and Vlad turned to the stranger.

"OK. I must tell you that we go to a place that is very dangerous for me and we will bring a lot of trouble on ourselves. In truth we may be killed doing what we are doing and if you choose to travel with us you too may share the same fate, do you understand?"

The stranger nodded to Vlad. "Okay. so you have weapons and we will leave you some food supplies if you choose to venture on your own, so which will it be, are you with us?"

The stranger nodded again, he felt he had no choice he knew no one but the two who had freed him, and what Vlad had told him during their walk through the facility, the world had become a different place then he could remember though his memory was hazy. Elves and dwarfs walked the earth, it was like something from a fairy tale, and now the world was governed by an alien race, the Greys he had called them, and it had caused him to have another memory flash that caused a pain to his temple. It was of a grey's hand reaching towards him. He did not know if these visions he kept having were real memories, but the Greys he knew were not good. So, he felt he had made the right decision, and all three of them began to walk in the direction they all knew would lead to Ipswich.

Crawling up from the tunnel that lead into the underground facility came a hand. The being had known that it would not survive. Its internal injury was far beyond repair, and it used what little power it had left to climb up out of the tunnel digging its fist into the side of the large hole giving itself leverage to help it climb upwards. It had one mission in mind and it was to reach the top so it would be able to let out a short radio signal. It was program to do this in the event of trouble. It had not left the hole fully, it clinged to the side and focused sending its message, but before it could fully complete its mission it lost its grip on the side and fell backwards down into the dark making a loud thudding sound on impact with the ground.

    The creatures battery power had failed and its last visions were of a blue sky looking up through what could be described as a black pit. Within its left eye electronic symbols blurred a little of its vision, it was a written language programmed by its makers. It understood the words as system terminated. All power had shut down and all went black. The machine time here had ended not knowing if the message it sent was fully received.

6

The Dome City, Ipswich

Nathan was a blond haired pale faced man of the age of forty. He had been brought up not to trust. He had faith in very few people especially those of authority. The only good thing he could remember about his upbringing was his father, who was killed when he was a child by Elfin guards. They had accused him of being a member of the resistance because he spoke out openly against the Greys and the way humans were treated on the earth. His father was a proud man and believed he was entitled to his own opinion, even though that opinion had got him killed. When his father had died his mother treated him with little respect, showing no love to him and saying he was as stupid as his father. So at the age of eleven, he left his mother in the countryside of Ipswich never to return, and headed to the city centre. It had been here he had spent the rest of his life. As a child he worked hard for a Sarron who he respected and who had taken him off the streets. He gave him clothes, food and a job. He tended to tables at the Bell free Inn, cleaned toilets, serving drinks and kept rooms tidy. He had learned everything possible about the inn business and as Tcepser the Sarron had taught him, it was the only business to stay wealthy and not get killed over.

Now a Sarron was an alien being, they were taken from

their home world hundreds of years ago by the Greys and were enslaved by them. They were used as soldiers, abductors and whatever else the Greys could think of. The Greys had promised them freedom if they placed all their efforts in helping to win the war. When the war was won they had expected to be taken back to their home world, but they were deceived. They were given the choice of freedom to roam earth a world they knew nothing about, a world that seemed to be slowly dying. Or to stay in the services of the Greys. The Greys had expected them to stay, but all Sarron's left the Grey's Mother ship and made their home on this planet. They survived the best way they could. They were tall thin creatures, and not ugly to look at. One could almost say they were cute looking, their colour varied, there were those that were green, some even had a light purple skin colour, while others had a brownie reddish complexion. They had wide eyes and long shaped heads, and all had very straight hair coming from only the top of their heads.

Tcepser was an honourable Sarron he worked hard all his life but he was old for his kind, he was 700 years. They were kept in chambers to stop them from ageing by the Greys, as they travelled great distances through space, and were let out when needed. Their real life spans were around 300 years. So when Tcepser pass, having fathered no children, he passed his business onto Nathan who he had come to love like his own son. And Nathan now ran the Bell Free Inn. He had little trouble from the elf's or the Orcus at his inn. Some human inns had to put up with all manner of treatment when Orcus entered. Some Orcus even refused to pay, as human was seen as scum to them. But none had ever done this in the Bell Free. He believed that it was because it was once Tcepsers inn, and it was believed that even in death they could avenge those that harmed those they loved. It was said then when they passed they only ascended to a high form, and that they were still amongst the living and sometimes make them self known. So Nathan had peace at his Inn, he served Elves and Orcus with a smile though he despised them very much.

It was on a bright hot sunny day when Nathan was crossing the city square after coming from the butchers where he had just purchased some fresh chicken for one piece of silver, that he first saw the image on the city hollow screen. The hollow screen was a holographic projection of images. It was Grey technology and they placed them in every city and town and some villages too. They used these screens to advertise the most wanted people, criminals against the Grey and Elfin justice system. Nathan laughed to himself every time he heard Justice System, because he knew like everyone else there was none. But for the last few years the image on this screen had only changed between two people, one was the well-known man of the sea, captain Gill.

All humans respected him and whispered stories to their children of the captain and his adventures at night while they slept. And the other was a man they called Kir, he was light skinned man but it was clear he was black and he had dread locked hair. No one had been sure of what his crimes were against the Greys or the Elves. Everyone had known the captain's crime was because he had a ship of great war technology and he had used it against Orcus many of times. But Kir, no one really knew, all Nathan had heard was that he was the last in the bloodline of a warrior breed that went back during the war. But today there were new faces on the hollow screen. Three men— none of whom could clearly be seen. What was noticeable about the black one was his hair. It too was locked like Kir's but it was only on the top like Tcepser's hair, and the little one was clearly a dwarf. There was no such thing as a human dwarf anymore, if ever one was born and it grew and it became apparent that it was a dwarf, he or she would be killed being mistaken as a non human dwarf, or just murdered because the Elves wanted no confusions, unless the mother could somehow get the child away to safety but this rarely happened. And the Last was another human he believed, he was slim and dark haired, but none of their features was made clear on the screen, a reward of a thousand gold pieces was offered to the capture of these men.

"Those men must be real rebels if they are offering that kind of money" Nathan thought to himself, he knew that with the money you could live in the best part of the silver city London and have anything you want for the rest of your life. He felt sorry for the men; because he knew that every bounty hunter and any fool who uses greed to run their lives would now be out hunting them. He turned away from the screen and went back to his inn; he had work to do and beings to serve.

It had not been long since the three men had left the facility and started the journey along the road that lead into dome city. They knew that they had not many miles to go. All could see the amazing gigantic force field that went up into the sky creating a bubble shape. Vlad had asked the stranger if it would be okay if he called him Xela. He explained that in his language it meant warrior with no fear, and as the stranger did not seem to talk and could not tell them his real name he felt it was appropriate to give him one.

When the stranger nodded in acceptance to this name Vlad then went on to explain to both Leron and the stranger that the force field they all could see now stretched out for miles and miles and protected the City and a lot of surrounding lands from the weather of England. He explained that it was first made with stolen alien technology by humans as protection in case of attack during the war, but the technology had not been fully integrated with the technology the humans already had and was not functioning at a hundred percent. So when the war came to Ipswich and London who both had the force field Technology, it protected both cities from the overwhelming attack the Greys unleashed from the skies. The attack burnt up or destroyed most towns and cities in England.

The Greys then unleashed a ground attack on both cities using Elfin guards who had no problem passing through the force field as it was not a fully working dome. So after the war when the Elves ruled, the Greys fixed the technology to protect the cities from the burning month. He explained that it was only in these cities that a human person could stand outside and watch the wonders of a few weeks that rained fire and made explosions in the night like fireworks.

Leron had asked Vlad how he knew so much about these things being a part of a race that had to hide from the world. He answered that his people have trusties. A few human people whose parents had fought during the war lived in his city and grew up with them. Also some had taken partners with dwarf's and had children that was of normal human height, and these people went out into the world and brought back supplies and other things they could use but most of all tell them the news that had been going on in the world. He explained also that his cousin Mada had a half human girlfriend, who he hoped one day to marry, and that she was posted in the dome city to work for a year and to bring back supplies and news. They continued their journey silently all still looking up into the sky and the great dome force field of Ipswich.

The stranger had taking to the name Xela, he had no name as far as he could remember and he was pleased that his new companion had taken the time to think of something to call him. The world he had known had truly changed and more than often he wondered if this was all for real or was he in some bazaar experiment aimed at making him crazier than he already felt. They were close now to the city, and many times already they had left the road in hiding from oncoming travellers and soldiers going to the dome city. Orcus, drones, humans, gnome looking beings and all types had travelled the road riding on horses towing carts full of all types of stocks. Some had food and drink they had brought to sell at the market place while others filled their carts up with their family members. Those that did not possess a horse or a cart travelled on foot carrying the few little belongings they could manage to bring with them. The soldier Orcus travelled through on their hover machines staring as if they were inspecting every being they passed, so it was a wise thing for the three men to hide off road whenever anyone was near. If anyone would have noticed the dwarf they would have all been discovered and passing into to Ipswich would have become almost impossible. But it was not too long before they reached the dome and once again hid off the road down a small slope. They looked over the top and could see the long queue of beings waiting to pass through into the dome city one by one through a small opening in the force field which was the entrance that was guarded by two Orcus and four drones.

Drones were a scary piece of machinery, they were tall in height and had bulky builds. Their face to Xela was like one big strange shape crash helmet for a motorbike rider with a dark tinted glass so you could not see inside. Their arms, body and legs were clearly mechanical made of a dark silvery grayish type of metal, but they revealed no wiring, and when they moved all you could hear was the mechanics working inside them. The technology for these was not as advanced as the humanoids that Vlad, Xela and Leron had fought with back at the military base in Woodbridge. Yet these huge bulky machines seemed just as intimidating. One of their arms had a huge weapon attached to it, and none of them wished to see what kind of damage the metal hulk could do with that kind of firepower.

The Orcus seemed to be asking everyone for I.D papers which was needed to enter the city. Burning months was all but a few weeks away and people flocked to the city early to get under the protection of the dome. The three of them was now stuck with a dilemma, of how they would enter the city with a dwarf and no papers.

"I have a way." Leron said quietly

"You do? Then share it with us please," Vlad had been racking his brains trying to come up with an idea and did not seem to have much patient with Leron.

"I am not sure how long I can sustain what I am about to do, I was a poor student of this art back home, I was hoping there would be another way."

"What art?" Vlad was becoming frustrated

Leron went into Vlad backpack and took out one of the folders he was carrying.

"No time to explain, tell Xela to pick you up and follow me"

And Leron stood up and walked over the slope onto the road and stopped at the end of the queue. Both Vlad and Xela were puzzled.

"Xela I think we should do as he says if his plan don't work we can always fight our way in." he laughed and Xela smiled.

Vlad words rang interesting to Xela and as much did not matter here he didn't think it would do any harm to play along for a little while so he picked Vlad up and walked towards the end of the queue carrying the small dwarf in his arms. It was a surprise that no one paid much attention to the dark stranger holding a member of the most wanted race in his arms a dwarf. They stood in the line for around two hours as more and more being's came and queued up behind them. Vlad was wondering why no one tried to kill or capture him and surprised also that Xela had stood carrying him for so long without getting tired. Dwarves were small but they were heavy, being such muscular beings but Xela had a strength where nothing much seem to bother him. The guards were checking everyone's papers one by one before they let them pass, until finally they came to Leron and his two companions. The Orcus looked at them suspiciously.

"Papers" The Orcus said in his deep ugly voice. It was always hard for Orcus to speak English as it was not their first language and most only knew a few words, like Papers, or drink, sleep or food, words like this filled up the vocabulary of a Orcus speaking English.

Leron passed the Orcus the folder he had took from Vlad backpack and this now made Vlad even more confused.

"And who is this that travels with you," A drone said. Its voice sounded as though it came through a radio speaker.

"These." Leron smiled as he looked at the both of them. "This is my wife," he pointed to Xela "and the one she is holding is our child"

The look on both Vlad and Xela face was one of complete shock, and they were more stunned when the Orcus handed back the papers and let them through. They were puzzled, and said nothing while they walked into the dome and along the road that ran through the centre of the countryside of Ipswich. When they had passed out of ear and vision shot, Xela put Vlad down.

"What just happened there?" Vlad half shouted.

"I created an illusion, we are trained well at doing this though I make mistakes but it makes us weak and I must continue to do this until we get what we came for please don't make me lose my concentration."

"Weak, what do you mean? How weak?" Vlad continued to question.

"If I don't get the sufficient time to recover it could seriously affect my health, it is easy when it is just one person, but I must create a big illusion for hundreds maybe thousands."

"This won't do, this won't do" Vlad paced up and down "we can't have you in bad condition we may need to fight our way out."

"We have no choice Vladlin if we hope to find what you need?"

Xela stood quietly listening to the both of them talk trying to understand how Leron could perform illusions. He listened carefully, trying to learn all he could about the both of them. Vlad was silent for a moment deep in thought both Xela and Leron waited patiently before Vlad spoke

"Okay. This is what we will do" the Dwarf took charge of the situation, "Leron you will stop creating this illusion this very moment., There is no one here to see me, and while we travel towards the city if we are sighted you may use your illusion trick but we will stay off the road and head through the fields and woodlands. When we get near the city I will find a place to hide for the night and you two will enter and look for a fair haired girl named Manue. She is my cousins girl she will help you find the information you need, just give her this." Vlad handed Leron a gold ring with the symbol of the axe he carried in his pocket so the glint would not alert the animals while he hunted "Are we agreed?"

Both Leron and Xela looked at each other knowing that if they did this they would both have to learn to get along with each other, but they both nodded in agreement with Vlad, knowing that this was the best course of action.

Vlad with his hand still in his pocket felt a chain of some kind pulling it out he lifted it into his vision and it was the chain his father had worn while he was close to death. After he had woken he had questioned only a little if all he had experienced during the days he was unconscious. If the events were real or something he had just dreamt up, but now in his hand was proof, proof that he had met his father in another realm a spirit realm, and now he fully believed in the importance of finding the survivors of his men.

"What is it?" Leron asked wondering why Vlad had become silent staring at a chain.

"Nothing" he said quietly to Leron not willing to share his thoughts. He spoke as if unsure of himself. He was still deep in thought about the event at the gateway to Valdarrior. He placed the chain around his neck and the three of them left the road and crossed through a field of green grass and yellow daffodils, heading closer and closer to the city centre.

Nathan's Bar was an attractive clean place for one to drink in, from the outside it had the homely look of an old fashioned country cottage, with a thatched roof and a clean white painted face with wooden support beams built into the brick work. Hanging outside was the sign with the words in elegant lettering "THE BELL FREE INN".

On the inside it was just as pretty and homely as the impression the outside look had given it. As one entered the inn he would see before him only a few paces away the serving counter, with plenty of mugs and jugs stacked neatly along a shelf at the back of the bar. The counter was made of a mahogany wood and three barrels laid neatly in a holder on top beside each other with taps ready to release the beverage that they held inside. To the right of the entrance were big wide steps that lead upwards to the inns rooms. All rooms were neatly kept and tidied regularly, pillows were always fluffed and clean bedding every night was offered to make the guests stay as comfortable as possible.

It was rare to find rooms such as this in any inn at the dome city, most inns never kept their rooms this well. This is why Nathan charged a higher rate for guests to stay in his clean tidy homely rooms. It was mainly those who were better off than others that spent nights at the Bell Free. This also helped to keep troublemakers and riff raff out of his bar. The stairs were wooden also and the banister was made of oak wood. The floor to the whole downstairs bar was made up of giant slabs of stone put together like brick work. Nathan had the floor scrubbed daily so there was never any dirt build up to destroy the cleanly look of his humble abode. The walls inside were painted a warm cream and the dark vanished frame support oak wood beams could be seen on the inside just like they were on the out.

On the walls hung photo pictures in glass frames, pictures of old that had been collected and sold at the market place. He had pictures of the dome city before the force field was made. Pictures of men drinking merrily in bars took up most spaces on each wall, but his most outstanding pictures were those of the flying machines. He had a picture that was taken during the war of many Grey alien flying machines gliding through a bright sunny day time sky casting dark shadows on the land below. However, his greatest pride was a rare picture to find, a picture of the human flying crafts flying to do combat with the enemy. The symbol R.A.F could clearly be seen along each side of the planes as they flew gallantly across a red sky at dawn.

An Orcus had almost smashed the picture shouting that it was rebellious for him to have this up in his bar, but Eed an Elfin commander, had ordered the Orcus to leave the pictures alone. Eed had always showed respect to Nathan, he even tipped his head to him when he sometimes saw him on the streets. This is something that none of his non human customers ever did. That night Eed had said to the Orcus if Nathan put a picture up of their Grey Flying crafts why was it not right for him to put up flying crafts of his own kind. The Orcus did not respond, nor fight with him, he was a commander and had authority over them.

The Orcus left the picture alone reluctantly, but the same creature still came in every night and walks to the picture, looks at it and then stares at Nathan, like as if it were making a threat, warning him that one day he would get Nathan for this insult. He had often wondered if Eed had done this out of respect for the inn and Tcepser as Eed and the Bell Free inn's former owner once spoke often. Or had it been for the fact that Eed did not like Orcus like most Elves and wanted to assert his authority. Nevertheless, his pictures were rare and many found themselves staring at them and imagining another time a better world, a world when mankind still had hope and freedom.

The Bell Free was lit with candlelight, there was no electricity allowed to humans. All electrical power were in the hands of the Elves and anyone who had the intelligence to make and build generators or anything technological were taken and never ever returned. Behind the serving counter was a door and through the door was a small hallway that led to some steps that went down into the cellar. It was here all the barrels of ale beer and bottles of wine were kept. The beer was brewed by Nathan himself but he purchased the wine and ales and some spirits from farmers and vineyard keepers on the outskirts in the country side of the dome. Sometimes when his stock was too low he would send his barmaid to them with two horses and a cart.

Once a month they would come to his Inn with barrels and bottles for him to purchase to replenish his stock. The Bell Free inn had many large oak tables with wooden chairs that had knitted cushions fasten with straps to the back and the seats making it comfortable for guest's to sit in groups while they ate and drank. Nathan had two wonderful cooks one of which was his main barmaid, she had done most of the cooking for the Bell Free but she also did most things around the inn. She was an amazing worker so Nathan had hired Lydia to come in and cook three days a week, giving his barmaid a little time for herself.

The Owner of the Bell free that evening had been cleaning his bar and washing the mugs, it was a job for his barmaid to do but this night they were short handed and he needed her to tend to the toilets and bedrooms. The inn had a maximum of ten rooms, and normally around this time of the season he never had a spare room, but tonight was different. Only five people all of whom were human had booked themselves in for four weeks. They were here to outlast burning month in the most comfortable way possible, but there was still plenty of time for others to arrive and book into the finest Inn in the city. Besides, he knew as always his bar would be filled within the next hour. This was the only bar Orcus and humans and any other species sat in together and drank. All those who had disagreement with each other kept their opinions to themselves and drank at separate ends of the bar. On rare occasions fights had broken out but only between each other's groups. For example; Orcus would fight Orcus and human against human. Elves sometimes fought with Orcus, as it was well known they had little trust between each other, but Elves never ever fought amongst themselves as they were a disciplined race. A race that showed respect for each other. An Elfin life was more precious than anything to them and this showed in the respect they displayed for one another. There was a rank given to each elf and all amongst them respected this. None seemed to seek power over the other. If an elf was appointed commander over you by the king it was respected and no questions asked.

Nathan was glad for his barmaid as she worked really hard and helped to keep the place spic and span. He had just finished cleaning the mugs, when his barmaid came down the steps.

"All done shall I open the door?" She said with a smile on her face.

She was right it was seven o'clock in the evening and a few people had gathered outside ready to come in for their drinks.

"Yes as always you are punctual, you can open up." Nathan informed her.

He watched her as she opened the door to let the customers in. She was such a pleasure to have around as she brightened up the place with her happy friendly smile. He had often wondered what she had to be really happy about in this life, and what kept her smiling. He had great feelings for the young barmaid but not in a way a man feels for an attractive girl but more like she was his young sister. She was small in height but most women were and she had a cute rounded face with wide blue eyes. She was adorable, and he would take care of her anyway he could. Her story had been similar to his.

He had found her wondering the streets one day asking the market stall keepers for a job, all ignored her. Something in her reminded him of himself, so he took her in and gave her board and paid work, and there had never been a day he had regretted it. She had told him that she had been abandon by her father when her mother died because her father had said he had no money to feed a daughter. In truth her dad had become a drunk and spent all what he had on alcohol from inns and taverns like Nathan's own. She beamed a beautiful smile at him and skipped youthfully back behind the serving counter and began to serve the customers the drinks they had ordered. The customers that had entered were all human. They were the ones that choose to drink early so they could leave before Orcus and Elves arrived at later times.

The inn was opened till all hours in the morning and it was past midnight that most Orcus and elf guards came in after finishing their guard duty at the Elfin guard station. The guard station was more like a castle. The Elves had used the Orcus and the poor people of the city to build the humongous building not long after the war. It once had seemed out of place compared to the rest of the buildings in the city centre. It was huge and stood way above any other building that was known in the dome city. It was made of bricks and strange metals. Towers protruded from each corner of the complex and casted shadows across the streets like great giant guards watching over the people. The walls were lined with Elves watching as if they were expecting an attack. Of course that was impossible now, the rebellion had been crushed and no one dared to attack an Elfin station, no one but the captain off course.

The city was governed by Eniamaj Dendoor the Elfin governor of dome City. He had command over troops made up of Elves, Orcus and Drones, making his men around two thousand. He called his men the city police, but they were more like the city bullies taking advantage of all and anyone they pleased. But though Eniamaj was rarely seen, it was believed that he was a fair governor for an elf. He had elected men to rebuild the city sewers and filtered fresh water from the lakes to reach the taps of every home in the city. He had shown general concern for its people and if he ever heard of an injustice by any of his men he made a public example of them. But people feared his men and rarely spoke out against them. They had terrorised humans and taken their earnings, abused those that had no homes and there were humans that had disappeared altogether. Everyone knew that the Orcus had executed them. They had a jealousy of humans, they despised them and did not hide this fact.

It was well known that the resistance had been

eliminated many years ago, and no human dared defile the Greys' rule. The Orcus continued to search out people and accuse them of being a member of a resistance that clearly did not exist. They threatened shop keepers and market sellers, and in fear for their own lives some would give a name of anyone and say they were part of the resistance so the Orcus would leave them alone. Others went to Orcus and gave a name of someone they hated, saying to them they heard that Mary Jacks had spoke out against them, and that would be the last anyone would ever see or hear of the poor person.

There were people in this city that were just as evil and ruthless as any Orcus or elf, and deep inside it sickened Nathan. He had learned many years ago to keep his hatred and distaste to himself, never uttering a word against the creatures that ran the city because he knew no one here could be trusted. No one but his pretty barmaid.

"Hey Govner," said the barmaid

This is what she had always called Nathan, he was the governor of the inn to her, and she liked to call him this, and Nathan did not mind it.

"Yes dear what can I do for you?"

"Don't be cheeky Gov, this barrel is empty, and customers want more beer" she said with a smile.

"I am sure by now you know where the barrels are, and I know you have no problem getting one." Nathan replied.

"Okay. sir I just did not want you to think if I went down into the cellar that I was slacking Okay." She said with a hint of sarcasm and giggled as she went through a door that was behind her and down some steps into the cellar.

Nathan smiled to himself. She was quite cheeky at times and he liked this. He was also amazed at her strength. He himself had problems carrying one of the beer barrels from the cellar up those steps. He had always had someone to help carry them, but this barmaid carried them on her own and had always made it look easy. She had explained to Nathan that since she was little she worked on her parents' farm and did all the carrying and this had made her strong.

Since it seemed no effort for her to carry these barrels he made her do it all the time. He watched as she returned carrying the big barrel, in all the time she had been doing it he still marvelled at such a little women carrying such a large object, and he smiled at the expressions on his customers faces when they witness such a sight. She placed the big barrel in the barrel rack and then turned to two men that were in awe at the sight.

"So what will it be then lads?" She beamed that wonderful smile again and began to serve.

Many people had ordered a bite to eat and as Nathan was short handed the only food on the menu was a delicious stew that his barmaid had cooked earlier and kept in the air tight warmer so it would not lose its heat. She began serving it up with freshly baked bread. It was while she had brought some stew and bread up to those customers who had ordered their food in their rooms that two strangers had entered the Bell Free.

It was not uncommon for strangers to enter his inn in this month as many strangers came to the dome city around this time, but he could not help but feel there was something familiar about the two. They both wore very expensive coolant hooded cloaks, and though the slender dark haired man removed his hood on entering the other who happened to be a dark skinned man did not.

"Two mugs of ale" the one who had un-hooded himself said.

But the still hooded one shook his head indicating he did not wish to drink.

"I feel I will be drinking alone." The slender man was well spoken and very polite.

Nathan served the man his drink.

"I was wondering" the slender stranger said to Nathan without touching his drink but placing two silver pieces on the counter.

"Yes" Nathan was very curious about these two. "I was wondering if you had a spare room we could share for the night"

"Yes I do I have a room with two single beds but I must warn you my prices are not cheap, especially for only one night at this time of year."

The slender man placed on the counter three gold pieces. Nathan was shocked at the currency these men were willing to give.

"I know I said I was expensive but for three gold pieces you could stay here for two weeks with food and drink with this amount of money" Nathan chuckled.

"Consider it a tip, for your services and maybe for a little information" replied the stranger.

Nathan became wary, those who seek information often came to stir trouble. Bounty hunters were the first thing that came to his mind.

"Who is it you are looking for?" Nathan asked.

"You are very perceptive to know we seek a person, But this person we seek we believe may be here in your inn"

The barman felt insulted, bounty hunters accusing him of harbouring a criminal; such slander could get a man killed.

"I harbour no criminals here bounty hunter so if I was you I would forget the room as you are not welcome here." He shouted

"Woe woe calm down good fellow, I am no bounty hunter and the person we seek is my cousin. I have not seen her for a while and as I was passing through the city I thought I would look to find her and see how she is."

Nathan became calm and entertained the idea that the

man maybe telling the truth.

"And what is this girl's name?" Nathan asked curiously.

"Her Name is Manue" Replied the stranger.

Nathan was stunned for a moment. Manue his barmaid, she had never mentioned anything to him about a cousin. She had told him she had no family left, someone was lying and Nathan was not quick to trust anyone.

"Mmm, I don't know. I might have a guest here by that name let me go and see if I do and I will tell her that you have arrived," He went to walk away.

"Wait one minute please, it has been a long time since I have seen her. We were children and she may not recognise me, but if you give her this she will know it is me. It's a gift she gave me when we were young." Explained the stranger holding out the item.

Nathan looked at the thin outstretched hand of the stranger. In the palm of his hand was a gold ring with an axe on it, he became suspicious as he knew the symbol, but did not let on. He reached out and took it and went up the steps. He had found Manue in the hallway carrying an empty tray back from one of the rooms.

"Manue"

"Yes Gov" she said as she watched Nathan approach her.

"There are two men downstairs for you" He began to explain.

"For me?" Manue seemed surprised.

"Yes one says he is your cousin"

"I ave no cousin" She became worried

"Are you sure because he gave me this to give to you" he opened the palm of his hand he could tell she immediately recognised it, and without thinking she took it from his hand.

"Oh my goodness, Gov it is my cousin." She said excitedly

"But you said… "

"I know but I thought my cousin was dead, that is why I said I ave no cousin, but if he gave you this he is alive, quick Gov please take me to him"

Nathan now knew something was wrong, she had recognised the ring and also agreed that the man downstairs was her cousin. Things were slightly falling into place about his barmaid though a lot of it still did not make sense, he wondered for a minute if she was a dwarf that just looked like she was human. This would explain her strength, but then he knew this was not possible.

Dwarves had distinctive features that she clearly did not possess. She knew the dwarves and the men downstairs that ring bared an emblem of a dwarfin house. He knew this for his father had taught him as a child about these things. He had been told great stories of the great warrior dwarf named Korin The great one, from the House of Bowen who fought alongside men and won great battles. This was the sign he wore upon his armour and on his breast plate, and if those men had shown that ring to an elf they would have been dead already. He took Manue to the men and watched how she ran out to greet them and gave them both a big hug.

"Oh cousin it's been a long time," She said hugging the stranger.

"Yes Manue I have missed you,"

"Come we ave plenty to talk about. I will take you to my room." She took the stranger by the hand.

"No Manue," Nathan put his foot down

"They have booked a room for the night and there is no exception for family. I am afraid they will pay like everyone else, and you have work to do, so you may show them to their room and return to work please." Nathan went behind the bar and served a customer.

Manue had known Nathan long enough and not once had he ever spoken to her like this; she knew he knew something was not right.

"Okay. Gov, I am sorry I will take em to their room and I will return."

She walked away up the stairs leading the stranger by the hand as the other one followed. Nathan picked up the mug that the stranger had purchased and found that he had not touched a drop.

"What kind of man does not finish or even start his ale?" he thought to himself as he began to wonder what he should do about the whole situation.

Manue had taken the two guests to their room, and told them to make themselves comfortable. The slender one had sat on one of the beds near the chest of draws that was in the room and the hooded man sat on a chair in the corner of the room by the window. She walked over to the chest of draws, and sliding the draw open she retrieved a knife that were in all guest rooms, (some guest felt they needed a blade for protection while they slept). Holding the blade she quickly turned and placed it to the slender mans throat. The man did not move a muscle— did not even flinch he just looked at her calmly.

"Who are ya and what ave ya done with the one that carried this." She held the ring up in her other hand.

"We are friends Manue. We have not come here to harm you." His voice was almost childlike.

"I know bounty unters and their dirty tricks." Manue replied.

"If I was here to harm you, would I not have done it by now?" The slender man replied.

"And ow would you do that while I'm holding this blade to your neck"

"You forget there are two of us" he pointed out.

She looked up to the hooded man in the corner, and before she could get the chance to blink he was gone and she felt his hand gently on her shoulder. She turned her head to face him. He stood tall over her with his hood over his head and she was startled. She turned her head back to face the man on the bed and to her surprise the blade she had carried was now at her own throat, and in her hand she held a scroll that was on the bed in every room stating the rules of the inn.

"If we were here to hurt you I would not do this"

The man threw the blade up only a little catching it again by its sharp end offering the handle to her, she reached for it slowly dropping the scroll and taking the blade, she did not hold it to the man in any threatening way but she kept it at her side for security.

"Okay. Mr, you have my attention, who are ya?"

"I am Leron and my companion here is Xela. We were sent here by Vladlin Bowen who I believe you know well, as I know you are half dwarfin"

"Is he Okay.? Where is he?" Manue asked anxiously.

"He is well and hiding outside the city centre but it is for your man Mada we fear for the most"

"Mada, what has happened?" Manue had become seriously concerned.

Leron continued to explain the past week's events and what had happened to the hunting party, and that they had learned that Mada and five others were still alive and that they had been transported to the dome city. Now they have come in hope to devise an escape for them. All the information overwhelmed Manue and now she was crying, crying for the danger her future husband was in and the danger that Vlad had put himself in coming to the Dome city.

"Vlad told us that you would help us find out what you can about his men"

"I've heard of no dwarf been brought ear in the city. I would have found a way to report back home if I did, but tomorrow I will inquire subtly, but please you must find em and help em escape." She wept.

"I promise you I will do my best" Leron answered.

Outside the room door where Leron and Manue conversed, stood Nathan. He had listened to most of the conversation and now he sneaked away quietly back down the steps, knowing that trouble had walked into his bar a long time ago.

7

The Great Escape

Vladlin Bowen, was settling in for the night in the woodlands on the outskirts of the city centre. It had been many hours since he had sent Leron and Xela ahead without him and he was slightly concerned for their safety.

On their journey to the centre they had come across a hollow screen and they found that they were the three top most wanted men; they found it baffling how anyone would have known about them and got this information to the Elves. The only beings that had encountered all three of them were the humanoids and Vlad resided to the fact that they had played a major part in this. Their features were not clear on the screen but it would not take much for anyone to notice Xela's hair, so he had given them all the coolant cloaks he carried and made them both wear one and advised Xela to keep his hood up at all times. The rest of the cloaks they could sell on the market to any market stall keeper, knowing that even if they were sold cheaply they would receive more than enough money for what they needed.

He had also given them the silver pieces; he had left believing that if they did not find Manue right away they would have no problem getting a bed for the night. It was a clear night as most nights were and Vlad laid in the woods on a cloak and used his back pack for a pillow. He looked up and marvelled at the stars and the full bright moon.

He never paid much attention to the moon shaped ship that could clearly be seen in the night time sky, though it was high up in space it was an unpleasant reminder to all of the atrocities that earth and all its occupancies had been through and were still going through. He felt a cold wind wisp across his face and he marvelled at the technology of the see through force field that was the dome. It was amazing how it was calibrated so that rain and air could pass through it but fire and blast weapons and beings could not.

Because it did not rain often in England the Elves had made it a condition that the Greys make it rain at least once every two weeks. This was so that the farmers could grow vegetables and water their lands and so the lakes and reservoirs would also never go dry. It was said that on the Greys' ship they contained huge amounts of water and they sent crafts to release H_2O from high up in the skies cause rain directly over the dome city and the city London.

Technology was an amazing thing to Vlad and it was understandable why the Elves and the Greys' did not want any other being to have any as it was another way to keep control of the populace. To keep every being in line how could one fight against beings with such amazing weaponry? Vlad turned over on his side, he had not made a fire, because he did not want to give anyone any sign that someone was sleeping out here in the woods.

He pulled his cloak around him to shield himself from the breeze, and he listened to the owl tooting in one of the nearby trees. It was the continued hoot of the owl that had made him begin to drift off, but when the owl had stopped and it wings could be heard fluttering as it left the branch it was perched on flying away into the night, the silence had brought Vlad out of his semi conscience state and made him on full alert. He listened closely. The crickets and the night time creatures had all gone silent, something was wrong. He laid still and slowly reached for his blade.

"I would not if I was you, I would prefer to bring in a live dwarf it is not good to have a dead one."

Vlad sat up to see who had spoken, Standing all around him were at least seven tall slender beings, with white long hair fluttering in the wind and clear bright white eyes peering at him. They all stood arrows pointed at him holding their bows firm. There was no chance for Vlad to escape this many. Slowly in plain sight he took out his blade and threw it down, and slowly standing up he raised his hands clearly showing the Elves that he was their prisoner and he was not going to fight.

Leron and Xela sat quietly in the room, Manue had gone about her work and left them to devise a plan for the morning. It was clear since the moment they met that Leron had not liked Xela but Vlad had sent them both on this mission and Leron was forced to communicate with him. At first on their journey through the city centre Leron had spoke to him as little as possible. But the more they walked the more he found that he spoke with him not getting a reply back, still Xela had nodded or shook his head in answer to any questions that Leron had asked him.

They had sold the remaining coolant cloaks to a market stall owner who seemed pleased to pay them the gold pieces they had asked for. Leron found that it was comfortable for him to have a companion that did not speak back to him or argue like Vlad often did. He felt that Xela was more like him in many ways. He was calm at all times and did not show any expression of anger or annoyance, he could be almost Fairrien, he had thought.

It was because Leron was missing the collective mind of his people. Spending his whole life in a range that he could hear the thoughts of his kind and they could his. They had always been like this it was the Fairrien way, no fairy had secrets from each other; it was like they were all really one, and agreed on everything as a collective group. It was a group decision to send Leron out here on this mission and befriend the dwarf. But now he was out of range of his people for the first time in his life and he could not hear their thoughts and follow their advice. He was on his own and alone and had to use his own single wisdom to overcome whatever challenges he may face. At first it was difficult having no voices in his mind but then he slowly became accustomed to the quiet.

It was in the calm mannerism of his new companion Xela that reminded him of his own kind, and the way Xela had moved to protect him if needed when Manue had the knife to him that proved to Leron that he was honourable. He had decided to give the stranger Xela a chance and except him as a friend. After all the young man was lost now in a time he knew nothing about and it was the Fairrien duty to help those who truly needed it.

He wondered for a moment on what age Xela was it was hard to tell, he looked young but then maybe he looked older it was strange. At times he looked as though he were a young man of the age of twenty and then other times Leron could picture him as almost a thirty year old human. He decided then that this being was really at least a century old and thought himself silly wondering about his age. It was while these silly thoughts were wondering through Leron's head that there was a gentle tap at the door of their room. Leron had not expected Manue back so soon, and he could tell Xela was suspicious as he moved quietly and with great speed to stand at the side of the door so he would be behind it when it opened.

Leron walked to the door and placed his hand on the handle.

"Who is it?" he said

"It's me Nathan the Inn keeper, I have information for you."

Leron was slightly puzzled; the only information he had asked from the innkeeper was about the girl Manue. He opened the door and saw Nathan standing looking very suspiciously in the hallway.

"What Information?" Leron was curious.

"Information about dwarfs" the man whispered.

"I think you better come in" Leron open the door wide and Nathan entered.

Leron went and seated himself and Xela closed the door behind the man after he had entered. Nathan jumped a little he had not seen Xela behind him and it startled him.

"So what information have you for us good fellow and what makes you think we are interested in Dwarves."

"I know everything Manue told me, she told me everything. I have no hatred towards dwarves, and Manue knows I can be trusted."

"What can you tell us?" Leron had become very interested; if Manue trusted this man and she was part dwarf then he would not be reluctant to trust him also.

"The dwarfs you speak of they had arrived here I overheard one of the Elfin guards speaking of them three nights ago. They are being kept in the north east tower at the Palace."

"Palace" Leron questioned.

"Yes the elf station but we call it a palace because it is built like such, but if you are to rescue them you must be quick because they are not to stay here long. They will be transported under heavy guard across the sea's."

"Do you know where too?"

"No, but I believe the only chance you will get is tonight at Midnight. It is the changing of the guards and while this change happens there is a five minute gap in which the tower is guarded by only two. The only problem you would have is getting past the gates to get on the palace ground. This I think will not be easy."

Leron considered what he was being told, things were moving too quick. He would have liked to have watched the palace and made a sufficient plan, but the innkeeper had told him that this was his only chance.

"What does Manue say of this?"

"She agrees with me" the Inn keeper went on, "But she must stay here so there is no suspicion on her, already a few Orcus guards have entered the Inn. Neither I or her must be missed."

"I should speak with her" Leron stood up.

"No you must not be seen speaking with her again if you are caught or recognised Manue and myself will both be executed"

"So what do you suggest?"

"Look, the only way to get on the palace grounds undetected is to scale the west wall. It is very big and only one guard sits this side of the wall, they expect no trouble from anyone and that wall is almost impossible to climb,"

"We have ways to climb a wall such as this"

"Then it is settled at five minutes to midnight you will leave via the back entrance and if your mission is successful do not return here. I will arrange for four horses to be on the south side of the wall, take them and leave but never return." The innkeeper turned and faced Xela; looking a bit frightened he squeezed past him and left the room.

Leron considered all that he had heard for a moment, he then looked at the wooden clock that hanged on the wall above the bed, it was eleven thirty time was short. He then decided to go with the plan, it had been the first real chance they have had during their whole journey that gave him hope in saving Vlad's men.

Xela was not so certain of this, and felt that Nathan had not been completely honest with them; it had bothered him so much that he opened his mouth as if to speak to say so, but nothing came out. He decided there was no point in stopping any of this, because none of it really mattered.

Vlad's hands had been tied firmly with some type of glowing wire. He secretly tried to use his strength to break himself loose but there was no hope this was Elfin magic, and his bonds were not meant to be so easily broken. He walked now under guard with three Elves behind him arrows still ready to be used if there were any trouble. Ahead and beside him rode the other Elves on pearly white horses and all dressed in different dark colours. It was like this with Elves they had no uniform they wore whatever colour suited them that day. But all their clothing was made from the finest of materials specially woven in the Elfin home land, a land that was once Vlad's people's home too. His tied hands were attached to a rope that in turn was tied to the head elf's saddle. They had not harmed him in anyway but he was sure this would come when they interrogated him.

They had now entered the city and Vlad's leather strapped shoes had been removed, they felt this would slow him down if he found a way to run. His feet were becoming slightly sore as they trotted along on the rough cobbled stone ground of the city centre. The city was actually quite clean and well kept, Vlad had been surprised that after all these years the place had not fallen to ruins. The Elves here had put an effort in maintaining a good condition of the city. Light in taverns and bars and homes lit up the streets making Vlad wishing for comfort of a nice warm bed. As they neared what could only be described as a huge castle, the streets up ahead were lit by what appeared to be street lanterns. "This place is well taken care of indeed" the thought entered his mind. They moved along for a short while until they found themselves at a very large iron gate.

"Who goes there?" A guard shouted from up above the castle gate.

"It is I your superior, Commander Eed" The Elf who had strung Vlad up to his horse replied.

After a short pause the gate began to lift upwards allowing the Elfin guards and Vlad to enter the castle grounds. On the other side of the gate Vlad found a small army waiting, all armed and ready as if to go to war, there were at least two hundred.

"This all for me" he said looking to the commander he now knew was named Eed.

"No they have another mission tonight" Eed looked down at him and smirked.

They came to a halt at the bottom of a tall tower.

"Take him to the dungeons I will tell the governor he has arrived." Eed ordered three of his men. He then walked away across the courtyard.

The Elfin guards opened the metal door before them with a big key of the likes Vlad had never seen before it seemed more like a small weapon rather than a key. It had sharp spikes coming from the end in all directions. They turned the lock and made Vlad enter beyond the big metal door. There were stone steps spiralling up wards towards the top. But the Elves took him the other way and made him walk the steps that spiralled downwards. The tower went deep under the ground; it took them a bit of time to reach the bottom.

When they had finally reached the end of the steps they came out upon a short passageway that was dimly lit by flaming torch light, and on reaching the end of the passageway they came to yet another metal door. One of the Elves banged on the door with his fist making a thundering echo along the passageway. After a moment a slot in the door slide open. It was an Orcus on the other side; these creatures had always made Vlad feel ill. They were ugly monsters that had no understanding of emotion, creatures that went against all the laws of nature. The creature looked at them all, and peered at the prisoner.

"Another one" it grinned.

It appeared to speak good English though its voice was still hideous. It spoke as though someone had placed their hand around its throat and squeezed tight, there was no emotion in its voice. Vlad was slightly shocked that a creature of this kind could master any language it was very uncommon for Orcus. The creature then opens the door from the other side.

Vlad noticed the blood stained leather apron the creature had over its dirty brown rags that it wore. This thing had done a lot of butchering, and he knew it was not animals it had been cutting to pieces. It let them pass through into the large dudgeon forcing upon them the overwhelming stench of death, dying human and non-human body waste that came from every cell they past. Vlad raised his tied hands to cover his nose, the Elves had covered their noses before entering as they knew what to expect.

He was surprised at how many prisoners were kept here. As they walked along the corridors of over packed cells he noticed the humans caged up and crammed tightly together in small cells looking underfed, skin sagged and the composition of their bodies were made up of bone with barely no muscle tissue. They were all unclothed except for some who had ripped small pieces of cloth to cover over their sexual organs down below. Men, women and children already half dead peered back at him. As he past their cells they sat and stood on dead bodies of their once and past cell mates or family member.

"There is more than enough space in here to house them all separately." The Orcus had noted the expression on

Vlad's face as he stared at the horrifying sight of the cruelty this thing had bestowed upon the humans.

"But it takes the fun out of keeping humans as prisoners." The creature hissed a giggle as he took pleasure from what he had created here.

Vlad saw creatures of all kinds in the dungeons as they walked that corridor, Sarron's, Ganomes, and amazingly locked in a cell and chained to a wall was even a Rock creature, one of the most fearsome races ever made upon this earth. Vlad knew that this creature could not have been easy to catch even for the Elves. Rock creatures were rarely seen these days. They grouped together far away from any being, living off what they could but killing any that came near them. They always travelled and moved in groups knowing no one not even the Elves would approach them, as they were wild and dangerous. Even ogre's who could be twice the size of them thought twice about fighting these creatures if they ever had to face one. Their strength was amazing; Vlad knew it was Elfin magic that held this creature to the wall. He must have been a wanderer, one of those that sometimes left the pack in search of better soil. These creatures could go months without eating, and although they ate meat and fruit, they also ate good quality soil, it was this that sustained them and what provided enough of what they needed to keep the outer layers of their skin solid rock. The genetic makeup of these creatures was amazing, only Grey technology could have created a creature such as this. Vlad stared at its rocky body; the creature stared back but did not move or make a sound. They were trying to break this creature, put it under their control, and by the looks of it they were almost there.

They put Vlad into an empty cell. When he had entered, the wire around his wrist lost its glow and fell away leaving his hands free. He turned as the metal bar cell door slammed shut and the Orcus jailer turned the key.

"Any trouble from you and we will put those back on"

The Orcus pointed towards the wire before he and the Elves walked back down the corridor of cells to the entrance. Vlad sat down in the rat infested cell on rotten hay that smelt as if many beings had urinated on it. This place was a germ infested trap, and he sooner be hanged then to spend much time in this cell. The smell of the place made him gag; he was sure that if he had much in his stomach it would have been wrenched from his belly through his mouth and onto the cell floor by now. The rock creatures cell was only a few yards away from his, Vlad looked around at the cruelty this creature had done here as the dungeon keeper. He then promised himself that the first chance he gets he will kill it and make it pay for what it had done.

It had gone five to midnight; Leron and Xela had snuck down the back stairs of the inn and now were crossing the city square, headed towards what was known as the palace. They moved fast and silently across the square, ducking and hiding behind objects as they approached the palace making sure that they were not seen. They reached the front of the building and observed two Elfin guards patrolling the front gate. They would have to be quick and quiet; Elves have very sharp vision and great hearing. They could hear a pin drop a hundred yards away. Leron knew he could move silently but he wondered if his companion could be as quiet as he needed to be.

They waited a few moments, hiding behind a market stall, waiting for the right moment. When the time was right and the guards were not facing their direction they sped from their hiding place across to the palace's west wall. They paused there for a moment while Leron peaked around the corner making sure they had not been heard. They had succeeded, the guards seem oblivious to their crossing to the wall. Leron turned and signalled the sign for Xela to wait. They had planned beforehand that when they reached the wall Leron would get on top and lower the rope he carried down to Xela so he may climb up. There was one guard they had been told, on top of this wall and Leron would have to take him out silently and quick before he could lower the rope, the more time they wasted the more likely it would be that they would be discovered.

Leron stood for a moment, eyes closed, Xela had wondered how Leron would get on top of this wall and now he knew. Leron's figure began to shimmer and before Xela's eyes after a bright flash he changed shape and became a small tiny ball of light. The rope, clothing weapons all vanished with him. Xela was surprised and really knew he was dreaming. He watched as the yellow ball of light flew upwards towards the top of the wall. Leron was in his energy form, it was the way his people mainly travelled; a Fairrien being could maintain this form for three days, but when carrying objects such as ropes and weaponry, it shorten the period of how long one could maintain the form, it really depended on how much was carried but in Leron case he could only stay this way for one and a half to two days at the most.

This form explained the everlasting rumours that fairies were little people with little wings, (it was not true of course but seeing a fairy in this form kind of explained why people would be mistaken). Within the ball of light was just the energy of his mind and soul no shape could be seen. Leron floated up now to the very high top of the wall, on reaching the top he was surprised at what he saw. The whole west wall was filled with Elfin guards, ducking down so they would not be seen. It was a trap! They had known they were coming, and only one other person knew what they would be doing this night.

Leron started to change his direction so he could float

down and warn Xela of the trap that had been set, but before he had the chance an elf jumped through the air with a glass jar in his hand catching Leron off guard. Leron found himself in the jar and before he could zip out of it, the lid slammed shut and the elf twisted it closed. Fairriens in this state did not need to breath for one whole day but the elf made holes in the tin top jar, they did not want him to die yet, not without interrogating him first.

Xela was at the bottom of the wall, he could sense something was not right, there was a sound to the right of him he turned around to look, and before he could even get a chance to run, he was surrounded by at least a hundred Elves and Orcus arrows and weapons all pointing at him. He tilted his head up as if waiting for Leron to come back down, but now standing on top of the wall with all arrows pointing in his direction where at least another hundred Elves. He was surrounded. It did not bother him, he had half expected this; he knew that Nathan the innkeeper was not telling the truth.

He considered for a moment fighting his way out. There was a small chance that he would make it, but he decided to let them take him were ever they wanted. It did not matter, nothing did. Maybe if he did not play the game he would get out of this mind state quicker. He dropped his weapons and let them tie his hands with a glowing wire; Xela smirked a wicked smirk and walked along with the Elves under heavy guard.

Manue had already gone to the room where the visitors and hopeful rescuer of Mada were staying. She had found them gone and on returning back downstairs to the inn she noticed that the whole inn were peering through the windows, she walked to the front door of the inn and opened it. She could then see what the interest was. Under a heavy guard of Elves she could see the one named Xela being escorted into the palace. She was fearful for them and poor Vlad out in the woodlands, he would be stuck.

She ran into the back room crying, crying for Mada, with these men captured Mada was sure to die. She would have to go and find Vlad and tell him of what had happened. She had started to get ready taking some food in a sack to feed Vladlin if he found himself hungry. But just then Nathan came in.

"What are you doing?"

"I have to go gov it's a family problem" she replied turning her head away from him trying to hide the tears that were rolling down her face.

"Your cousin's friend seems to have been arrested."

"Well he is my cousins friend nothing to do with me." She held her sack and went to walk out of the door.

"I can't let you go,"

"What you mean govna; I must go my family needs me."

"Do you mean the dwarf that waits in the woods?"

Manue was shocked, how had Nathan known about this.

"Don't bother go he would have been arrested by now and you will get arrested to if you go out there."

"Nathan what have you done?" Her voice became no longer playful or giddy. She spoke like a woman now, with serious concerns, her smile was nowhere to be seen and she became almost a different person.

"I did it for you dear, it was only a matter of time before they were caught, I saw them this morning on the hollow screen. They are the most wanted men now." Nathan seemed sorrowful.

"They were my only hope they were... "

"I know friends of your family, I know you are half dwarfin and it does not matter. You can stay here with me no one will ever know, if those men would have got caught here we would all be dead and the Orcus would have learned of your bloodline. I had to save you."

Manue's faced changed to one of anger and hatred.

"You stupid old man, you have become one of those that you hate, the ones you go on about who betray each other for money to the enemy, isn't that what you call em the enemy, I thought you were a good man, but you are just as sick and twisted as the rest of em out there. Now get out of my way."

She pushed past him knocking him into the wall, he knew she was strong and she could have done a lot worse to him. She ran upstairs to her room, there was no hope for her lover now, Mada would surely die. She laid on her bed with her face in her pillow weeping, she had never felt such sorrow and it struck a pain into her soul.

Nathan sat in the back room, the words of Manue sunk into his heart. She was right he was as bad as the ones in the village who turned people over for money or just because they didn't like them. And what made it worse was that he had turned over three men that had done him no harm. He had sent them to his enemies so that they may be killed. It was the love he had for Manue that had drove him to do such a stupid thing, and now those men stood in the hands of his father's killers. He had become to accustom to this life that he lived, he had it better than most and he had wanted it to stay this way until he died. He wanted Manue to have his inn after his passing. But this was no excuse for what he had done and he knew it, he sat and cried at the ugliness that was inside him, the selfish beast that had driven him to this mess, he then became sick at himself. And there was no way he could fix it. Not now it was too late, or was it?

Vladlin had watched the rock creature standing silently

chained against the wall, it stood motionless as if it were a statue. He had sat the last thirty minute devising ways of escape, and now his attention was fully locked on the subdued creature.

"Ohh ow ichi owe" Vlad spoke, his people had learned this language many years ago when the rock creatures had began to evolve. They had once been intelligent creatures in their prime of evolution, before the Greys noticed them. Man themselves believed they had once as a people evolved from this species but the dwarf knew that had not been true. Apes they were, they began to evolve around 2010 and had broken away from all apes that did not take to their ways. There had been a fight between the species, evolving species fought and over powered what had become the lesser species of apes, they had devised their own language, and began to dig holes in the ground and covered them with branches and leaves as a roof for their homes.

Man had discovered this amazing change in the apes and went out hunting them and taking them back for study, many were caught and were taken to all corners of the earth, but here in England they ended up in zoo's a place where humans came to watch animals. But the apes were smart and while they were being observed they themselves were observing their captures, they learned what they could about the dominating species before they devised a way of escape.

They were all male silverback apes; they had grown larger in their evolving and walked up right with hunched backs. Their muscular build was amazing. They were the dominant male apes and it was only in these males that the evolution process had begun. But rather then they all fought and killed each other as was expected of the male silver back species to prove who was the real dominate male, they worked together and formed their escape taking along many female apes to keep their lineage going. They lived in the shadows being hunted at every turn. It was the Dwarves that came to their aid giving them a safe haven from those who seek to capture them.

They lived with the dwarves a short time, and it was within this time that the dwarves had learned their language and became a friend to the new species. But that was during the beginning of the war, which was when the creatures knew themselves. It was the Greys that had abducted them, changing their genetic makeup, trying to develop a stronger mightier soldier to fight and kill men. When they were returned to earth they were an unrecognisable fierce creature.

At first killing all they could find following the orders of the Greys, but then there was a change in them and they turned on their masters, killing Orcus and breaking drones. They did not want any part of this war, they just wanted to be left alone, and from that moment they had killed any species that came near them, they were like wild creatures, and it was foolish for the Elves to try and control them again. Vlad spoke the language of the evolved apes, hoping that deep down inside there was still some kind of remembrance of what it once had been.

"Ohh ow ichi owe" he said again, this was a greeting from one friend to another.

The creature lifted its head, the first movement the rock had made since Vlad's arrival in the dungeons.

"Ohh ow ichi owe" Vlad said again.

"Arrrh owe ichi arhcow." The creature spoke making the deepest sound with its voice; they had all become deep voiced beings now. It had not been like this before the change. Vlad opened his mouth to say more, but he heard the Orcus walking along the corridor, he had others with him, they were Elves.

"Come now." The Orcus opened the cell "Governor Eniamaj Dendoor has requested your presents" the monster hissed.

Dendoor, Vlad knew this name, he began to walk along the cellblock looking to the rock creature as he passed its cell. He reached the dungeon door and was about to leave with the Elfin guards when the Orcus stopped him.

"Before you go tell me what did it say to you?"

"Who?" Vlad answered back to the Orcus.

"The rock thing I heard you trying to speak with it, what did it say?"

Vlad looked the beast in its eyes, "it said there are no friends here, and when it is free it will kill you."

Vlad had added the part about killing the jailer; he wanted him to feel fear. The jailer stared back at him looking a little worried, before he began to giggle its hideous sound.

Vlad and the Elves exited the dungeon hearing the cruel giggle of a seriously demented Orcus echoing throughout the tower.

Eniamaj was a slightly overweight averaged height tanned skin white eyed elf. He was known to be an arrogant and at times very naïve governor of dome city. He considered himself a good leader, he still believed in the old Values of the old ways before Maxius was king amongst his people. He believed and had faith in his king to one day restore the earth to its natural glory, so that all could live peacefully on the earth, new and old creatures included. What he had accomplished, since being ruler of the dome city, was to mark a beginning for the rest of a New England and one day the rest of the world. He had been good to the people, and they lived in harmony with his men. The city had kept its beauty and nature flourished all around. On the outskirts of the city, fields and meadows and farm land stretched for miles and miles. There was little the people of Ipswich could ask for so he believed. Many years ago he had found it hard to be a firm believer in the Elfin campaign against the dwarfs. They were their distant cousins.

They were once creatures of nature, brilliant sculptures and architects. They had designed and help build the Elfin home city, and joined magic forces with the Elves to create amazing weaponry to fight during the war. How quick it had been that the Elves turned on them was a surprise to Eniamaj. But when he had heard what the dwarves had done, and what they also kept from the Elves, he began to understand the determination in finding their new city.

He had now believed that it was necessary to find them because they held what was needed to restore a true peace on the earth, and they had to pay for their crimes. He sat in his hall which was more like a large throne room that had solid golden pillars to support its roof. The walls were decorated with satin red silky material and gold engravings ran around each wall, engravings of Elfin hero's that had fought and died in great battles. The ceiling of the hall arched upwards with golden beams to support and make the arch, but in between the beams were great paintings of an Elfin battlefield, fighting beside Men against Orcus. It was an amazing piece of art, and if it were anyone else that had this picture painted it would have been seen as an insult towards the Greys.

But Eniamaj was a firm believer in history; he kept his own personal Library of ancient books. Books of ancient human and dwarfin philosophers and ancient human dwarfin and Elfin history. He read often on the great people that played a major part in maintaining good morals amongst the people of this planet, and had learnt the necessities of wars to uphold these values.

Eniamaj sat in his great throne like chair which was made of gold, wearing his silk purple gown, with the golden symbol of the house of Dendoor. Upon the right side of the gown, a golden pattern also ran around every seam of the outfit, making the gown an outstanding piece of art itself. Everything Eniamaj wore or did was related to some sort of art. He respected any being that showed artistic skills, he believed art was the essence of all things even nature. There was a knocking on his hall room door.

"Enter" Eniamaj shouted, his voice echoed through the whole room as the acoustics were designed so all could hear when the Governor spoke. He had expected them to bring the Dwarf to him, he had ordered it. He believed that maybe he would have more luck trying to get information from this one then he did the others. But as he saw the dwarf they entered with he knew he would have no such luck. Standing before him at the bottom of his large steps that lead up to his chair was Vladlin Bowen, The last full male member of the house of Bowen, unless he had children of course. He had known him once a very long time ago; they had been friends before times of war. Eniamaj heart was saddened for only a moment, he knew he had to do what was needed and expected of him as the governor. He had to try his best to get information for his king, regardless that this dwarf had once been a friend; he fixed firmly on the words his king had shouted to his people on the day of victory.

"There are no dwarfin friends, they are all now the enemy, and we will seek all until peace is restored to us." Maxius had shouted, and these words now held firm in the Governors mind.

"Vladlin Bowen, this is an unexpected surprise." Eniamaj spoke as though he was a young human English king.

This had been the voice that Vladlin's old friend used when he mimicked the sound of posh English kings. This had not been his real voice. He had changed, even his appearance, he had gained weight which was a very hard thing for an elf to do. It was very rare to have a slightly plump elf, it was practically unheard of.

"I see you have changed in many ways Eniamaj" Vlad said looking to his belly as four Elfin guards stood around him.

"Arh you mean this," Eniamaj rubbed his belly. "It is the compliments of good living, I find that these days I eat a lot, I think it has become a habit of mine." He smiled.

Vlad kept stern faced and did not smile, he was a prisoner, and he knew that there was no longer a friend in any elf.

"So what is it you want of me, because there is nothing I have to offer?"

"Oh come now Vladlin, I am sure there is something you have for me" smiled Eniamaj

"There is nothing so you may as well kill me now as there is nothing you can do to make me talk". Vlad said defiantly.

Eniamaj stood up and walked to a chest of draws that was near his great chair. He opened the draw and pulled out a Snipe blade.

"Have you ever seen what a snipe blade can do to a being when penetrating the right part of the body?"

Vlad stayed silent

"You are reluctant to answer, so I gather you don't know so I will explain." He walked slowly down the steps caressing the blade as though it were his lover. And now he stood before Vlad blade in hand.

"If the blade is forced to the lower abdomen of any species and twisted at the right angle so that the light could reflect upon it, it begins to slowly burn the being from the inside out, causing scrutinising pain, it could take many hours for the being to die."

Eniamaj placed the blade on Vlad's cheek catching the moonlight that came through his large colour glass windows causing a small fire bolt to be released from the blade along the side of Vlad's face. His face began to bleed a little, but

Vlad did not wince or yell out in pain, he just gritted his teeth.

"Is that supposed to scare me, Huh do your worse."

"Oh Vladlin" The elf removed the blade from Vlad's face and began to walk back up the steps to his mighty chair. He sat down and faced the dwarf once again.

"Why would I want to hurt an old friend?"

Eniamaj then clapped his hands and the sound echoed. A few moments later the hall doors open and in marched Eed and ten Elfin guards and in the centre of them was Xela, looking unbothered by his surrounding escort. Eed was carrying a glass jar with a bright little light inside it. They all stopped at the steps.

"Hmmm, are we a little surprised Vladlin, are these not your friends."

"These, I only see one" Vlad asked.

"Oh so you do not recognise the Fairrien in the jar"

Vlad almost laughed. "Don't be absurd Eniamaj"

"Oh but it is true, Fairriens can change their form to what you see in the jar, it is their essence made up of just energy."

Vlad looked to Xela, and Xela nodded to confirm what he had just been told.

"It is not you my friend I intend to use this blade on, it will be this one," he pointed his blade towards Xela, "I am also interested in why we received a partial message from a humanoid telling us that this one here must be stopped. They seemed more interested in him then the two of you. I just want to cut him open to see what he is all about, but maybe I won't?"

"And why would that be?" Vlad stared at the elf with pure hatred; he could not believe that this thing before him had once been a friend.

"COME ON VLAD!" Eniamaj shouted as he rose to his feet once again and rushed down the steps letting loose his furious voice into Vlad's face, "Tell us where your city is, tell us so we can retrieve what we need, and I won't hurt your friends. Did you know that a Fairrien cannot maintain that state forever, and when he begins to change back he will be crushed to pieces. Give us what we want and your friends will be unharmed"

"You will never find our city, and you will never retrieve the sacred book" Vlad spat in his face.

Eniamaj raised his hand as if to strike him, but changed his mind and wiped the saliva of his face.

"We will see Young Bowen" His voice became calm "we will see, you will have a day to think this over, and then your friends die" He turned to Eed "Take them back to the dungeons" he then started once again back up his steps.

"What happened to you, all of you" Vlad shouted as he was being escorted out of the hall, "We are cousins, we were friends, and yet you all fall under the power of one evil elf. Does this mean you must all become the same." He shouted as he was being ushered out of the room.

"Halt" Eniamaj shouted. "What happened to us, as if you don't know. It was your kind your people who murdered King Lithor. You think we did not know, you murdered the greatest Elfin king that ever lived, and for this your people will never be forgiven."

"Ha" Vlad shouted back "You believe anything this twisted little elf king of yours tell you these days. What nonsense, think about it why would we murder a great king who let us live side by side as a people. A king who had the sense to know what was good and what was bad. Our people to this day still hold tribute to the great King Lithor, he was what we call a true elf. I wonder how many of them are still left if any at all."

Vlad turned and walked and the guards walked with him and Xela, leaving his words in the mind of a naïve governor. The words of the dwarf rang through Eniamaj mind, was there truth to what he had said, he contemplated it for some time, before realising it did not matter the Dwarves still had the book and this book was needed by the king to make the earth whole again. His naivety made him lose sight of the real picture.

Nathan had gathered his horses from his stable at the back of his inn, he owned five horses, but tonight only four would be in use. He had saddled each horse but one, and wondered if what he was about to do was the most foolish thing he had ever dreamt of. He was going to rescue the strangers, he was going to put things right with Manue, and he was going to put things right with himself. He knew the probability of his survival was next to nought. But he would do his father proud by doing what he knew in his heart was right, he had caused this mess and now only he could fix it, or try, he had thought through many plans and all had many flaws, he had not quite decided on which he would attempt, in truth it seemed impossible to help them escape, and one would have thought he had created himself a suicide mission, but he cared little now for his own safety. If he was just and true of heart God would guild him and help him through this one, he always had, it was God that had lead Tcepser to him when he had nothing and nowhere to go, and it was God that really kept his business flourishing. Now he was doing the right thing he prayed for Gods help once again. He finished bridling and putting the saddle on the last horse and after tethering each of the horses to his saddle he then put his foot into the stirrup as he mounted the horse. He was now ready to go, he had closed the bar early sending the non booked in guests off to their own homes, on the bar he left a note in an envelope signed Manue, this note was for her and what should happen if he did not return, he held the reins on his horse gently, then tapped his feet against the horses side, the horse took off at a slow trot, and the other horses followed behind with their lead ropes attached to Nathan's horse, this was the moment and there would be no turning back for him.

The streets were quiet, as he trotted across the square all was silent but the odd drunk vomiting in the corner outside of one of the many taverns that surrounded the city centre. It was late and most beings were in the warmth of their homes, his long black leather jacket fluttered in the cold night wind air as he approached the castle gates. Two Elves were on guard duty, and had been alerted to his presence way before he had reached them. He pulled his horse to a halt outside the gate.

"What is it you want here human?" One of the Elfin guards pointed his bow and arrow towards him.

"I am he who told you of the strangers, I have found their horses and brought them to you, I wish to speak with your commander, I believe there is a reward for me."

"I know you; you are the keeper of Tcepser's inn. I never thought you were one to talk much, you have surprised us all; bring the horses through the gate I will find the commander for you."

The big gates opened and Nathan went through with all the horses he had brought along with him, the guard had made him wait in the court yard while he went to find the commander. Across the courtyard to the back right of the complex Nathan could see the entrance to the tower which was rumoured to be where all the prisoners were kept, one Orcus guard alone paced up and down in front of the great iron door which he knew would be locked, he had gotten this far, but to get any further would be more than a challenge. He had brought a hand gun that he carried in his jacket, he was in luck if it had been an elf guard he would not have been quick enough to shoot it, but with an Orcus he stood a fair chance. He was scared and his heart began to race. He considered for a moment not to go through with it. He looked around and saw the Orcus and Elfin guards that stood high on top of the walls, but all seemed to have their attention peering out over the outside of the palace. Why would they look inside, no one would expect an attack on an Elfin station, especially from a weak pathetic human. He gathered himself together and trotted across the courtyard with his horses to where the Orcus stood.

"It must be a bugger standing here all night?" Nathan said to the Orcus that was outside the tower.

"Human, go" It grunted.

It spoke little English and was very hard to understand, Nathan used this to his advantage. He dismounted and approached the hideous looking creature.

"I am sorry my hearing is not too good." Nathan stood now right next to the creature.

"Human go" It grunted as it began to raise its laser weapon, but before it could Nathan had pulled out his hand gun and placed it to the Orcus head and fired. Its brains splattered against the door, this was the quickest way to kill an Orcus, he had heard stories of how an Orcus could survive multiple gunshot wounds but if you shoot them in the head they die immediately. He was smart to put a silencer on his weapon he had made it himself using the aid of a plastic bottle to help suppress the gun shot sound. He was sure that any elf in range still heard the wisp his weapon made but would not have guessed that it was a gun being fired, and he was right. He quickly took the key that creature had worn at its side, and found that it did open the door to the tower, as he entered he dragged the Orcus body in with him so the creature would not be found if any investigative elf wandered by, and then he locked the door with the key from the inside. He had done it, he was inside the tower, there was no way he could back out now. He had killed an Orcus and the Elves would find out sooner or later, his life in the city was over and he hoped that Manue would not be a suspect in all of this. He looked around and saw the steps that spiralled upwards, and he then saw the ones that went downwards under the ground. He wondered for a moment if the cells where the strangers were held would be up in the tower, he then decided against it.

Time was short, and the best places for cells and prisoners were always underground where it was dark and dirty. He took the steps that lead down, around and around the steps went and he wondered if they would ever come to an end. He began to move quicker, he was worried; an elf had gone to fetch Eed. On his return they would notice he was gone and see the horses he had left outside the tower, they would know something was up when the guard of the tower could not be found, and they would sound the alarm. He rushed now almost slipping on one of the steps, but he kept his balance and before he knew it he was at the bottom of the steps, there was only one way to go once he was at the bottom, and it was along a narrow passageway that led to an iron door. Nathan had already planned for lock dungeon doors, and he knew there had to be a jailer on the other side and he hoped there would not be more than one. He pulled out the plastic explosive he carried in his jacket, he had known one day this would come in handy, he had brought it off a trader many years ago, the trader had told him he could use it for mining, but if one day he found himself hungry he could go to a lake and throw it in and he was promised the explosion would give him enough fish to eat and to sell. But Nathan did not buy it for any of these reasons, he just liked the weapons of old and he had planed one day to take it somewhere quiet and blow something up just for the fun of it, but he never found the time, he had forgotten about it for years until this very night. Now he would get to see the explosion he always wanted to see. He stuck the explosive to the iron door, and then he knocked with his fist before he began to run up the passageway. He needed to get to the steps so he could be out of the way of the blast. As he ran up the passage way, the Orcus jailer came to the door and opens the slot to peak out; all he could see was a shadow of a being running around the corner of the steps way up the hall. Before he had time to think about it any further, Nathan pressed the detonator that had come with the purchasing of the explosive, it still worked, and the iron door flew in wards and fire ran along the side of the walls of the passage way. Nathan had covered his ears and when the fire had stopped he looked down the passage way, the door had blown off its hinges and now Nathan was running into the dungeon, he stepped over the door that had landed on the Orcus, it had appeared dead so he did not think twice about it.

Vlad had been sitting silently in his cell. They had put Xela in the cell with him but they had not released him from the magic Wire. They did not trust him and it seemed as if they sensed something about him. Vlad knew they were right not to release him he had seen the man fight and he was no push over. He was trying to devise a way of smashing the glass somehow on the Jar that the Orcus jailer had put high up on a shelf when his prayers were answered. A loud explosion echoed through the dungeon, and the Orcus jailer came flying past their cell with the large iron door, it landed on top of him and Vlad hoped the creature was dead. In the explosion the jar had fell to the ground and smashed and now standing before his cell door was Leron, rope staff and machine gun in hand.

"That's a neat trick you have there, why did you not tell me about it" Vlad shouted,

"You never asked" Leron smiled back.

It was then unexpectedly Nathan the innkeeper entered the cell; Leron immediately grabbed the man by his throat and held him high off the ground.

"Please I came to save you," Nathan squawked.

"What are you doing" Vlad shouted at Leron

"This man set us up it is because of him we were caught and you too most likely"

"There is no time for this he is here to save us now let's debate this later, get us out" Vlad was insistent.

Leron let Nathan go but stared at him with a fierce look. The key to the cells were on the jailer but as they lifted the door off the creature to get the keys it sat up and knocked Leron flying into a wall. It was still alive and Leron being in his energy form for so long carrying equipment had made him a little weak and slow.

Nathan pulled out his gun and shot at the creature but did not aim high enough; the creature grabbed the weapon from him and slammed him against a wall. It was at this point that Xela seemed to have woke up from a daze, it was as if he had said to himself I am bored with being here it's time to go. To everyone's amazement he pulled his wrist apart breaking the unbreakable Elfin wire with ease, he walked to the cell door and knocked it off its hinges with little effort. He grabbed the Orcus who had let go of Nathan when he saw Xela approaching him, and pushed it aside. The Orcus creature flew into a cell door knocking it down with the force and power from Xela's arms. The only words that came to Vlad's Mind was "Shit, who is this Man, all the time he had sat in this stinking cell, he could of tried to escape anytime but yet he did not," it appeared that this being was stronger than when he had fought with Leron and if it was so Vlad wondered where Xela drew his power from. Leron was back on his feet and Vlad and Xela grabbed their belongings and weapons that the jailer had kept in the dungeon.

"The Elves will be waiting for us topside, they must have heard the explosion" Nathan shouted.

"There will be too many we must let all the prisoners out, including the rock creature," Vlad shouted

"Are you mad?" Nathan knew the danger "The thing will kill us all too."

"It is our only hope; it will keep the Elves occupied while we escape."

Xela did not think twice he was already busting the cell doors open, letting out all the prisoners, it was a monstrous place a dungeon full of cruelty, and he had wondered what part of his mind could create such a nightmare, he busted open the cell where the rock creature was kept, and broke its chains like they were pieces of string. The creature seeing its bonds broken immediately became alive and vibrant, filled with anger and hatred it moved its arm instantly to strike Xela. Xela held its arm firm preventing it from striking him.

"That's impossible" Nathan whispered. No manling could be as strong as a rock creature, the creature had used all its might and realised its strength was not as great as this being before him, Xela was the dominate male, and it turned its attention away from him smashing walls and cells as it headed out of the dungeon and up the stairs. There was little time to stand and wonder in awe at the strange being Vlad and Leron had found in a Cryo-Chamber

, they had to escape and no matter how strong Xela was, dealing with at least seven hundred Elves Orcus and drones was not going to be easy, they ushered the prisoners out of the cells and up the steps not fearing the sounds of screams up ahead of them, they knew that this was because Elves and Orcus came face to face with the rock creature, the ancient primate was unknowingly clearing a path for them. They had left the injured and sick behind; there was nothing they could do for them, staying to help them would only get them all killed.

There were around fifty prisoners a mixed group of

different races, they were scared and all began instantly to run for their freedom up the steps, there were too many blocking the pathway of the steps all running ahead of their four rescuers, as weak as they were, adrenalin pumped through their bodies using their energy to climb the steps. This was not good there was no one ahead of them to fight any danger they may run into, They all moved as fast as they could, climbing over the dead bodies of the Orcus guards that had already entered the tower and had been killed by the rock creature, the Elves had been smart they sent in the Orcus while they probably waited outside probably up high on the castle walls, waiting with their arrows ready to plug holes into anyone that came through the tower door, Up ahead a great thundering sound echoed through the tower, It was the rock creature, it had reach the tower door and had smashed through it, now it was outside fighting its way through the real enemy.

Vlad had become really concerned for the prisoners and was now shouting for them to stop, he knew they were reaching the top and feared they would just run out into the open, but his pleas were ignored, some of these beings had spent years in these dungeons, surviving off rats and whatever slop the Orcus had given them, and now the only thing they could think of was their freedom. They scrambled up the last of the steps and ran around to the wide-open gash in the wall where the iron door had once stood. For a moment those up front hesitated, pausing as if some kind of logic was trying to reach their brains, trying to warn them of the danger that awaited outside, they could see ahead the rock creature fighting and killing and stumping and crushing many Orcus and drones that attacked, and arrows flew down from high up all around and into the creature, but it seemed unaffected, smashing its way towards the large gate that lead to freedom.

There was no time to think straight for the front leaders

of the prisoners, outside was freedom and that was all they could think of, they ran out blindly hoping to make it to the gate, and all behind followed, women children of all species, running towards freedom, running towards hope. Vlad Leron Nathan and Xela had finally reached the top behind the prisoners, Vlad and Nathan screamed out for them to stop, but they had known it was already too late, they watched as the prisoners ran into the open and the Elfin arrows flew down into their frail bodies, Drones mighty guns fired explosive bullets that on impacted blew the being to pieces from inside out, laser bolts of the Orcus also burned holes into the running prisoners, it was a massacre, beings with no weapons no strength, what threat were they to the Elves, there was no honour in this killing and there was no mercy given, tears found their way to each of them except Xela, his eyes became glossy but he refused to let a tear drop. He would make them pay with the might of his own weapons. Nathan could see the horses to the side of the door; they had moved but were unharmed.

"Quick the horses are to the right," he shouted.

All four raised their guns and began firing into the oncoming Orcus and drones, as they exited the Tower; it was their turn to kill their turn to inflict pain for those that had died before them. Leron and Xela stood side-by-side shooting high at the Elves and low at the Orcus and drones, as Nathan and Vlad readied the horses, the rock creature had already smashed its way through the gate and now half of Eniamaj's army were outside the gate trying to stop the creature from escaping, Vlad and Nathan had mounted their horse and brought the other two to were Leron and Xela stood shooting to cover them from the incoming weapons fire.

"Come on get on and let's ride out of here." Nathan shouted.

In a blink of an eye Leron was on his horse, all three

mounted men fired bullets towards the enemy to give Xela time to mount the last of the saddled animals, But just as Xela put his foot in the stirrup, he heard something, with his extra sensitive hearing, through all the gunfire and laser blasts, he heard the sound of a little girl crying. He turned and looked ahead of him, where all the prisoners had been murdered, amongst their bodies sat a young human child, sitting on top of a dead women, that was most likely her mother, something In Xela snapped, it was wrong even in dreams a child like this should not face such atrocities, a child should never have to face such monsters under any circumstances. Xela had forgotten the horse and was moving now with such speed and rage, using his bare hands to deflect the powerful Elfin arrows that rained down towards him, everything about him was human, but his energy his speed and his power, he dodged bullets and Laser bolts like they moved to slow for him, he ran through drones breaking them to pieces with one single blow, he had to save the child, he had to take her away from this mess, he had to take her to a better place away from this nightmare, he was almost there he was so close he could smell her tears, just then at that moment when he had almost reached the child, Xela was struck in the shoulder by a laser bolt, he went down, a little shocked that it was possible for him to get hit, and surprised that he felt pain, he shrugged the feeling off and got to his feet, he was then pieced by an arrow in his right leg. He dropped to one knee, he was surrounded now by Orcus, and he fought them on one knee tripping them over and hitting as many as he could in their throats, he raised his machine gun that was strapped over his shoulder and started firing at them shooting them in the chest and cleanly in their heads, it was a blood bath. Vlad and the others were already riding towards him with the spare horse shooting at the surrounding Orcus and machines that were trying to kill what they now knew was a very dangerous being. But Xela was on his feet again, telling himself that there was no pain, ignoring the arrow in his leg he began killing the creatures with whatever means he had, he shot them and Twisted their heads if they came to close, he was moving now, not so fast as before the arrow had slowed him and he was limping, the girl was still there alive, he had reached her, he picked her up with one hand while he shot at the oncoming enemy with his weapon, but as he put the child over his shoulder, an arrow pierced the child right through the front of her head protruding out of the back causing blood to drip on Xela's shoulder, he had felt the child go limp, and swung her around to see if she was alright. She was not, he dropped down now in the blood of the courtyard battle, on his knees, no longer firing or concerned with his own safety, they had killed the innocent while she was in his arms. There was no hope in a place like this, he was in no fairy tale story where the good always survived, he had no control over lives here. He laid her down gentle in the arms of the dead women where he had found her, he had assumed this had been her mother, and it was best that they rest here in each other's arms. He wondered what would happen if he was killed now, and sat there and closed his eyes. While he closed his Eyes he was yanked up high, it was Leron he had pulled him from the ground and lifted him up to the back of his horse.

"This is yours my friend, now ride." Leron had said before he leaped from the horse he had been riding to the spare horse beside him.

They rode now all four of them through the courtyard guns blazing, cloaks fluttering behind them; they were at their strongest when they all stood together. They rode towards the gate; up ahead they could still see the rock creature fighting off its enemies, smashing into buildings.

High up on the castle walls walking through one of the tower doors on the Westside of the castle came the Elfin Commander. Eed had heard the alarm but was ordered to let his men deal with it as he was in a meeting with Eniamaj discussing their next move with the prisoners. So he was surprised to find on reaching the wall that the courtyard was filled with bodies and his high walls was stained with the blood of Elves, he was furious who was brave enough or even skilled enough to kill Elves in their very own station. It was then he saw the four, on horseback riding towards the gate, guns blazing like they were fighters from days of old, it was then that he realised who had done this. Eed ordered his nearest man to give him a bow. He took his bow and aimed at the last rider, He had never missed a target in all of the three hundred years that he had lived, he followed the horse but he pointed his arrow a little ahead of his target compensating for the fact that it was a moving target and adjusting for the wind, then he released the string of his bow. The arrows flew through the air with such speed, Eed could have been firing a gun, "These are not days of old," he whispered as the arrow went straight through the side of the last rider.

Nathan slumped over his horse, as it galloped through the gates, he had been hit and he was now finding it hard to breath, blood wept from his side and he felt the arrow that was sticking in him, he knew it was very unlikely that he was coming back from this place alive, but at least he had helped the strangers escape, Maybe God would forgive him for what he had done now, maybe Manue would forgive him also. His horse followed the other riders as they galloped through the streets.
The streets were alive now with many beings, they had heard the commotion in the night and came out of their

homes to see what the disturbance was, the great rock creature had torn down houses and building with its own hands and was smashing and killing Orcus and drones that had surrounded it, Vlad could see that the creature would soon be overwhelmed as more and more drones came rushing through the street weapon hand ready to attack and fire upon the once primate creature. The Rock skinned creature had unknowingly helped to cause a diversion for their escape and Vlad felt that it deserved a fighting chance; he grabbed a grenade that he had retrieved with the rest of his things from the dungeon and threw it into the crowd of Orcus and drones.

"Oww chu cicci" he shouted to the creature.

In English it would be understood as big bang. The creature moved quick out of the way understanding, and the explosion lit up the streets like a large fire work, Orcus and drones were destroyed and the attack came to a short halt, it was enough time for the creature to run and make a bit of distance before they could catch up with it again, now it was their own skins Vlad worried about. Leron had shouted "to the Inn" as they cross the city square, Leron was leading them now his horse in front, he turned down an ally knowing that they were being pursued by Elves that had mounted their own horses, they had made a small distance from them and Leron hoped to lose them through the allies and the streets, he turned left into another alley, Vlad Nathan Xela trailing behind. He was quick to make a sharp right, and followed the next ally to its end and turned left again. All four horses kept tight together as they left the allies and came out onto a street,

Leron was good with directions, he had taken note of the city centre streets when they had arrived, always looking for the quick way out or looking for ways to lose anyone that may pursue them, He believed it was always better to be safe than sorry, and in this case they were heading towards safe, as it seemed that they had lost the Elfin Guards that had been chasing them, they turned right short after exiting the ally, and followed the street until it lead right back to the inn, Leron lead them all around to the back of Nathan's beloved home and business residence to the stables. It was when they had dismounted that Vlad noticed Nathan still slumped on his horse with a serious injury; he had an arrow going right through his right side and out of the other side of him, it was a lethal wound and after Leron had looked at it he was not too sure if it would be too late to try and save him.

"Manue is here," Leron said to Vlad.

"Try your best to keep him alive, we can't stop here long, I will get her." And Vlad ran into the building.

"Manue" he shouted as he ran up the stairs

Manue was still weeping in her room when she heard the call she could recognise this voice anywhere, it was Vlad, she ran out of her room to greet the dwarf in the hall way.

"But ho..."

"No time to explain you can't stay here gets some things together, you must return home, and tell them what has happened." Vlad ordered.

"But what about Mada?"

"He is no longer here; they are taking him across the seas to France. I will go after him"

Vlad had asked about the others while he was in the cells, the Orcus was all too pleased to tell him of how he beat them and wanted to cut them open but he was not permitted to, and now they had left two days ago headed to cross the seas to France from the port at Hastings, and that Orcus would take great pleasure in cutting Vlad open as he had been promised that he could.

"I have always wondered what the inside of a Dwarf look like" the thing had said,

Vlad smirked at the thought; he knew if the creature still lived it would still be wondering. Manue had gathered her things together and took some food for her journey, she came down the stairs and noticed the note on the bar that Nathan had wrote before leaving to attempt the rescue, she picked it up and slipped it into the pocket of her beige trousers that she had changed into, there was no time for dresses when it came to travelling. She followed Vlad as he led her out the back to the stables. When she saw the three men that awaited at the back of the Bell Free inn she found herself confused and a little surprised, the last she had known both Xela and Leron had been captured, she had believed on seeing Vlad that they had not caught him in the woods and he had somehow made his way to her, but know she knew this was not the case, she was shocked at the injury Nathan had received.

"Did you do this?" She faced Leron and sounded furious.

"No he came to rescue us, I don't know why; after all he set us up. He helped us escape" Leron Told her.

She had known why, it had been what she had said to him, She knew he was a good man who had made a mistake and he had known it too, he went back for them because it was the right thing, and she knew now that he cared about her more than she had believed.

Leron had broken the arrow but left the stick inside the wound, He then put what look like herbs on the injury and then bandaged Nathan as quick as he could, the man was unconscious and did not feel a thing.

"You must take him home with you," Vlad said, Manue looked a little surprised. "Blindfold him if you must but if he makes it they can save him it is the least we can do for him"

Manue agreed and saddled and mounted the horse that was still left in the stable.

"Foolish man, why did you do such a brave thing?" She smiled at Nathan as she tied the reins from his horse to her saddle.

"You must change the dressing once a day and put this on the wound" Leron passed her a little pouch that contained some of his herbs.

They all mounted their horses Xela had already pulled the arrow from his leg and Leron had patched him up the best he could in such short time, he had planned to look at the shoulder wound later when they had escaped from the city but now they had little time to spare they all must ride hard and fast before they are caught. Vlad pulled his horse up beside Manue and kissed her on the cheek.

"Ride fast now and don't rest until you are clear of the city, hopefully they will concentrate on following us."

"You will need a ship and someone you can trust,"

"You know of such a man?" Vlad spoke quietly to Manue.

"I met such a man a long time ago, his location is a secret that he revealed to me so I would know how to find him if I was ever in trouble"

"Tell me his name" Vlad insisted

She whispered in Vlad' ear telling him all he needed to know, she had known the strangers for only a short time and now she never knew who could be trusted.

"You must have done this man a great service for him to tell you were he resides." He had heard of this man, who had not? But none knew where he could be found.

"I helped the man once don't ask too many questions." She winked.

They hugged each other and then they parted as the three horse man headed south out of the city and Manue and injured companion Nathan headed north, each riding as fast and hard as they could.

As they rode through the night Vlad could not help but feel concerned for Manue, he would never forgive himself if anything happened to her, she was a smart girl and he hoped and made himself believe that she would make it. He had other concerns he had to think about, the Orcus must not reach their Flying ship in France with the five dwarves. He leaned forward and rode with the others through the streets and out of the city centre into the dark surroundings of the countryside, the moonlight lit the road making sure Vlad's horse did not stray from its path, tonight the horses would be ridden like they had never been ridden before, so three mounted manling silhouettes rode off into the moonlight with one destination in mind, Dover.

8

Dreams, Voices and Heroes

Luceria had ventured into the world of dreams, it was a plain that her people often travelled to share thoughts with one another, and also to be intimate with partners of the Nemlaer, the Nemlaer were a tribe that Lived in their forest and worshiped them like they were Goddesses, they were warriors and would protect each and every one of Luceria's people with their lives,

The Nymphs often took partners with the men of this tribe and had taught them how to sail the plain of dreams, it was with these men that gave the Nymphs the ability to procreate, as there were no male child ever born to the mystical beings. A man had to be pure of heart before a Nymph could be fertilised by his seed, it was a custom for the Nemlaer men to be raised as such, and it was an honour for the mother of a Nemlaer male for her son to be picked by a Nymphet, the tribe celebrated this event and had made it a ritual, it was these times that Nemlaer and Nymph came together to dance and be merry in a three days celebration.

The men that were chosen would then spend every night for many of years with his Goddess, making passionate love as it could take up to ten years for a Nymphet to be impregnated. But at the precise moment when the seed had been planted both beings joined as one in a spiritual union of ecstasy leaving their bodies and becoming spirits for only moments that seemed to the participates like many hours of intimate bliss, this was known as Arcarem. It helped the males mind to transcend onto a higher plain of consciousness understanding the rules and secrets of nature and awarding him to become a guardian, being able to take on the form of whatever creature nature had suited to him.

Some could become birds, the owl, the hawk the eagle, while others could become wolves, panthers, and other spiritual creatures, Luceria's Farther was the King of the Nemlaer and though they lived separate from one another they conversed many of times on the plain of dreams, or when she could she followed her mother whenever she went into the forest dwellings of the Nemlaer, her mother the queen of her people loved Werdna Taylor Lucy's father with all her heart, after the mating process it was natural for Nymphs to take on other partners, but her mother had refused this and only mated with the one man she loved.

All Luceria's sisters had the same father, this was a rare thing amongst her people, Lucy had often wondered about the love her mother had found for her father and though it was rare she wondered would she too ever get to feel the feelings her mother had obtained. The Nymphs were a powerful race but never used their skills or Knowledge to harm others; it was against their beliefs and against their ancient laws, it was why Mother Nature had provided the Nemlaer with the abilities to protect them and had given the ascended Nemlaer males the gift of eternal life, so they would always be there to protect natures most mystical beings.

The world of dreams had many plains, there were even plains of future and past, only those who had considerable skills could master these levels of the vast dreamscape, learning and understanding the choice of paths that lay before them, or seeing the mistakes of the past, Luceria had the skill to glimpse pieces of the future, she had not yet become a master and was learning, but she also had the ability to travel many different paths and now Luceria Ventured out of the safety of the dream plain that was guarded and protected by her people. On the Nymphs plain nothing could harm them, here they controlled all that happened, but when a Nymph with the ability to pass beyond the barrier ventured out on her own, this left her to the opportunities of considerable dangers, there were other beings out there who had the ability to travel the dream world, and they also had the ability to harm others that travelled these Paths, and Lucy knew that these were dark days, something had stirred in mother earth, something bad was starting to happen, but at the same time hope had shown itself in the face of a young pretty girl, a youth that had found her way on the plains of dreams into the nymphs own guarded and protected plains, a youth with a destiny, she had senses something in this girl when she had spoke to her, and there had been a link, a link to another being, and now she searched the plains to find this link, to make certain it was of a good soul. She had told the young girl to bring him to them but now she was not so sure, she had seen darkness follow the girl, and no longer did anything seem clear. She had to be sure she had to know who he was.

 She floated now beyond the barrier into the great darkness, concentrating hard it was not long before she found herself before the strings. The strings were bright long thin lines that flourished with many colours and went on for eternities, there were so many it would be impossible for anyone to count, but each path represented a time or place, it was only the truly skilled that could navigate the strings, if a mistake was made a soul could be lost forever never to return to its natural body. Lucy knew only a few of these paths and she entered one of the strings that she knew represented the present day. Nothing seen on these paths were always clear, there were points were there were moments of clarity, and things sometimes revealed themselves in different forms, but not even the very wise could understand all they saw, for some images could have more than one meaning. It was clarity that she sort after now a present path of the now happening, these paths normally represented themselves clearly, she did not need or want any complications. She flew now through skies that riddled themselves with clouds and bright shiny days, as she drifted at high speed over the seas and across deserts, images of obscure beings floated past her and around her as she followed the powerful link that she had made with the young girl the night she, Katie had come to them.

She had passed now into night time skies, she was close she could sense the girl, and she could also sense another power, something had energy greater than she had imagined, she wondered if it were the child, and knew then that it was not, there was a dark energy here, dark and empty, she drifted, she was no longer over the sea she had found land, within a split of a second she was amongst a battlefield, human men were being slaughtered and fought bravely to fend off a overwhelming swarm of Orcus, it was a horrid sight, no mercy was given even to those that begged, there was nothing she could do here to help, not in this form, the human fate was their own, she was here for another reason, she moved now away from this scene, and found herself in some kind of tunnel with many passageways, she floated through walls and doors, and could hear that the battle had found its way inside these tunnels also.

"Where is she" She asked herself, and before she knew it the scenery had changed, she was now in one of the homes of the people that lived in these tunnels, and she could hear the sound of a young girl humming a tune, it was a tune she knew, and had not heard she was a young root, many years ago. She followed the sound to a door way and peered inside, there she was, the girl Katie, she was laying in the arms of a dead women, Lucy could see the women had died a horrible death, something had bit into this women's chest, Blood paved the floor of the room like an overflowing tub of water on a bathroom floor, but it was not water and it did not come from a tub, it came from a human body and Katie night dress was stained with the blood of the women, this women was someone close to her and Lucy knew it was more than likely that this was her mother, Lucy's heart Was saddened, but she also noticed that something was clearly not right with the young girls behaviour, there was dangers in this place and Katie was in danger. She was their only hope, she was not allowed to be harmed, Lucy had to make the youth aware of the danger she was in, she had to make contact with the young girls mind.

The Nymph had travelled far and she could feel the strain of her natural body trying to pull her back, but there was no time she had to stay and try to help, she moved now over to Katie, and seeing her dull Aura, she moved her own Aura into Katie's making them both as though they were one, she had entered the girl and she found herself in a dark place, here in the youths mind there was nothing but a dark empty space, it was unusual, something was always in one's mind, the brain created images constantly on a subconscious level, but here in the Katie's mind was nothing just blackness, and then she heard it, the weeping of Katie, she moved through the darkness until she found a small light, and there in the light sat Katie crying.

"Katie you must wake from this you are in danger" Lucy's voice echoed through the darkness.

Katie looked up and seemed a little surprised to find Lucy in her dream.

"Why are you here I did not dream you to be here leave me alone" Katie curled up in the light and continued her crying trying to ignore Lucy's presence.

The Nymph now knew where she was, she had seen a mind turn like this before, this was what happened to a person when their mind began to break, pressures of life or some major catastrophe could bring any being into this state, but here in the smallest part of her mind Katie had created this light with her own image inside, this was the last part of Katie's sanity, if the light was to go then there would be no hope for the child but in death.

"Katie you are in danger if you don't wake the Orcus will find you and harm you."

"Gooooood" She screamed "Good let them find me, let them harm me and kill me like they did my mother, that way I will get to stay with her, isn't that how it is meant to be, should a daughter not stay with her mother?" she wept and turn her head away from Lucy.

"Katie" Lucy pleaded.

"Go A-WAAAAY!" she screamed.

And at that moment an invisible force pushed Lucy from Katie's mind, and Lucy found herself before the young girl in her mother's arms once again. Someone need to help this child, and Lucy's time here was short, she moved now within second floating along the corridors of the maze, she floated towards an energy that she had sensed earlier, it was him, and be his purpose good or evil he was the only one that could help her at this moment, right and left she turned, feeling the growing strength of her natural body trying to pull her back, she had to last a few moments more; he was close, she could sense him, and as she turned the next corner she saw two figures moving with speed towards her along one of the many passageways that riddled through the whole construction of this complex that seemed to be built into the earth. It was the tallest out of the two, it was him, a tall dark figure, he was dark in skin and appearance. They both had almost speeded past her but, the tall one stopped, as if he could sense her, The little one beckoned him to keep moving but he did not, he moved slowly now walking around the area where Lucy stood, he could sense her, it was unusual for a human to be able to sense any being in sprit form while they were fully conscious.

"What is it Xela?" The little one spoke.

But the dark one did not reply, it was Lucy last opportunity, she moved now towards his ear and whispered, she had barley finished her sentence, when the overwhelming force of her natural body yanked her back with and incredible force, she floated now, at high speeds like a stretched elastic band retracting back to it natural shape, within moments Lucy found herself back in her body sitting in the centre of the forest next to the old wise Oak tree that had been a teacher to all of the young forest maidens.

She stood now in her open flowing see through white dress, her tinted green skin blending in with her environment; she turned and laid her hand upon the great Oak.

"I must report what I have seen, dangers are coming you have told me that much already, we must help them, I will talk to mother,"

She kissed the tree gently, and bowed her head as though she stood before a great king, and then turned and skipped away merrily, with her dress flowing in the wind exposing more of her already exposed body, she giggled loudly as she danced and twirled to the natural music of the forest, she danced now to find her mother, there must be a meeting tonight of all, Nemlaer and Nymphs, there was no celebrations but these was serious times and things needed to be discussed.

Eed Resarf, was a commander in Eniamaj own personal army, he was a tall elf, but did not have the slender build of most of his kind, he had worked on his muscle tissue for centuries building up a strength that went beyond the normal amazing power that all elf had been born with, his sharp pointed Elfin features, were distinct, the cheek bones of his face were high under his eyes and the dip in his facial cheeks went deep along the long length of his thin jaw as though the creator had chiselled and sculptured his face to stand out amongst his own kind, he was a leader, and he held a position of authority, and there was no way that he was going to take heed to any superstition that was believed amongst his men and the rest of the dome city population.

Superstition had no truth to them, it was a made up fantasy to send fear into the hearts of beings to control their behaviour, he should know, he had started enough of them in the past to control the populace, so why would he take heed to the whispers that echoed down every hallway of Eniamaj Elfin station, Eniamaj palace, he half laughed at the thought. Eed paced down the long corridors that led to the private chambers of the governor, he had requested to see him, but to Eed this was the wrong time, he had been organising the Orcus and putting together a hunting party, and there was no time to lose, the longer they waited the further and further the three men would get away from them, and these stupid rumours of superstitions did not help at all, it was as if his men were afraid to be involved with him, and had tried to keep their distance.

"Puh stupidness" He mumbled to himself as he reached the beautifully painted door of Eniamaj chamber room.

He found once again that he marvelled at the creative art work that had been painted on this door, it was said that

Eniamaj had painted this himself, but in all the time Eed had spent here he had never once seen the Elfin Governor pick up a paint brush and paint, but he found the artwork amazing, every time he had looked at it he found that he noticed something he did not notice before, and he wondered if someone was continually painting this door adding more and more pieces to the painting, the door way was riddled with valleys and trees, and hills and all kinds of beings on different sections of the door. It was great work, but there was not even time to stop too long even to look at great art. He knocked on the door and then entered the room.

Eniamaj sat at a great-vanished oak wood desk; it was here where he wrote his orders and stamped his seal for the couriers to take to his men that patrolled different parts of the city. Every three months he would spend hours at this desk writing the report that was requested from him by the king, keeping Maxius informed of the full current situation of the growing dome city Ipswich. And now Eniamaj sat with his elbows on the desk and his hands interlinked resting his chin between his fingers starring stern faced at Eed.

"You requested my presence Sir" Eed was being formal.

It was the Elfin way now, but there had been a time when all elf's were called by their first name no matter what position they held amongst their people, even kings were addressed by their first names, but those times had gone and it had been by the order of Maxius that higher-ranking Elfin leaders were to be addressed as sir, or whatever title they held, this was to show that their position was recognised and respected.

"Come, take a seat Eed." Eniamaj leaned back in his chair.

"No if it is Okay. With you sir I prefer to stand, time is short and I am anxious to get back to the men so we can leave to catch the criminals"

"Arh I see," The governor paused for a moment as if thinking before he continued to speak.

"Well it is actually your going after these men, or should I say not going why I have called you before me."

"Not going?" Eed seemed puzzled.

"Yes not going, it has come to my attention that the Orcus now fear to be under your command, and believe if they travel with you they would all be doomed."

"But sir you know it's just stupid superstition."

"Superstition it maybe, but one that is taken very seriously amongst the Orcus, and also many Elf's believe this superstition too."

"Sir it is important that I lead this mission, if I don't go who would lead them."

"I have taken care of that, I have sent Imrarge to lead them and take a few drones with them to"

"But you cannot be serious sir… "

"You question my judgement?" Eniamaj raised his voice slightly.

Eed thought for a moment before answering.

"Yes sir I do, you are about to unleash 800 Orcus out on their own with a psycho sergeant Orcus to lead them, there will be no one to control them, they will harm innocents if they get the chance."

"Remember your place!" Eniamaj rose to his feet.

There was silence in the room as both men stared at each other; it was the governor that spoke first.

"Your concern is well noted" he spoke calm now. "But Imrarge is a capable leader and has assured me that he will hold true to the Elfin law, no innocents will be harmed under his command."

Eed had come face to face with this Orcus more times than often, this Orcus was unstable, to many times Eed had to use his rank to keep Imrarge in line, he was a menace, and no good would come of this, Eed knew it and wonder how it was the Eniamaj did not know it too.

"If you say so sir, so what will you have me do?" He knew there was no point in arguing with the Governor; it was very rare that this Elf ever changed his mind.

"You will stay here and protect the palace, by now the Orcus have already left to catch the escaped prisoners, and I suggest you find time to make peace with the spirits or pray that this superstition is just a superstition."

Eed was angry now and wanted to shout at the foolish naïve Governor but held his tongue and did not say a word, but Eniamaj could see the anger in his pearly white eyes.

"You are dismissed," he ordered.

The commander turned and walked to the door he paused as if he were to say something more.

"I said you are dismissed commander" Eniamaj cut him off before he even got to say a word.

Eed exited the room and now walked away from the governor's chamber thinking that he worked for a complete and utter fool. He stormed down the hallway before he came to a stop at one of the many windows that ran alongside the corridor. The last of the Orcus were leaving in desert vehicles, they were fast machines, it would be no time the governor believed before they caught up with the criminals, but one was a Fairrien and Orcus had no idea how to deal with such beings, he did not believe they would return as soon as the governor had expected. He turned from the window and continued his walk towards his own bed chamber; he did not want to show his face today to his men, the Elfin guards already knew their duty for the night he was not needed. But it was then he heard the voice echoing along the corridors of the Palace.

"EEEED! WHAT DID YOU DOOOOOOOO" the voice echoed.

"Who's there?" Eed shouted.

From around the corner came one of his Elfin Guards.

"You there! why did you call my name?"

"Me sir?" the Elf looked confused.

"Yes you, who else is here?" Eed was losing his patients.

"But sir I just came up from the court yard, I did not call you"

Eed stood puzzled for a moment and he believed the guard spoke the truth.

"But did you hear it; did you hear someone calling me?"

"No sir I heard nothing," The guard seemed as though he feared Eed.

It was strange there was never any fear amongst Elves, an elf would never willing harm another elf, but Eed had known it was something else that made him fear, it was the rumours, the superstition. He did not say another word to the guard, he just walked away wondering if he really had imagined the voice and all this talk of superstition was just getting to his head.

^
—

The captain had expected a blade to cut along his throat, and was surprised when his attacker did not kill him, there had been a bounty on the Captains head for years, they had called him the last of the rebels, all over the world there had been images of him on the Hollow screens, claiming he attacked Elfin stations at random. It had not been true, he had killed Orcus, many of them trying to protect his ship, and he had fired upon Elfin station from great distances so they would not be able to use their short range communication system to call for help, all he had done, was for the protection of his ship and his men, he was strong minded like his father before him, it was in their blood, the desire to be free and to be able to do as they pleased ran through many generations of Gills, and no one was going to tell them that they were not allowed to have Technology, or that they were not allowed to sail the seas in a great ship like the Daring.

He needed his ship and the weapons onboard, he knew this is what made the Elves want him so bad, they knew he had Missiles aboard, missiles that could cause great damage and destruction, most of these powerful weapons were retrieved by the maids from many sunken ships, the maids were masters of technology and could repair or make almost anything that the captain could think off, and once they had understood how the missiles worked they continued to make them for the Daring, building and restocking his ship with these mighty weapons whenever he needed them. But it was for his weaponry he had believed he was about to be killed for. The stranger had taken away his side arm and released him. Now the captain stood before the man that had sneaked up on him, he was a slender man with black short hair and a thin moustache ran along his upper lip, but there was something almost elfish about him, but Elf's did not have dark hair the Captain knew this.

"Who be you lad and what be you wanting wid me." Captain Gill demanded.

"Have no fear Captain I am not here to harm you, I am here to ask for your aid"

"Huh aid, aid tis not su-um I be given out freely these days, particularly to err, half Elfin men" The captain took a wild stab in the dark, hoping to find out if this being worked for the Elves.

"Come on captain you are a man of the world, we both know there is not such a thing as an half elf, it is a crime for the Elf's to mix with humans and it is said that there genetic makeup is not compatible for such an act to even happen, if you really want to know my kind I will tell you, we, I mean I am Fairrien"

It had been a long time since Leron had heard the collective voice of his people, and it was only now that he was getting use to being one rather than many.

"Fairrien puh" The captain almost laughed. "There be no such thing, they died or disappeared years ago, those beings be only remembered in fairy tales."

"Why do you play these Games I know who you are and I have been led to believe that you are an intelligent man, you know our kind exist and weather I am Fairrien or not it is not the point, My companions and I are in need of a ride on your ship."

"How be it that everyone knows where I might be found, me location tis meant to be a secret"

"My name is Leron and one of my companions is a dwarf, he received this information from a distant relation, a young Girl by the name of Manue, she sent this message for you, she said that you are to help us because you owe her."

"Manue, I remember that Girl, Blond, strong, pretty little ting and be you right that girl dids me some great honour, but if you travel with a dwarf then you should have said, I would help any dwarf that be needing aid, t'were great warriors they be in times of wa… "

A great thundering sound echoed through the shallows, it was the sound of an explosion.

"What be that?" The Captain looked to Leron.

"We have been hunted by Orcus and it is no doubt that they attack you now, we must hurry."

The captain grabbed his things and left his apartment and headed down the corridors of the shallows with Leron tailing behind, they were heading to the ship, and Leron knew now that Xela and Vlad would be on their way.

It had been almost two weeks since the most wanted three men in England had left the Dome city Ipswich; they had been pursued at every turn, by Orcus and every bounty hunter that had seen their image on the hollow screens.

Along the way they had met new allies and new enemies, and had been forced to hide out in many different places, all to get to where they were now. They had reached the great Dover Village, and had left their horses at a great distance so they would not be noticed when they approached the human colony.

Leron had gone in ahead of them to find the Captain; Vlad had told his two companions everything that Manue had told him and it was apparent to them that the captain and his ship was needed if they were ever to cross the seas to France, but now the Village was under attack, the Orcus had passed into the caves that were built into the hillside that went down into one of the many cliffs of Dover, they were monsters, it was as if they did not care about catching the three of them at all, they were driven and determined to kill humans. Since they had left the dome city these creatures had roamed the lands killing and raping and mutilating every man women and child they came across, and any other species that happened to be in the way.

But now Vlad and Xela had entered the complex via a rear entrance that the Orcus had not yet detected. They had to find Leron and the captain, and they chose to follow the sound of weapons fire to find someone who could lead them to the captain as the underground corridors were like being in a maze. They ran now with great speed time was growing short and it would not belong before the facility is overwhelmed, they turned left and right always moving towards the sound of gun fire, they were close, it appeared as if the weapons fire was just up ahead of them, Vlad hope that they came across the humans first rather than the Orcus, but it was in the middle of his thoughts when Xela came to a halt. Xela began to act strange; he looked around as if he was sensing something.

"What is it?" Vlad address the bemused Xela.

He had known it was hopeless to ask the man any

questions, as he had not spoken a word since they had first found him, but it was obvious something was bothering him, then without any indication Xela speeded of towards the gun fire, but not at the speed to keep in rang of Vlad, he was moving now as fast as he could, not quite his top speed as the injury to his leg was not fully healed, but still it was too fast for Vlad to keep up. Xela ran now like a cheater chasing after its prey, he had sense a powerful presence and had heard a voice whisper in his head, "hear the girl, save her." It had whispered, his hearing then became tuned and he could hear through all the weapons fire and the commotion a child humming a tune, he knew that this child was in danger and he had to save her, he had to save her to make up for the child he did not save in the dome city, maybe then and only then would he wake up from this nightmare, he failed to save an innocent and now he had been given a second chance.

He moved now as fast as he could, but came to a stop when he found himself in the mist of humans at a barrier that had been put together with many kinds of furniture and other things. The humans were under heavy attack and the Orcus were almost through the barrier, there were not many men left fighting, most were children and women that held the weapons now, leaning on the dead bodies of the many that had fallen before, some were maybe their husbands and fathers and mothers, but they continued to do what their dead brethren had been doing before them, defend themselves, they all seemed shocked and a little surprised to see Xela standing beside them, they did not know him and nor he them but he would now give them time to regroup.

Xela jumped high somersaulting over the barrier into the middle of the attacking Orcus, firing his weapon he wore around his shoulder he killed those that were at the barrier forcing the others to back off for a moment, and then he charged at them shooting and hitting them as he speeded through the whole army leaving behind him what looked like a pathway made of dead Orcus, within seconds he was gone, speeding along one of the many corridors that riddled through the Shallows, Many of the Orcus now had turned and began to pursue the being that had run through them as though they were nothing, while the others continued their attack on the barrier.

Billy had been shocked at what he had seen, a black skin man that he had never seen before had jumped into the middle of the Orcus and killed many before escaping from them. Was this a dream had he seen what he really though he saw, if that had confused him what happen next made him wonder if he was really just having a strange nightmarish dream. Charging from behind them came a dwarf, firing a machine gun with accuracy cleanly shooting the Orcus in the head, if it had not been for this little man the Orcus would not have backed off, to prepare for their next charge, the little man had saved them for only a moment. But who was he? And what was he doing here in the shallows, too many questions had entered Billy's mind he had to take charge here, Knarf had not returned and the safety of the remaining Villagers was down to the next few orders he was about to give.

"While we can we must retreat." Billy shouted.

"NO, YOU MUST HOLD OUT A LITTLE LONGER" The dwarf bellowed.

Billy had a choice to make, and right now he did not know what to do.

Knarf had left Kir and the others many minutes ago, he hoped his two right hand men had found the other council members and the captain and were now on their way to the captains ship, but now he approached the door that lead to

Yenned's apartment. He turned the handle, but he was not surprised to find that it was locked; he had no time to knock or shout, he raised his gun and fired at the lock on the door making multiple bullet holes, the door then swung open. Inside was dark, no candles had been lit, and there was no sign of Yenned.

"My lady" Knarf said quietly as if he expected someone to over hear him.

There was no reply, he looked around and did not find her in the main room of the apartment, so he made his way to the bedroom, it had been the first time he had entered her quarters uninvited, but this did not concern him now, there was no time for grace or manners. He moved into the bedroom, but when lighting a candle that was on a table he saw nothing, as he turned to leave the room believing that it was possible that Yenned had already left her apartment he heard what sounded like a whimper from underneath the Lady's bed.

"Yenned is that you?" He moved closer and knelt down peering under the bed. It was Yenned, curled up like a frightened small child with tears rolling down her face.

"My Lady we are under attack we must go quickly you are in danger here." Knarf was sincere.

Yenned had felt a fool, and now felt embarrassed that Knarf had found her crying, and hiding under her bed, she was their leader, and now he must of thought that she was weak, she turn her embarrassment to anger and attacked the concerned Knarf with vicious words.

"How dare you enter my room without my permission," She wiped her tears from her face pushing Knarf over as she crawled to her feet from under the bed. Her face now twisted with anger.

"My lady… "

"Don't my lady me, I will stay where I damn well please I am in charge and I order you to leave, I can take care of myself."

Knarf rose to his feet, he turned as if he was going to leave, but common sense took a hold of him.

"No"

"What was that" Yenned looked furious.

"You heard me I said no so why don't you shut the fuck up!" He was shouting now, "for years I have followed your orders, even when I thought you were in the wrong. I have stood by you at every turn defending your name and your honour, and in this moment of danger again you wish to treat me like your lap dog. Fuck you!" There was a moment of silence as both stared at each other in the flickering of the candlelight.

"We are under attack and in these circumstances I am in charge and I order you to follow me and make your way to the captain's ship."

Yenned was taken back, Knarf had never spoken to her like this before she was almost frightened of him, but she wouldn't take orders from anyone she was stubborn and her stubbornness would not budge even if it led her to her own death.

"I am going nowhere, so what are you going to do about it." She lifted her head high and stood proud challenging him to try and make her go.

"I am sorry my lady but I have no time to argue such foolishness I thought you were smarter than this."

Knarf raised his fist and then punched Yenned in the face, she dropped like a sack of potatoes, it had hurt him to do this, he had never laid a hand on a woman before but these were desperate times and time was very short. Yenned was semiconscious, but she was in a state where she was unable to move or talk, this made it easy for Knarf to pick her up and carry her over his shoulder, he had found Yenned, now he must get her to safety. He moved as Quick as he could towards the great door were he hoped to find the captain waiting.

Navi was almost at the door that leads to the captain's ship and the deep underground tunnels of the Shallows, The horrid memories of Hayley's death kept running through his mind. He carried Noel in his arms, the last of the bloodline of Hayley's family, it was why people had children, so after their death their children would live on with the memories and lessons taught from their parents, in this child Hayley would be immortal, and Navi knew it was his responsibility to keep that bloodline alive, the child was silent and still, he had hurt his head when his mother had dropped him and now he was unconscious, but he would be all right Navi hoped. He was worried, the footsteps he had heard behind him seemed closer now, it seemed as though they were gaining on him, and he started to wonder if he could open the great iron door and pass through it locking it behind him before his pursuers could get in. they sounded to close and he knew it was unlikely he could do this. He would have to stand and fight. He moved still as quickly as he could, he was nearing his destination, and found comfort in the whispering sounds of human voices up ahead. There were people waiting at the door, there was hope now he would not have to fight alone. He turned the final corner, and was half pleased to find Kir waiting with weapon ready as if he was about to fire, Kir relaxed as soon as he saw Navi.

"Navi, thank god, I almost capped your ass." Kir's voice was deep and had a hint of an American accent his great grand parents had immigrated from America and came to England but the family accent was still a part of him though he grew up as English.

"Keep your gun raised, enemy, coming, behind." Navi was breathing hard.

He was tired and out of breath, he walked through the small group of people and pulled out the bunch of keys he had in his pocket, he had to open the door and get to safety.

Kir raised his gun ready to shoot anything that came around the corner, but it was lucky for the captain that Leron had moved ahead of him, and within seconds he was in front of the long dreadlock haired dark skinned man pushing his gun up as he pulled the trigger, no one was hit by the bullets and Kir released the trigger, a bit stunned at how fast this man had moved to avoid the awful bloodshed that would have occurred. The captain and Knarf's rights hand men Zepol Heffer had came around the corner with four of the other council members, Mr Lopez, Mr Graham, Miss Cordea and Mr Teltnarg grant, all tailing behind.

"It be a good thing this gentlemen can be moving fast," the captain said on approaching the door. "Or I'm sure you would have shot me by now".

Kir never replied, he just lowered his gun, and took a moment to slow his heart rate. Navi had opened the door and was ready to pass through.

"We must wait, we can't leave without Knarf" Zepol looked to Navi.

"We must go it is dangerous here," Navi's thoughts were only for the child that he carried bringing this child to safety was all that mattered to him now.

"No, he be right Navi we must give Knarf a chance."

"And I also have two companions who I know would now be on their way." Leron spoke calmly.

"Well that's your fucking problem; I am going to the ship." Navi continued to move through the door.

"Me men will not be letting you on board Navi, not without me, they may be even shooting at ya, your be passing into cave that be not permitted even by you."

The captain was serious and Navi knew he spoke the truth, to go through the tunnels that led down to the captains ship was against the agreement the captain had with the council, anyone passing into these tunnels without the captains or Yenned's permission could be shot these parts of the caves belong to the captain, and Yenned had her own secret here as well no one else ever went down there without speaking to either first and no one would even dare board his ship unexpected.

Navi sat down in the doorway; there was nowhere for him to go without the captain.

"Okay. I will wait." Was all he said as he lowered his head holding the child in his arms whilst he sat in the doorway.

"Good then I will take Zepol with me and we will bring back the others that hold the Orcus at bay." Heffer spoke.

"If they're still live" Navi mumbled.

"I go with you" Leron stepped out with them.

"Who is this?" Zepol looked inquiringly to the Captain.

"He be trust worthy take him, you be finding you may be needing him, hurry back I'll be given ya ten minutes and then we be gone and this door here be locked behind us."

After hearing that the three men moved off down the hallways of the shallows to save what was left of the Dover villagers.

Xela moved fast along the corridors of the shallows being led by his tuned acute hearing to the wonderful melody of a young voice humming. The sound was so sweet and musical it almost sounded like more than one person was humming in harmony with another, although he clearly could tell that the sound came from one voice he couldn't help but feel drawn to its rhythm bringing him closer and closer to where the melody originated. He felt like a sailor on a ship being drawn by the magical sweet call of sirens, hypnotised by the voice of beautiful maidens drawing the sailors closer to the rocks so the ship would be sunk.

He hoped that he too had not been placed under a similar kind of spell that would lead him into some kind of trap, after all he wondered, where had the voice come from that had alerted him to the voice of the girl? He had seen a shimmer, an outline of a figure of a women almost ghostly, he lingered on these thoughts only momentarily before dismissing any beliefs he may have had on this matter, nothing was important here and he should not waste time trying to work things out. But if that was true why did he desperately need to save this girl? Why? He continued to question himself and his own actions as he moved speedily along the corridors, giving himself only one answer, because it would take him away from this nightmare and help him to believe that good can prevail even in bad dreams, he knew this or he believed this and this is what steered him now.

He could hear back in the distance the horde of Orcus trying to keep up with him, they were fast but they were no way near as fast as he was and he began to like that fact that here he had amazing speed and strength and if anything he would take pleasure in this, every step he took he left them further and further behind. This way and that, he turned corners and moved along corridors, he was in a maze and he hoped he would find his way back, but back was not going to be easy. She was close now the humming was very close; the musical sound of her voice seemed to ricochet of the tin wall of these tunnels causing her humming to be amplified as though her voice was being played from a Compact Disk through speakers. The sound flowed all around him and he felt overcome by emotion, it would not be long now before he reached her, "keep humming" he repeated in his mind, "keep humming that way I know you are still alive, don't let it stop."

He passed now into a corridor of mutilated bodies, the smell of blood and guts almost made him gag, but he moved on, looking at the unfortunate humans that never made it to the barricade, it was like the dome city all over again, bodies filled this corridor, men women and children, men's heads were decapitated and left laying beside their bodies, the women's stomach seemed to be cut open and the entrails and guts were dragged out of them, it appeared that these beasts had bit into these women as though they had been eating them, they were truly monsters, but the saddest sight were those of the little children. Xela looked away and kept on moving, what kind of creatures could truly do this to any child with no remorse. He came to a door that was half opened, it was here the humming was coming from, he had made it here and the child was still alive, he moved now into the apartment and followed the sound to the right of the room.

Passing what appeared to be a kitchen to the right of him he came to an open door that lead into a bedroom, there he saw a young girl who appeared to be a young lady, he had expected to find a small child but here he had found a girl who looked seventeen maybe eighteen, she was laying in the arms of a dead women who had been horrifically mutilated, blood covered the both of them, but the young girl seemed unaffected, she just rocked back and forth paying no attention to his presence. He moved to her taking her from the arms of the dead women and placing her on her feet he checked her to see if she had any injuries, the young girl looked right through him while he looked for injuries as though he was not there, it was like she was blind but he knew this was not the case her pupils were focused but not on him or anything else. There was something wrong with her, her mind was not right, her mind was gone or was going, She had witness atrocities that no young girl should ever witness and this had affected her Xela understood this, she was in a state of shock and he did not doubt that the women dead before him was someone close to this young girl. He picked the girl up and carried her over his shoulder, she was not heavy but here Xela was strong he had amazing strength, so carrying her would be no problem, but now he had to go back the same way he came, and he knew the Orcus were coming towards him. He was worried, he did not want to stand and fight them for he feared the young girl would be harmed, he did not think he could face the death of another young person he tried to save.

He walked out into the corridor of dead bodies, and set the girl down once again on her feet, she was still humming her tune but it did not seem as magical or as powerful as when he had heard it in the distance; he held her face in his hands and stared into her eyes. Removing one hand from her face he placed his finger to his lips indicating for her to be silent; she ignored him and continued to hum. The Orcus were getting closer and he had little time to reason with her, he slapped her hard in the face, she had to come out of it she had to or she may die. But it was as if she did not feel the strike, her head moved to the side from the force of the blow but she was silent for only a second and then she faced him again and continued to hum. She was in shock and now he had to shock her out of it, he slapped her again but this time even harder almost instantly a big red hand mark appeared on her face.

"Errrrrrrrrrrr" She roared, throwing her hands and feet everywhere hitting Xela every where she possibly could, she was hysterical tears poured down her cheeks and she continued to hit Xela frantically with her head down not daring to look up. Xela allowed himself to be hit, she had to release her pain and he was the only one around who she could take it out on, he gave her a moment and then took her by her shoulders and made her face him once again. He wanted to tell her it would be all right he wanted to comfort her but he could not. She lifted her head to face the man who had struck her, and it was as if she had seen Xela for the first time since he had arrived at her apartment. Xela once again put his finger to his lips indicating for her to be silent, she understood and tried to calm herself, she was scared and confused, she had stopped the humming and Xela made her lay down amongst the bodies and he laid nearby her covering them both under the dead bloody bodies of the young girls neighbours, it was an unpleasant thing to do, but it was the only way, he indicated once again for the girl to be silent, and then the horde of huge footsteps came charging down the corridor, stepping on and over the dead bodies that filled the hallway, they were looking for Xela, there must have been a hundred of them as both Xela and the young girl lay silently waiting for them to all pass by so they could return to the barricade.

Vlad had convinced the young boy and the others to keep fighting, he had no idea where Xela had gone but he was certain that the strange man would return, he was a friend now who was lost and alone in a time he did not understand and he felt a deep responsibility to look out for him and help him come to terms with a future where men were not the most powerful living force that walked the earth, it was clear that Xela could take care of himself but he still had no one in this world he could trust but Vlad and Leron.

The Orcus had began their attack again and things were not looking good, the numbers of villages that were left were around the fifty mark and they were diminishing, dying from the laser weapons of the Orcus, the monstrous beings knew now that these villagers were weak, they had picked off and killed most of the men that mattered in this battle and now they were not going to let up on this attack until they had totally overwhelmed the people that stood brave behind the barricade. The laser blast were coming at them like a hundred thousand fire flies with great speed hitting and killing those that did not find good cover, but the barricade itself had become weak filled with laser holes it would not hold up much longer. Billy knew this and something had to be done.

"We must pull back we can't hold here any longer."

Vlad knew the truth of the situation and did not move to argue, The young man had his people to think of, and only Vlad was concerned for Xela, they had did well and held their position longer than he had expected them too, he too now had to fall back with the rest of them.

The Orcus now were on a full out attack, Billy was shouting to the young children and women that had now become his soldiers to fall back, but it was hard as many moved backwards they were hit by laser bolts burning holes through them instantly. The small corridor that the villagers had stood and protected for minutes which to them had seemed like hours, was overwhelmed by the smell of burning flesh, more and more villagers fell as they rushed to make the retreat, it was over, they all knew it. It was only a matter of time; this was the last small space they had to hold back the Orcus and now they had lost the position. Billy had not expected them to retreat and hold ground further back, the shallows corridors beyond this point were wide open spaces, they would all be slaughtered and they knew it, the villagers ran, they were running for their lives now, in hope to find some hiding place and maybe escape the shallows later, maybe someone would make it he hoped.

The Orcus now were on top of the barrier, and were trying to break through it and climb over it.

"Run" Billy shouted to the villagers, his only concern now was for them. He stood his ground at the barricade, he had started this day as a young boy, and now he stood firing his weapon into the oncoming Orcus— ready to die like a man, in order to protect what was left of his people and his home. Vlad was overcome by admiration for this young lad, to see such a young boy filled with honour and a sense of decency, who could stand and act so brave in the face of certain death to give others a little time and a little hope of escape, in this moment there was no selfishness in this boy and it had been rare for Vlad to feel honoured to stand and fight beside such a young human male, but he felt more than just honoured, he felt proud. He stood beside him, beside this stranger this youth, though the boy might of felt that this was not his fight and though he too should have retreated with the others he felt that staying was more of the right thing to do though he knew that the boy and himself did not stand a chance, after all Vlad believed this was his fight if it were not for himself and the others these Orcus would not be wandering the country side killing people in order to capture them, this was his fault it was him who had brought this horror on these innocent people, so it would be just if he were to die here beside this boy.

Orcus now gathered in line trying to breach and climb over the barricade, the villager had gone, moving into the corridor. Both Vlad and Billy stood firing and holding back the Orcus giving the others as much time as possible to get deeper into the shallows, Billy was amazed at the strength of the dwarf, it was true that these being were strong, as Orcus came over the barricade this little man was twisting their necks and firing his weapon into them and with mighty blows knocking them down to the ground, Orcus were known to have super strength and for this little man to be able to do this showed to him how powerful dwarves really were. But even for the strong dwarf there were too many for him to deal with, they came like a wave breaching the barricade, knocking Billy's gun out of his hand and hitting him full blast in the chest the young man flew backwards into the corridor of the shallows, Vlad fought as hard has he could but it too look like the end of him, Billy laid now in the corridor behind him, the villagers were nowhere to be seen, they had moved deeper into the shallows, he was unable to move and he found it hard to breath, he watched as the little man was picked up by a Orcus, and was about to be smashed to the ground, when with lighting speed something moved from around the corner from the right hand side of Billy where the Villagers had all ran too, but it moved so fast that Billy could barely see what it was until it stopped moving for only a second as it smashed the Orcus that was holding the dwarf back behind the barricade into the hundreds of Orcus that was behind him.

It was a man, a dark haired man, He moved so fast and his power was amazing, he produced a staff and was now deflecting laser blast and fighting and killing the clones with it, he was fast and though the dwarf was on his feet now firing his weapons at the Orcus and fighting beside this super fast man, it seem that they could only hold their position for so long, as some Orcus slipped past them and now headed towards Billy who found that he could barely move, he was injured badly and he knew there was no where he could go, and just as he thought there was no one to save him now, Zepol and Heffer, Knarf's men came storming around the corner, firing and hitting there mark with precise accuracy, Orcus dropped dead from bullets that hit them cleanly in the centre of their heads; these men were professional, they had trained for combat, and they had sail the sea with the captain on many occasions.

Billy believed they had fought many battles before, they were all the back up the dwarf and the fast man needed, they stood beside them firing into the Orcus, but the Orcus would not back off, the barricade had been broken and they refused to reassess the situation, how was it possible that four men could hold back this mighty force. They attacked with a ferociousness that was beyond Billy understanding, they attacked with pure hatred with such an energy that now the four men found that they were moving backwards, they could not hold the position and if they moved back to far the Orcus would move into the wider space and then all would be lost they would be surrounded, there was no hope and three time this day Billy had lost hope in surviving this day, and he believed now that there would be no other chance, he closed his eyes and prayed for help from god and by some miracle god must of heard his prayer and answered.

When Billy opened his eyes much to his surprise almost unbelievably the first dark-skinned man appeared came from behind the Orcus, moving almost casually he carried a girl, it seemed as though he was walking slowly through the horde of monstrous killers as the girl wrapped her legs and arms around him as though she was giving him a big hug, he carried her at his front holding her with only one hand, she laid her head on his shoulders and closed her eyes, it was almost impossible to see exactly what it was that this being was doing to the surrounding Orcus, but all that could be seen was his one free hand moving, shimmering and all beings around him just fell dead at his feet. Vlad was amazed it seemed that the more angry Xela became the more powerful he was, or maybe it was possible that he was growing stronger every minute that he spent out of the cryogenic chamber, it was a thought that Vlad did not hold onto long, as he was fighting his own battles against these beings, Billy could see that the dark skinned man had now reached the barricade killing as many of the Orcus as he could he then turned and pushed one of the Orcus with such force it flew backwards into the gap in the barricade that the Orcus had breached knocking all that was climbing through the breach backwards.

For a moment a split second the attack had stopped it gave the others time to retreat the dwarf took many explosives from a pack he carried on his back and stuck them to the walls in the corridor, Billy knew what they were, Knarf had used the same thing to seal the other corridor of the shallows, Billy could see now that the girl the funny haired stranger was carrying was Katie, the girl who had so often made fun of him Zepol moved now and helped Billy to his feet and then the stranger carrying Katie, Billy and Zepol moved now down the corridors of the shallows. Billy was finding it hard to breath he was certain he had broken some ribs and maybe something more. Heffer the dwarf and the strange speedy man all stood and held back the Orcus as they attacked the barricade once again.

It had been maybe around three minutes before Billy heard the explosion back down the corridor of the shallows, he hoped that all had survived and were now making their way to them, the corridors of the shallows were long and windy they turned many corners with Zepol who helped Billy to walk on his feet led the way. They were headed towards the door that was forbidden Billy knew this it was the only possible place of an exit that lead this way, it had always been in his mind and many others what the secret was that laid beyond the door, it was obvious that the captain used this door so it was more than probable that beyond the door could take them to his ship, but he believed there was more than this, there was something else and maybe now he would get to see.

They reached the door to find a few people waiting, already the captain had moved people into the tunnels and had left, Kir, Knarf and Yenned to wait for them, they had arrived at the door not long after Zepol had left, and Billy wondered how Yenned's face had become so swollen. Soon after they reached the door the dwarf, Heffer and Leron arrived behind them.

"Time is short" the dwarf said, "we have sealed of the corridor but it will not take them long to break through and I know they have drones with them they will be sending them ahead of them from now on and I have seen what their fire power can do."

"Then we must go quick into the tunnels that is beyond this door little man." Knarf seemed surprised to find a dwarf in their midst, and also the other two strangers but there was little time to question what had happen while he had gone to find Yenned, so all moved beyond the doors and down some stone steps that went down into the dark. Knarf had been given the key to lock the door when the last had passed through, and this is what he did, he also rigged the top of the steps with explosives he was going to seal this entrance so no one would ever find these tunnels.

^

Eed sat in his chair peering out of the wide window with many things on his mind; one of the things that plagued him right now was the whereabouts of the Orcus troops that Eniamaj had sent out after the three escapees, it had been almost two weeks and burning month was almost upon them, he did not worry about the Orcus lives, it was the damage that he knew they were capable of doing, if they were to go out there and kill needlessly it would reflect on the Elvin campaign to bring unity to all beings, and could possibly start a rebellion here in England, this was the last thing that was needed right now, not when everything seemed to be going so well, why did the Governor not listen to him? He needed to go, by now he would have caught them and brought them back with little harm to anyone.

The foolish governor was naïve and thought he knew best about everything. And to make matters worse, Eed too was slowly beginning to believe in the superstitions that had kept his men at a distance from him, he wondered if it was his mind playing tricks, but he kept hearing the voice, calling his name and accusing him of a crime, even now when he slept the voice plagued him even in his dreams, bring him weird vivid nightmarish dreams of blood covered faces and death, he feared now to sleep. It was taking its toll on him, tiredness had crept in and he continuously forced himself to stay awake, the voices and the worry about the Orcus, it was all bringing him to the edge of insanity, it had been days since he had a proper wash and cleanliness was a must amongst all Elves, his appearance had been lacking, and he knew it would not be long before he would be brought before Eniamaj.

It had been days now since he saw to any of his duties and he had left all his work to Nrethsa, his captain, and apprentice, he had taught him all he knew since he had arrived fifty years ago here in the dome city, and he knew the youngling could take care of business while he tried to get himself together. Nrethsa was the only friend he had in all this, not fearing the superstitions he came to the tower and gave Eed a report on daily events that had occurred in the dome city and asked advice about what he should do. Nrethsa was a good elf, and a good leader; he would do well as a commander one day. Eed had spent most of his time in his tower that was located at the north side of the west wall of the Elfin castle. His tower consisted of two rooms one was his sleeping chamber and the other was his study were he did most if not all of his paper work, he had chosen this tower when he had first arrived at the city.

It was the ideal location in the whole castle to keep an eye on everything down below in the court yard, also the view from the windows of the tower extended far beyond the castle walls and he could see way out and even beyond the city buildings, he often used his telescope to watch the daily lives of the people, and at times had caught crimes being committed, not just by the people but by Orcus too, and there was nothing more he liked than to catch a Orcus breaking the rules, it strengthen his case that they were undisciplined and not to be trusted and forced the hand of Eniamaj to punish and even execute the culprit in front of the public. He hoped that the Orcus unit that had gone in search of the dwarf and his men were caught outside when the fire rained, not all of them were wearing their protective armour that could protect them from the intense heat, and this would kill at least half of them, the fewer Orcus there were in this city the better, then maybe the people would believe that the Elves here were now trying to help situations and not make them worse.

There was a knock on the door to his tower room, Eed did not wish to see anyone today and would rather be left alone to his thoughts, he decided not to answer it. But the knocking came again, but harder and louder.

"Go away I am not seeing anyone today" he shouted.

But there was no reply beyond the door, but the knocking came again, he was annoyed and bothered by people's ignorance to respect his decision, he moved from his chair with a mind to tell whoever was beyond the door exactly how he felt. The knocking on the door had become faster and louder not stopping at all, someone was determined to make him angry, while the door was still being knocked he pulled the door open quickly with a fury ready to pounce, but when the door was opened he did not speak a word, he was surprised to find that no one was beyond the door.

There was no sound of footsteps retreating down the windy steps of the tower, and he had opened the door while it was still being knocked, was he going insane, was there really ever a knock at his door, he closed the door slowly and walked back to his seat beside the window and sat down, stunned and bothered, he did not know what was real anymore, every day he believed more and more that he was being haunted, and just as this thought was in his mind, the voices started, but this time it was not accusing him, it was saying something different, but it was now more than one voice, it was many all whispering the same thing but out of zinc.

"Go after him. To the north, to the north, redeem yourself, your self redeem to the north, the north redeem, go after save to the north, yourself go, the north the north the north the north the north."

The words rolled around in his mind, making the room seem as though it was spinning, everything was whirling now spinning around he was losing focus, and then came the Knocking at the door again over and over, his eyes started to close he could not keep them opened he was going to pass out.

"Why the hell did you not answer the door to me?"

In that instant the voices and the spinning stopped and turning around slowly Eed found Eniamaj standing before him, with a look of puzzlement and annoyance on his face. It took a moment for Eed to get reoriented once again with his environment.

"Did you hear me commander, I said why did you not answer the door for me?" Eniamaj said once again.

"Sorry... sorry sir I was... sleeping." Eed could not think of anything else to explain what had just happened to him.

"And you still sit in your chair?"

Eed moved to stand to his feet.

"No don't bother stay seated, you are obviously not well"

Eed stayed seated while the governor walked around peering at Eed's belongings as he spoke.

"I had heard rumours about you, so I thought I would come and see."

Eed wondered for a moment if the governor had someone carry him up to his tower, as the steps were long and winded around until they reached his chambers, and many had found it a bother climbing these steps, and he could not imagine the heavy weighty Governor climbing these steps on his own.

"I was coming to see you today sir I have a request"

"Well for goodness sake clean yourself up then come and see me, you look terrible and you smell, I never knew an elf could smell this foul if we tried."

"I never knew and Elf could get that fat if he tried" the words wisped through Eed's mind but he never spoke them.

"Eed come and see me when you have fixed yourself up, we must speak you are jeopardising your position here."

Eniamaj then walked to the door and left the room.

The foolish Governor was right about one thing he needed to clean himself up and get his act together, he had a plan now a plan to get his sanity back and he needed the Governors permission so he must look presentable and seem clear of mind or he would not get what he needed. Eed went into his bedchamber where he had a bathtub; he pulled a chain that hung over the tub and warm water came pouring from a wide pipe. He would bath and think of his next step carefully. The Elfin commander had taken his bath and put on his best colours, a dark blue long bodied and long sleeved silk round neck garment type shirt with shiny ivory type buttons, The shirt had the symbol of the Hawk in black woven into the material, and white silk loose trousers using a black velvet sash to tie around the long shirt and around his waist holding the shirt and both the trousers up. These were his best colours and he wore these proudly, when his men see him they would think he was back on track. Now he walked along the corridors of the castle head held high, his men watched him as he passed as he strode proudly to the hall, Eniamaj imaginary throne room, he had things to discuss and today he will be heard.

Eniamaj watched in amazement from his great chair as Eed enter the great hall, looking clean and confident like the

Eed he had known before, it was a remarkable turnaround from the character he had just spoke with no more than an hour ago, something was on his mind and he had come here to vent his thoughts and re-establish his position once again as commander of Eniamaj's soldiers, so the governor thought but he did not intend to make it easy for him, he had let his position slip over the last week or so, and now he would have to do more than dress good to convince him that he was still worthy of the tasks at hand.

Eed stopped at the bottom of the steps that lead to the great chair and knelt down on one knee, showing Eniamaj more respect than he deserved.

"My Lord." Eed spoke in the custom of old English leaders who spoke before their kings.

It was a fashion that Eniamaj was proud of and took a liking to almost the same way as Maxius, the ways of old English human Kings had found its way in to the heart of Elfin leaders, and Eed did not think too much of this behaviour but chose to play the game if he had any chance of getting what he wanted this was the only way he could do it.

"You may rise" The governor took pride in playing a king and was quick to act the position.

Eed stood looking up towards Eniamaj sitting on his great chair, the Governor stared at him for a while as if trying to probe his mind trying to understand what game Eed was playing.

"I see you have cleaned yourself up well, and now you look presentable to speak with me, no doubt you have something of importance that is on your mind. Speak and let me hear."

"My lord, I know you believe that I have not been of sane mind this past week, and you may feel that I am no longer capable of being commander over this army"

"Ar huh, I knew it, you have come to plead to keep

your position here, but after your recent behaviour I am not so sure you are really capable of doing this job."

"You have me wrong my lord."

Eniamaj seemed confused, he had secretly intended Eed to continue his work here in his castle but he wanted the great commander to beg and prove himself worthy, the governor knew himself that there was no one who could run the Elfin station and command the men as well as Eed has, and though Nrethsa was doing a good job he was not as efficient as the famous Eed adopted to the house of Hawkindoor. Eed had a history, that not many knew of, he was adopted by the legendary Earthsha Hawkins, cousin to the king himself Maxius Millidor, The Hawkindoor house had honours that went back centuries, that had defended the throne and performed great deeds in the honour of all Elfin people.

Eed's parents were Resarfs, the last of a tribal elf family that choose to live separate from the rest of the Elfin people, but Earthsha had travelled many times to see this family and had some secret with them that was not spoken of, but one night Eed's parents had died due to a fire no one knew how or why it had happened, it was never mention or even spoken of, and it was then that the Hawkins adopted Eed, and though Eed would always be known as a Resarf, there was a part of him that was a little proud to also be a member of the house of Hawkindoor. It was the king himself who had sent Eed here to be the commander, and Eniamaj worried a little that Eed did not intend to keep his position here, He would be the one to feel the wraith of Maxius, because his adopted cousin has left and wish to return home, Eniamaj was quick to question Eed.

"What do you mean I have you wrong?"

"My lord I do not wish to continue for now as the commander here"

"What?" The governor was outraged and did not seem

to hide the fact of his disappointment; it was as he had feared.

"You wish to leave here and run back home as a failure what would the King say?"

Eed remained calm and did not forget to show respect to Eniamaj, he spoke well mannered and worthy of an old English Knight.

"My lord, it is not quite as you suspect, I have indeed come before you to ask your permission to leave here, but I do intend to return and it is not back to Laysenia I wish to go."

"Oh?" Eniamaj said inquiringly, Eed had taken him by surprise and he did not know what it was Eed exactly wanted.

"Where is it then you wish to go?"

"My lord I have received recent information, that strangers left the city by the North gate the same night of the escape, I believe that this man was the dwarf and had separated Himself from the others knowing that we would follow the group that headed south, The dwarf would be on his way back to his people and as an excellent tracker I come before you to plead that when the rain comes and goes that I be allowed to track him."

"Where did you hear this information, how could they escape the city so easy"

"A guard revealed this information to me" He lied "and I believe they exited the city the same way they had entered, it is believed they used some kind of science, or old folklore magic."

"Preposterous, dwarves have forgotten the old ways they no longer have these skills I am sure most of their wise ones died during the war, and during the great hunt, even our people struggle to wield the science we once had"

"As always you are right my lord," Eed said humbly as he bowed his head in respect.

Eniamaj knew Eed was playing to his emotion to the proper manners and respect of the old English ways, and he knew that this mission was for some reason important to Eed. But if what the commander had said was true it was also important to him, it could lead to the discovery of the dwarfin kingdom, something had to be done and weather he sent Eed or not someone would have to track Vladlin, he needed time to think.

"I will consider your request and I will summon you when a decision had been made, but for now I expect you to return to your duties."

"Of course my lord." Eed bowed before the governor once again before turning to leave.

"Oh just one more thing" Eniamaj called out. Eed stopped in his tracks.

"Yes sir how may I aid you further."

"Well I was wondering how are the voices in your head are you still hearing them"

Eed was shocked, how did the governor know of this he had told no one, but then the sudden realisation of the time when he had accused a guard of calling out to him, and other times when he had been caught by guards shouting out at the voice telling it to shut up, and it appeared to them that he was mad, they had reported this to Eniamaj, this is how he knew, he had thought his men would of keep his behaviour quiet for at least a little longer.

"Voices?"

"Yes, I here you have been talking to yourself of late and I wondered if your mind was right now, I mean right enough to make the right decisions."

"I did think at one time that I heard something, but these were just whispers most probably from people in the distant, I hear no voices, I just have been worried about the Orcus and wondering why it was taking them so long to return and had let myself go with worry and my behaviour had become inappropriate, I realise this now but I am fully mended and ready to work hard for your cause, our cause the cause of the Elfin Nation to bring unity to all, This is still our cause governor, am I right"

"Yes you are right and I am glad you are back with sound mind, I will have a decision for you before burning months is over, you may leave."

Eed walked towards the great doors of the Eniamaj's great hall, feeling a little relieved, he had lied and put on the best performance he possibly could, and now he hoped the governor would make the right decision.

9

Fire Skies and Bon Voyage

Down below a small bright light came into the vision as the small group of people took care with their movement as they walk slowly and carefully down each damp slippery stone step that laid before them, feeling the moist stone walls for some kind of support encase of a slip, they all continued moving down the steps for what seemed like hours when in fact it had been more like thirty minutes, it had been slow moving for the group as most of the surrounding was covered in absolute darkness, and only those who walked ahead with Leron had full advantage of the light that was produced from the staff that he carried, there had already been an injury, miss Yenned Had taken the young girl Katie from the arms of Xela, not feeling comfortable around the stranger, but both Yenned and Katie had slipped, Yenned now was forced to use Knarf to support her in her steps as she had injured her ankle, while Xela was quick to take the young girls hand who had been fortunate to have only scraped her knees during the fall.

    Katie had not uttered a word to the stranger in fact not to anyone since her mother's passing, but she took time to brush the white dust from Xela's hair that had covered them all when Knarf had ignited the explosives at the entrance to these dark damp caves that they had all found themselves in, piles and piles of rock came down and sent an overwhelming wave of dust and dirt down the passage way of steps that lead deep into the cliff and below the shallows covering each and every one of them in a pale grainy substance that came from the rock, but the only emotion that Katie had shown was that for the dust in Xela's hair and while he carried her she gently brushed the dust aside with her hands and when she had finished she laid her head once again on the strange mans shoulders and closed her eyes.

Up above Orcus rampaged through every corner of the shallows searching for any living human they could find, to torcher and make them suffer for their fallen comrades, but all they would find were the dead that had already fallen, while the small group of people were slipping away from their grasp right below their feet.

The explosion at the entrance to the steps that lead below the shallows hand done its job, Hard rock boulders had fell knocking the door down and falling on top of it making it impossible for anyone to know that there was ever a door there. To the Orcus it appeared like a rock wall that could have been there for years and they had no idea where the men that had held them back for so long had disappeared too, but little did they know that the small group of people had reached the bottom of the steps and found that the bright light was a burning torch held by the captain as he stood waiting for the last group of people to reach him.

When they met they all followed the captain through winding passage ways, the tunnels below were just as bad if not worse than the shallows, there were many different paths that lead of in other directions and Vlad was amazed that anyone could remember their way through this maze of caves, around ten minutes later they came into a large opening filled with many burning torches, it was a wide grand space in the caves that made Xela and the others feel like small creatures passing into a land made for giants, the Cavern was filled with at least a hundred burning torches lighting every corner of the gigantic space.

Looking up Xela could see the high roof of the cave riddled with stalactites of an amazing cream white colour, Katie too looked up she had never seen anything like it, huge giant white stalactites hung from the ceiling of the cave as though they were decoration, but the most wonderful sight was the huge ship docked in what seemed like a small lake in the middle of a cave, it was surreal, and Leron wondered how they had got the ship in here as there were no visible entrance for such a huge ship to pass through. They walked around the lake to the right side of the ship and found all the survivors of the shallows gathered together around a few well-placed fires, tending to those that were wounded, and comforting the children that had lost their parents. Yenned stared at the group, this was all that were left from a population of eight hundred, grouped before her were no more than a hundred including men women and children, it had been a massacre, families that had grown up here who's fathers had helped to make the shallows what it was had been killed murdered slaughtered and Yenned could not help but feel that it was her fault, tears rolled down her cheeks, she was useless she had coursed this she told herself.

Knarf noticed the sadness in Yenned and moved to comfort her she shrugged him off.

She decided there and then that she would no longer be weak, it was now the people needed a leader someone to help them survive and live through this disaster, someone who in the past Yenned had not been, but now she would make it all right, now she would make up for her own selfishness it was the people that needed her now and now she would be there for them.

Leron was still scanning the walls for some sign of an exit for this large ship that was beside them, it was like a riddle, and he wanted to solve the puzzle.

"I see that some of ye be baffled in awe of me ships docking." The captain smiled. "But don't be worrying ye selves tis a very well hidden entrance we be havin in these caves, as those that will leave with me shall see."

"Are we not all to leave with you" Navi was shocked still holding the young child in his arms, which had still not woken.

"It be not possible for you all to be travelling wid me and me men, I will be on a dangerous voyage that we may not be returning from"

"But we will die here if you leave without us" someone shouted out from the crowd.

"Don't be daft, you would surly suffer if you were all to be travelling with me, I have not enough food or stock on board to support another hundred, and me be travelling with a dwarf and these two men" He moved his hand in the direction of Leron and Xela.

"Who incidentally be right now are the most wanted men on this here planet, if communication could reach the Greys I be sure they be even send one of their giant airships to deal wid us. Now who here is ready to face the Greys, you think the Orcus were bad enough."

There was a gasp amongst the people, fear had struck them, some would not be leaving with the captain and those that did may face a certain death, there were chatter and words of confusion spreading amongst the group no one seemed to know what to do.

"But if you leave us we will starve or be found out by the Orcus and they will kill us" Another voice echoed above the murmurs of the crowd and all went silent waiting for the captains reply.

"Be not that silly, did you not think that you council members had not prepared for the day when the shallows be over run, wake up people! This is a dangerous world you be all living in, long gone are the days of niceties when your fellow man would ask yer for a mug of water, this day and age he would first be cutting your throat, then be asking if you mind."

All was silent it was as though that captain was speaking in the council chamber, when he spoke the council listened but now all of the surviving villagers was silent and hanging on to every word the captain was saying.

"Your council Know of the world beyond the shallows and know there are worse and more powerful things to worry about than just the bandits that used to attack us once in awhile. And when Navi be travelling he learned and survived many a dangerous situations, ask him he would be tellin yer, and because of the danger out there your council made plans long ago to be taking care of its people if such a sad occasion like today would fall upon the gracious people of the True Dover Village. But why am I speaking I will be gone, it should be she that leads you that should be given you the choices you have. Come Yenned."

Yenned was still a bit shaken and devastated by the deaths of her fellow villagers. But she understood the importance of what the captain had been saying and he was right it should be her to tell the people what options they had, and it was about time she stopped letting others lead and took the reins herself to prove not only to herself but to her people that she will be once again a good leader. She stepped to where the captain had been standing as though it was a stage, the captain stepped aside and all eyes were on Yenned, she saw hopeless eyes facing her, a worn and suffered people, and now she must give them hope.

"The Captain is right; we have planned for this day for years, though we hoped this day would never come. Here in another section of these caves hidden and kept secret from all except those that needed to know, is what we the council members have named the Shallowed."

The people began to murmur once again "The Shallowed what nonsense is that, we need hope not foolish talk" a voice shouted and many people murmured in agreement.

"No you misunderstand, it is called the Shallowed because it is a smaller version of the shallows, there are small apartments there to house around three hundred, and we have been storing stocks there for years in fact there is more stock in the Shallowed then what we had up above."

A sound of surprise went through the crowd it was a sign of hope, and the people clung to it like gold

"What about the Orcus they will not leave so easy they know some of us are still alive and they will hunt us and maybe find these caves." A Voice amongst the people spoke out loudly tearing the hope away from the others.

"It is highly unlikely the way to the Shallowed is very difficult for those who do not know these caves to find and even then the entrance to our new home if you choose it to be so is well hidden and virtually impossible to see,"

The captain stepped forward.

"And also when me ship be leaving the Orcus will be seeing it on the channel waters and assume that all the survivors would be on board and it will be me they will seek and they would leave this place, so you be have no fear of them be hunting yer."

"I am not saying it will be easy" Yenned continued to address the people. "In fact it will be hard it would be like starting the shallows all over again, but we must take care of our children, so that one day our children's children will grow and the Dover village will one day again flourish with many men and women and children brought up to honour the human way to take care of each other, and maybe one day they will return to the shallows and maybe even beyond that, but here in Dover we are the hope of the human race and we have a responsibility to carry on and live and grow for those who died so that we may live, so please people take your chances with the captain or follow me to the Shallowed I will begin the journey after the captain and his men have left."

There was silence Yenned waited for a response from the people but there was none, she waited a moment more staring at them as they stared back at her before she turned to walk away but as she moved a single clap could be heard amongst the survivors then another than the whole crowd was clapping and half smiling there was hope in their eyes and they were thanking Yenned and the members of their council for pulling through for them and giving them the option of a second chance. Tears rolled down Yenned eyes, she was overwhelmed by the thanks the villagers were giving her, and she still felt that she did not deserve it.

An hour had past, the captain and his men had spent their time preparing for cast off, Navi sat alone away from the group still clutching the child in his arms, the boy had not woken and a fear had crept into his heart.

"Wake up" the words circled his mind like a whirl wind " wake up" he kept repeating, he was no long thinking it he was whispering it to himself, sweat dripped from his forehead, and he began to rock back and forth with the child in his arms.

"Wake up" his voice became louder as he began to become agitated.

"Wake up wake up wake up wake up," he was crying now working his voice and his emotions into a frenzy.

Yenned who was only a few yards away over heard Navi's ramblings and became concerned, she approached him.

"What's wrong"?

"He won't wake up" Navi began to cry frantically "Wake up damn you wake up" He screamed. The cave had become silent the villagers were looking curiously towards Navi.

"Wake the Fuck up Noel wake up" he was shaking the child now like a rag doll.

"Navi stop it" Yenned shouted she moved to take the child from him.

"No stay away don't you dare put your hands on him, he is my responsibility mine you hear." He spat his words at her as he rose to his feet holding the child under his arm as though he was protected the child from Yenned.

"Okay. Calm down, we are all friends here" Yenned put her hands out as if to calm him with her gestures, she could clearly see that Navi had become unstable and she was uncertain how he would reacted if she breached the distance that Navi had made between them.

"I just want him to wake up thats all" He said not directly to Yenned and maybe not to anyone in particular.

"We know" Yenned continued to speak calmly trying to help Navi to think rationally, by this time Knarf Vlad and Leron had gathered behind Yenned curious about the commotion.

"What's the problem?" Knarf asked. There was an unsettling feeling for Yenned when Knarf stood beside her, she felt like she did not want to be near him.

"There is something wrong with the child and Navi won't let me near to see if he can be helped"

Knarf stepped a little closer.

"Come on Navi we are your friend we have the child interests at heart let us take a look at him we may be able to help."

"No stay back you, you and your master, it was her fault all this happened, it was her fault that we were not prepared, I lost the love of my life and all I have left is her child, and you will not take him from me." His face twisted with hatred and anger.

His word hurt Yenned deep like a knife being stabbed back into the same wound, she was feeling the pain already for not letting the villagers know that the Orcus were on their way but to hear someone else say it made it hurt that much deeper.

"Look Navi you must let us see the child we are here to help you."

"I told you bitch stay the fuck back! don't you understand, fuck about… " he trailed of as though he was in his own little world.

"Something has to be done" Knarf whispered back to Vlad.

"It's done" Leron intervened, and before Navi knew it the boy was no longer in his arms Leron stood next to Yenned with the child.

"What the fuck?" Navi lost his mind, a few villager ran forward to restrain him, and he knocked them flat on their back, he rushed towards the child screaming and ranting when he found himself held tight in the arms of Vlad, he could not move it was as though he had been locked in some type of vice, he was trying his best to break free, struggling and exerting all his energy scream and shout with madness foaming at the mouth he screamed.

"You fucks you fucks leave him alone you fuckers!"

All watched in amazement no one had ever seen Navi like this before, but the stress of the nights events had brought many already close to breaking point, and Navi was the one that finally snapped, and most people understood this, it was a short while before Navi exerted all his energy and calmed down, Vlad released him and he slumped to the floor in tears, Leron had examined the child and he confirmed what subconsciously Navi knew in his heart already, the child was dead.

He had died back in the shallows when his mother had dropped him, Leron confirmed this when he explained that he had almost died immediately from the head injury, he had landed on his head and the force of gravity had broke the Childs neck, it was a quick death, the Strange Fairrien had said, as though this was meant to comfort him, he had saved no one but himself, Hayley had died and her son too and he had lived, why was I not there to protect her? Why did I leave her on her own, he cursed himself? And made a vow, to himself that many more Orcus would die by his hands or he would die trying. He sat alone once again crying in the darkest part of the cavern.

"Do you think I should go and talk with him," Yenned asked Leron standing yards from where Navi sat.

"No I think sometimes it is best to let a man grieve until he realises when it is time to move on." Leron walked away from the concerned Yenned, to help more of the injured Villager who Vlad was already tending to. Julie looked towards the dark corner at the crying man on the cavern ground. Her heart went out to him and then she too turned and went to help what villagers she could.

A few hours had past the captain and his men had readied the ship, Leron and Vlad had done all they could to help those that were injured.

"We will wait here before we continue on down to our new home, take care captain and sail safe and swift, our hopes and thoughts will always be with you." Yenned said sincerely

The captain took her into his arms and hugged her.

"Yenned, it is time for you to be a strong leader take care of your people and hopefully one day soon we will return."

The captain then turned to Knarf.

"Take care of her as I know you will."

"Actually" Yenned interrupted "I am ordering Knarf to

go with you captain"

The look of surprise was clearly registered on both the captains and Knarf's face.

"You what?" Knarf half raised his voice to Yenned. She stepped back as if she expected him to hit her again.

She could not deal with having Knarf in her presence, he was her best friend once, her confidante and now she felt she did not know who he was, and she no longer felt safe around him, it was the best course of action for him to leave with the captain.

"I am sending you Knarf with the captain, to escort the dwarf on his mission, I have heard the importance of his mission, and it is vital for him and his whole nation, and as he and his friends had done so much to help us I think it is wise as a leader to send our best man to escort them and help defend them on this journey."

"Madam," Knarf became formal, "have you not seen the skills these men possess, I feel there is little I could add to help them in their mission."

The captain felt the need to intervene.

"And besides me lady would Knarf not be need here in the defence and the rebuilding of this here shallows."

"I feel there would be no need of defence and besides we have men here trained by Knarf who would be able to take up his position while he is gone, and in answer to your question Knarf I feel you and your team have a lot to offer to help these on their mission, you are all excellent marks men and you have the best human military expertise on a battle field known, maybe in all of England as far as I am concerned, this is my decision and unless you wish to go against me this is what you will do, I order it." She said sharply "Good day to you captain and Knarf may you too also sail safely" And with that she turned and walked away to stand amongst her people.

Knarf stood shocked at what he had just heard, he

stared at her hard and she in turn looked to him with coldness in her eyes. He was almost willing to tell her no, but he had been ordered and it was his duty to obey. He called to his men and the two approached there used to be three but they had lost a man during the battle. "Come" he said and he and his men boarded the ship and did not look back.

"All aboard" the captain shouted.

Leron and Vlad said their goodbyes and boarded the ship, Xela stood for a moment with the young girl still clutching him tight, she did not want to leave him, and he half did not want to leave her, there was something about this young girl something that made him feel connected to her, but he knew here was her place and it would be more safe for her here than where they were about to go. Yenned noticed the inability of the two to separate and walked over and reached her hands out to take Katie hand from Xela. Xela let go and allowed Yenned to take the girls hand but Katie struggled from her grip she did not want to leave him she felt save with him, she knew him though he did not her. Xela watched for a moment as Katie struggled free from the grasp of Yenned's hands and ran off into the crowd he felt sad to leave her but it was best. He turned without a word and boarded the ship.

The people of the shallows watched as the ship lifted anchor and a rumbling echoed throughout the cavern, at the far wall two huge giant cogs on either side of the wall began to turn two great giant chains, and then all was understood, the mystery of the ship in a cavern was revealed, as a crack appeared in the centre of the wall and began to open outwards, the wall was a great doorway disguised as part of the cliffs, it was amazing to watch as the ship slowly set sail out towards the great Gates that lead out into the wide scape of the sea, the people off the shallows began to cheer and call out the names of their new found heroes, Lerons name could be heard Knarf Vlad and Xela's name was called, but most off all they all hailed and shouted out to the captain the loudest, he was the main hero of the people and they would forever tell stories to their children of this great captain that went out to sea to make the Orcus believe that the whole village had left with him risking his life and that of his men because the captain ship was sure to be attacked.

"Three cheers for the captain and his men" Someone in the crowd shouted. "Hip hip hooray" The crowd joined in. This was a moment of celebration for them for a while, they all knew they would have little else to celebrate for a long time. The ship sailed smoothly out through the gates and into the sea, the cogs began to rotate the other way and the great doors closed slowly behind them, Yenned watched as the last bit of sunlight they would see for sometime disappeared through the smallest crack as the gate closed.

"now our journey begins" she thought to herself, she turned to the people "Come now we must gather ourselves together and leave this place." The crowd gathered together and followed Yenned and her new guards through a secret door made much like the door way for the ship disguised in the same fashion, the villagers all passed in one by one into a narrow tunnel that would lead them to their new home.

∧
=

It had been two weeks since burning month had started, think gassy clouds filled the skies making the landscape dark and gloomy, and then within those clouds light formed as if lightning was striking within them, and then the great explosions started lighting up the whole sky like fireworks and the fire rain poured bouncing and sparking high up in the sky as it could not find its way through the force field of the dome city, many nights people came out in the streets and watched the awesome wonderful site of burning month, beings partied and celebrated many nights in the city as a ritual to the safe harbour of the dome city, giving thanks to whatever god they believed in. burning month did not in fact last the whole month, it last around to two three weeks, and when it was over and the clouds past for some strange reason it was followed by bitter cold nights, so for the weather to become normal if you could say the weather was ever normal at all, one would be wise to wait a whole month before journeying back to their outside homes, that's if their homes were made out of the right materials so it maybe still standing when they returned.

Eed had waited to hear word from Eniamaj, and yet nothing, he needed to know if he would be permitted to go as Burning month could end anytime soon and he wanted to be prepared, as soon as the heat went he too wanted to go, he did not fear the bitter nights he had endured worse weather back at Laysenia in the outer regions where he used to play when he was a child, the cold did not affect Elves as much as it would other species. So he waited patiently for Eniamaj and while he waited the voices did not let up, taunting him night and day giving him no rest, around the men he ignored them and acted as normal, but at night alone he found that he shouted at them telling them to leave him alone, What did they want him to do run out of the city in the burning fire. Days went by and the voices had let up, it was only the one voice he heard now on occasion, always reminding him to go north. These spirits were real and he had broken the cardinal rule, his future his sanity depended on leaving.

Eed sat quietly in his tower, it had been a busy day, there had been a commotion in the streets some drunken villagers had started a fight with a bar owner, and his customers became involved and the fight escalated out into the streets and it took the smart and calm response of Eed and his Elfin guards to put the matter under control, without harming any of the people. He smiled to himself, wondering if Eniamaj recognised the benefits of have very few Orcus in the city, if they were here, many people would have been killed. He had realised how relaxed the people had become since the Orcus left the city in search of the dwarf and his friends, even the Elfin guards had started to be friendlier towards the people of all species including humans; some even greeted them when they saw them on the streets. He then began to wonder as he stared out of his tower window how things would change when and if the Orcus returned, just then when he was deep in this thought, high up in the sky, the fire stop raining and the explosion in the sky ceased, the clouds were dissipating the gasses had burned themselves out, Eed leapt out of his seat and ran down the steps of his tower as fast as his leg would carry him speeding along the corridors of the castle until he found himself at Eniamaj chamber he knocked.

"He is not there Commander"

Eed looked to his right, to find the young Elfin guard that patrolled that corridor.

"Where is he?"

"I don't know he headed down toward the east corridors about ten ferns ago"

Eed did not stop to thank the young guard he was too impatient, he rushed back down the corridor and turned right running through the doors that lead to the steps that went down to the east corridors.

Eniamaj had decided to take a stroll down to the east side of the castle, he hardly ever visited this side, but it was the eastside of the castle where most of the guest or women were housed, Elfin and other respectful honourable beings that had come to visit the great Eniamaj to do business or trades resided here. It is said that the east hall was the life of the castle; it was here were all came to be entertained. And as it was rare for Eniamaj to let himself be entertained he rarely ventured to this side of the castle, he had left the entertainment of guest for the Elfin women to arrange. Many people who came to see the governor would wait weeks or even sometimes up to a month before he would allow them to meet with him, and it was the entertainment and the friendly social talks that kept his honourable guest waiting to meet with him for so long. He was close to the hall. He did not know what had made him decided to come to the hall this day but today he felt sociable, he could hear the music being played on old Elfin instruments echoing through the eastern corridors and towers, the Elfin musicians played a string instrument called the Teao, it was made on a gold winding shape base and had only four strings, it takes almost a hundred years to learn how to play one note on the instrument but once the lesson are understood one would find it easier to master this art. Certain Elves dedicated their whole lives to music, some could even wield sounds as a great weapon but only true masters, but now just on these four strings came a sound of a twenty people playing many different instruments to create the most wonderful music any being could imagine. He smiled to himself; humans had never under stood how one person could play such an instrument that made the sound of so many playing. As he approached the door that had two guards standing either side, he heard footsteps running up behind him.

"Oh I wondered when you would find me." Eniamaj said without even turning to see who it was. He continued to walk toward the doors.

"Wait Eniamaj"

The governor stopped and turned to face Eed.

"Yes what is it?"

"If you knew I would come then you also know why I am here, do you give me your permission?"

"Eed you have proven that you are still a worthy elf loyal to our cause, I have had reports of your conduct over these past few weeks and I must say that your behaviour and conduct have been admirable, it seems that you have proven yourself."

Eniamaj turned once again to continue on through the door.

"So does this mean I can go" Eed requested once again for an answer

"Oh my dear Eed how could I let such an admirable being and commander leave my service now in pursuit of what may be a dangerous and desperate criminal, I have already told Lykle to leave tomorrow with a small escort in pursuit of the those that left by the north gate, you have no need to go anywhere you will stay here and continue your duties." A wicked smile crept across the governor's face.

"How could you?" Eed moved closer to the governor in an almost threatening way, before taking control of himself.

"What is the meaning of this do you move to threaten me" Eniamaj half laughed.

"No my lord." Eed had taken control of his senses and decided to play the game out.

"You are right as always my lord I only meant how could you let me go, I am truly needed here yet again you have shown me why you are law here, your wisdom is like no other."

"Well I am glad you understand now let me attend to my business" and Eniamaj turned and enter though the great doors."

"I won't go huh" The words whispered through his mind "we will see about that"

Eed found his way back to his tower as quick as he could he grabbed a small brown travel sack and put some important things in it that he would need for his trip, he was going and there was nothing Eniamaj could do about it he will find Nathan and the dwarf for now was not his concern, he would leave immediately this would give him almost a day ahead of the Lykle and his men, Lykle was a young skilled ambitious elf, he thought himself one of the best hunters amongst all Elves, and he was loyal to Eniamaj he would do anything the governor told him, but Eed did not think it wise for a smart man to follow anyone so blindly. He gathered his things together and went down to the stables, there he saddled and mounted his horse, leaning over he whispered into the horses ear.

"Elwine swier gohall grander" which in the Elfin tongue is to mean Go swift and noiselessly great Grander that is his horse's name. And with those words the horse took off at great speed making little noise as it moved swiftly across the court yard, the guards immediately recognised that it was the commander and asking no questions they opened the gate knowing that he did not intend to stop and answer any questions and out he rode into the night wearing a hooded cloak up the streets as fast as he could towards the north exit of the city.

Katie sat quietly behind a large sack in a dark corner; a few men had past her and had not been aware of her presence. She had ran off into the crowd and circled back to the ship, and seeing a long chain that went from a hole in the side of the ship into the water, she dived in and swam to the big thick chain and climbed her way up into the hole, it was a damp dark place where she had found herself and she was cold and wet, so she crept along corridors climbing steps trying to find her way upwards to the deck, but she heard footsteps and found herself opening the nearest door which appeared to be some kind of store room and as it was dry she stayed there ever since, she would find her way top side as soon as the ship had sailed out a little further too late for them to turn back and bring her to the villagers. She had an urge, she knew deep within herself that she had to stay with the dark one they called Xela, it was as if he was a magnet and she was the metal object being drawn in, she knew him, the man from her dream, It was no coincidence that she dreamt of this man not too long before she actually saw him and realised that he really existed.

She wondered if all this had been a dream and that maybe she was still dreaming. After all when she was drifting, drifting in her mind to a place that she did not know if she could ever return from, the girl who had also been in her dream had come to her too, Luceria whispering to her words of hope, but she refused to listen. It was when the man had come it was him there was something about him, something that made her not want to die, but honour her mother's wish, it was curiosity, it had always been this that had driven her throughout her life, the deep overwhelming feeling of knowing the truth of things and find out about the unexplainable.

She was curious about the dark man, and now her senses came back to her she was curious about her father, her mother had said something about him, before before...
but she could not remember clearly, she did not want to remember too much, she did not want to think of her mother like she had last seen her, but maybe yes maybe it really is all a dream, she said to herself, but she knew this was not true, she began to understand the reality of what had happened and the shallows was no more, she began to cry, the images of old friends and elders their bodies and their blood, she had laid with them used them to hide her from the beasts, and now she started to feel sick.

She leaned over into the corner and was sick throwing up what was left of any food she had eaten earlier. The images of the dead flashed before her again and now she saw her mother, "no I don't want to think this no," she tried to tell herself, she began to cry hysterically, but then a sound like a musical voice drifting on a breeze, whispered by her ear, it was comforting, like when her mother use to sing, it was as if her mother was with her. Now her mother's words was in her mind, "you are special you are different" she clung tight to the memory of her mother's voice and curled up and closed her eyes and fell into an uneasy sleep.

^—

The horn creature sat at a great table as though he were a king,

"Marchtar keeba" he ordered.

His men rushed around to bring him more food. He had already eaten live chickens from the stock of the humans, and different types of food that had been found in other rooms of the complex, but what he really wanted was parts, his favourite part, a delicacy that most Orcus never get to taste, the sweet succulent breast of a human women, he had fed on this much this night, and he had a taste for it that never seemed to let up. He pulled another chicken from the basket before him, and twisted its neck so it would stop squirming, and with no care for the birds' feathers, he tore his shape teeth into it as the birds' blood dripped around the great beast mouth. While still chewing the bird in his mouth he shouted at his men.

"Marktear fromo keepapa Huma? Darkie darumbo feboola!" he roared ferociously.

You men cannot find the humans? They are here find them, is what he had said, and the group of Orcus before him rushed out once again to search the many corridors that riddled throughout the shallows. There were already hundreds of Orcus searching the tunnels for the survivors, and he knew there were survivors after all some of them put up a great fight and killed many of his men and for that they will be found and killed, they had been searching all night and dawn crept up slowly on them, as the great Orcus beast continued to eat away at the raw chicken, another Orcus entered the great hall that the beast had taken for his throne room.

"He arr" (What is it?) he moaned not taken much notice of the Orcus that had come to him.

"Graff Imrarge, der ark semo der da soaka" The Orcus had come to tell sergeant Imrarge that there is something on the sea and for him to come and look.

Imrarge swallowed down the last bit leaving only a few feathers in his hand that he discarded on the ground, and stood to his feet. He himself was a giant amongst his men, Orcus were naturally tall and deformed looking they came in all shapes and sizes but it was still hard to tell them apart, but Imrarge was the tallest and bulkiest of his men, he followed the Orcus that had come to him and they walked the tunnels of the shallows followed by every Orcus they passed along the way. They crossed the star ways and stepped over the bodies of their fallen comrades and continued out through broken walls to the outside world. The sun had just began to creep over the horizon and daylight crept across the village grounds lighting up the many dead bodies of Orcus and mostly humans, the air was foul the foul smell of death wavered across Imrarge holes in his face that some might call a nose. He breathed in deeply as if smelling a sweet odour and smirked, if it was possible for a reject clone to smirk.

"Taki der" (look there). One of his men pointed out to the sea. And before the sergeants eyes he saw something that he had not seen since the days of old, it was a warship a human war ship sailing on the sea, only one man was believed to have such a ship and now all had been explain where the villagers had disappeared too.

"Tasha mokka drones" (Send the drones quick) and with that Imrarge and his army rushed as quickly as they could to find their way to the beach.

The ship sailed out on the sea and the captain made sure

she held her course steady, but he was no fool he knew the Orcus would sight them as they headed out, and he hope this would make the Orcus give up the hunter for the villagers. The Orcus carried remarkable weapons some may even reach the ship from the beach, they needed to make distance and pick up as much speed as they could to get out of weapons range. He stood looking through his binoculars and watched as the large mass of Orcus formed on the beach, they had seen them and they were readying their weapons. The captain had been prepared for this and already had two of his men ready to keep reloading the ammo for the 4.5 inch guns, he went into the tower and picked up a radio, "get ready to commence fire wait for my order", just then a great explosion occurred just off the stern of the ship, making the ship sway and rock as the waves from the explosion rocking the ship, Damage report the captain shout on the radio, a voice came back through, "no damage captain clean miss". They had already started to fire and now the seas around them kept rocking the ship as the Orcus continued firing at them. They were trying to get the right aim and distance, and they were already close still firing at them repeatedly.

"Fire all guns fire" the captain bellowed over his radio.

The great thundering sound of the ships guns echoed throughout the whole ship, it felt as if the ship itself was in a middle of an earthquake, great explosions hit the beach but over the heads of the Orcus and maybe killing only a few that were further back. "Reset, reset" the captain shouted "Get that BAE system going immediate fire" The firing mechanism for all the weapons on his ship were run by a computer, the computer would work out the range of its targets and reconfigure itself to make a higher success rate of finding its marks, the gun battle had begun but the captain was just trying to stall time so the ship could get out of range.

The ship began to shake and thundering sounds echoed throughout the whole vessel causing Katie to awake. She opened her eyes terrified feeling she was in a nightmare, it was almost like the sounds she had heard back in the shallows, explosive sounds making her now feel scared. Frightened for her own life she knew she needed to find Xela only he could protect her, now on her feet the young girl ran from the store room finding her way to some metal steps that lead upwards, she began to climb. When she reached the top the door was open, walking through she found herself on one of the lower decks surrounded by men rushing around everywhere. No one had paid any attention to her, they were busy she guessed trying to save the ship. Peering out to sea it seemed to her for a short while that they were in a thunderstorm, the sounds of thunder clashed all around her causing the ship to rock back and forth making It hard for Katie to keep her footing. Water came from the sea or the skies she did not know which one but she was getting soaked, holding onto things the girl moved slowly and carefully along the deck having no idea where she was going. As she walked a great crash hit the sea besides the ship as if a monster had stirred the water throwing waves high up and causing the ship to tilt at such a speed Katie never had time to grab anything to hold herself steady. The young girl lifted off the deck and flew through the air and just as she nearly went overboard she grabbed hold of the railing on the outside of the ship as the ship once again became level. She was hanging from the edge holding on with all her might. Katie's arms felt weak clinging to the side of the ship holding onto to a slippery wet rail, she wondered how much longer she could hold on and this made her think of what it would be like to die.

With each moment that passed she felt herself slipping and soon she would find herself in the sea missing, no one never knowing that she was ever there, she would just drown in the sea with its mighty waves and be forgotten. Her only hope was for one of the crewmen to come past and find her. She looked over her shoulder noticing something strange, there was something in the sea, there were many things in the sea, at first she thought they were maids come to save them, but her hopes of maids all vanished when one of the things jumped from the sea and clung to the side of the ship below her, it was horrible, it was made from metal and it dug sharp claws into the side of the ship and began to climb up like it was climbing a ladder. The thing climbed fast now and it would soon be on her, this was it this was the end for her she felt it, why did she come here?

Just then as if in answer to her question, she looked up and before her, stood Xela, reaching his hand out to her. It was as if he knew she was there, not hesitating Katie grabbed his hand and he pulled her up as though she was a feather and swung her around onto her feet behind him. She clung to his hand tight, just then the machine thing reached the top and found Xela's gun in its face, it paused, as if confused, Xela paused as if he was given the thing time to come to terms with its confusion, then he smirked and pulled the trigger, the thing went falling back into the sea, whether that had killed it or not Katie did not know but now Xela was moving swiftly, so fast that while holding his hand firm she was sure her feet did not touch the ground, there were more of the metal things lots of them climbing up from the sea onto the deck they were everywhere ripping into the ships metal and attacking anyone in sight.

Men were firing at these things with guns but there was little affect. "Fire in the hole," someone shouted and Xela pulled Katie to a side and ducked down and covered her, there was an explosion on the deck and bits of the machine came flying by them. They had found away to stop them by using more powerful weapons but still there was too many of them. Xela left Katie then, indicating for her to stay where she was. He ran to help the men that were fighting, he moved fast destroying them as he went but there was so many, they were surrounded by the creatures all raising their arms as if ready to fire great weapons. These were drones, Katie has heard of these machines in Navi's stories. But once again Katie watched as men died before her, images of her mother flashed in her mind causing her emotional pain, looking to the beach Katie could see Orcus and knew it was them. It was them that had caused all this and it was them that had killed her mother, and now they wanted to harm the captain and his men, and the dark one.

"No" she began to whisper.

"No not again" her voice became louder.

No not again she shouted or she intended to shout, but it was as if she shouted these words but something other came out. Her voice became like a song, a wailing musical song that echoed throughout the seas and the land, all that could be heard above the roar of the sea and the fighting and the killing was the wailing song of Katie's voice. She was upset and an emotion surged through her body a power an energy that she had never felt before or even knew she had. Everyone stopped fighting and the Orcus were puzzled by this sound, just then Katie began to glow.

Xela stood looking towards her confused; she was glowing like a light bulb he thought not understanding what was happening to her. And as if she used her last breath she sighed releasing a blast of energy, that did not harm no one but the creatures on the ship, they disintegrated right before everyone's eyes, and the circle of energy continued to expand outwards towards the beach, the Orcus on the beach began to run for cover some hid behind rocks while others had nowhere to hide, and within moments many Orcus disintegrated too. Katie dropped to the deck unconscious; Xela rushed and picked her up.

"Look up my friends" It was Vlad he was beside Xela with Leron, clouds had formed and they all knew what type of clouds these were.

"Quick everyone below deck" The captains voice echoed over the ship through speakers. Every crewman moved as quickly as they could and Xela carrying Katie moved below deck too, with Leron and Vlad behind him locking the hatch.

Imrarge stood and looked towards the ship, what power had done this what creature, his vision was sharp; he had seen a girl child on the ship. This energy had come from her. He looked back and found the beach covered in black dust, and now dust fell all around him as though it came from the sky, it was the remains of many Orcus, his men incinerated before his eyes, he looked around at his survivors, and estimated that he had no more that two hundred men left. As he watched the ship sail away in the distance he utter a curse and a promise of catching all those that were on that ship, but just then there was a great clash of thunder, and the whole sky light up like fire.

"Rockoo, rockoo marcar" (Run, Run to the caves) Imrarge shouted as he and his men moved as quickly as they could. Fire rained from the skies; it had begun— burning month, and there was only little equipment for only a few of his men to survive out in this heat, not all these men would be coming on his great hunt— he knew this now as they all ran to the shallows for cover.

10

The Cat, the Monk and the Trurh

Far across the seas and high above the lands, in the coldest and deadliest of mountains in the cavern of a cave sat an old dark-skinned man crossed legged wrapped up in the fur of a bear by a burnt out fire. The man sat motionless with his eyes closed, he had been sitting this way for a day and a half, locked in deep meditation, the cold had crept into the cave and he was beginning to freeze. He was in his meditative state while his life was draining away unaware of the danger he was in, flashes and visions came to his mind. He saw what appeared to be a human heart in the palm of a thin grey hand, the heart began to beat and grow and grow until the vision changed into three men different in shape size and origin, then he saw a forest, a forest so big it crossed wide along the lands.

    He was still deep in his meditative state unaware that his fire had burnt out when a creature with white fur and sharp white teeth slowly walked into the cave on all fours, with its yellow eyes locked on the old man it approached him, the old man was to deep in his world of visions and dreams to notice the great Paw of the creature raised towards his head, and with one movement the paw knocked the old man over, immediately he woke feeling the ever dangerous frost that had been biting at him for many hours, he had no feeling left in his fingers, and he began to shake uncontrollably.

"Ttthank yoy you Llli Light" His teeth chatterers as he struggled to speak "I... I had hoped you would of... of... of come sooner"

The white panther pushed the man's fire powder pouch towards him with its nose

"Please fetch me... fetch me wood from the... ... ..." he said weakly still shivering, before he could finish the large cat was gone, but soon returned with bunches of twigs clutched in its jaws. It laid it down where the previous fire had been lit, the old man struggling poured the powder from the pouch over the twigs, and then struck a rock on another rock that also contain the powder and caused a spark that immediately lit up all the powder and began to burn the twigs. Again the cat left and returned with a small log dropping it in the fire.

"You may... have saved my life... this day old friend," he said faintly before he passed out.

A whole day and a night went by before he woke finding himself covered in more of his furs and his fire still burning and the large cat laying beside him waiting patiently.

"Good Light you have kept the fire burning".

The cat was not his pet, but his companion and trusted friend, it had intelligence high above that of any other animal, and the old man would gladly give his life to save that of Lights. The man stood up slowly feeling the blood flowing through his veins; Light raised her head glad to see her friend back on his feet.

"I have had strange visions light and I fear these are the times we have waited so many years for."

He placed his hand on the panther's head and closed his eyes, moments passed as if his hand had connected them both physically.

"You must go to the black forest and find them protect them until I see you again" He removed his hand from the cats head and the cat leaped up as quick as it could and turned towards the exit of the cave and out into the snowy ice felt mountains.

The old man left the cave and stood at its entrance at the top of the mountain holding his staff a snow blizzard blew all around him, he watch the white cat head down the mountain leaving paw prints in the snow until it became nothing but the snow itself.

"Your journey has just begun my friend," he said as the blizzard blew his fur cloak making it flutter in the wind.

A gentle breeze blew across the trees making a cacophony of rustling leaves making one almost believe that the trees were whispering amongst themselves about the commotion that was going on before them in the clearing of the forest on this warm starry night. Gathered together sitting on what appeared to be tree stubs around the front of a never ending burning fire were at least a hundred people, and sitting on the opposite side of the fire in wonderfully carved throne like chairs sat Werdna Taylor and his lifelong partner Isnat bizoumous Queen of the nymph with their daughters and five other nymphets.

Standing tall and speaking so all could hear was a dark skinned man, wearing a shawl of tribal traditional colours of brown and green. Woven to detail into the shawl was the image of the great bear which represented their king. This man that stood before the throne was known as Ola Nosredna he was adviser and good friend of the king, and all listened to him because when he spoke he spoke with wisdom.

"So you would have us do nothing" Werdna asked Ola.

"No your greatness I say we prepare ourselves for the

worse, and wait, rather than to go out and bring trouble to us, remember we have an oath to protect our fair goddesses so why would we go out and bring unnecessary trouble to our lands."

"So you feel we should wait until trouble comes and destroy us all" a few mumbles could be heard amongst the people, as Luceria spoke, it was rare for a goddess to speak directly to anyone Nemlaer at an official meeting, the only one that had spoken was the queen and usually she left all to Werdna, he knew her thoughts and she his.

"I am sorry wise one if I have offended you" Ola kneeled down averting his eyes from the beauty of the nymph princess.

"It is no offence for one to speak his mind," she giggled

"Luceria please it is not our place to speak here amongst men they are our guardians it's their duty to decide." Isnat spoke sharply her voices carrying its self on the breeze almost musical.

"Mother times are changing and I suggest we change with it, the forest lands beyond ours are diminishing, being destroyed by powers unknown to us. I have seen it while travelling the plain of dreams, surrounding tribes and species are being annihilated for no reason at all, we would be fools to think trouble will not come to us, even the great oak worries."

"May I speak" Ola pleaded.

"Yes please today is no ordinary meeting today men and nymph will converse on matters that seem gravely important to us all." Werdna had spoken.

"But does not the powers of your greatness and her kind protects these lands we live in, and is not the place of the Nemlaer a hidden place disguised by the magic's of our great goddesses and mother earth."

"Yes Ola you are right these lands are protected none

can penetrate our realm and yours is hidden by our powers you will not be discovered." Isnat spoke calmly assuring the people.

"Yes mother that maybe but it is not wise to believe that mother earths power cannot be crushed, we all know the prophesy and I believe these are the days, there is strange powers in the land and I have seen this power in that of a girl, and if she falls into the wrong hands we will all be doomed our forest and all that is protected will be lost, not even the maids in the sea will be safe, I think we should extend our protection further, we need to protect more of the forest and its inhabitants why wait until dark days fall on us"

"Tell me more of this being you have seen" Werdna was known for his wisdom and took all into consideration, he was king of his people and his decisions protected the nymphs and Nemlaer, all that was spoken this day would be considered and then he would decided what was to be done, this was the way of his people and the nymphs as the greatest protector the nymphs had always trusted his judgment and went with it.

Luceria explain to her father and the people of the night Katie had come to her and how then she had sensed a power beyond that what was known to any beings, she also talked of the night she went beyond the realms of their lands and saw devastation on the earth, as she past lands and countries she saw ogres becoming enraged destroying and killing any creatures that came their way, they were destroying the out regions of the black forest. Dark beings had brushed past her on her travels beings not known to her, dark in every way with an evil so deep it had frightened her, and then she saw Orcus killing humans as though it was sport.

"These are indeed grave times," Isnat agreed, "if all these things be true then it is the Nemlaer's duty to investigate."

"Ola the wisest of my council take eight men and investigate beyond the realm help those who need it but most important bring to us the child, their fate is now in your hands." Werdna said

Immediately Ola bowed to his king and turned and left,

"The prophesy has come to us, now is the time for all to prepare meeting is adjourned." Werdna rose from his seat and all stood. The stubs as if they were never there retracted back into the earth.

For days Adnohr had travelled from the high cold mountains of the Himalayas, running on all four paws at a steady pace with nothing but the fur on her back to protect her from the winter cold weather that came with the high peaks of the mountains, stopping only to rest and hunt food when it was needed, but always heading north west, after days of travel moving at fast speed she found her way from the cold Himalayas and crossed over the border into Tibet, she knew now she had to be alert, big cats as herself were rarely seen in the land of beings, and though she was a hunter herself it was amongst men that she had been hunted before, these days beings would risk their lives to catch and kill even the wildest and most dangerous of animals. And for many beings she would be a prime target to be a meal on a hungry families table.

She travelled long hour's through Tibet before seeing a living soul, but when at last she did she avoided them continuing to move steadily northwest until she came to a village of humans. She stopped at a distance and watched patiently, she had seen something that had made her curious, an old human vehicle. These things had been known to her once before, before she was the way she is now, it was a different time then and a different place, but the vehicle was the same kind, it was a truck, and it made her watched patiently as all the villagers gathered around the truck and the small oriental man that had entered it. She needed to know, she wanted to hear what was being said, but for this she had to get close risking the chance that she may be exposed. But she was tired and if there was any chance the truck could be any help to her she would have to risk it, she walked slowly entering the village creeping soundlessly towards the truck and the gathering villager.

A small child stood amongst the adults who were all excited about the driver and the truck that was about to leave the village, the little girl stood beside her mother, wondering what all the commotion was about. Soon finding herself bored of the event her mind wandered to a bird that had caught her eye and she followed it, turning her head towards the south entrance of the village, it was that moment that she froze losing track of the bird and where it was going, and focused all her attention on the big tall yellow and black dotted cat that had entered the village and appeared to be walking straight towards them, she began to pull at her mother's dress.

"Mama mama." She called, not turning her head away from the large cat; her mother ignored her still too interested in the truck and its driver.

"Mama mama." She called again, and just as her mother turned and knelt down to see what her child had wanted, the cat vanished right before the little girls eyes.

"What is it dear," The mother asked.

"A big cat I just saw a magic big cat," She shouted excitedly to her mother.

"Yes dear ok maybe you can play with the big cat later" The mother said dismissing the Childs story as a childish game. She lifted the child from the ground and held her with one arm letting the child use her hip as a seat, and then she turned her attention back towards the truck. But the child was no longer interested in the truck she continued to look into the direction she had seen the cat, wondering where the magic cat had gone she continued to look southwards.

Adnohr moved silently knowing now she had become invisible to all that might be looking her way. She had the amazing skill to blend in with any background, reflecting light around her, making the illusion that one could see right through her as though she was never there. It was not her only skill, she could change colour depending on what mood suited her, but for now the illusion of invisibility was all that was needed, and it had allowed her to get right close to the villagers and the truck, hearing all that was said.

"Okay. Ponchi" Said a tall man standing at the door of the truck talking with the driver.

"Drive safe, and look out for bandits, I here China is becoming crowded with creatures of all kinds."

"It's ok I have Shelly" the driver said lifting up the shotgun he had in the seat beside him.

"Well get back safe and with our stock and drive well" The tall man shouted above the commotion of all the villagers.

"Ok bye everyone", the driver said as he began to drive of slowly, waving at the people as though he was a king driving through a crowd of his worthy subjects. Adnohr saw her chance, as the truck drove of picking up speed and while some of the villager ran beside it waving their goodbye's, The large cat ran at a fast pace gaining on the truck it lifted itself into the air and landed on all four paws in the back of the truck with a small thud. She had made it; she will catch this ride to China and rest until she got there without losing time. She knew her task, it had not been human words that had showed her the way, but it had been a power a link that had always been between the old man in the cave and her, he called her Light but if he knew her real name things would be different, they were both here in this age at this time for a purpose and now with one touch the old man had shown her it was time. She knew what had to be done and she would do her best to fulfill this mission or die trying.

The driver of the truck had heard a thud at the back and for a moment considered to stop and investigate. But then quickly dismissed the idea as he believed that it was probably some of the villagers banging on the back of the truck as a farewell, forgetting all about it he continued his journey straight to China.

The driver headed north, towards the Chinese border, it was more than likely that he was a farmer of some kind sent by his people to bring back stocks and seeds for planting, it would explain his need for the truck that Light had hitched a ride in, some villages in Tibet had recently had problems growing enough food to support their families, seeds for planting were scarce and China was an ideal place for purchasing and trading such goods.

The large Panther slept through most of their journey, only leaving the truck when the driver stopped to fill his water tank on the vehicle. She moved silently from the truck stretched her legs and made sure she was back in before the driver was ready to continue his mission. She wondered very little about the man who owned the four wheeled truck, he was of no interest to her, He was a small oriental man with black hair and rags for clothing, and that's all she knew or cared to know. There were more important things that had to be done, and the driver was a means to an end.

The journey became long and weary and the sun began to burn down on the back of the vehicle making Adnohr in desperate need for water. It had been the second day of their journey and as the previous day before she once again dreamed of night fall and cooler temperatures, Cats were engineered by mother nature to tolerate both heat and cold, in the hot weather while the large cats sweat the cool breeze would vibrate along the dampness of their furs helping to keep her kind cool, but without water this was useless it was not enough, she would de-hydrate and then eventually die. It was her luck that on the second night the driver stopped and made camp for the night giving his truck time to cool down, it was unnecessary to push such an old vehicle beyond its limits when there was no need. But to Adnohr's delight he made camp right beside a small lake and there he filled his water canisters, but also in the moon light of a very starry night, if one looked closely you could see the outline of a very large wet leopard who had just bathed in the cool lake and now bowed her head drinking as much water as she could.

The next day brought hope and promise to both the driver and his unknown guest travelling with him. The sun was not too hot this day and they both had had their fill of water, and now before them they could see the vast boarder of China, for as far as one could see stretching long and far across the plains separating Tibet from China was a huge massive electrical fence. No one came into China without the proper papers, China's riches belonged to the Grey's but it was here that the creatures allowed all species to trade with one another on the Chinese market in the only standing city in China, Beijing. There was one road that leads straight into the city through the wasteland that made up most of the country, and this was the road they travelled but first they would have to pass through boarder control.

The country was now a desolate land it was not the war that had caused this, it was something unnatural that had made it this way. When the Greys had laid claim on this once beautiful and marvelous country within weeks it had become a desert, part of which had un-breathable air, if one travelled off the roads and took a wrong turn they would find themselves unfortunately dead. The gases that lingered in certain areas were lethal to all beings except for the Greys, but Beijing was left standing and protected for the residents of China to live their lives.

The driver slowed and came to a stop at boarder control; two Orcus and a drone approached him.

"Papers"

The driver handed his papers to the drone, starring maybe a little too hard at the Orcus before him. It did not matter how many times he had come across these creatures, it still amazed him that such an ugly crooked faced grotesque being could exist or even want to live in that state. The other Orcus walked around the side and looked in the back of the truck and found nothing, he waved his arms giving the all clear and the drone gave back the papers to the driver with a warning.

"Do not stray of the road, this is punishable by death" It said in a mechanical way.

The gate before them opened and the small Tibetan man drove in while the gate closed behind them. He had entered the complex where the boarder Orcus lived. This was the only way from the south into China. He drove forwards slowly towards the second gate that would allow him out of the complex and on the road to his destination. But then came an awful screeching voice.

"Stop that vehicle" it had screeched, the voice echoed all around the complex and it was pain to the driver ears. It was like a hissing screech, immediately Lights ears perked up, she knew this sound, and now she crouched in the back of the truck in attack mode ready to pounce. She looked to her right through a gap in the side of the truck, and noticed a young girl being searched by the Orcus, but she could not see the thing that had made the sound. But then she felt it, an overwhelming presence engulfed her, it was as if she had been surrounded by evil. Her heart began to pound and she gritted her teeth her muscles tighten and she bowed lower to the floor ready. The driver in the front began to sweat as the dark hooded creature came towards his truck, he felt a presence too it was a bad feeling that had come over him his hands were shaking and his heart was beating at an incredible rate, this was dark and without seeing what lurked under the hood he knew it was pure evil. The presence of this being had struck fear right into the heart of the small Tibetan man causing him to wet himself as he sat in his seat shaking. The hooded being stopped a few yards from the truck.

"There is something in there!" its screeched, its voice echoed— sending chills into the bones of the small driver, as the dark being pointed a pale finger at the back of the small man's vehicle. The being walked slowly towards the back of the truck. Light was crouched low and ready, it would be a shame for her to die this way not even making it to her destination, but if she would lose her life this day she would do so fighting. Her teeth were showing and her claws dug deep into the wooden floor of the truck. The being moved slowly and smoothly closer almost as though it was floating across the ground, closer and closer it came to the truck, the panther scratched claw marks into the floor, but just as the dark figure was almost there, as if some strange prayer had been answered the dark thing stopped in it stead, and turned to look back at the commotion that had begun behind it. It was the young girl the Orcus had tried to take something from her, something she carried and now she was fighting them, and surprisingly she was winning, she was knocking them down like she was squatting flies, using little effort, her style, her technique her movement it could only be ... . Before the cat could think it, the dark being hissed.

"She's Shaolin"

And with that more guards attacked to no avail, she moved with grace and fluency that was flowing as if almost dancing to a strange music that only she could hear, turning and striking effortlessly, killing Orcus with just one touch, her movement was almost magical, no matter how many Orcus attacked they could not handle her. A drone aimed its weapon at her, but the dark one raised its hand indicating for the drone not to shoot, then it seemed to float over towards the fighting young girl, the Orcus backed away and the girl stood untouched and bold holding in her hand what appeared to be a scroll.

"You fight hard to protect that which you carry" The dark thing squealed at her, the sound unpleasing even to the Orcus ears.

"Your evil does not scare me," The small girl said with courage.

"Let meeee see that" and with a quick movement of the creatures hand, the scroll flew from the girls hand and into the slender pale hands of the hooded being. She moved instantly to retrieve it, but with a movement of the dark ones other hand she flew back as though she had been hit by a great force.

The creature took little notice of what he had just done to the girl, but instead stared at the marking on the scroll immediately recognising it, his red eyes became yellow as though flames burned deep within them.

"Where are you taaaaking this" it said raising its hand, the girl lifted from the ground into the air clutching at her throat as though she was being chocked.

Adnohr Light watched through the side of the truck, the young tanned skinned Asian looking girl, with short black straight hair wearing dark orange baggy trousers and some type of brown shawl that could be described as a poncho was Shaolin and that was all she needed to know. It was her duty, and without giving it another thought she leapt from the back of the truck and dashed straight towards the evil thing jumping high she landed on the back of the creature knocking it to the ground, the scrolled rolled from its hand and rolled along the courtyard floor, Light also recognised this scroll. It was important and this scroll could not fall in the hands of the dark ones. The hooded creature was back on its feet and moved with such speed that it was amazing that it did not retrieve the scroll. Just as it reached for it, it flew back across the ground and up into the air into the hands of the young shaolin girl.

"We too know the arts," She said with a half smile.

The creature waved its hands with the intention to do something to her, but she waived her hands also as if blocking and invisible force.

"Attaaaack her" The creature screeched to its Orcus raising its voice to a mind shattering peek.

It seemed to Adnohr that the young girl could handle herself against this dark evil thing which was rare for even shaolin but with a Orcus attack as well it was doubtful that she could win, the cat moved in position between the young girl and the attacking Orcus and de-cloaked itself making itself seen, all was surprised at the appearance of this huge Leopard that had appeared out of thin air, the shaolin girl was surprised too but she could feel this cat was on her side and now understood why the creature had fallen to the ground when it could have killed her. The Orcus came forward and the cat disappeared once again. Orcus found themselves attacked and torn apart with one gash from Adnohr's mighty claws they tore into them like extremely sharp knives, it was hard for the Orcus to fight an enemy they could not see. The girls hands moved quick and began hand to hand combat with the hooded creature knocking it to the ground, she rushed for the truck pushing the driver over to the other seat and finding herself in a wet puddle, she whistled loud for the invisible cat, and when she heard the thud in the back of the Vehicle she put her foot down and speeded crashing through the gate that lead into China.

The dark Creature stood up and peered into the direction of the escaping shaolin girl. "There is nowhere for them to go" it thought to its self.

It knew that leaving the road was almost certain death in these parts and they would never survive the gases. They would radio ahead and have drones meet them along the road. Believing that they would not get far, its concern was mainly for the scroll, it knew there were more of them and that someone was bringing them together.

"These are truly the times." It thought before it turned and moved towards the hovercraft he must tell the others.

∧
—

Through the lands and across the plain he had travelled tracking his prey he was in his element. As a child he had hunted and tracked animals of all kinds not to capture or to kill but to understand the way of the beast, to understand the basic animal instinct to survive and avoid capture. His adopted father had taught him many things and showed him how to use his senses to track beings long after they had gone, using his supernatural senses such as hawk eye vision to see things in the earth that others would miss. It was his amazing senses that had lead him on the path he was now on.

He had picked up the trail two days back and now he moved silently on foot leaving his horse behind, his prey was close maybe only a mile ahead. This pursuit has lasted for days with no rest or sleep always moving onwards desperate to gain ground, so determined he was his horse had become tired and did not seem to have the stamina that he possessed, forcing him to leave the animal behind, it would rest and then catch up to him when it was ready.

There were others out on the prowl not far behind him; he had to make sure he reached those that he had tracked before the others. Why? He asked himself as he moved with much hast, every step bringing him closer and close to his mark. He himself did not know why or what he would do when he would catch up to them, would he capture them and take them back with him? No he knew this was not the reason he had begun this venture. The voices for a reason wanted him to find this man and by the tracks he now knew there were only two of them, he was being sent to save them, Eed knew this would be the only way they would leave his head, leave his mind in peace, if he saved Nathan then the spirits would forgive him. Up ahead through the dark Eed could see a small light in the hollow of an old building, "they are burning a fire, not a smart trick if one does not want to be found" he thought to himself.

Manue had travelled north towards her home, bringing with her Nathan her boss and friend who was now dying, their travel had been slow and she was forced to stop many times to clean the wound and give him fresh bandages, they had spent to many nights resting only five miles outside the city walls, waiting and trying to stop the blood that was seeping through Nathan's injury. The potion that Leron had given her had helped but Nathan was in no condition to be moved, so she gave the potion time to work its magic. Nathan had been drifting in and out of consciousness but on the third day he awoke fighting the pain and insisting that they continue their journey implying that he was well enough to travel. Not believing a word he had said but understanding the importance of reaching their destination Manue took the time to find what turned out to be a large piece of rusting metal from the old building nearby it was about six feet in length and would be very hard to lift if she was not so strong. She had no idea what it was before but now it would become some sort of carriage for her injured companion. Using the rope that she had carried with her when they had left the city knowing that it would come in handy, she tied it to the metal hinges of the large metal slate and then tied it to her horse in a fashion making it a perfect harness.

She knew it was not good for Nathan's wound if he travelled slumped over a horse. She helped him lay down on the rusty metal and then climbing into her saddle and taking hold of the reins of the horse that had once carried Nathan they continued their journey at a very slow pace. The journey was taking its toll on Nathan, Manue could see this and she began to wonder if he would survive the trip. Keeping a close eye on him she moved forever forwards headed towards the secret home of the dwarf nation, believing to herself that things could not get much worse but she was wrong. Whilst moving through daylight with the sun burning down on them thick clouds started to form in the sky casting long shadows not just on the ground but also in their hearts. They both knew what these clouds meant and they also knew the consequences of being caught unprotected at this time of year. Nathan had all but given up but Manue had not finished yet and where there is life there was hope. She moved the horses at a faster pace towards what she believed to be a road that once passed through a long gone village or town. The sky had become dark with gassy clouds and light began to flicker as if like lightening, lighting up the sky but not yet had it displayed any explosive reactions. Manue stopped on the gravel covered road and dismounted and began searching in the dirt as if she had lost a precious jewel or something.

"Alas she has gone mad" The thought crossed Nathan's mind.

But Manue kept looking, and soon she jumped up with glee.

"I knew it; I knew I could find one." She shouted.

She went back and picked Nathan up like a doll from his resting place and carried him over to what she had found. It was a hole, a hole in the ground causing Nathan to look a little confused.

"I had been told once by the elders that men had tunnels under the ground in every town village or city. It was where they washed all their bodily waste away— they called 'em sewers. We will be safe under 'ere."

The explanation had appeased Nathan confusion he did not say a word it hurt him too much to speak; he let Manue carry him down an old rusty ladder under the earth, laying him down she told him that she would be back taking herself back up the ladder she left Nathan alone.

Minutes had passed and she had not returned. Nathan became worried and prayed the fire from the sky had not started and that she had not been burned alive, but to his relief she returned sliding a metal round circle over the hole above her. And she descended down the ladder.

"I had to take care of the horses" She winked at him, and with that the sky above could be heard roaring as if with fury. It had begun burning month and they would be stuck here in this hole until it finished. Manue hoped they had enough supplies to last them the whole time they were down here and she knew the extra meat she had just obtained would help a great deal during the time they would have to spend underground.

Weeks past and burning month ended, the half dwarfin girl and her injured companion had spent the whole time underground living of the rations they carried and the rats that so frequently past through the tunnels, with some rather tasty meat that Manue produced often which Nathan had no idea where she had got it. But with every moment they spent waiting Nathan's condition had worsened. But now they were back on the road Manue dragging Nathan along on her home made cart without wheels, it was fortunate she had dwarfin blood flowing through her veins because dragging Nathan along on a cart with no wheels whilst running had very little effect on Manue until the first five miles, but then she became weary and she began to tire night time was falling and she needed to rest, it would not be long before she would reach her destination another day and she hoped she would be back in her long missed home.

She looked back at her injured companion and wondered if he would last that long, he had spent most of the trip unconscious mumbling crazy words in his sleep as a fever ran through him, he was in a bad way sweating and coughing up blood, the signs were not good given that all the treatment she had for him had finished the day before. She had been grateful for Leron's potion and knew that if it was not for its healing power Nathan would not have made it this far and would be dead already. Now all she could do was clean the wound and change the bandages when it was needed.

They found a place to camp and began to make a fire knowing it was risky, they knew it was possible a fire would give their position away to anyone that maybe searching for them, but the nights after burning month had been so cold, it was possible that the cold itself could kill Nathan, knowing this Manue wrapped him up tight in a blanket the best she could, feeling the cold herself she ignored it and continued to make her fire.

Eed was moving quickly now he had been wrong the others were closer than he had thought. Dawn was creeping slowly across the eastern skies and the others were almost on top of him, he could hear their almost silent movements with his sharp sensitive hearing and they were moving fast, if anything just as fast as he was they had spotted the camp fire. Desperate to get there before them he rushed now at an incredible rate forgetting about stealth he did not care who heard him. He raced manoeuvring himself at his top speed navigating the rocky path before him with wind rushing past his ears he felt determined. Still moving so fast and carelessly it should have been no surprise when rushing out to those he had been tracking for days that he found himself winded and flat on the ground. The girl had heard him coming and had hit him with a devastating force with some kind of metal log, the impact had sent him flying back through the air a few yards landing hard on the ground, the blow had slowed him down but he knew time was too short to lay around. Catch his breath he got straight back on to his feet trying to approach the girl, shouting warnings, but everything happened too quick, too fast.

Out of nowhere five of his white haired brethren came almost floating, leaping on the girl that was holding the large log as a weapon, it was surreal, Eed could not work out if the blow had made him hallucinate, the girl was rather small but she held a log that was one and a half times her size and she held it like she was holding a twig. And further more to his surprise and that of his brethren was that fact that after jumping on the girl all of them found themselves flying back with kicks and punches hurting each and every one of them. And then it dawned on him in the flicker of the campfire as daylight crept but had not quite reached them.

"She is dwarfin she must be, the girl at the Inn was dwarfin all along and no one knew or even thought," his mind raced as he almost half laughed getting his thoughts together he approached her once again.

"Wait" He shouted.

Manue was not about to listen to anyone let alone an elf, she stood bold ready to swing at any of them if they came to close, but before she could do anymore damage headed straight for her at a Gallop came Lykle, the elf Eniamaj had given charge to track this pair— and probably also Eed himself.

Lykle reining his horse to a stop as he aimed some type

of big gun at Manue pulling the trigger, Before the Half dwarfin girl could react an expanding net came flying from the weapon covering Manue, Entangled she fell to the ground she struggled but found that she could not break the bonds.

"Lykle what is the meaning of this, these are my prisoners".

"You are in Violation Eed Resarf you have left the city against our governors orders" Lykle's voice boomed deeply as if he were a judge issuing a Punishment.

"Never the less I am still the ranking officer here and I demand you free her and let me bring them back."

"Ha ... " Lykle laughed his voice deep unlike most of his kind "You exceed yourself Eed Resarf of the house of Hawkindoor. What happened to you, I once respected you but now you are a shadow of what you used to be let them go? With you Huh you must be joking."

"Men" Eed turned to the Elves that had accompanied Lykle "As your commander I order you to release the Prisoner"

The white haired beings stood almost uncertain but never the less they did nothing.

"You see Eed, I forgot to tell you, you have been stripped of your command by Eniamaj himself, I am now commander these men follow you no longer."

He turned to his men "Ejai hum caflu swysine".

Lykle had ordered them to arrest Eed, moving slowly and still uncertain they came for him, he had been their commander for as long as most of them had been in the dome city. He had taught most of them all they knew about being a guard it was him that had trained them in the art of war, and now they were being forced to arrest him, there mentor and respected leader. But when they approached him they did not have time to change their minds. Eed moved with swift speed fighting them with the Elfin style of Swasari, Eed was a master and none could match him with the possibility of Lykle who had also practised the art since elflinghood. Quick and fast was his movements striking his men in order to disable their actions.

From the ground still entangled Manue could not believe what she was seeing, the great elf Eed fighting against his own men, with swift movements he fought blocking their attacks and then countering finding the right pressure point and paralysing them with one precise touch. She watched as four of them became as statues standing in the exact position as their last movement, alive and well but unable to move, this was so his men would not be harmed the effects of such attacks wore off after around thirty minutes, but it gave Eed enough time to break the bonds that had held her.

"I am not your enemy do not fight me" Eed said quickly before releasing her.

"Swarar Windward" Lykle was shouting to the remaining three men who had been reluctant to engage in the fighting. Lykle dismounted and all four men headed for Eed.

Manue was free, she came to her feet Quickly leaving the Elf to his battle she turned and in one swoop she picked up Nathan and carried him over her shoulder and she ran, not even looking back.

Eed defended himself as long as he could from what he knew was a losing battle with Lykle fighting him also he knew he could not possibly win, he had already received several strikes to crucial parts of his body and he was tiring. fighting three well trained Elfin guard and a master was taking its toll, he gave the girl as much time as he could to escape and then he too turned and ran in pursuit of the strange dwarfin girl and her companion Nathan, behind him came three of the men he was just fighting not willing to let him go so easily.

Lykle did not pursue Eed himself right away he stopped and touched each of the four men that were paralysed releasing them from their trap.

"Come quick" he told them and leaping on to his horse they followed.

Manue had not been running more than ten yarns carrying a very sick Nathan on her shoulder worrying that she may kill him moving him this way, she could hear movement not far behind, it was impossible for her to outrun Elves, on their feet they were much too quick. She came to a rocky place that was riddled with thousand of big rock Boulders and beams; it was as if someone had once tried to build a humongous structure here. It was a maze and she was sure that if she hid within this place and stayed very quiet it would be a task for anyone to find them but as she moved to hide amongst the rocks a hand grabbed her and another placed its self around her mouth, more hands pulled Nathan from her shoulders and she found it incredibly hard to struggle against her assailants.

Eed being very closely tailed came to the rocky place and dodged in and out and around rocks and pillars fast and silently trying to lose his pursuers. He looked back and saw no one and began to sneak his way through the rocky maze looking for the bar girl and Nathan. He moved listening very closely for any sounds of movement but he heard none, and soon he found himself in a clearing amongst the Pillars.

There were steps that led down a short way into some kind of large square and at the centre were a few old extinguished campfires. He moved amongst them and deduced that Beings had been there recently, not feeling comfortable knowing he was too much in the open he began to feel like sitting Prey for all those that were looking for him and began to move quickly to cross the square to begin climbing the steps at the other end to get back amongst the tall pillars and rocks. But as he crossed, out stepped all eight Elves four behind and four in front at both ends of the square at each set of steps.

Lykle spoke as he and his men walked slowly— closing in on him.

"You will not escape this time not only have you committed an offence against our governor by doing so you have committed an offence against our king, you are now declared a traitor against our people. Take him," he shouted at his men.

Eed began to fight once again but this time to no avail, it was only a distraction so Eed would not see Lykle pointing the same weapon he had used earlier on the dwarf girl at Him, and within moments Eed found himself entangled in the same bonds swisewire only Elfin blades could cut such bonds and Eed was finding it hard to reach the blade he carried on his ankle.

"We will find the girl and her companion and bring you all back to face Elfin justice" Lykle said proudly.

"Well here I am come and get me" A voice echoed amongst the tall pillars that surrounded them all.

When Lykle looked up he found himself surrounded. Standing in plain view was the girl accompanied by around thirty well-armed Dwarves. Lykle was beat, it was not possible for so few Elves to defeat so many dwarves though Elves were faster the dwarves had the strength and many arrows were pointing in their direction. But many years of religious training and belief kicked in and took over from Logic, the hatred of the dwarfin kind, and the pain it caused Lykle to see so many free and standing bold like they were better than he was, like they were equal to him like they had rights made the new Elfin commander act irrationally, twisting his face almost to an unrecognisable state his eyes became red like many of his kind had before him, barking orders in an almost devilish like tone he ordered his men to attack and like a wild beast he charged forward with his men to engage the dwarfs in battle, the dwarves let loose their arrows.

The Elves were quick and began to dodge and move through them but they were not quick enough there were too many arrows and it was not possible for any being to navigate his way through such a shower of arrows, his men fell almost within a few steps of their attack, arrows prelude from the rib cages and foreheads, an arrow went straight through the eye of the man closest to Lykle and ten more followed hitting him in various places. But Lykle determined, continued forwards dodging, an arrow hit him in the shoulder, but he continued to move then another went straight through his left hand; he ignored the pain and unsheathed his sword with his right hand, as he raised it up his right arm was hit and then his legs. He dropped to the ground as the shower of arrows stopped, all stood and watched as the mad elf still with arrows in him dug his sword in the ground to use as a crouch to raise himself up. And with his last burst of energy he raised his sword shouting the words "Swyinta farar quib" (which is to mean for our King) and he burst forward as 10 more arrows pierced his body and Lykle dropped dead in a puddle of blood that he and his men had made.

The dwarves surrounded the Elf in the net one turned to another; "What shall we do with him?" he asked.

The other replied "Take him with us".

As soon as it was said the dwarf hit Eed with a great club, knocking him unconscious. They tied him up and blindfolded him and carried both him and Nathan, with Manue beside them to the secret kingdom of the dwarf nation.

∧
—

Seven wolves rushed through the forest at an incredible rate, these were no ordinary wolves the mere size of them was enough to intimidate any being. They averaged the size and muscular build of a tiger and though bulky and strong they moved with the agility of a common cat, running and leaping as if they were as light as a feather making hardly any sound as their paws touched down on dry leaves and dirty gravel, they wisped through the forest silently making no sound but the patter of their breaths. Up above their heads circled a large hawk its wing span was so enormous it overshadowed the doglike creatures as they travelled undeterred to their destination they had orders they had a mission and nothing would stop the completion of their task.

Eed awoke with a sharp pain thudding in his head, his vision was blurred and he lay still for a moment giving time for his head to clear and his eyes to adjust to the dimly lit four-walled room that he was in. He placed his right hand on his left temple to find the spot where he had been clubbed had been dressed and a bandage was wrapped firmly around his injury. He could not decipher the purpose of the room he had awoken in, was it a cell? Was he in some kind of dungeon or a bedchamber? He sat up slowly and groaned from his pains and aching body, he was surprised to find that his clothes had been removed and a bandage was also wrapped around his ribs bringing back the memory of the blow he had taken from the dwarf girl. At the end of the bed he found some clothes neatly folded, a pair of lose brown trousers and a brown shirt and beside his bed he found a pair of foot wear, leather and suede bound together making it a comfortable fit for his feet, he took his time dressing himself carefully as not to irritate his injuries, he had found his bed surprisingly comfortable considering that on closer inspection it was made from stone with a straw mattress and warm sheets for bedding. The whole room was made from stone, not brick blocks of any kind; it was as though someone had chiselled the rock, hollowed it out to create the lair he found himself in; it almost had the effect of a small cave.

Two lamps shone dimly on either side of his bed they were electric lights, these people must have a generator of some kind, he pondered when the thought came to him to smash them and use the glass as a weapon, but the lights were imbedded in the rock wall, with a thick glass covering them and no matter how hard he hit one of them the protective glass would not break. Looking around the room he found that there was no clear visible door, it was as if the rock had grown around him but he knew the idea was absurd, they had put him in here and they would be coming for him soon, but he could not understand why he was still alive, Surly they hated Elves as much as his people hated them. He stopped wondering and focused on his escape, he went from wall to wall trying to find a secret door, which had to be there. There had to be a door how else would they come and get me?

Just as he felt that he would never find it he noticed a small thin crack that went a small way down in the wall to the right of him, he would have paid it no mind but the crack was too straight to be natural. He dug his nails into the crack and pulled hard, some of his nails pulled away from his fingers and his hands bled, but he felt the rock give way and moved slightly towards him, so he gritted his teeth and moaned out loud refusing himself from letting go he pulled harder, and his determination paid off. The rock gave way and pulled out like a small door on hinges. But it was no door; behind the rock was a window, glassed just as thick as that which protected the lamps. But what he saw through the window to his left made him stand still and stare in awe. Blood dripped from his fingertips as he stood and glared. He rubbed his eyes in disbelief or maybe to adjust to the bright lights he was staring at. Off into the distance about a mile and a half away from his present position in what appeared to be the largest cavern in any cave that he had ever seen was a large beautiful city of lights, lighting the huge cavern up like a human Christmas tree in a dark room, it was beautiful he could never have believed that such a place existed.

"It's wonderful isn't it?"

Eed tried to turn quickly to see who had entered the room, but felt sluggish and moved slower than he wanted to. To the left of him now visible was a door and standing in its path was a dwarf and behind him stood six other dwarves all with the hands on the hilt of their swords.

"You will find that you are slower than usual and your senses may also be a little slow," The small man continued. "It's because you have been drugged, it's not harmful but it was the only way we knew to slow you down."

"What could I do even if I had speed" Eed replied.

"You Elves are witty and your build is unusual for your kind, though your strength still is no match for six of my guards, with your speed you may concoct some idea of escape and that we can't have."

"I am Eed Resarf commander of the Dome legion and who are you that address me." Eed respectably stayed as formal as he could.

"Just think of me as the one who wanted you dead as soon as you arrived, you are a security risk."

"So why did you not just kill me?"

"Well fortunately for you I was overruled but come with me and you can ask the council that same question, they have requested your presence."

Eed was escorted from the room taking only three steps down before finding himself in a hall way. To the left of him were more doors to other rooms maybe like mine he guessed, and before him was a large window that ran all along the corridor, it allowed him to see the vast underground landscape that was before him. Multiple stone lodges and homes laid out before and around the massive city, like thousands of pebbles scattered along the ground.

Smoke flowed out from what appeared to be chimney's and swirled around high like ghostly dragons up and up until it was sucked into a hole that had been created in the rooftop of the cavern, he wondered for a minute if the smoke led to the outside world, and wondered how he would get so high to find out.

The area of homes before the city was a busy place and small dots like ants moved in and out and amongst the houses with purpose, it was amazing to him that so many dwarves lived that so many dwarves had survived the war and survived the mass killing by Eed's own kind. They had procreated and made themselves strong again but how? He wondered, it took many years for a dwarfna to conceive a child like the Elves. There bloodline were once almost the same this is why the Elfin population was so slow to grow, to bear a child for a female in Eed's own race was followed by great celebration as it was a rare thing these days. But the Dwarves they must have been breeding like rabbits but then the thought of the Dwarf girl came to him the one who could past as a human girl for all those years in Nathan's bar. She was taller than most dwarves but still small in height but past off as a small human girl easily, they have interbreed with humans and it had worked they have created a new generation, and more worrying possibly an army. Eed took a moment to admire the great glass structure that curved over the city, making the city remind him of a toy he once had, it was a city in glass and water and when he shook it, the illusion was made that it was snowing in the little city in the palm of his hand.

This great place was not in water and it was no toy, it was a monument to the achievements that these beings had reached with all the odds against them, he had always known that dwarves were resourceful but it did not occurred to him and less likely to anyone else that they were this resourceful. He stood only a short while admiring from high up in what now appeared to be some kind of tower. The dwarves had allowed him to admire their work but soon after moved him on, they turned to the right in the corridor and walked a short way until they came to some wide stone steps that seemed to go down and down a long way. The idea did past his mind that this would be a good opportunity to try and escape, but as if reading his mind the one who seemed to be the boss of the guards ordered three of his men to stay behind him at all times while two others would walk in front of him and the leader himself and one other would walk very closely beside him. But before they continued down the steps the small man stared at him with a face so serious it could have been carved from stone itself.

"If you have any ideas of escape believe me I will not hesitate to kill you."

Eed now knew that this was not the time to try an escape, with the effects of the drug still making him sluggish he had no chance so he let himself be led peacefully down the steps.

"We never imagined to ever have prisoners so really we have no dungeons or cells, this tower was not constructed to hold captured beings to be moved back and forth along corridors and steps, if we had intended to hold people such as yourself we would have constructed some kind of lift for this facility."

The little man went on to say as they descended the never-ending steps.

"This is one of our ten seer's towers these were the first buildings to be constructed when we first dug our way to this cavern, each tower holds two hundred men all trained and experienced soldiers." He bragged "we are now walking along the outside of the complex but I assure you inside is actually a lot bigger than it appears, if we were ever discovered it would be here the battle would begin as there is only one way in and one way out."

Eed could not believe the arrogance of the small being beside him, giving away vital strategic information to the enemy, he seemed too smart to do such a thing, so the elf concluded that either the dwarf lied and wanted him to believe there was only one way to attack or he believed that Eed would not be around long enough to tell anyone anything that he had learned, and he feared that it was the latter that was correct.

The dwarf continued to brag about the greatness of his soldiers and their training drills that they were made to do every four hours of the day, and their techniques at fighting and there weaponry, until at last after twenty minutes they reached the bottom of the steps, and much to his surprise waiting on small tracks that riddled down a long slope and far off into the distance amongst the Dwarfin homes and into the city was a small train and its driver, it was made similar to the humans black steam engines of old, and had three carriages but the train was made smaller with only three rows of three seats in each carriage.

"Oh yes we have our own rail system here, it helps people to get around much easier, but this track is strictly military so we have no stops and no worries about picking up civilians along the way, this will take us straight to the city, so please step on."

One of the guards went before Eed and one followed after making it a tight fitting for all on the leather made chairs that was tightly confined and fixed down to the train.

The other guards came on the train seating themselves in the rows behind him and in front of him all with their swords unsheathed ready for anything that Eed may try. The last to enter was their leader who Eed found much too talkative for his own liking.

The wheels on the track began to spin before they took grip and the train began to move off slowly, they were on their way to the city and Eed could not help but marvel at the Dwarfin kingdom. The city itself was obviously further away from them as it first appeared to be, it was either that or the train was ridiculously slow. But Eed knew this was not the case, the train pulled its three carriages along with ample speed along the whining tracks, he was intrigued by the little people in their little homes as the train past through their villages, Crowds of people stopped and stared as the train went past, many younglings getting excited pulling on their parent's clothes and pointing at the elf on the train as they past them by.

"It's was as if they had never seen an elf before" Eed spoke out loud.

"Many of them have not, most have been born and raised in theses caves and many have never seen the outside world, but have no fear all knows about their ancient evil cousins" the talkative dwarf said glaring at him daring Eed to challenge the truth of his words.

Eed had plenty to say on the matter but did not feel the urgency to argue his and his peoples case. He felt strangely relaxed as if it were the first bit of peace he had in years, it occurred to him that it may have something to do with the fact that he had not heard the voices since he came into contact with the girl and Nathan before he was captured, but he also resided to the fact that this place, its wonders and beauty tapped into a peace that was within him, reminding him of home his homeland a place he had not seen for years, though it was differently designed, he clearly recognised that these people had a hand in the architecture and designs of the Elfin homeland, This place was giving him the calm he so desperately needed. He turned away from the dwarfs glare and continued to enjoy the views of this strange new world. He decided whatever plans they had for him the one thing he will cling to was this peaceful moment this peaceful time.

At last after around twenty-five minutes the train slowed down and came to a stop, a group of armed dwarves with bows and swords had stopped the train at what looked to be like a checkpoint right before the city gates. Two of them approached while the others angled their bows at the train.

"Papers please" one of the dwarves said to the driver of the train.

"Its ok Carshawl we have orders from the council" the talkative dwarf said raising his voice so he could be heard at the front.

"Oh general Mirezz" He said surprised "I did not see you their sir, please forgive me, of course you may continue."

"Have no worries Young Ravin, your father would have been proud, one day your thoroughness will save the day, carry on soldier." Mirezz said with a smile. The dwarf Carshawl saluted Mirezz and then waved his men to let the train through. As the train moved off slowly once again, Eed found himself marvelling at the great glass gateway that was before them. "This glass dome must have took them years to make" he pondered not giving to much thought that it had been around a hundred ninety years since the dwarves had been in hiding in this city.

The train passed through the gates and into the city of lights, it was wonderful, every building designed in a similar fashion to those buildings back in the Elfin kingdom, but the material was different, most were made from stone or glass or even stone and glass depending on the building or the object, it was as if Eed had entered some kind of future world where everything was clean or even sterilized almost until it shined. Even the stone used as the base of most of the homes had a gleam as if it were marble. There were pavements for the people to walk on so they did not get in the way of the many trains that passed along the many tracks that riddled throughout the city. It was busy here, there were trading markets and shops, it was like a world away from all the troubles and poverty that raged throughout the entire world up above. Mirezz noticed the surprise on Eed's face and felt he needed some explanation.

"You see elf" he half spat the word. "This is the only world that my people have, so the council over the years have made an economy of sorts, we continuously send out hunting parties that travel far and wide to bring back good stock, we also have half breeds."

"How is that possible?"

"Well it was through the hatred and mistreatment from your kind that made it possible. Many human dwarves were mistaken for our own kind and banished and slaughtered throughout lands, we found them and took them in and found that our genetic makeup was compatible with theirs thus making it possible for us to procreate quicker than we once did, but it was soon realised that a person born of dwarf and human dwarf blood could also procreate with normal sized humans, so we allowed for a few trustworthy humans to stay with us, those who were running in fear hiding their dwarf like sons and daughters from the likes of your kind and the humans or other beings that would hunt them. And here they found love and lifelong partners thus having off spring that is taller than the average dwarf, but could easily pass as a human.

So many went out in the outside world to find work, to learn to do anything that would help our growing society anything to keep it strong and make it stronger. We now have stock supplies delivered at certain locations all over England, we then give a percentage to every person in the dwarf nation and they do with it as they please, some trade stock for other things at the markets, whilst other have skills in sowing and sweet making or baking and opened up shops of their own. There is not one man or women who has nothing to do in this place, those who feel they have nothing to do become soldiers or cavers, the ones who help create new parts of our city to enlarge it for our growing population. So you see your people, your ways has helped us find our own way and most of us are glad we no longer pay homage to Elves."

Eed did not say a word; if he had, the words would have been "Truly remarkable."

^
—
Yatnahc, stop the truck in the middle of the road, Ponchi the owner of the truck was in a state of shock as the stench from his wet trousers filled the truck with an unpleasant aroma.

"Let me out I will walk from here" he pleaded with tears streaming down his face, he was scared and terrified and Yatnahc could understand this but she could not let him go.

"If I let you go they will force you to tell where we left the road and then they will kill you think about it, you know I speak the truth."

"Leave the road!" he screeched in shock as if he was about to pee his pants again.

"Calm down Mr, do not be to shocked leaving the road is our only means of escape we must turn north west from here."

"Leaving the road is certain death so either way we all die." He slumped in his seat and began sobbing more hysterically.

"I came just to get food and supplies for my village and now I will never see them again, and who will know what happen to me."

"Tell me your name."

"My name is Ponchi"

"Well Ponchi I am Yatnahc of the new Shaolin order,

and I tell you this that this day you will not die, I have a map to get us safely through the Misty Plain and a mission that will save more than your village, you don't know it yet but all in this region is in danger, and I go to get help."

"So what choice do I have?" he whimpered

"You have only two, come with me and maybe live and become a hero of your people or stay here and die at the hands of Orcus."

He wiped his tears from his face and looked her in her eyes

"Is not much of a choice" he paused a moment "I am with you."

"Good my friend Ponchi now take these soap leaves and this water and remove your trousers and clean them before we continue, to travel this land and survive takes concentration and I can't concentrate with that stench."

"I am not a brave man Yatnahc I am sorry my cowardice shows so easy"

"Courage and braveness come from those who act when it is needed my friend I am sure before this journey is over you will learn more about yourself."

Ponchi clean his trousers as quick as he could and they began their journey, turning the truck into the misty plains that reared off to the left of the road a great dark mist engulfed them and from the roadside they could no longer be seen.

The Train began to slow as it moved smoothly along the curves of the tracks that led into an archway of a fantastic building. It was the tallest building in the entire city; the peak almost reached the roof of the enormous cavern. The building itself was composed of crystal glass, which was riddled with many colours reflecting all the brilliants and magnificence of the dwarfin architects. It was amazing; a skill that all the world would appreciate.

The train came to a halt and the guards exited escorting Eed through the great doors of the building that was surely the pride and joy of all Dwarfindom. On entering they were met by even more guards who joined as part of Eed's escort making the guards surrounding him around twenty. With this council he now knew that they were not willing to take any chances with him.

"I see Mirezz that these council members must be very important." Eed said with a smirk.

"Yes they are" He spat "And I won't hesitate to kill you so please give me an excuse, oh and its general to you."

Eed smiled, he had overheard the soldier back at the city gates call the dwarf General Mirezz, and knew to call his name would irritate him as the dwarf had refused to give him his name on their first meeting. At least if they were to kill him he would take satisfaction from seeing the annoyance and the loss of composer from Mirezz.

He walked along the wide corridor that was elegant itself with its white marble floor and red carpet that ran along its centre. Old pictures of long dead war legends and heroes some of whom Eed had seen once, hung on the silver walls in great Glass frames. Korin the great, Excordor the merciful, even great ancient dwarfin kings hung in this corridor, and beside them stood Ancient armour of all kinds, ranging from Dwarfin to human and even thousand year old Elfin armour long forgotten and never used these days stood proud amongst the other artifacts. It was like this corridor was a museum of old relics and old times when men were heroes. They walked until they reached the end of the corridor at yet another great but well decorated double door that was guarded by four tall guards whom were almost the size of Eed himself. "Humans" he wondered.

"These are four of our best soldiers. They are part of an elite order that train only for the protection and the bidding of the king, all are dwarves but carry the human gene, the tallest children born from such couples are selected to be trained from their tenth year. It is a great honour for ones parents when their child is selected to be part of the Kelkorion order the Kings personal guards."

Mirezz felt the need to show how well organised they were. But Eed believed it to be showing off and he was not far from the truth.

"I thought there was no longer a king amongst the Dwarf nation."

"There is always a king as there are always equal decisions amongst the king and his council. He ordered it this way, a wise king he is."

The doors were opened and Eed was marched in like a lamb to the slaughter with his escort of twenty all poised and ready to kill him at the slightest sniff of any trouble. He moved forward into a great massive hall. The hall was so wide it did not surprise him that up above and all around in a full circle were rows and rows of seats. But what did surprise him was they were all filled with angry looking dwarves. This was no private council meeting, what happened here today would be known by all in this kingdom. All went silent as they watched the Elf enter, this was an audience all came to see if the elf would put on show before his untimely death.

At the centre of the hall before him was a Tree of stone or something of the likes. It was clearly made from stone but it was designed like the branches of a tree that spread out in different directions and on different levels, but its branches curved from the trees centre like two hands poised ready to catch or great fingers about to close, and on each of these branches were well made seats and on each branch sat a dwarf and the braches were fourteen so fourteen dwarves sat on the stone tree all able to see those who stood at the centre of the hall clearly, and most importantly he who sat at the centre in the great seat that rose up many steps from the base of the tree. And he that sat there was familiar to Eed, he had seen him when he was elfling when there was once peace between elf and dwarf. He was Alex Cordeadoor, King of the dwarves, a legend that was long believed amongst the world above as dead. It was believed that he had died in the battle of blood at Colchester, when the Elves came to claim Suffolk during the war.

There were stories of a great battle in Essex and it was the dwarves that held the last line at Colchester and their king led them. It was known as one of the worse massacre's in history, very few dwarves escaped, drones came with the Elves and showed no mercy, eye witnesses reported Alex being shot by laser but he continued to fight on, then it was said he was pieced but continued with an arrow sticking into his chest, he fought sword to sword with three Elves, no dwarf had ever been known to possess such speed as he did. He died after killing two that he fought with; he received a blade through his centre from the third elf. The elf was Eniamaj himself, his name was legend for killing the dwarf king, but now it appears that it was not so. To further Eed's surprise, above the king hung a great huge golden frame, an in it at its centre was a picture, A picture of Lithor the most famous and respected Elfin king, Hero of all Elves, Eed lost his composure. "How dare you" he shouted and moved a step forward aggressively only to stop in his tracks when twenty blades rose immediately to his throat. He had forgotten in his anger that he was in hostile territory, but the emotions he felt at the mockery of his king were overwhelming. They dared to hang his king in their hall; they did this to mock him and his true king that died at their murderous hands.

All of Maxius's teaching rose to his mind, reminding him how these dwarves had hated Elves for centuries plotting for the day to kill Lithor so they could take over. But when the Elves had discovered their treachery after they had murdered their king the dwarves escaped taking with them the sacred Book that Lithor himself had kept. Only the great king had read it and known its secrets, and when they stole the book it only proved more so that they had killed him at Laguna. But now before him they mocked the greatest king that ever lived, hanging him at the centre of their hall as if his death was their Victory.

"You are dangerous, now you die." Mirezz raised his sword to strike at Eed's head.

"No"

Mirezz held his sword steady but still inches away from ending Eed's life, all around him voices of the dwarfin people screamed and chanted KILL HIM KILL HIM. But the king had order him to stop and it would be foolish to ignore a royal order. He leaned in and whispered.

"You are lucky elf for now but your time will come very very soon."

He turned to face the stage with the council members and his king.

"Have we become monsters and butchers that we would execute a being without first hearing him speak, and here in this sacred and blessed hall?" The kings' voice boomed throughout the whole hall and silence fell.

"I am sorry my lord he moved aggressively, please I ask your forgiveness." Mirezz dropped to one knee.

"Forgiveness, we shall see. Now bring him closer," Alex ordered, his voice echoing through the hall and murmurs went out amongst the people.

"You dare to move against us, you should and most probably die for this Insolence." The king stared stoned face at the Elf from his high throne making the elf appear small to him.

Indeed Eed felt small surrounded by the council members, he felt like small prey caught in the wings of a great eagle but this did not stop him from his boldness.

"Insolence, Huh" he spat "is it not you that is Insolent?"

The people rose to their feet. All around him shouted violent and vicious words at him.

"He must die" a voice could clearly be heard from the crowd and all followed in suit saying words similar insisting on his death all stunned and shocked at the arrogance of the elf who spoke to their king as though he was a common farmer.

"Silence" Alex boomed once again. The crowd quietened down until there was silence once again.

"I should have you killed where you stand, but though I am king in this kingdom there will be lawful rulings on such things."

Alex rose to his feet and spoke loudly to his council.

"What say ye?" He roared like a performer on a stage "For this Elf shall it be life or death."

He looked to each and every one of his councilmen, and one by one in turn they held out their hands with dark grimacing looks upon their faces, holding out their thumbs and pointing it downwards. There was a momentary silence from all before a great cheer went up amongst the crowd, they rose once again clapping and cheering, after a few moments the king held up both arms as to silence the crowd and the people complied.

"It seems elf that your fate has been decided. You shall be taken from here to the far pillars of Ulsaw and shall be beheaded immediately, a quick and firm death."

The cheer went up again through the crowd and Mirezz turned and smirked at Eed.

"There is no compassion here for Elves, I will try and make it quick and painless, try." He said with sarcasm.

"Wait my lord," A women's voice shouted down from the crowd, all who heard went silent in shock.

"Wait" She shouted again and this time all heard and

murmured amongst themselves.

"Who speaks" the king shouted up into the audience.

The crowd seated themselves so that the girl maybe pinpointed by all and their king. And standing alone was a blond girl, one who Eed recognised immediately.

"I am Manue Bowen distant cousin to Vladlin of the house of Bowin and fiancé to Mada Cree."

"I know you child you have done well in providing news and stocks for your people, what is it you have to say?" Alex said curiously.

"I asks that I may be allowed to speak for this elf if the court will hear me, and my Uncle."

"You're Uncle"

She turned to the old man who was beside her and helped him to his feet, he was thin for a dwarf, it was also apparent that he had many years with him as his aged showed from his movement and the white long wiry beard that went down to his feet. He held a great gold staff and wore a hooded brown cloak; he pulled his hood back to reveal his face.

"I am Gustavius Tnarg high priest and keeper of the sacred scrolls in the west temple."

There was shock and whispers all around them, Gustavius was a very important being, he was the oldest of all dwarves that lived, he had knowledge and practised magic's of the old ways that had long been forgotten by most dwarves. It was also common knowledge that he seldom left the temple, even the king himself would not summon him but went to his temple instead to speak and seek spiritual guidance in times of need, and now the wisest man stands and asks to speak for an elf, one who had shown arrogance and insolence before the king and his people, the people murmured at the disgrace of such an act, but none dared raise their voice to speak out against him, there was rumours that he could kill a man with just a stare.

"Gustavius is that you." The king struggled to see high up into audience.

"It is I your Highness."

"Then come down with your niece and speak what you have to say, as it is only a foolish man that would not hear the words of a man such as you before we condemn this elf, don't you agree?"

He looked to his council. All nodded uneasily. Most council members did not like the relationship between the king and the keeper of the Scrolls; they feared his advice was more powerful than that of any council member.

Manue and her uncle worked their way through the seats to the steps and began their decent and after moments they reached the bottom and walked across the floor of the great hall until they were in front of Eed and the soldiers and before their king who had now seated himself intrigued with what they had to say.

Eed was surprised that the girl would speak for him but he was sure it would make no difference. Manue cleared her throat and began to speak clearly and loud so the acoustics would carry her voice so all could hear.

"As you know my lord I have spent many years in the great City Ipswich, relaying information and helping to provide provisions and stocks for our people." The king nodded at the truth of her words.

"It was there in that city that I had observed this Elf the one they call Eed, right hand man to the Governor. And in all those years I had learned that this one was and is different to most, he had shown compassion like the stories of Elves of old, I have seen him treat others as Equals and defended even the weak against Orcus that was under his own command."

"It may be true my dear but it is not enough to save him from his insolence here."

"My Lord I owe this elf my life."

Whispers spread through the crowd like wild fire. Manue continued.

"When I travelled here to bring the news of Vlad and his hunting party and to save a life of a dear friend, I was captured and the Elf freed me and stood to fight his own kind while I escaped, I do not pretend to understand his actions but I owe him my life and I would never find peace if I did not get the chance to repay my debt."

"Silence" The king shouted at the crowd who continued to talk amongst themselves.

"These are strange actions for an elf I must agree" Rehsa Hurdin high councillor and most trusted friend to the king stood up and spoke.

"But what would you have us do, spare his life? And then what would we do with him send him home? Ha he cannot be freed the whole Elf kingdom would be down on us."

All respected Rehsa, and most importantly every council member did too, his words here had weight amongst the others.

"Well as I understand it Rehsa this one was Blindfolded and knocked on conscious before he was brought here we could easily just do the same and bring him back to where he was found." The King spoke throwing out some options to be considered.

"Yes it may be true, but Elves my lord have great senses as you well know his tracking skills could surpass that what we expect, he has had a scent for this place how do we know he could not find it now."

"Rehsa let it be known that your words are deeply noted, though no decision has been made yet." The King explained

"My Lord may I say one more thing."

"You may speak."

"It is important for us for your people that this elf be

executed, not just for his insolence before you, but for the spirit of the people, let them know and believe that we will not tolerate the Elves hunting and killing us, let the people know that an elf has paid for the murders of our best hunting party let their families have some redemption for the wickedness of Elves."

The people roared out with cheers once again at Rehsa speech.

"Quiet you wild people!" Alex boomed again. "We are not here to act as animal" he said when the crowd had silenced. "One more outburst and I will make an example of one of you for ignoring your kings order."

There was no longer even a whisper up in the audience. They all knew the king would keep his promise.

"Now Rehsa I have heard your words and so has all here but I will have you all know that to take a life of any being! Would bring no peace and nor will it bring back any of those that have been lost to us."

"King Alex" It was now Gustavius that spoke.

"I ask that you leave this elf in my charge." If the people would dare to speak or whisper, they would have expressed their shock at the Scroll keeper request.

"And what cares ye about this Elf wise one?"

"I sense good spirits with this one, I heard their voices the moment he was brought to the city, echoing calling to me, the dark days are soon arriving my king I have foreseen it and I fear if we kill this one it will bring doom on us all."

The great hall had become so silent that one could hear a pin drop if it were to fall. No one spoke and the king sat quietly in thought.

He turned to his council.

"What say you now my trusted advisors?"

There was a discussion and quiet talk between the council members and then Rehsa stood.

"My lord six members Voted that he should live whilst

eight members vote that he should die."

"Mmmm I myself vote that he should live, I myself know the dark times that Gustavius speak of I have read it in our most sacred texts and I believe too that these times are soon to come, and If Gustavius believes that this Elf is important then I over rule the council."

Now it was the council that was shocked and spoke out in horror. But Rehsa Voice was the Loudest.

"But my lord you cannot… "

"Cannot what!?" The king stood angrily. "Cannot, do I hear one of you tell me what I can and cannot do?" There was silence no one spoke, the fury of the king made them each tremble not one of them had seen such display of fearsome power from him for many years and all was taken back.

"I have overruled this council and I will not be questioned. I do this because I see the importance of today even though you do not." He turned to those before him.

"The elf known as Eed will be sent in Gustavius charge and confined to the temple and its grounds where he will always be escorted by two of my own personal guards and he must submit to taking the elixir once every day without complaint. Do you agree to this Elf."

Eed had remembered how blind arrogance had killed Lykle and decided it would be best to submit until he could find a way of escape.

"I agree" He replied.

"Then it is settled, Mirezz you and your men will escort him to the temple and take two of my guards."

"Yes your majesty" Mirezz bowed and turned on his heals with his escort taking the elf with them they left the hall.

"Thank you" Manue said to the king before her uncle and herself followed after Eed and his escort of dwarfin soldiers.

Eed paced up and down his bedchamber, it was a small room but quite comfortable giving his position. The room was furbished with a desk and writing materials that he had requested, curtains to block out the bright lights of the city that came through the window into his chamber. He had a very comfortable bed with sheets that were regularly changed, though gratefully he was treated very well he did not feel much like a prisoner; he was welcome to move freely around the temple as he pleased as long as he was under the escort of the two guards that waited outside his chamber. It had been two weeks since he had arrived in this place and already they were playing with his mind, trying to interfere with his values and beliefs, making out the dwarves to be innocent in all this.

He had spent many days with the old man of the temple, quickly feeling drawn to him he felt safe in his presence. Gustavius was full of knowledge making it interesting for Eed to spend many hours talking with him and listening to stories of old, mostly about the times when elf and dwarf lived together in harmony he had even claimed to have once been a great friend and advisor to the Elfin King Lithor before he had died. The old man had told him that the picture of his past king in the great hall was not mockery but held at the centre above their king in tribute to the person king Alex respected more than any other living being that ever lived. Eed had always believed that all dwarfs were not evil believing that all should not pay for the crimes of the few. He had felt until recently that the Old man was one of the good ones, but the last two days Gustavius had continued to plague his mind with talks of Maxius his king. Filling his head with stories of plots and deceit, wrong doings and betrayal, some of the things the old man said made sense to Eed, confusing him enough to almost break down all his defences. For a few moments he was willing to except the possibilities that there was truth to the old man's words. But here, alone now in his chamber he had thought on all that he had been told and came to believe that Gustavius was a liar. The lies he told were part of a greater plot.

He believed they had drugged him everyday not just to weaken his speed but his thoughts as well, and then the old man played his part filling his head with brainwashing material against his own king and many of his own people and with all that talk that he had shown him no proof.

"They think I am stupid" he spoke the words aloud.

"Stupid you are" the words echoed and whispered around his room vibrating through his mind.

"Who's there?" he looked around though he knew he was alone.

"Stupid stupid" The words crept up from a whisper becoming louder and louder. It was the voices he had thought they had left him; he had hoped he was free of this madness. Many of them rose now to high monstrous voices flooding his mind with wicked words. Had Nathan died? He wondered would he now be plagued like this forever.

"Stupid Stupid Stupid" they chanted, sweat dripped from his forehead, he was bewitched and it was taking its effect of his mind physically, his head began to thud and pains shot though his brain like he had received a sharp blow from a pointed object to the back of his head. He placed his hands over his ears as if to stop himself from hearing the overwhelming loudness of the voices that sent shudders through his brain.

"Shut up" he whispered, "Shut up" He raised his voice, and now his whisper had become a shout.

"SHUT UP SHUT UP SHUT UP!" He screamed.

His chamber door swung open and the voices stopped. The guards stood in the doorway but before them stood Gustavius.

"Whom do you shout at?"

"You old man" Eed was quick to cover his behaviour.

"Me"

"Yes you think me a fool to believe the lies you have been telling me these last few days, but the truth of it make sense to me now."

"What do you mean Man speak?"

"Mean, what do I mean Ha ha," Eed giggled like a man on the edge of madness.

"You know very well what I mean, I had wondered why an half dwarf girl would speak on my behalf" he paced the room with his head down and his finger to his chin as though he was a detective revealing his findings.

"And I also wondered why a wise dwarf such as you would also help to save me. But I realise now that I was never meant to die that day when I was sentenced in your great hall am I right?"

"I don't understand" Gustavius seem genuinely confused.

"I was not meant to die you and your king and his council had planned this, a great show for my benefit before your people to make me believe that the two of you actually cared about me, that your niece really felt that she owed a debt to me."

"But we do"

"No there is no need to play anymore games, I have worked it out, I know your plans to trick me and to brainwash me against my own kind. What did you plan to have me do once you turned me? Did you expect me to assassinate my governor, or even worse send me home to assassinate my king Maxius like you did to our king before?"

"I do not lie Eed, yes I hoped you will see the truth in all this, so that when the dark days come you would stand on the right side and fight, but I have not deceived you, I have genuinely grown fond of you and Manue has too."

"Dark days what nonsense, and me fighting on the right side, and I am sure by the right side you mean your side the side of the dwarfin people. I see what is going on here, you are building an army, your people intend to make war with us."

"Eed the right side will be the side who tries to save this world and weather your people will stand with us or against us no one knows, that is for fate to decide. But for now I will waste no more time to convince you, come with me and I will show you all the proof you will need and then if you choose not to believe then I promise I will not teach you anymore of the things we know to be the truth."

"Take me to this proof, you will find that I am not an easy man to convince."

"I fear you are not ready for it but I will show you and hope your spirit will not be crushed too much, come."

Gustavius turned and left and Eed trailed behind him followed closely by the king's best guards.

They had walked down the great steps to the ground level of the building, walking along the corridors they passed many doors and Eed wondered why this place had so many rooms. He had seen no more than around ten people passing through these corridors since he had arrived at the temple. It was a quiet place and he wondered if the people that resided here spent most of their time in meditation. They turned two more corners and travelled the hallways.

It was a vast wide holy building riddled with great halls and wide corridors. Gustavius opened the door that was before him at the end of the hallway and they all entered, the door had led them to a wide room with a large table at its centre that was covered in scrolls paper work and maps. The room was filled with shelves of books all around.

"This is where I do most of my deepest thinking, it is

my study, please follow." The old dwarf continued to walk to the end of the room and stopped at the opposite door from where they had entered. He then turned to the guards.

"Here you two may not enter"

"But... " One of the guards began to speak.

"Have no worries young Luap, this door is the only way in and the only way out, please you must wait here."

The tall dark-skinned half dwarfin male Luap seemed suspicious but nodded in agreement and placed himself and the other guard at either side of the door, as if they had just began their guard duty.

Gustavius did not produce a key as there was no clear visible keyhole, neither did he reach out and turn the door handle as there was also no handle on the door, all the old man did was whisper, Eed's sharp ears caught some of the words, and realised it was not a language known to him.

"Shue yeska Rushoo" Gustavius whispered.

And as though obeying a command the doors swung open.

"Old magic" Eed commented.

"There is no such thing as Old magic Eed your people know this, come now." Gustavius entered and Eed followed.

As Eed entered he looked back to watch the doors close behind him with no aid from any physical being, but when he turned his head forwards to look around he stood still in his tracks. The massive size of the room was overwhelming, it appeared to go on and on for miles, the room was filled with rows and rows of shelves filled with books that would have rose high to the ceiling if there were one. As Eed looked up the bookshelves seem to go up so high that the end of them faded into the clouds that covered possibly the ceiling, it appeared as though there was no ceiling and the shelves had reached the skies, which he knew was not possible as he had just been on the floor above and they were on the ground floor of the building.

"But how?" The elf was confused about the size and the length of the room; he had seen the building from the outside and knew it was not possible that it could hold a room this size.

"All things are possible if we first go back to nature; do not place your mind on impossibilities." Gustavius continued his walk after giving the elf something to ponder.

The Elf followed the dwarf along the pathway that led through the centre of the shelves until they came to a small gate; it surprised Eed further to find that the rest of the room was filled with water. The shelves still rose from the riverbed high into the cloudy ceilings of the room and the pathway beyond the gate filled with water formed a mist in the distance. The Elves once knew this magic it was taught amongst the greatest of their people. Even Eed himself once knew how to bend nature with small effects. But things had changed since Lithor had past, nature did not bend to their will so easily these days, only the very few still wield the power to do such things like create rooms larger than the building itself, and it appeared that only the Redeye had this power and it was world known that more and more of Eed's people were being inflicted with the so called gift of Red eyes.

Gustavius stood at the gate and held out the small silver whistle shaped like a bird he wore around his neck, and placing it to his lips he blew on it. The sound that flowed from the instrument was a sweet sound, a self-melody played on a single breath of magical air, swaying and dancing all around. The sound brought images of meadows and wonderful rivers and magical places that Eed's homeland was once filled with.

"We must wait here," the old man had told him.

"What is this place?" Eed had to know; he had not seen anything so marvellous since he was last in Laysenia.

"This Eed is Unyara, the Library, the one true library; it took a lot of power and energy to have it moved here from our old home."

"So it still exists, I have heard stories of this place my mother told me about the wonders of the dwarfin library in the city of Roses, she told me that it was filled with ancient mysticism and magic's, all the Elves that entered its walls marvelled at it. We lived far from the city, I rarely went there, but the library disappeared when your people left so I never got to see it until now. How could such a place be moved?"

"With a lot of help from what most would call Magic." The old man winked at the elf making him feel like a child learning a school lesson.

"Is it true that this place has every book ever written?" Eed felt now like a child on an outing eager to learn more and he did not mind that fact being in such a marvellous and rare place.

"No not every book, but here you will find nearly every book or a copy of most books ever written and published, it is the library itself that brings the books here, it strives to have every book." He lowered his voice to a whisper. "But that my friend I fear is an impossible task but don't let the library know I said so." He finished leaving Eed to think if he was being serious or not.

They both stood at the gate for awhile until Eed observed swirling in the mist and ripples flowing along the water that was once still only moments ago.

"Ahh about time where have you been?" The old man shouted out into the mist.

"Learning wise one learning" Came a smooth husky voice from within the mist, Eed paid full attention and watched as a raft came forward and stopped at the gate, and standing tall with his long oar in hand was a Sarron also known as a spook, Green in colour wearing a long gown as if he were a monk in an old human monastery.

Spooks lived all over the globe, they were peaceful beings and Eed himself had spoken to a few who had resided at the dome city. He even went as far as to call one his friend, the one he believes now haunts him, some friend the thought past through his mind. But here in the dwarf city would be the last place he had expected one to live. They were once workers for the Greys and he wondered how could the dwarves trust a Sarron, who knows how many still worked or did favours for their former slave masters. But the elf soon came to realise that the Spooks loyalty would not be in question because if he had been a traitor the Elves would have known their cities whereabouts a long time ago.

"You look startled." Gustavius observed the Elf.

"Well… no it's just that I had a friend once who was a Sarron."

"Was" The Spook spoke with its husky voice. "I sense he is still with you and many others too, it is strange for so many to follow one."

Eed felt slightly embarrassed that someone knew his secret, and sense that the Sarron must also know the shame that make the spirits taunt him, he turned his head looking out into the water feeling uncomfortable.

"No time to discuss such things please step aboard and I will formally introduce you to David."

Eed complied with the old man wishes and stepped onto the raft looking confused.

"David?"

"Yes David, meet Eed the elf." Gustavius smiled.

"But is it not a human name?"

"Yes the dwarves found it hard to pronounce my real name and so here, I am called David, or farthing, Gustavius calls me only David he has grown accustom to it."

"I see." Eed wondered how difficult a name could be to

pronounce.

The raft glided smoothly through the waters carrying the dwarf and the elf that stood silently holding onto the rails of the small boat to keep their footing steady.

The tall Alien being continued pushing the long stick like oar into the water, reaching the bottom aiding the raft to continue moving smoothly in the direction the old man needed them to go.

They rode silently for many minutes until other rafts began to appear in the mist, all dwarves poling slowly along and around the shelves. Some rafts were bigger than others being able to contain tables and chairs. There were rafts tied up to shelves while there owners sat at wooden desks reading books under dimly lit lamps and taking sips of some warm brew from rather large mugs. But the whole place was silent, no one made a sound, the only noises were the gentle sounds of poling oars, rippling water and the rafts that glided through it.

"How do they reach the books if they needed one from high up?" the elf whispered, Not wanting to make any sound loud enough to break the quiet ambiance that was all around.

"There are what you may call lifts, you ask for the book you wish and the lifts will take you to it, but do not ask me how it works only the Library knows."

It was the second time Gustavius had referred to the library as though it was a living entity; the dwarf's ways held a familiarity of someone once close to Eed but at the same time his ways were still strange.

They continued on until they reached a wide opening amongst the shelves that formed into a circle of shelves rather than rows. There were four paths that lay before them and the Spook David steered them to the right along the right waterway that continued with rows and rows of shelved books like the others before.

Moments past and Eed wondered if they would ever reach their destination. He began to think of how annoying it would be to come and find a book that one needed which happened to be at the furthest end of this place on the highest shelf. It would probably take them hours if not days in these slow floating rafts. He had become fidgety feeling confined and bored on this small slow raft and found more amusement at fidgeting with the sleeve of his garment and in doing so the Old man recognised his impatience.

"You know this place is only for Scholars of the arts and keepers of the truth. All here has learned that to find real truth one must first find real patience. Some here spend days looking for what they need, while others have been here for years. In here there is no concept of time. Nothing beyond this realm should interfere with patience."

"I am no Scholar why am I allowed to be here?" The old dwarf now had Eed's full attention.

"Because my friend you have the heart and the abilities to become a great leader, but first you must know truth."

"To many riddles dwarf I am starting to lose my faith in your proof though I believe there is nothing that could convince me that you have even spoken any truth to me."

"You are impatient, the truth will find those who wait for it, unfortunately you cannot, so we are rushing you to it. And my only hope is that it does not cause you too much distress."

"What do you mean?"

The old man would not divulge any more information, all he did was put his finger to his lips implying Eed to be silent. "Enough said." was his final words.

They rode on for a few more moments until they came to two great Pillars and between them was a thick Grey smoky cloud. The Spook slowed the raft to a stop. And all looked up at the two huge wide yellow Eyes that appeared in the smoky cloud. Eed took a step back to the back of the raft, showing a little fear and concern.

"It is a spirit," the elf said putting himself on guard.

"It is known as the gate keeper." David replied showing no fear of the thing before them.

The great yellow eyes peered down from a great height as though a great giant looking upon some ants.

"WHO GOES THERE?" The deep thunderous voice bellowed from the mist.

"It is I Gustavius, keeper of the temple and guardian of the truth old friend."

"AH I SEE SO IT IS, AND WHO TRAVELS WITH THEE?"

"The Liberian and a seeker of the truth" Gustavius shouted out.

"YOU ARE A WISE ONE AND YOUR JUDGEMENT OF PERONS HAS NEVER BEEN AT FAULT, YOU MAY PASS."

And as if someone had opened a window and a breeze passed through, the mist cleared up all around, and before them at what could possibly be the centre of a long high silver wall stood a great golden gate. That stood as high as any of the shelves, so high it was not possible for anyone to see where either the wall or the gate ended.

David began poling the raft towards the gate and as they moved smoothly forward the gate began to open inwards giving enough space for the raft to float through to the other side. A moment after they passed through the gate clanged shut sending small waves along the water rocking the small boat they travelled in, but not too much so that any of them lost their footing. It took only a few minutes for the waves to die down before Eed took the time to notice his environment. The place they had entered expanded far and wide but before them on the smallest of Islands stood a small building. Eed found himself amused at the thought of a building within a building, if in a building he really was.

The raft stopped at a wooden platform that was at the bottom of yet again some more stone steps that led up to the front door of the stone facility.

"Wait here for us" Gustavius, told David.

The old man stepped onto the platform and began climbing the steps. Eed did not ask but just followed looking around as he went. He looked up and found that the clouds had formed and opening here above the building and as if he were outside on a clear night the stars shone brightly high up in what appeared to be a night time sky. It was hard for Eed to understand, was he really looking at a night time sky within a building? It all had to be some kind of illusion did it not? He questioned his own logic.

Bright fire lit torches burned either side of the steps and above the door to what Eed believed to be a small house. He did not think to ask why there were fire lit torches when dim electrical lamps had lighted the rest of the library. The reason behind it he knew was of little importance. But what he was brought here to see undoubtedly would be the most important thing for him right now and he felt he had some Idea of what was hidden here.

The old man reached the door and raised his arms high as though he were worshipping a God. The doors opened making Eed realise that he had long been impressed already that this dwarf had kept his powers and practises of the old arts. It was something that Eed would have liked to practise himself.

They entered through the door into the house and it was no surprise to the elf that the building had only one room as it appeared very small from the outside. But at the centre of the brick clayed room was a gold alter of sorts, and on its centre with light beaming down on it from above stood a great book as large as Eed's waist to his feet.

"Do you know what this is?" Gustavius stood beside the book facing Eed with a stern face.

"Is it what I think it is?"

"I don't know; tell me what do you think it is?"

"Our people called it Swylegra"

"Yes the book of truths, so you know its power?" Gustavius answered.

"Yes it was our king Lithors, no lie could ever be written on its pages, our king wrote much in it."

"No your king wrote nothing in it. The book is magic to its own self, no being could put ink on its papers, the book writes itself. It is not known where the book came from but what is known is that the book held secrets, secrets that if were known by the wrong people could cause a worldwide catastrophe."

"My people need this book to bring unity, why do you not give it back and all this hatred will end." Eed pleaded

"Do not be fooled by what Maxius tells you, no earthbound being has ever been able to decipher the words written there in but king Lithor and he knew that this book could help lead the Greys to what they truly want, and that secret is why the Greys want this book. Maxius your king has other reasons why he wants it."

"He needs to bring unity all knows this, with the Greys help this book will bring peace and equality to all." Eed expressed

"Come on Eed, I thought you were one not to be blindly led. Think man think your own words not what others has put in your head."

"And what for then do you say my king needs this?" Eed raised his head and looked down the end of his nose at Gustavius, feeling arrogant enough to indicate to the dwarf that he will not believe a word he says.

"What most of your people did not know, is that after spending much time reading and touching the book the book became familiar with its new owner and began to write and document all the important events that happened in Lithors life. This is why your king wants this book, because Maxius knows what is written on the last few pages."

"And what is that?"

"Here take these gloves, the book cannot be physically touched or it may begin to write your story. And we do not know what will happen when its pages are full."

Eed took the black gloves and placed them on his hands.

"I will await you outside" Gustavius walked away from the altar and outside closing the door behind him.

Eed was almost scared to turn the books pages to read. He was scared of what was written. The book had many pages so he decided to open it at its centre but found the pages blank. He turned a few more pages back until he found words, the book had only half been written. He decided to read five pages from its end, and so he began each page making his heartbeat a little quicker as truths beyond his own beliefs were revealed.

11

Mountain Due's

Yatnahc had been driving the truck at a slow pace for more than an hour through the deadly mist also known by her people as the mist of the damned. She had left the vehicle on a number of occasions to hide their tracks, so it would be hard for those looking for her to follow through this dark murky dangerous wasteland. She checked often in the back of the truck to find the big cat visible and silent, it showed no aggression and sat silently as if waiting, waiting for us to clear this dark place I am sure she pondered.

Ponchi was silent also shaking almost continuously he was terrified. The rumours of this place had stuck with him since childhood; people went in here and never ever came out. Sitting in prayer he prayed that the gods would protect them.

Driving through this place was not an easy task, Yatnahc found it hard even to follow the map she had been given by the seer monk. Here it seemed as if it were dusk verging on night all the time though she knew it was not even mid day. The murky mist filled every inch of the land before them and all around them but as they travelled they could see mist to the right and left of them that was so thick it had become black, it made her concerned about nightfall. It was clearly marked on the map that these dark spots meant certain death, and at night all these land would look the same, she had decided that when night came they would have to stop. The map before her showed directions by landmarks such as the moon faced rock that was a huge stone with carvings of some ancient writing that had also the picture of the moon carved into it. Such landmarks were only recognisable when within two or three metres of the object thus continuing to make their journey carefully slow.

As she travelled the almost vanishing path that laid out before her they came to a dark overwhelming shape, at first she thought it was another place where the mist had gone black, but on closer inspection she could see it was a tree, in fact a black willow. She had never seen such a sight before, not even in the Zhao chen (the place they called the Black forest) she had been there before when she was a child and saw strange and wonderful things but nothing like this. The willow was not dead its leaf's flourished but all of its leaf's were as black as coal, it was as if it was a silhouette against the dark grey mist that was all around. The thought of anything surviving in this place was puzzling to her even something so obscure. She looked down on the map and it was clearly marked, (turn left at the black willow) she was moving for sure in the right direction, she turned left and continued driving slowly.

The mist's was a dead place; there were no sounds of life. Here it was silent not even the normal whisper of the wind made a sound; All that could be heard was the sound of the trucks engine. But when Yatnahc turned it off closing her eyes to rest, none of them had ever experienced such complete silence in their lives. Even Light was disturbed by the silence and groaned and roared from time to time to show her discomfort, it was as though some dark magic ruled here and each of them would feel a relief when and if they finally left the mist of the damned behind them.

They travelled all through what they realised as daylight

and rested during night fall, it was so dark at night that the camp fire they made using wood from parts of the truck gave off little light leaving them with little worries that anyone could spot their fire from a distance. Light came from the back of the truck on some of these nights and lay beside the fire absorbing the warmth that it gave off. Ponchi still worried about being in the presence of such a large cat stayed well away from her and sat close to Yatnahc as though she was his protector. It had been by their own estimate three days since they had entered the mists and it was starting to take its effect on them, The cat became more agitated in the back groaning and roaring thunderous roars from time to time. On the fifth day Ponchi began to lose it.

"I can't take this anymore!" he screamed in an almost high-pitched womanly voice.

"I want to see something further away than three feet in front of my face I need to get out of here!" he began to sob.

"Quiet man I need to focus"

"Focus!" he became angry almost manlier, Yatnahc admired this attitude rather than the whimpering coward she was used to.

"You don't even know where you're going you have got us lost; we are all as good as dead I will take my chances on my own."

He grabbed the door handle to jump out of the moving truck with illogical plans to run off into the mist and for a while it all made sense to him, this girl was not here to help him, she and the cat had caused his problems, why should he trust her? Maybe she planned to kill him, maybe she planned to kill herself but did not want to die alone, of course it made sense. Why it made sense he did not know. But it did, and he felt the need to get away, but before he could go any further Yatnahc hit him on the back of the neck and knocked him unconscious, he was getting hysterical and she knew the sleep would do him good.

On the 6th day Ponchi was thinking more clearly and felt stupid for how he had acted the previous day and apologised, but then it was Yatnahc that began to act strange. She had started to see things in the mist and admittedly she had seen them yesterday, but not as often as she was seeing them today. They rushed before the truck and dashed in and out of vision amongst the mist, they floated almost spirit like, dark ghostly shapes all around them, she became scared frightened for their lives sweating all over she stopped the truck.

"What are you doing?" Ponchi said as she exited the vehicle.

He followed her.

"Its Okay. I will protect you from them I will fight them don't worry"

Ponchi was worried she was sweating like she had a fever and acting strange

"Fight who? Yatnahc fight who?"

"Don't you see them they're everywhere are you blind?"

He realised then that Yatnahc was not feeling well; he put his arms around her.

"No I see nothing there is nothing there Yatnahc."

"But there is there is we are in danger I see them."

He had never seen her so unhinged since the moment he had met her.

"This is not you it's the mist it is playing tricks on you, on all of us it wants us to lose our minds, believe me please believe me there is nothing there, I need you Yatnahc without you thinking straight we have no hope of leaving this place."

She calmed down and seemed more at ease.

"Really you see nothing they're not real?" she questioned still a little unsure.

"Truly there is nothing" he assured her in a surprisingly

calming voice.

"Come back to the truck and rest awhile I will drive a short time I saw on the map that it is straight from here until we get to the lighting in the mist."

She agreed and went back to the truck almost instantly falling asleep.

Ponchi had been driving for over two hours, feeling terrified he did not think to wake Yatnahc and let her know about their recent dilemma. Yatnahc had consented to let him drive falling asleep almost immediately leaving Ponchi to follow the simple instructions that was on the map. The directions read:

Go forward five miles along the path until you reach the lighting in the mist; there will be four paths leading in four different directions.

It was marked clearly on the map that they were to take the second path to the left, but in fact Ponchi had not even reached that point, as he had been driving a long time now and had not reached any point of anything significant. To make matters worse the path before him had faded into the mist so he had stopped and exited the truck to have a closer look, assuming the mist had just got thicker making the path slightly harder to see, but on closer inspection this had not been the case, the path before them had disappeared, there was no longer any path or any clear sign of a man made road, all he could see was dirt and rocks there was rough ground ahead of them, He wisely thought it would be best if the turned around and retraced their movements in hopes of finding the paths or road believing that it was possible that he had missed them, but to his amazement there was no road or path behind them either.

"The mist has eaten the road," he whispered.

Sweat dripped from his forehead as the overwhelming sense of fear took root throughout his entire body.

"It does not want us to leave; the mist has eaten the

road." He kept mumbling these words under his breath over and over again trembling whilst in a state of shock he returned to the truck and continued to drive, in the direction he believed to be North West, but in truth he had no idea in which direction he was driving.

It had been a short while since Yatnahc awoke to find an almost crazy Ponchi driving them on an invisible road to nowhere, she had tried to get some sense out of him but all he kept mumbling was the mist had eaten the road. She knew then that they were lost and there was no sign of any road, she began to shout at him to stop the truck but he ignored her still mumbling. So she jumped over into his lap slamming her foot down on the breaks. The truck skidded a little then stopped, Ponchi did not react or do anything but mumble the same words that had started to make Yatnahc slightly irritated.

He let her guide him from the driver's seat out of the truck and around the vehicle and back into the passenger's seat, she was worried for him he was losing his mind if he had not already, a place she could have been if Ponchi had not made her realise what this place was doing to them, and how it was effecting their minds driving them to the edge of madness. She decided she would not let this happen to him, like her he just needed to rest and forget the worries of this place. She seated herself in the drivers' seat and thought for a few moments. "The compass" it came to her, there was a compass on the top of her knife that was given to her by Brother Fei before her departure.

Her mind wandered to him for a moment he was her best friend and mentor at the temple, he had taught her things the others would not. The memory came to her remembering how eager she was to take up this mission, to go out alone on this Adventure and now her mind longed for home, to be in the temple again with her brothers and sisters. She caught herself daydreaming and instantly put her mind in order whilst removing the blade from her boot. Unscrewing the top she revealed the compass that clearly showed the way northwest, their only hope now was that this place did not affect the magnetic works of the compass. She turned the engine back on and took a moment to look at her Human travelling companion who was staring wide eyed out of the window ahead of them still mumbling.

"We've got to get out of here" the words rang through her mind as she continued their journey driving in the direction the compass pointed out to be northwest.

It had been so long now that none of them could remember how many days or weeks ago it was when they had first entered the mist, they had all been surviving on the rations Ponchi had carried in his truck as Yatnahc small supply of food had diminished a long time ago. There was worry amongst them, the food they had left was too little to feed them all and they estimated it would last another day or so. It had been probably over a week ago when the last of the fuel canisters had run out and they did not recollect how many days it was when the truck ran out of fuel itself. It was in bad shape the tyres had worn and burst as the terrain was too rough for it, they continued on a short while before it gave up on them, forcing them to leave the truck behind and walk it on foot. The mist had not let up in anyway and Ponchi began to worry what the Cat would do when it realised there was little food left to eat in the sack that he carried. He stared back at the cat that walked so closely behind them and felt uneasy at the thought that the cat could attack him from behind and he would never see it coming. Yatnahc was focused on the compass and was sure it was leading them somewhere, it had been long overdue since they had seen any landmarks that were on the map and Ponchi believed that the compass was leading them all to their doom, still worried and frightened he tagged along beside Yatnahc like a small boy to his mother.

Light walked closely behind her new companions, hunger had crawled through every inch of her body making her weary, she had never known hunger like this before and in this place there was nothing to hunt. She had overheard Ponchi telling the Monk that their supplies were low and though the little snacks they had been feeding her had sustained the hunger for short moments it was clearly still not enough. The small driver looked back at her and all she could see was meat, had she turned that hungry that she would consider eating a human? The thought made her cringe and she shook her head as if to discard herself from the idea. There was a time when she was not the way she was now. Sometimes it was like another lifetime ago, unclear and distant while other times she could remember certain things clearly, the clearest memory she held was that of the old man and her true name Adnohr. He had been with her before she was what she is now but he does not recognise her, he does not understand what draws them together he does not even remember why their bond was forged. But she could in parts, but mostly the important parts, but she knew one day it would all become clear to her and most importantly the old man. She held on to these thoughts, the thoughts of the old man brought her comfort and helped her think less on food, they pushed on all three of them, they pushed on because there was nothing else they could do.

It had become difficult for the three of them to constantly head northwest. They found as they moved on the black mist became more frequent, and in some places went on for miles forcing them to change direction in order to navigate their way around the dark black places. It was on one of these occasions while they moved in the western direction (according to the compass) besides what could only be described as a Black wall of mist that they found hope. The line of the thick murky black smoke like substance was so straight it gave off the suspicion that something wanted it to be this way; some being of a sort had their hands in the making of this wall. It went on for miles and miles and they forced themselves to move along side it. Many hours they had walked and they were certain that night-time would fall soon, and while Yatnahc was considering camping down hope lit up the mist. There were flashes of light in the black mist northwest of them, making Yatnahc determined to move on. They walk west along the wall until they came to what they had been looking for, the lighting in the Mist and the roads spread out before them. It was the paths that had been described on the map and at last the long lost roads. There only dilemma was which road they would have come from had they not lost the road. Ponchi insisted that it would have been the road to the left of them it seemed to be heading south and it was that kind of direction they had come from. Yatnahc agreed and they pushed on taking the second road to the right from the south road. These were the important landmarks, the ones that showed them that they were going the right way, and further more according to the map they had not far to go before they came clear of the misty plains.

"Two miles it says here and we will be clear" Yatnahc said hopeful as they walked.

"I pray it is only two miles or I shall surely die, I can't go on much further, we have no food and I have been struggling to walk."

The monk knew there was truth to Ponchi's words, he had been struggling to walk for many miles now and it had been she herself that had encouraged him to keep moving to keep walking, he had stopped many times for the last few hours and would have been happy never to move again, she had noticed a difference in him, it seemed to her that he had lost his fear of this place, he had calmed and seem to have his wits about him for the first time since they had met. The monk could not tell if it was simply because he was too exhausted to even care about his own life, or he clearly realised that there is nothing to fear here but the black mist because nothing lived here nothing at all.

Following the map they continued their long journey. Complete darkness soon fell forcing them to camp down for the night, tired hungry and exhausted the three slept conserving what little energy they had left.

What they believed to be morning soon arrived, bringing themselves to their feet trying to shake off the chill of last dark they pushed on. They had had no campfire since they had lost the truck, and before then they had stripped it of most of its wood, so now when they slept they cuddled together under a large blanket that Ponchi had in his truck for cold nights. It was these nights that Ponchi was glad for the cat. Its fur offered some warmth and though he still feared her he wouldn't have minded if she killed him quick in his sleep. Many more hours past whilst they travelled and their pace had dramatically slowed forcing Yatnahc to the realisation that they would all die of starvation before they could find their way free of this place.

Ponchi had been a well fed man when she had first met him, and now he was next to skin and bone, even the cat had become very slim, and herself was the thinnest of them all. It was pure determination that kept her moving; determination to complete her task, the scroll had to be delivered the worlds fate may depend on it. They moved along the road slowly until they came to the end and found themselves at the bottom of what possibly could be a mountain.

"This is not on the map," Ponchi said wearily.

"Yes but according to the map we should have been clear of this place a long time ago, it's as if... "

"Go on, as if what?"

"It's as if these mist have spread further since this map was made, it's like it is growing."

"Heaven forbid if the world gets full of this mist but here anything is possible. So what do we do now go around it."

"We don't know how big it is, but we know we must get to the other side." Yatnahc said certain of what they must do.

"I don't know if I have the strength to climb."

"We must Ponchi we must."

Adnohr took off finding her way along a steep path that led up into the mountain, within moments she was gone from their sights.

"Has it abandoned us?" the small man inquired.

"Who knows" Was all Yatnahc replied before she too began to follow the path upwards with Ponchi trailing behind.

Yatnahc and Ponchi had been scrambling and crawling their way up the mountain, they had seen no sign of the cat and wondered how the creature had found its way up this Rocky steep mountain. Both had found it hard climbing, in some places they were forced to climb almost completely vertical cliff faces using their feet and hands grabbing onto the rough knots and crannies that the craggy surface mountain had to offer. On more than one occasion both of them had slipped and almost fell to their deaths. The Lack of food or water had taken its toll and as they climbed higher the only satisfaction for all their efforts was that the mist seemed to be thinning out the higher they made themselves go.

Now around them from time to time in odd places they saw vegetation, green plants were growing. Here the mist was not strong enough to effect life, as it had done below. Not caring for their own safety both at the brink of starvation scrabbled to whatever plants they could find tarring them from the mountainside and stuffing them in their mouths chewing very little. They ate like wild animals chewing on a carcass. But only there was no meat here it was green plants and none of them really knew what effect they would have on them. Almost immediately Ponchi felt sick and brought back up from the bowels of his stomach the plants that he had eaten. Shortly afterwards Yatnahc did the same. But this did not deter the two from eating the plants they found. They were dying from lack of food, thirst and exhaustion. Their lips had become dry and cracked, knowing their fate they knew their only hope was the juice the plants could provide, that was if it did not poison them first. Both crawled now along the slope, as the mountain became less steep. Time in this place had been pointless neither of them really knew how long they had been climbing, they crawled using every piece of energy they had left in their weak and tired bodies but Ponchi stopped and Yatnahc looked back to him to see why.

"I… can't… can't… go on." He barely managed to squeeze the words through his mouth.

"We… must." Yatnahc was tougher than the driver but as she said those words really knowing there was no point anymore. They had come as far as they were going to go, they had tried and failed and it would be here they would die. The monk crawled back to where Ponchi had stopped and lay beside him.

"Let's … rest a little." She struggled to speak.

Ponchi did not speak but nodded in agreement he was no fool, he could feel his body shutting down, he knew this rest would be one he would not awake from.

"This… was… different" Were Ponchi's last words before closing his eyes.

Yatnahc turned over onto her back and laid on the mountain slope looking upwards and outwards. She could see something through the thin mist, just a little higher but far away from the mountain that was under her. She could not quite make it out but it was large very large and black and it had to be floating. She thought for a moment that if she could get a little higher she would be able to see what it was, but sensibly resided to the fact that she had no energy left to move anywhere. She laid back staring out at the shape feeling the strong pull of tiredness. Her eyelids felt like someone had tied small weights to her lashes and she struggled to keep her eyelids open, but soon she succumbed to the overwhelming-ness of exhaustion. The black shape was the last thing she saw from the slope of the mountain.

Light, had left the others behind many hours ago, She knew none of them would survive a day without food or water and focused all her attention on finding these two things. She longed for the taste of meat and believed that the mountain heights would rise above the mist leaving open the possibility that vegetation could grow. And where there was green there was water and also mountain goats, birds and other animals of the likes. She intended to feed herself first and then bring back food for the others, fruit of anything she could carry in her mouth.

She had found a small crevice in the mountain and squeezed her way through. To her surprise she realised that beings had been here before. Artifacts covered in dust, filled the cave all around. Jars made of clay, painted and decorated with unique and detailed delicacy, grand statues of humans with swords standing bold like guardians lined up along the two sides of the cave walls. The dim light crept in through the Crevice illuminating parts of the walls lighting up the amazing artwork that covered every inch of the cave. The pictures seemed to be telling a story of many men battling a beast demonstrating the many deaths these people had suffered. She looked around the cave her sharp eyes penetrating through the dark as if she had small torches in her sockets instead of eyes. She was now aware of what this place was paying more attention to the rows and rows of bed like slabs that filled the centre of the cave, she realised that people had been wrapped up and placed here, some were more than likely just bones now but all had been mummified. This was a burial ground, and if all these bodies were here there had to be easier access to allow those who needed to bury their dead.

Light continued forwards and was not disappointed to find that she was right, she had found some steps that led upwards and without wasting time she began her ascent not knowing how long it would take her to reach the top.

She moved fast at first clambering the steps as though she was in a race, her run soon became a trot and hours later she found her trot had become a slow walk. Each step hurting her now, her muscles ached all over her body and nothing could express how relieved she was when she finally reached the top. Taking a short rest she realised that all that stood in her way was a wooden door, painted on the inside like the paintings in the cave below. Using her head she pushed against it gently and was not surprised that it was locked. Walking back a few paces she ran at the door leaping in the air throwing her mighty body weight against it. The door bent outwards some, but did not break leaving the cat to fall back on the ground bruised and hurting. She would not give up now she had not come all this way for nothing, her companions needed her and there was no time to go back and begin climbing this mountain again. She picked herself up and walked further away from the door and this time she would use all the energy she could muster speeding at the door as fast as her legs could carry her, leaping high she roared out loud as her body came crashing through the wooden exit shattering the door to pieces. Almost instantly she found herself blinded by the bright light of the outside un-misty world, landing on all four paws she squinted. It had been a long time since she had seen real daylight and she knew she had made it high above the mist. The large cat made herself comfortable and laid awhile on the ground stretched out like a cat on a rug, adjusting her eyes and resting, listening to the sweet sounds of the many birds that flew around or were sitting in the many trees that was all around her. It appeared that she was in a mountain forest and her mind was working on a plan to capture a bird in her jaws.

She had spent the next hour trying to creep up on birds using every hunting trick she could possibly think of but her efforts led to no avail. The birds were too quick and though she made herself invisible, they still sensed that she was there. After many tries she decided on one final attempt before trying to find some water or some prey that walked on all fours and had no wings. She hid herself in a bush and sat patiently still like a statue. Not moving even a fraction she controlled her breathing leaving very little margin of error for the birds to detect her presence. She had picked a good spot, small nuts of a strange kind had fell from some of the trees and laid on the ground all around the bush were she waited patiently under the cover of her amazing skill to make herself unseen. There was no doubt in her mind that a bird would find this ideal place to feed.

It had been around thirty minutes and no bird had come close enough for her to make her move, hope was diminishing fast and hunger was making her impatient. She almost gave up on the idea contemplating finding water instead; this place flourished with green and it was obvious there was a stream or something of the likes nearby. Just as she moved slightly, ready to de-cloak and expose her position, trotting through the forest nearby came a large boar. The animal stopped in its tracks, it had sensed something and considered it to be dangerous. Adnohr heart began to pound; this was her chance to eat well, adrenaline pumped through her veins as she watched the pig like creature move slowly closer and closer to her position.

The cat dug her claws slowly into the earth leaning her body weight back on to high hind legs ready to pounce. Her eyes now were locked on the boar; even the bird that had landed on the bush now so close to her head did not make her shift her focus. Her mouth began to drool like a starving child anxious to bite into a big red juicy apple. The boar came closer and stopped once more; it was too late it knew it had already made its last mistake. Before the tusked pig could fully turn around and bolt, like a flash the large leopard came leaping from the bush beside it digging its claws into its back slicing its side open like a butcher with his carving knife. Adnohr slammed her mighty jaws around the back of the pig's neck, blood poured from the boar as it kicked frantically with the last breaths of life as the great leopard swung it around in its jaws like a wild dog tearing a rag doll apart. The boar's neck snapped and the creature stopped kicking. Adnohr Light now tore into the large boar with her great jaws eating as much as she could. She had long needed this food and it will help sustain her a good while longer. Blood dripped from her mouth; she had become accustomed in the past to eating cooked meat that the old man had made for her. She would hunt and he would cook for the both of them, but this day the taste of blood and raw flesh had never before tasted so good.

"... .shall we do with her?" A man was speaking.

"Well we can't turn back."

"I be thinking lads you be all missing the point." It was the captain.

Katie stood with her ears pressed against the metal wall listening to the men speak in the other room. She had woken to find herself in a bed baffled of how she had gotten there. She remembered everything up unto the point she watched Xela and the others fighting against the metal monsters that had boarded the ship and now it was her that was being discussed, why? And what happened to the monsters she thought, thinking that they would be a better topic to be discussed.

"What point is that Captain?" someone else had said.

"The girl did show us a strange thing and further more we be owing her our lives."

The captain's statement had stunned the young girl. They owed her their lives how why? She listened curiously.

"Well we have to decide what is to be done with her." It was Knarf Katie knew his voice anywhere.

From there they all began to debate in turn or over each other, it was suggested that some of the crew thought her to be unnatural while others were frightened. It was all too much for Katie to take in or even understand. She grabbed a blanket from the bed and wrapped it tight around herself, then left the room heading for the main deck for some fresh sea air.

Katie turned the metal circle that opened the door and stepped outside. The sun was going down and far in the distance of the red sky she could see fire clouds sparkling and lighting up the heavens. They had sailed beyond the seas of England escaping the hot fires of burning month leaving behind her home and her people leaving her to wonder if she would ever get to see Dover again. Her mother was gone there was no family there or even here who would look out for her? These thoughts made her heart sadden leaving no room to think on what the men had said about her down below, her mind was with her mother now and a tear rolled down her cheek. Memories of happy times they had together came in flashes, visions of herself with her mother sitting beside a fire on the beech singing songs of old and eating warm apple pies that her mother had baked with Apples she often took from the apple tree they grew on the shallows farm, though she knew it was forbidden she risked it so her and her Katie could have those special nights. Her mother had been the one to inspire her to be adventurous without knowing it, many nights she sat and told Katie stories wondrous stories of the little boy named Peter. She had told Katie that they had been passed down through generations to remind adults of the child within and so children would learn to accept a loss of a loved one. "After all" Katie could almost hear her mother's voice on a breeze drifting by. "Death would be the greatest adventure."

The young girl prayed that her mother was on such an adventure, the best adventure anyone could imagine she tried to smile at the thought but only found more tears.

"Don't be sad young one."

Katie turned to find the dwarf behind her.

"I'm sorry I just feel a little… " she began to sob.

"It's ok come sit with us."

Vlad put his arms around her, he would have let her rest her head on his shoulders but she would have to bend down and it would be difficult to walk in such a manner, so he just comforted her as they walked to the stern of the ship. As they walked men were still rushing around repairing damages as best they could, the battle with the drones had made a mess causing damages to vital parts of the ship which the captain had ordered his men to fix immediately. Upon reaching the stern Katie was pleased to find Xela who was sitting beside Leron on a bench. Instantly Katie left the arms of the dwarf jumping into the arms of Xela hugging him tight, she felt and odd feeling like she had known him along time and she knew him well and he her, there was no understanding to the feeling, she did not know how or why but there was something unsaid between them and he had saved her twice now.

"Thank you for helping me I knew you would come."

Xela did not speak; he just stared into her eyes.

"There is no words to be heard from him young lady, he is mute," Leron said.

"He can speak I heard him."

"What" Both Fairrien and Dwarf said surprised?

"When?" Vlad asked.

"Before you came, before I saw any of you I saw him in a dream and he spoke to me."

"I am sorry but that was only a dream," Vlad said certain of himself "one I am sure you had of someone else that you have confused with him."

"No it was him"

Katie placed her hand on his face and looked back into his eyes and for a moment she felt like she could feel and hear his thoughts, it were as though they were connected she found herself continuing to speak.

"He is not from this time; this era is new to him."

"What do you mean?" Leron became curious.

"He feels, or felt like he is, was asleep and this is a dream. He believes or believed that you're not we're not real."

"Ha Ha" Vlad almost keeled over with laughter "Preposterous how could she know such things" Though he found it amusing he did not feel that either Leron or himself should entertain the idea of this young girls game.

"I don't know but she is right."

Leron and Vlad stood with their jaws wide open in shock. It had been Xela that had spoken.

"But it is not a dream is it? It's all real a dwarf a fairy the creatures that attacked us, and you the special girl whom I feel I have vowed to protect. It's all real isn't it?"

The large cat watched from amongst the trees as five pale skinned tribal men with painted faces wearing little clothing lifted her companions from the ground and carried them away. At first she was ready to pounce warning them to stay away, but she realised that they may help them in ways she could not. Making herself Invisible she followed them closely not willing to allow any harm to come to the monk and the driver, she followed them past trees and through bushes moving upwards for what seemed around a mile or two until the ground began to level and the tribal men carrying her companions stepped out into a clearing that led down into a valley where a community of people had made their homes. Light sat amongst the trees and watched. It was a beautiful place, surrounded by the simplicities of mother earth.

The homes were made from timber and large leaf's weaved together to make roofs. A stream ran alongside their village and a half naked village Shepherd watched over his herd of mountain goats beside it while they grazed and drank from the stream. Most women wore long thin gowns of either brown or green but showed no skin like the men who seemed more primitive in their attire than the women. The people gathered around the men who had returned home carrying Ponchi and Yatnahc, they were curious and Light knew it was very likely that they had not seen any other people apart from their own kind in these mountains, and such an event would arouse interest and change to their routine life. Light watched curiously as a tall man more primitive than the rest wearing a head garment made from the head of a boar, pushed his way through the crowd. The people backed away from him, this indicated that this man had power here. He shouted something in a language unknown to Light making the people disbursed, turning his attention back to the men who were still carrying Ponchi and Yatnahc he began to speak calmly, then shortly after the boar headed man called to some of the women and they came and took the monk and the driver from the men carrying them in to one of the timber made homes.

The tall cat stayed close, she wondered into the village undetected at night making sure her friend's were safe and stealing a goat she retreated back to the trees, she would stay around for a week or so making sure her friends were well before she would continue her journey even if that meant she continued alone.

Yatnahc had started to regain her strength; it had been three days since she awoke to find herself in this place. She had no idea who these people were but they came to her and Ponchi often caring for them the best they could. The women had bathed them fed them and gave them clean garments and constantly provided them with lots of fluids, she had no idea why these people would help them and neither did she understand their language, they just came and tended to them then left and for their kindness she was grateful but unfortunately Ponchi was still not well. He had become ill with a sickness that did not seem to be improving no matter what medicines these people gave him. It was hard for Yatnahc, on some days whilst speaking with him he seemed not to know whom she was talking about people and places she did not know or had never seen. Sweat covered his body as the fever became worse, he continuously mumbled in his sleep and there was nothing that could calm him but pure exhaustion when he became hysterical in the night. Yatnahc felt bad, it had been her that had brought the poor man into this mess, she had taken him away from his life and now if he were to die? She did not dare to think he would get well he will be better she convinced herself. It was not his destiny to die she knew this, they had important things to do and he would help her, it was fate that had brought them together for this reason fate would not let him die not this day and not this way.

On the fifth day Ponchi had a moment of clarity calling for Yatnahc, he knew who she was and his mind seem well, she sat with him and he laid his head on her lap, he was finding it hard to breath but he spoke never the less.

"Promise me Yatnahc... promise me... that if I do not make it you will help... help my people get food and stock."

"I will"

"No" he grabbed her hand firmly "Promise me"

"Yes I promise" Yatnahc answered and with that Ponchi took his last breath.

He had died with his head on the monks lap eyes wide open, she moved her hands over his face closing his eyes as tears rolled down her cheeks, he had died here in an unknown land and to her it was her fault and there was no forgiveness to oneself.

They buried Ponchi on a mound not far from the village; the people had been kind and performed a ritual ceremony as if he had been one of their own, the women bathed his body in scented water then whilst chanting some kind of prayer they painted symbols of a strange kind upon his body, once they had finished they massaged or rubbed an oily substance over every inch of him, then singing in wonderful harmony they wrapped him in yellow dyed cotton that had been dipped into some kind of think gooey opaque liquid making Ponchi completely mummified. It was at the ceremony that one of the women spoke to her in English. English was Yatnahc second language, her first was both Cantonese and a Tibetan dialect called Lhasa. Leong a family friend that had raised her after her parents had died had told her that her family on her father's side were originally from China from a place called Canton that no longer existed. But it was necessary once for all to speak English, as it was believed it was the universal language of the world and so it was a tradition that all in the family should learn it and this tradition had been passed to her. But it had been a long time since Yatnahc had found the need to speak English and felt a little rusty, but clearly not as rusty as the young tribal girl that now spoke to her.

"I am Maya, understand do you English?"

"Yes I speak English" She was pleased at last to be able to communicate with someone here though she wished it was happier circumstances.

"My English is not so good I am... err am one of two here who speaks it."

"It is good that we can speak, it is a sad time for me." Yatnahc explained.

"I offer from my people and me our errr sadness at the friend of your loss."

"Thank you." Yatnahc understood what she had meant to say.

Maya went onto explain the ceremony the best she could in English, Yatnahc understood that first the body was cleansed to show purity to the spirits, the oil they had massaged over Ponchi was scented with the essence of a flower they called Aquilegia, which they believed was the favourite scented flower of their gods. The symbol they had painted on him the girl explained would ward off evil spirits who often came to claim the souls of the dead. They had mummified him to maintain his body, as they believed that in the new world the dead would return and if there is no vessel the soul would be lost forever.

Yatnahc watched as the men entered wearing the paint of the dead, covered in symbols similar to those they had painted on Ponchi they picked up her companion who had been laid on a wooden slate that had carved handles and carried him out of the shack. The monk had asked Maya why the men had the marking like those they had put on Ponchi, Maya explained that this would protect them from bad spirits that lingered around the dead, Yatnahc, Maya and the women that tended to the body followed behind the men. The rest of the villagers awaited outside playing drums and chanting strange words and all followed behind the body that was carried up onto a mound away from the village, there awaiting was a hole already dug and at the bottom they had placed some kind of dark mud, Ponchi was lowered slowly into the grave and Yatnahc cried as she said her last goodbyes to her companion and friend.

    The following night Yatnahc laid unable to sleep in her hay made bed in the shack that she once shared with Ponchi, she wonder where the cat had got to, she was better now and soon she would have to make preparations to continue her journey hoping the tribal people would provide her with provisions. The tribe were a strange people, Maya had told her that their people are called the Yarazk which meant hard to break they had once lived on the grounds below the mountains many years ago, so long that only the oldest of their people remembered. But the mist came from China; Yatnahc had not been surprised to find that they had passed way beyond the borders of China but did not expect that the mist had carried itself so far. They had passed into Kazakhstan. Mayas people had once lived further east but the mist spread further and further over the years bringing with it a darker mist of death that had killed many of their people. The strong survived and climbed this mountain Maya informed her and they were pleased to find that the mist did not reach above their new found land, so it was decided that they would stay here believing that the mist would one day cover the whole world and only those that lived above it would survive. Yatnahc had asked Maya did she know what caused the mist.

    "Yes all here knows Mist black rock it comes."

    "Black rock what do you mean?"

    "Black rock that fly shows you me."

    Maya had took Yatnahc late yesterday afternoon to a high spot far from the village and they sat on a hill and watched the flying black rock, she had seen it before, the day they had climbed the mountain, it was the dark shape she had seen in the mist but now she could clearly see that it was some type of flying craft, one like she had never heard of before, it was a slick shiny black and triangle in shape with no visible windows or burning engine. It hovered high up in the distance making it hard for Yatnahc to work out how big it really was, its only purpose seemed to be just for making the mist which continuously came from the bottom of the ship polluting all the lands below. It all meant something, the scroll she carried, the black ship she already knew something bad was happening but she had no idea how bad things were going to get. Laying in the hut she pondered over the all these things including the words Maya had said to her earlier that day, "Today you must prepare." Prepare for what? She had asked but Maya refused to reply and now it was late, very late she had slept little and the sun would rise in less than two hours. Turning over and closing her eyes she tried to force herself to sleep, but when she found she could not she opened her eyes to find many men standing around her bed holding her at spear point.

"What's the meaning of this?"

A female entered the hut carrying a burning torch, it was Maya.

"We helped you now you do to help us come."

The monk girl let herself be led from her bed and outside where the whole Village awaited. They led her to the centre of the village where they had prepared a large circle of burning spears, which illuminated the circles centre. They forced her into the centre while the entire village stood around the outside of the circle as if awaiting a show.

"What help do you want from me?" Yatnahc shouted to Maya.

Maya stood inside the circle.

"You have said a warrior you is first prove this and all we will tell."

"Prove? How?"

"Our people came from east of these mountains in a time that once was, some eer ... Traditions we have kept, Fight will you are best warriors."

The tribal leader sat high on a special made throne that rose outside and high above the circle giving him the best view of the Monk and Maya below. He shouted out in his strange tongue and Maya left the circle leaving Yatnahc on her own. All fell silent, not a sound was made but the fast movement of a pair of feet picked up by Yatnahc sharp hearing. They were coming from behind her and closing in on her position, she did not turn or move an inch, she just waited, waited until she heard the feet that was now close to her leave the ground. It was at that moment that the monk fell back onto the ground lifting one foot high into the air placing her foot in the groin of the man that had attacked her with a flying kick. He dropped, rolled over and forced himself back to his feet showing excruciating pain only in his face. Yatnahc too was back on her feet.

The painted skin attacker took a deep breath and breathed out loudly as if composing himself then made his stance. It was Eagle fist, this stance had surprised her making her wonder how anyone in such a tribe could know this form of kung fu that had been lost to all for years except Shaolin, but she had little time to think, he moved and he was upon her instantly attacking the head and legs Simultaneously, Yatnahc was fast blocking his attacks with ease almost playing with him, drawing him in making him believe he had the advantage, his style was good and he was a great fighter but not good enough, the Shaolin girl waited for the next strike to her head and rather than stepping backwards she side stepped moving her head only inches away from the strike pushing her attackers striking arm down with her right hand while she chopped him in the throat with her left. Gasping for air he bent down, raising her knee fast and hard Yatnahc made contact with his head knocking him flat on his back and out cold.

There was stillness for a moment as if all was shock by the quick defeat of their warrior, the Peoples leader from his high throne shouted out to his people and as if complying with his words a long wooden pole was thrown to her and drums began to play. Yatnahc caught the pole firmly in one hand spinning it around in one motion she dug the pole into the earth to the right of her and stood tall holding it as if demonstrating her good posture. Two more painted men enter the circle carrying poles also, moving one to the right and the other to the left they attacked the Monk girl from both sides, but Yatnahc was a truly talented fighter, she dodged and moved around them almost dancing using the pole as an extension of her arm she blocked the deadly strikes of their attacks. These men were good she thought, great even but she had a hidden talent they had not seen yet one she would only use if she felt it was necessary. The three continued striking and counter striking looking to gain the advantage over the other, the two men worked together like one unit as if they had one mind knowing where and when to striking in unison with the other. "How had they come to learn this Kung fu?" The thought kept running through her mind.

She blocked the strike of the man to the left of her with her pole then spinning around low she swept at the feet of the other who jumped her pole as if he were expecting it, but her strike at his feet was a decoy still continuing in the motion she completed a full spin hitting the feet of the man to her left tripping him over continuing to spin but raising up high onto her feet she struck the man on the right clean in his head knocking him backwards, stopping her spin she quickly turned back to the man she had tripped who had flipped himself back onto his feet, she moved fast and kicked him hard in his chest lifting him off the ground he flew back breaking some burning spears and landing in the crowd he did not get back up.

The people, shocked at the power of her kick, stopped the drums while the man she had knocked hard in the head attacked her in anger charging and striking his pole down on her, The monk caught the pole as it came down with her right hand and dropping her own pole from her left she used her left elbow to break her attackers pole, grabbing hold of both parts of the broken pole she spun around ripping the part that was still in her attackers hand away from him leaving her with two sticks, he faced her and she hit him repeatedly in his chest like she was beating some drums and finishing him with one more final blow to his head putting him out of action, it was a hard strike and she hoped she had not killed him, as he lay motionless on his back.

"Yetki, Yetki!" Their leader shouted.

The drums began again and five men entered the broken circle with swords attacking charging at her instantly, she dodged the first mans sword and using her whole arm she hit the next man in his neck relieving him of his sword she stood and defended herself against the four men that were still standing.

Light had been asleep resting beside a tree up in the hill in the woodlands when the drums began to play. She had eaten well that day stealing another goat from the villagers herd, it had taken a moment while stirring before she awoke fully and stood casually peering from the trees into the valley, but when her sharp eyes detected Yatnahc defending herself against some tribal men, instantly she was moving fast on her feet becoming invisible as she went she raced down into the valley as fast as she could.

Yatnahc was in her element, her greatest skills as a warrior was with a sword. She had exceeded all the other students at the temple when it came to sword techniques and styles and she had mastered every one of them. So much that the Abbott had given her a title to teach the other students the techniques she had learned and had created herself, She was called Mistress Wind sword because her blade was so swift that one would never see when it would cut but would only feel it. The four sword men that attacked were incredible swords men, their skills were equal to most students at Shaolin, and being four great warriors she knew this fight would not be easy. She deflected strikes and countered and moved quickly and swiftly around and between her attackers, leaping when necessary and flowing with perfect swordsmanship she became like a branch in the wind bending but was certain not to break. The people of the village had never before seen such a display of skill and as the drums played they stood in awe at the fighters before them.

Yatnahc had found a gap in one of their defences and slipping under two swords and leaning back inches away from the third she reached the forth man blocking another blow from the man to the right of her with her sword she kicked the man to the left and while he fell back she power punched the forth man in his chest before he could bring his sword down on her. The punch was so hard he flew back as if a great wind had hit him causing him to tumble backwards he rolled in the dirt until he came to a stop. He lifted himself only a little as if he intended to get right back up but then fell face first into the dirt. It was at this point one of the swordsmen screamed out in terror as blood poured from his back. The drums stopped no one had seen a sword strike him but then standing before Yatnahc was a great Cat that had appeared from nowhere. The sword men immediately forgot about Yatnahc and attacked the beast that they believed to be evil.

"Nooo" The monk shouted and with one movement of

her arm the weapons of the men flew from their grasps over to Yatnahc and Landed at her feet.

Light moved to attack.

"Cat be still" she shouted and Light complied.

Both the magical cat and the powers that the monk girl had displayed took the people back. She had commanded the weapons of her attackers to obey her and this they had never seen before. There was a silence as the great leader of their village climbed down from his throne, and walked slowly towards the Monk and the Cat, when he reached within a yard of them he knelt down on his knees and bowed his head chanting. The villagers took their lead from their leader and they too went down on their knees and bowed, chanting or praying to her as though she was a God.

12

The Pirates of the Dead Seas

The ship sailed leaving England far behind so far that not even its burning skies were in view. The captain adjusted his course heading southeast their new destination Belgium, as they sailed calmness fell upon the crew while they continued their duties and repairs.

Vlad and Leron had spent the last hour throwing questions at Xela trying to understand who and what he was, the man they thought mute now had a voice but still seemed reluctant to use it. Though he was young looking Xela spoke with a deep warm voice of a man while Katie sat silently on his lap cuddling him as he answered very little of the questions that the Fairrien and dwarf asked of him. It was as if he had become accustomed to not saying a word, and the young girl could tell that he was already regretting that he ever spoke.

"Where are you from are you human, where do you get such speed and strength, what's your name." Question after question Leron and Vlad went on not even giving the poor man time to answer all of what they had asked.

"Stop it you two!" Katie raised her voice she had enough of their behaviour.

"Stop what?" the dwarf look sheepish like he had no

idea what she meant.

"You know what." She gave them both a stern look before she spoke again. "The first time he speaks to you, you want to interrogate him like he had committed some kind of crime."

"She is right Vlad we have been wrong," he turned to Xela "please tell us what you would like in your own time, you are our companion and friend and we have fought battles together forgive us for being so rude." Leron was sincere.

"I'll tell you what I can remember."

"Do you not remember things?" Katie was curious now.

"I don't remember much of anything, just the things that comes to me in vision and dreams"

"And your name may I ask, do you remember this?"

"No I do not remember, I have amnesia but I do remember the year is, was 2010 and I know this is not my time."

"So you are telling us that you are over two hundred years old and you are from the time of men, before the world is what it is now, do you remember any of it? Like what it was like then?" Katie was excited, a man from the past, he could tell her things that no one else could from the days of legends

"Yea I remember some of it."

"I remember what it was like; I have lived many more years." Vlad seemed a little jealous.

"Yes Vladlin you and I both but neither of us lived amongst the land of men, he has and there is knowledge in him that neither you nor me could know."

"The wisdom of Fairriens" The dwarf said under his breath. "Okay. I understand" he rose to his feet. "I am going to see what food I can rustle up on this boat."

"Ship" Leron corrected him.

"Does a boat not carry people and float on water?"

"Yes dwarf it does" Leron answered.

"Then I say we are on a boat, ship boat they are the same thing to me."

The dwarf walked off to find the gully mumbling to himself about the arrogance of Fairriens leaving Katie, Leron and Xela sitting at the stern of the ship gazing out at the sea talking about days of old and the great buildings of men.

It was not long before the captain sighted land. It was Belgium and knowing that the Belgium harbour was the base of yet another Elfin station he knew there was no possibility of them docking there. But around seven miles along the coast past the Belgium harbour the captain knew of a small secret port he had used before. It was run by a group of the most dangerous men that sailed the seas. The harbour was big enough to dock only eight ships and a few fishing boats, it was here that smugglers and people fleeing oppression came to find their way across the sea. If one had the right amount of silver they could catch a ride on either the Argol or the Sharron, two ships that were once originally cargo ships but were armed now with two 114 mm Mk 8 Mod 0 guns for bombardment and scaring boats and ships to stop or be destroyed. And four rotating high-powered turret machine guns at the bow, stern, port and starboard sides of each ship so the men that sailed the beasts could gun down any beings that did not comply to their wishes, These were Pirates ships ones that the Captain himself helped to arm.

The English Channel often had small boats containing supplies going back and forth between England and other European countries. The pirates lived off robbing such ships, most were men working for the government and few were people with their own boats risking the seas to travel to a new life with hopes to finding a better land. But very few slipped past the pirates and the only way to avoid them was to sail the dark waters and no one did this but the

Orcus as it was well known that those waters were home to leviathans and Krakens, though the clean waters were not always safe from such creatures.

The Argol and the Sharron were the two fastest cargo ships that ever sailed. They had once belonged to the United States naval forces before the war had started.

The captain spoke into a radio and ordered all stop down to the engine room. He had steered the ship between two huge pillars that led the way to some kind of cove. As the ship glided silently and swiftly through the waters all the crew fell silent while the new comers found their way to the bow to see where they were heading. Knarf and a few of the others spotted some men high up on the cliff. They were lookouts most probably sending word up ahead of the approaching ship. The captain shouted out from the bridge to a crewmember down beside the mast. "Signal" he had said and immediately the British flag that the captain insisted he sailed with was lowered and hoisted up in its place was the cross bones and skull pirate flag that sailed the seas on every pirate ship throughout the centuries. The captain was not and had never been a pirate, but this flag was a signal that allowed any ship to pass into the secret harbour where the captain had planned to dock.

They sailed on slowly for at least another mile. Knarf could not help but notice how well armed these people were. Before they sailed through the great archway into the wide-open space of water that had a small armada of ships all docked, he paid particular attention to the multiple large cannons that peeped out of holes all over and on top of the cliff walls that ran along both sides of the narrow canal they drifted through to reach the port, and more to his surprise after they had passed through the archway a great iron gate began to close behind them powered by great chains that went around a great iron cog and then on to a large handle that was being turned by two gigantic creatures. They stood side by side wrapped up in heavy chains linked to great metal cuffs that was attached to both their hands and feet and was fixed firmly in the wall stopping the great muscular creatures from moving far from their post. The cog they turned was so big that no human could power it, the question still remain of how these creatures were caught and forced into labour, their kind were the strong arm of the Elfin and Orcus forces these creatures were evil and worked alongside all that was dark, if they were ever freed Knarf knew they would destroy this place and all that was in it, ogres were a dangerous breed for anyone to attempt to keep as a pet.

The captain stood proud on the bridge looking on to his welcoming committee that consisted of around twenty to thirty armed men, armed with an assortment of rifles hand guns and a few machine guns, In the mist of these men stood Tony blackheart Gold, also known as Captain Blackheart. He captained the famous ship called the Sharron that helped maintain his reputation as one of the two most feared men that ruled and governed this harbour. He stood like a giant amongst his own men, tall and muscular wearing only a black vest and cut short green trousers his dark brown skin and his half bleached short woolly hair, a strange patterned black tattoo covered the left side of his face and made him appear to Xela as a giant African warrior.

The ship was anchored and docked at the first pier. Leron and Vlad, Kir, Knarf, Zepol and Heffer all armed accompanied the captain along the pier to where the group of men stood, walking through the crowd of pirates came Blackheart carrying a sawn off shotgun he stopped when he stood before the captain. No one spoke and a silence fell throughout the docks. Both men stared at each other like old enemies about to do battle. Knarf became uncomfortable.

"I don't like this" her whispered to Kir who was beside him. "Get ready"

The shallows soldiers were ready to draw arms while Knarf slowly reached for his side arm when Blackheart spoke.

"You dare come back here Mr Gill, I should gut you like a fish."

"What makes you be thinking I would not be gutting you first like a fish?"

Everyone was tense Knarf now had his hand on his gun and could see Leron and the others poised for battle.

"Because" blackheart replied, "I don't think you would know how to gut a fish as big as me".

Both men were silent once again but for only a moment before they both roared with laughter and embraced each other. Everyone else looked confused.

"It has been a long time my friend come bring your men we will eat and drink and be merry for it is not often we are visited by the great captain Gill."

"Aye it's been awhile there Tony."

Black heart went serious.

"Hey it's Blackheart when the men are around."

"Oh sorry me mind is forgetful."

They continued to laugh joke and chat as the captain and blackheart walked off towards a tavern. Leron Knarf and the others followed a bit bemused by the two captain's behaviour, leaving Xela Katie and Navi with the ship's crew watching them from the grandest ship at the docks.

The Port fellow Tavern was the only bar on the harbour, Knarf took note on how well these people had developed this small area, there was over a hundred or so homes and shacks riddle throughout the caves and amongst the cliffs making it difficult for any wide eyed flying crafts that may pass over to find them, these homes made some kind of small community for its residents. There was even a marketplace where one could trade sell or buy goods. It was a busy place there were people moving around working or boarding small fishing boats everyone seemed to have something to do making Knarf realise how organised these people were. The shallows soldiers though they appreciated the efficiency of this place in such difficult times still did not like or trust the looks of one person that crossed their paths.

They entered what only could be described as the busiest filthiest foul smelling tavern that anyone of them had ever the misfortune of seeing. Though it were a large building the tavern was still way overcrowded, filled with bearded dirty sweating men, most that had scars or mutilated in some way, with fierce looks it was obvious that these men were of the roughest kind, drinking ale and fighting and feeling up that half naked barmaids while they served drinks, even prostitutes did their business here, as the group entered a few of the black teeth women approached Leron and Knarf.

"A Copper piece or a loaf of bread for a fuck gov, you look wealthy enough, come on Ill make you nice an warm and you can fondle me all you please, he he." She grinned showing her almost all rotten teeth.

"Get out of here" Blackheart roared as he pushed one of the girls to the floor with such force she bowled over two rough men who fell and dropped their mugs. They got to their feet quick to start trouble with whoever had caused this distress but stopped still when they realised it was Blackheart.

"If my guests want women they would have one of my clean girls not you syphilis carrying scum."

The tavern was silent while Blackheart raised his voice.

"Anymore disturbances from you whores will result in your deaths. Now leave my guests and be gone."

"Sorry sorry please forgive me" the filthy girl picked

herself up and ran off into the crowd of men.

"Barmaid bring some ale for me and my guests and some wild boar, today we will dine like kings."

Seeing that the trouble was over the rowdy crowd continued whatever they were doing and the sound of laughter and fighting and good old drunken cheer flooded every corner of the inn.

The barmaids scurried around as quick as they could to fulfil the dark giants orders, while Blackheart and four of his men, Captain gill and the rest seated themselves at the biggest table in the tavern, the Ale was brought to them almost as soon as they found themselves comfortable in their seats. Zepol took a gulp of his ale and was truly surprised that such a dark dirty place as this could produce such great tasting ale.

"Hey it's good huh" The dark giant noticed the surprise on Zepol's face.

"Yes it is very good."

"We acquired barrels and barrels of it from a merchant ship supplying stock for the Elfin stations in France, it is fair to say that ship never made it Ha ha ha " he laughed and his men laughed with him.

"I am surprised that your partner in crime is not with us." The captain inquired.

"Paul you mean, that fool does his own thing these days, I swear he is getting soft, it's like he can't stomach the work we do anymore always talking about a better community Huh fool."

"There be nothing wrong thinking better for your people."

"People, my people all me and my men care about is money and loot, that's the life of a Pirate everyone knows that if we start thinking of others it would get us killed."

"Blackheart you're a Philosopher to yourself and your teachings I care not to understand, but while I be having your attention a little information I be seeking."

No one spoke when the barmaid came over and presented two large roasted boar and placed them on the table with huge bowls of roast potato and a jug of gravy. Immediately the men tucked in cutting chunks of meat off the boars with the knives they carried and scuffing down their food like they had not eaten in days, the stench of the inn was easily ignored as the aroma of their food filled the nostrils with moments of a better smelling place.

"What. Info_ you... are wanting?"

The dark giant mouth was filled with food as he spoke.

"We be tracking a group of dem Orcus that be travellin wid prisoners and probably a faceless one. They came across the seas from England maybe two weeks ago."

He had taken it upon himself to help the small man and his friends as much as he could their escape from the shallows had been down to the help from the dwarf and his friends and now the captain felt it was time to repay the favour.

"You should be asking bullet hole Paul."

"Asking me what?"

Everyone looked up from their plates of food to find a dark skinned bare-chested man. His large muscles bulged as though he had been lifting something heavy, while veins rippled along his arms up into his overly broad chest. His stomach muscles were so toned they looked like someone had replaced them with small rocks which in all gave the impression that his whole body had been chiselled to perfection by the gods when they had given him life. He was of average height wearing a rag wrapped tight around his head, across his body from left shoulder to right hip a belt hung with the attachment of a semi automatic rifle. There was no mistake why they had called the man Bullet hole. For riddled over his body were bullet wounds of at least twenty, old wounds that had long since healed leaving decorative scares leaving the on lookers to wonder was it really possible that a man could be shot this many times and survive.

"Arrh there he be the man I be just thinking of." Gill stood and greeted his old friend with the clenching of hands.

"What brings you these sides Gill; it has been at least two years or so since we last saw you."

Paul had always been fond of the captain he was a thinking man much like himself wanting to make thing better for everyone.

"Well some… " he stopped and began to eye the man that stood with Paul. He was a thin weasely looking pink skinned man. With the rough look of a drunken wino that you would expect to find in some city street sleeping in the gutters. But it was not his roughness that had held the captain's attention as most of the men in that place fitted that same description. Nor was it the three stubs on his right hand where three of his fingers from the little one to his middle appeared to have been cut off at the knuckles, Even his blond hair though it was filthy or his piercing blue eyes wasn't the cause of the captains distraction. In fact Gill was not quite sure what it was but he had a feeling, a feeling he was not sure of. Had he seen this man before? The captain squared up to him like a man about to brawl.

"What be your name boy?"

"Noititilop and I am no boy." He was fingering the hilt of his sheaved knife that was attached to his belt.

"Be that an Elfin name you be carrying boy."

His tone was deep and dark and Paul did not like where this was going.

"He is cool Gill he is cool chill, we call him Nape. He has been with us a while you can trust him, he is one of my best spies."

The captain seemed to relax a little returning to his seat he eyeballed the strange man once again before continuing to speak.

"I beg ya pardon, these have been strange days for me an my folk of late and I be not too quick to trustin strangers but if you say he is of good nature well that be enough for me."

"Well as good a nature as a pirate can be." Paul laughed and it seemed the whole table laughed with him.

It is strange how these men follow everything these two did as though they were sheep. The thought crossed Kir mind

"So what were you saying?" Bullet returned to matters at hand.

"Well some unfortunate events have been taking place that has brought us here to seek help from those I have helped in the past. We be looking for Orcus that maybe travelling to France with some unusual prisoners."

Vlad immediately turned his attention to the conversation of the captain. He was a good man and he was grateful that he would help him however he could.

"Orcus, you say?" Bullet found himself a seat and cutting a piece of meat from the boar he took a bite.

"I have spies all over the Belgium ports. It does me good to know what merchant ships be coming and going amongst other things, but you are in luck I have been told of a large group of maybe twenty or thirty travelling with one of those we dare not speak of. Ale!" he shouted and like a slave heeding to a master a pretty little barmaid rushed over with a mug of ale for the bullet pirate. Paul washed down the meat with a gulp of his ale before continuing to speak.

"They arrived twelve days ago at Knokke port it was said they had prisoners of a rare breed much like your friend here." He stared at the unique little man sitting across the table; it was rare for anyone to see a dwarf, so the looks Vlad had been receiving since he arrived did not bother him.

"Yes they are my kin and it is important that we stop

them from boarding the flying ship in France."

The entire company of pirates roared with laughter and Vlad did not take too kindly too it.

"Why do you laugh?" He stood on the table aggressively ready to pounce.

"Calm down little man we mean no offence but this group travels with one of the twelve."

"So"

"So my dwarfin friend it means there is no saving them, it would take an army to stop one of those creatures and you are but a few I am sorry but there is nothing you can do for them."

"If we cannot save them then I must… " he dropped his head as if he had just realised what the outcome of his mission would be.

"Must what?" Paul was curious.

The dwarf climbed back on to his stool looking sad he answered.

"I must kill them" he said regretfully "they must not reach the Greys."

"Well if that is the case small man their convoy left on horseback three days ago but you have a small window of hope."

"How so?" Leron inquired.

"I have recently learned from a good source that the ship in Paris has not arrived and will not be expected there for another month. So they will be forced to wait in Paris until it arrives."

Vlad got up from the table "Leron we must go back to the ship and prepare, if we are lucky we may catch them before they reach Paris."

The Captain Knarf and the others rose from the table.

"Thank you I am in your debt" Vlad said.

"You are welcome little man." Bullet grinned. "And you captain will you be leaving also."

"No I hope to dock here for a month or so if it is ok with you, I have some ammunition for your turrets as payment."

"Well then." Blackheart stood and shook the captain's hand. "You are welcome to stay as long as you like."

They said their goodbyes and see you later and heading back to the ship to make plans.

Katie had found Xela who had left her a while ago sleeping on the benches at the stern of the ship; she had found him below deck in one of the washrooms. He had not closed the door behind him and nor did he turn to acknowledge the young girl standing in the doorway. She watched as he stood staring into the mirror with a razor shaving the sides of his head she had found it interesting how his hair was long on the top and his sides were woolly like a sheep skin rug but now he was bald on the sides with just his long lock's sprouting from the top of his head reminding her of a story she had heard about some ancient American Indians they had once called the Mohicans. Once he had finished he put the razor to his face.

"Let me do that." She entered the washroom and pulled up a stool.

"But I am ... " Xela still did not feel comfortable speaking, he had spent so much time silent that he found it hard to find the words to say what he meant.

"No buts just sit." He was surprised how comfortable this girl was with him only a few days back it was next to impossible for anyone to get a word from her but since today she had spent hours sitting and talking with him about her life and the shallows and learning what she could from him about the old days. But he was pleased if she continued to converse it kept her mind away from the terrible things she had witnessed that had almost brought her to the brink of insanity.

She raised her hands up to his broad shoulders and

forced him down onto the stool, he did not protest. The young girl took the razor from his hands setting it aside she took that bar of soap that was in the basin and ran some water onto it from the tap then began to rub the soap in her hands making it foam. Then placing the bar of soap down she used the foamy cool substance that was left in her hands and applied it to his face. He had not thought to do this and he was sure to have left himself with a few cuts if he had continued to shave his face himself. He watched her in the mirror admiring her, she had faced such atrocities so much pain and her true sadness he could still see deep in her eyes but here, right now with a sad calmness upon her face he saw a strength that he knew would carry her through these dark days and hopefully lead her to a better happier life. He continued to watch as she gently applied the soap onto his face caressing in small circular movements with her fingertips keeping the substance foamy white against his skin.

He looked at her and himself in the mirror as though they were in a picture, and though it was almost surreal seeing her soft pink delicate hands against his own dark skin he felt a closeness to her, he could not explain it himself but it was almost as if he had known her all his life. She picked up the razor; she had never shaved a man before, once she had watched one of the elder women shave her husband down on the beach near the shallows, and though Xela had only very small stubble on his face she planned to be gentle making sure she did not cut him. She moved the razor across his jaw line with such grace the dark man felt comfortable to be in her hands, she shaved the rough from his face with perfection not touching his moustache and goat beard that went around his mouth to his chin. He was impressed with the outcome.

"Thank you." He moved to get up.

"You're not finished yet." She pushed him back down

and picked up some scissors.

"Your beard is way too long I will trim it and make it neat."

He did not reply he just stared at her while she faced him kneeling down to get close to make sure she was trimming his beard neatly, he stared at her brown eyes and her smooth skin he noticed her ruffled hair that had not been brushed for days. He had not taken any notice before but she was very pretty and the way she was taking care of him he knew she would make some one very happy one day and felt the need even more to protect her so she could have that chance of whatever passed as a normal life these days. She caught him staring.

"What is it?"

"Nothing"

"Come on what's bothering you?"

"Nothing really, it's just... that your pretty that's all."

She blushed and felt embarrassed that she even asked the question and saying no more she finished the trim.

"There, you are done." She handed him the mirror so he could admire her work.

"Thanks it's good, I owe you one."

She giggled

"You owe me nothing," She said as she skipped away headed for the upper deck.

She thought on the nice things Xela had said to her as she leaned on the railings on the port side of the ship watching the people of this strange place go about their everyday business and duties. Had he really thought she was pretty? Or was he just humouring her trying to keep her mind off the bad stuff. Her mind drifted to her mother causing her to feel a deep sadness making her feel as though someone had reached deep inside her and was tearing at her gut, she was feeling guilty that even for such a short while she had a moment of enjoyment, someone had said something nice to her and she had become all girly and pleased with herself. Pleased, how could I even be happy about anything that would happen in my life without my mother, she hated herself for letting herself feel any type of pleasure, but it was him Xela there was something about him that made her feel at ease what would her mother had said? And then she heard it, the whirling of a musical tone it was her mother's voice as though it was drifting on a breeze.

Find pleasure in any moment and hold onto it, it sang whirling and spinning around her so loud she was surprised no one else had heard it and then it faded until it was no more than just a breeze.

She was not quite sure if she had heard it for real or if it was just in her mind but in that moment she felt comforted and felt that her mother was really with her watching over her, she decided there and then that today she would enjoy the moment because she knew that her mother would of wanted it so. She would always be sad deep down she knew this but for now Xela thought she was pretty. She smiled at the thought then turned her attention to the returning group who were now boarding the ship, they seemed eager and she knew that her stop here would be short.

∧
—

She was slender and graceful with sharpness to her features that extended her beauty beyond that of most of her kind. Her hair flowed below her shoulders and though most her hair was snow white a black streak flowed along the left side of her face. There was no paleness to her skin but her skin was unblemished flawless and smooth, she walked as though the Linage of royalty was in her blood, and it was so. Wearing her chosen colours her gown was made up of bright blue, grey and a white shawl ran the length of her body and trailed behind her like a bride walking the isle. Grey represented the clouds, white the snow and blue revealed the mood of winter, the mood that she was feeling now. She walked the red carpet that led to her cousin's chamber and on reaching the door she passed through with not even a word from the two guards standing at either side, they knew better to question her or even obstruct her in anyway, they would leave that to her cousin. She wore beauty all around her it was as if the very air she walked through was affected by her presence, but though sweet and attractive all knew that she was a fierce warrior and her wrath was nothing to play with.

"Ah Anairda Grip what a pleasant surprise, it's nice that my distant cousin would pay her king a visit UNANNOUNCED!"

Maxius raised his voice so Elpoep and the Elf guard would hear his displeasure.

"Tis not a visit of pleasure why I am before you today oh sweetest of cousins."

She was being sarcastic she did not like Maxius, nor did she trust his rule of the people, she felt a darkness when she was around him and knew he dealt in nothing good, but her mannerisms were not as most who stood before him because she had no fear of him.

"So what do I owe the honour?"

"I am here because of the uprising in France, I wish to go and act as a diplomat?"

"Diplomat? With humans, huh they should be annihilated with their arrogance and insolence, how dare they defy me." He paced the room.

"Yes your lordship I see your point but it has been over six months and they still cannot be found, they have technologies of old and if stories of them reach other lands there will be more uprisings."

"So what do you propose?"

"Send me with three others we will seek them out and offer them a deal, our own lands are diminishing my lord and if we can stop this bloodshed and do some good maybe nature may restore some of our lands."

"Nature!" He stopped pacing and faced Anairda with a grim look upon his face. "You believe old folks tales, you think our mother has turned on us and is destroying our world. You insult me and your own kind as if we are the bad ones, IT WAS US! ME who saved this planet, if I did not help end the war we all would have destroyed each other and what would have been left of this world then, Nature! NATURE SHOULD BE GRATEFUL TO ME!"

Anairda stood back in shock had she really heard what she thought she had heard, Maxius the Elfin king insulting all that is sacred to the Elfin people. (Mother Nature should be grateful to him) She was almost sick at his arrogance but she hid it well.

"Never the less the problems with the humans must be dealt with, I suggest we offer them land in which they can be free in and plant, farm and govern themselves with our promise of no attack or interfering in their chosen way of life."

"And what do you think they will do with that? They would use their new freedom to build bigger armies to fight us."

"We will make them sign a treaty, the one thing I know about humans is that they will not break a bargain."

"You are silly cousin, first you will have to fin... " he paused as a thought came to his mind, and then a small smirk appeared on the side of his mouth.

"You know my sweet cousin you are right, find them and make this deal, may Mother Nature forgive our ignorance. I only ask that you take a small garrison of my men with you under your complete command and Lrac Also, I am sure he would like to travel for a while."

Anairda knew the king was up to something and assumed it was just to get Lrac out of the way, nearly all of the land knew his insecurity with the elf that could be king.

"Very well your majesty we will leave on the morrow."

She turned and moved gracefully from his chamber.

∧
‾

The sky had become dark and gloomy and for the past hour rain hammered down on the horse mounted group like thousands of small pellets splattering against a wall. They had been travelling for three days now along rough and difficult terrain with no clear visible road and an old map and compass to guild them. The map was little use for serious direction as it was ancient made in the times when men ruled. Much of the roads and landmarks had long since been destroyed, bullet had shaded out the areas on the map where it was not safe to travel, rumours and stories of the dark mist spreading across the lands poisoning and killing every living thing that came into contact with it had stopped many from travelling this far south.

They had joined the poor excuse for a road a mile or so past Antwerp, so not to arouse suspicion from any inquiring eyes taking note of strangers passing through. They followed the road to Limburg a small village where people bragged that their village had once been a great thrithing city before the war making the group feel pity for the way they lived now. Most of the people lived in filth and would lap up your piss if they thought it would earn them a piece of dried meat, their homes were mainly straw huts and old collapsing buildings, the village stunk, it stunk so bad that the group believed that people emptied there bowels everywhere and anyway even in the streets. They had arrived late in the evening and spent the night at a shack that someone had dared to call a tavern which served ale that was most likely one part piss and three parts dirty water, there was no way to describe the food they were offered to buy. On taking one look at the slop that others were eating, the small group decided to stick to their own supplies. Leron and Knarf had slept in the stables to protect the horses, having no doubt that the people of this village would of killed their horses in the night for meat to eat and to sell, and they were right they spent half of their night scaring prying villages away who had idea's that their horses were easy pickings.

They continued the journey at sunrise the next morning and travelled all day until the dirt track road turned into a dirt trail that ran up and down rocky hills and through swamp filled woods. Resting for only few hours they continued on their way all feeling miserable, and now the rain had made it worse, drenching their clothes and muddying the track making their travel irritatingly slow. All were miserable, all except for one. Katie did not seem effected or even a little miserable on that godforsaken journey and some might say she seemed even a little bit pleased.

The group had been reduced to seven. Kir and Navi had opted to stay behind to try life as a ship hand on the Daring leaving Xela, Leron, Knarf, Zepol, Heffer and Vlad to attempt to rescue the dwarfin prisoners. Captain Gill had given Knarf a long range radio with promises of being able to contact the ship as long as they stayed in Western Europe when the dispute had broken out. Navi had been insisting that the young girl should stay aboard with him, Katie refused and Xela spoke up saying he felt only he could protect her and that she was more safe with him. She was pleased that he had spoken so strongly for her, he was truly a good man and she did not want to leave him, she knew deep down that for this moment for this time they were meant to stay together. Gill accepted Xela's argument saying that she was old enough to make her own decision but the truth be told it was because his crew were spooked by her, believing she was a bad Omen waiting to happen. Navi had walked off swearing about stupid men sending young ladies on suicide missions and that was how Katie became the seventh member of the group.

But now she was pleased, almost joyous to be seeing the wonders she had never seen but only heard about. To be drenched in cool rain which was a rare thing back in England, and to go through a swamp wood, these were sights and sensations she had always hoped to see and experience, though their mission was dangerous she would for now enjoy and appreciate the things the others did not.

Knarf called the company to a halt to check the map and camp down for a while until the rain eased up. Leron and Xela were quick to make a small shelter with some sticks and a large plastic sheet that Leron took from the ship and carried in his saddle pack.

"Surly it would be easier to turn west now?" Zepol hated these lands and the quicker they reached France the better.

"You heard the pirate Paul as we all did" Knarf replied. "These shaded areas on the map represents the dark mist which is poisonous, they don't know how far it has spread so we were told to stay well clear, we will keep going south until we reach Luxemburg it has the only clear path from this country to France when we are sure we have avoided the mist then it will be safe to turn west."

They all knew he was right they had seen the dark mist in the distance from the sea; it ran along the coastline of the port the captain had called Oostende. He had said that once many years ago it was a vibrant place until the mist came. At first people had thought it was gas from the France coast left over from the war but spreading to their lands, but this mist was not green but dark like a black swirling smoke coming from a burning fire. Some people left Oostende and moved further up the coast to Knokke, but others stayed, as the mist at first did not do them harm. But then one day it became thicker, so thick one could not tell night from day, no one had known what happened to those that had stayed behind, but it soon became knowledge to all that what went into the thick mist never ever came out of it. The story had made them all weary of the dark smoke like substance they did not need to be told again to stay clear. The company grouped together under the shelter as the rain did not show any signs of letting up. Katie cuddled up to Xela and slept leaving the others sitting still watching the rain in silence.

The sky was a clear blue, and as the sun shone brightly not one cloud for miles could be seen. A great eagle circled up above casting a shadow on the green flourishing land below. Before her the land ahead consisted of green grass covered hilly valleys and beautiful exotic flowers and plants that she had neither seen nor been told about before. A clear wondrous stream ran alongside her down through the trees to the river half a mile ahead. It was amazingly pretty and wonderful, she looked behind her and was surprised to see grey gloomy clouds and rough terrain it was as if the path that she must of followed was in a different world or even a different time. She asked herself the question of how she had gotten here in the first place. She did not remember walking or riding here, the thought drifted with the rest of her unanswered questions as she stared back at the strange world behind, so strange she thought surreal even, only in a surreal world could you look back a few yards and see it pouring down with rain a thunderstorm she thought as she saw the lightning and heard the distant roar of the skies behind, but in front an untouched world, magical unaffected by such weathers, separate from what laid behind, it was as if this place was protected shielded away from the rest of the world.

There were people behind her in the gloom it the dirty

wet lands, something made her feel drawn to them a familiarity like she had known them once and they her, for a moment she was tempted to go into the gloom and greet them and show them this wondrous place but the land ahead seemed to be calling drawing her into it with unheard words and melodies whispering by on a cool breeze, filling her senses with sweet aroma's and overwhelming emotions and sensations that can only be described as happiness, A true feeling that she had escaped her for a time. She followed the sound of the whispering breeze enjoying its melody dancing and skipping down into the valley and through the trees until she came to the river, where a boat sat as though it was waiting for her. She did not know why but she climbed in. the boat drifted off as though it were steered and rowed by invisible oars.

The sun glistened along the river while small fish leapt up to bathe in its glory for only moments before going back under to repeating the process. She watched interestingly as she drifted smoothly lost but happily content with her environment. She had never thought that such a place existed anywhere on this earth if on earth she was, except maybe a fairy forest. Maybe that's where she was? Maybe somehow she had found her way to one of their sacred magical lands, she did not stay to long on that thought because her eyes had caught a glimpse of something, something moving amongst the trees alongside the bank to the right of her and the river, struggling to see what it was the great eagle above let out a cry causing her to look up. Even high above, the eagle seemed overly large and she wondered if eagles were normally this big, she took her attention away from the great bird to see where the boat was drifting then her heart began to pound with fear.

Just ahead on the bank where it seemed the river came to an end awaited seven of the fiercest looking wolves she could have ever imagined. She had only seen wolves in pictures or in old films back at the shallows and none of them had seemed so big. They were huge and muscular, only slightly smaller than the average size horse, their shapes cast dark shadows on the river and she was frightened. The boat continued to drift towards them and she panicked, almost certain they would eat her she prepared herself to jump into the water to escape the sharp teeth and strong jaws. But that was before she heard the song singing on the same melody of the breeze, it was the voice of a women.

"In potters lane the prophecy told, from ancient lands of warriors bold.

The heart and shell brings freedom and doom, the world falls dark unless the shell finds you.

Through love and hate one must die, to save us all from the Smokey misty skies,

The evil looms from white eye to red, like a plague it roams unless the truth be told.

La la la lala la lala la, la la la lala la la la la hmmm la la la la la, lala la la la hmmm hmm hmmmm... ."

Though the words of the song were dark the voice had calmed her almost putting her in a trance, the song the feeling it invoked were so strong nothing mattered all her questions how she had got here where she was going the threat of the wolves. She looked to them now no longer fearing them; it was as if she knew their purpose was not to harm her. The boat stopped alongside the bank and she climbed from it where the wolves awaited. They did not approach her or threaten her in anyway; one turned and walked into the trees then stopped and looked back at her as if to say follow. So she did and the wolf led the way, as she moved the others fell into place two either side of her and two behind, as though they were guarding her protecting her from dangers she did not know about.

Time went by or it did not it seemed as though they

could have been walking for hours but time here was different she knew this though she did not know how. Her legs did not hurt or ache not even a little she did not feel tired or felt she needed a rest, in fact it was almost like she was floating, drifting along to the strange women's song floating in a timeless place until she found herself in a clearing amongst the trees. The wolves stopped gave her one last look as if to place her face in their memories and then turned and leapt off running as though they had more important things to do leaving her alone in the clearing where there was nothing except a large tree in its centre. But the song the melody was all around her, so close that its singer could have been right next to her filling the air with its harmony causing the trees outside the clearing to sway as if they danced also to the song, and then it stopped and left only silence, not even the trees rustled.

"You have found your way to us again young Katie, though this time I had a little something to do with it."

She looked up into the tree in the centre of the clearing and saw a girl wearing a see through green nightdress that exposed all of her unusual green body; she had met her before but only in a dream. She watched as a branch from the tree moved as if it were alive wrapping itself around the green girl it carried her safely to the ground.

"Its Lucy isn't it?" Katie clearly remembered the strange dream she had one night in the shallows, the same dream she had seen Xela in and this golden haired girl before her.

"I am glad you remember me."

"Yes I do, so this is a dream isn't it?"

"Yes but not in the same sense that most people would dream. You have travelled on a path not many can find, but I called you to me because I can feel that you are closer to me much closer than before."

"Close to your home?" Katie wished and hoped that

this was all real to meet this girl and see the home of the fairies would be wonderful.
"Will there be other fairy's there?"
Lucy giggled and then smiled.
"We are not fairies pretty one, we are distant cousin to them, but you travel with one."
"I do?" Katie new she travelled with a dwarf but not a fairy
"I came to you two nights ago, it was the last time I was allowed to leave our own realm of dreams and I saw him the dark haired one with the pointed ears did you not notice." She giggled again like a small child.

It was strange that this being could speak with her and seem so mature and wise and within a moment she seemed so young so childish younger than Katie herself, but the green girl had brought news to her, Leron was a fairy and no one had told her.

"Katie" Lucy said once she had stopped giggling. "When you return to your body you must remember that this conversation we are having was and is real, do you understand."

Katie nodded; Lucy had become older and more serious once again.

"Bring the dark one and travel east go east and we will find you."

"East, we can't go east we have important things to do in the south."

Lucy seemed a little distracted not really paying much attention to what Katie had just said, looking around as if something were nearby, remembering the dream she had last time she was with Lucy Katie became worried.

"Are we in danger?"

"No not here I had you brought to our own realm where we would be safe, there are things outside our own dream realms that have become more powerful and dangerous, waiting to feed off someone like me so I have been forbidden to leave our own realm. But you, oh my sweet you and your friends are in danger, once again our time is cut short, you must return and I will be in trouble but I must take you or you will not wake in time, come take my hand."

Katie was worried her real body was in danger, she took Lucy's hand and did not asks any more questions she only wished to get back. Within seconds they were flying, flying high above the trees at a great speed, the breeze barely touching them, it was wonderful, to fly how great she thought but of course none of it was real, it was really just a dream and she knew this. They flew with the river beneath them and back along the stream where Katie had begun and now she could see the rain and the other people on the other side.

"From here I can go no further, it is too dangerous for me even to be this far from our own realm, but my people still control a lot of what happens here up to this point."

Katie pretended she knew a little of what Lucy was talking about and nodded in understanding thought she truly did not understand.

"Go now" Lucy continued. "And remember east you will have time."

And then she pushed Katie forwards like a master setting his pet free, and she was offended, Katie turned back but Lucy was gone, and then the darkness crept all around closing in on her like a poison spreading through the air finding every piece of light it could pollute and change, it became darker and darker until the last spark of light faded and then the rain drizzled.

Katie awoke with her head resting on Xela's chest. It took her a moment to realise where she was, lifting her head slowly she found all her companions were asleep, night had fallen and someone had took the time to light a fire she did not think about how strange it was that a log burned and hissed while small drops of rain fell upon it but the fire never went out, she was too tired to even think. She looked at her new friends, they deserve the rest she thought, and laid her head back down on Xela who also seemed asleep. But as she was about to close her eyes once again she notice something, there were people or something sneaking through their camp. They were all around, her heart began to pound and she opened her mouth about to scream when Xela's hand covered it.

"Shhhh" he whispered "Don't worry we all know, and are ready"

One of them came to close to Knarf and leaned over to maybe cut his throat while he slept, but found a shock when Knarf opened his eyes and said "Not tonight baby, I am trying to rest" Pointing his gun right at the things head he pulled the trigger and its head exploded.

And then everything happened too quick they were upon them Knarf, Zepol and Heffer were shooting into them as more and more of them came out of the dark, Leron and Vlad were up fighting also shooting and using physical strength when they came to near, but Katie soon realised who these people were, they were not people. Her stomach wrenched and she felt she was going to be sick. How had they found them? How had they gotten here? Before she could think a dart or something flew through the air towards her, but Xela was quick and grabbed her turning his back protecting her in his arms the dart struck him, he dropped to his knees.

"! Are you alright?" she shouted over the gunfire.

"Yeah I'm fine, I just.. I just feel a little weak" And then Xela passed out.

^
‾

It had only been three hours since the small group had left on their journey taking with them supplies and horses,

Nape was almost certain they would never be seen again and further more to add to his pleasure Bullet had agreed to his request to return to Antwerp for a few days to see what more he could find out about the Orcus and their captives. The weasel looking man had no patience for outsiders and did not care for the captain; there was a familiarity about him though he could have sworn he did not know the fella though his reputation was known worldwide.

Even on his trip to the America's people whispered stories about the captain and how one day he would save them all. Fools but then again most people were if he had his way he would have slit the man's throat. But he was smart, smart enough not to cause a commotion when he was so eager to kill the idiot captain. He never looked like much and he was sure he could take him, but like Nape told himself he was smart, smarter than all those pathetic excuses for pirates back at their lair. They had no clue, no idea that it was him that kept them safe, he was the only one that knew the ins and outs of things and while it served his interests the pirates could continue living the way they choose.

On reaching Antwerp he rode steadily through the outer city streets where human people lived like scavengers begging for food from every person that rode a horse or looked better off than they did. Thin underfed children were fighting over a dead rat for meat to bring home to their families. Here on the outer edge of the city everyone had the same as each other, nothing but the rags on their backs and their mud built homes. The nearby woods were off limits, it was forbidden to cut wood or hunt animals except if the Governor of Antwerp had personally given his permission. This was his way to keep the people in line, all waiting for his once a month charity where he would be escorted through the slums throwing bread and dry pieces of meat to the people as though they were dogs and sometimes he chose not to give anything.

"Please sir please, some bread for my mother and me she is sick."

A small girl clung to his legs as he rode slowly through the city slums. He pulled on the reins causing his horse to stop, intrigued he stared at the small girl. She was around the age of sixteen to seventeen; her hair was so filled with dirt one could not tell its true colour.

"Take off your dress." Nape ordered.

She seemed shocked and ashamed at the request looking to the ground she felt fear to meet his eyes, standing still she did nothing.

"Oh well" he said sitting tall on his steed. "I suppose someone else may feed your mother." He began to ride off slowly.

"Wait sir" She called and he stopped.

A few grubby looking men had gathered waiting to see if they too could beg from the stranger. She felt ashamed and embarrassed but never the less she unrobed herself dropping her filthy garment that looked as though it was made from a sack and probably was. She stood naked in the muddy streets of the outer city. Nape dismounted putting on just one riding glove on his left hand he approached the young girl. He stared straight into her eyes with a cold look upon his face as though she was nothing, she stared back and it seemed that time itself had stopped. Then she felt it, he had placed his left hand between her legs, she winched and he smirked as a tear rolled down her cheek. In his right hand he held one piece of Elfin gold, while he fondled her with his gloved hand as he held the gold so she could see.

"Would you do anything for this?"

"Yes" She answered feeling sick at herself, but if it meant that she would lose her virginity to this beast in order to feed and nurse her mother back to health then she would do it.

"What's your name child?"

"Justine" She whispered welling up with tears she found it hard to speak.

He stopped fondling her and gave her the gold, when he had mounted his horse she reached into the mud to retrieve her dress.

"No no no you pretty thing you have not finished yet" Nape said with and evil grin.

"You men" Shouting to the group gathered nearby. "have her till she bleeds."

But before she could protest they were upon her, fondling and groping as though she was a piece of meat, when she struggled they beat her, she did not know how many men had entered her that day but as she held tightly to the gold she also clung tight to the memory of the horse mounted man who laughed cruelly as he watched her being abused before he rode off into the inner city.

Nape past through the inner city gates undeterred by the Elfin guards, they had seen him often enough and knew well enough to let him be. It was much different in the inner city, People worked three times as hard as one would expect but life here was much better than those on the other side of the wall. The streets were always busy at this time of day people mingled everywhere like bees busying around a hive, the market sellers had set up their stools, the fish mongers were selling their early morning catch. Here under the Elfin regime life was better though secretly people complained about the taxes in fear of being accused of treason against the Elfin state, which was punishable by death they only spoke about such things behind closed doors. "So what that half or more of every beings stock went to the governor, the Elves must be fed" nape thought. He had no quarries with the White haired folk in fact he had done well playing both sides. He rode casually along the cobbled stone streets up passed Marche' aux Poisson, and then along Vlaaikensgang street until he came to the sheriff's office.

The Elfin governor, Ecitsujni, had strange notions, watching to many old human screenings he had become obsessed with what was once called the wild west, and so he had set up a sheriff office where the people could police themselves, only they did not because the appointed sheriff was an elf himself named Retisnimtpurroc Mostly known as Purroc who helped to enforce the wishes and the law of the Governor. He also had thirty human Deputies who were recruited from bandits that stole from and murdered anyone that travelled to close to their territory those that joined saw it was a great opportunity to continue being murders and thieves but this time it was called law. They were the local hit squad that relied on people like Nape to give them information, information about those who would speak out against the Elfin regime, or the whereabouts of certain pirates. Nape thought himself a double agent both an Elfin spy and a spy for the pirate, for some time now he had been playing both sides reaping the benefits of being treated well and paid good from elf and man, that was the main reason he had never foreclosed the details of the Pirates hideout.

He had lied to Purroc letting him believe that he had made friends with some pirate who he hoped one day would lead him to their true home, but every time a pirate pissed him off or caused him any grief he saw it as an opportunity to make money and give Purroc more belief in him by telling him where and when that pirate could be found outside of the pirates lair. Purroc's dream was to one day free the seas of pirate scum so that the supplies they sent or received across the waters would be safe. But nape for now while it served him had no plans to give up the pirate home, just the Captain that man had challenged him and now he would pay for that mistake.

He entered the building finding a rough necked Deputy asleep at the desk, waking the man up who was none too pleased he insisted on speaking with Purroc, waiting only a few moments on the lazy deputies return he was told to go through to the sheriff's office. Nape never knocked before entering, the room was dark with nothing but a small candle burning on the table where Purroc sat, the candle light lit up the Elfin features illuminating his deep red eyes as though flames burned in them. It was not unusual for the elf to sit in darkness, he said often enough that he found himself more and more attracted to darkness than light these days, he had boasted once or twice about how sharp his vision had become in complete darkness and sometimes the daylight caused him pains or aches to his head. Purroc was a show off and a babbler and if it was not for the long time they had been together and the money he made from him Nape would have cut ties with the foolish elf a long time ago.

"So what news do you bring?" Purroc was eating some kind of fruit.

"Strangers have arrived from across the sea, I have been told that it is the famous Captain gill himself, I await news for when he will come to the city to get supplies, but you must have your men ready." The pirates' harbour brought in a lot of money and he would be damned if he would see it destroyed over the captain, he would trick him in coming to the city.

"More, you know more I can smell it on you."

The sound was barely recognisable as a voice and Nape struggled to understand, someone else was with them. He stepped back looking for the exit behind him as the creature stepped out from a dark corner into the candle light. It was horrifyingly ugly, and though some had passed through these lands Nape had always kept his distance. These creatures were never posted here so it was rare for anyone in these parts to be so close to one.

"You see" Purroc spoke as he continued to eat what nape now recognised as a banana a rare and expensive fruit for anyone to be eating.

"My friend here has travelled far" The creature stepped a little close to nape casting a dark shadow over him.

"He believes you know more and his species are known for smelling fear and lies on humans. But he could be wrong and if he is you are of no use to him or me and I am afraid that I would have to leave you in his hands, and everyone knows Orcus take pleasure in killing humans slowly, very very slowly."

The creature grunted something and moved towards nape in a threatening manner. Nape was not brave but he was a true coward who took pleasure in killing and threatening those weaker than him but would run if he felt his life was threatened, he then wondered if he told them all he knew would they really let him live.

"… Purroc you be joking, right?"

"No, he is what they call the local police, why?" Bullet was curious of how the captain knew the name.

"That be an evil one he be. I be rememberin' many years back me ship needed repairs so I was forced to travel across countries from Russia to Amsterdam, it were the days me be buying me fine horse Distant. Ahh distant… " He paused for a moment thinking on his horse before continuing.

"I know Katie will be looking after her," he said thinking about distant and the young girl Katie journeying across the lands believing they would be safe.

"Anyway I had travelled far and fast crossing the boarders of Poland into Germany where I found myself in a town. Mainly humans be there and a small garrison of Elves were thereabouts. They paid little attention to me as I was only a passerby but I remember the name. It be a young man and his wife be begging." The captain's face became solemn as he stared into nothing teary eyed.

"Purroc, the man called, 'please' he begged. I hear his voice as though it was yesterday he called that name. I sat upon my steed wishing there was something I could do. But it was just me, me men I left guarding the ship. I remember his evil red eyes burning through the man with a cold heat. He took a poker that was heated on a blacksmiths fire and struck it through the mans eye and out the back of his head. The screams, his scream echoed through my head, the people gasp at the horror. This he said this is what happens if you human scum eat from my vegetable patch. They were a starving people and that was how he fed them with the body of their own fellow man and if the people were to survive they all knew they would cut up and eat that man's body and any other body that Purroc would kill. And the girl, the man's wife... The Elf told his human companion, the only human it trusted, he told him too… "

The captain stopped, stunned or shocked he did not speak. It was though a thought a memory had come to mind.

"What is it?" Bullet walked over and put his hand on his old friends shoulder. "Captain, what is it?"

"Oh no, may god have mercy on us all."

"Why what's wrong?"

"It's Purroc, Purroc and Suduj they called them the devil and his demon. Through the lands I travelled then, everyone had heard their names and feared them."

"So what's new, you had me worried for a moment Purroc is just as evil as he was then."

"My boy worried you should be, the demon I be remembering now where I saw him. The demon be your man Nape."

He was a long way away from England, it had been a (month or so) tracking the three escapee's across England across the sea and to this point, with an added bonus the young girl. The loss of his men at Dover would be worthwhile if he finished them all now.

While the skies of England rain fire Imrarge had taken a hundred men, and with their protective clothing drove across counties to the Hastings port, after a two day delay by Elves who held nothing but contempt for his kind, they were then permitted to commandeer a small steel cargo ship to take them to Knokke in Belgium where many more Orcus hating Elves awaited. But Belgium had reminded Imrarge of an elf that had once travelled to the dome city who had as much hatred for humans as any Orcus, they conversed and the elf said he hoped one day Imrarge would visit him at his station in Belgium. Remembering this he made the captain of the ship head for Antwerp bypassing Knokke. His plan was simple, get whatever supplies the elf would allow, and take weekly runs along the coastline of Europe in hopes of sighting the ship with his escaped prisoners. They had to land somewhere in Europe everyone knew the other waters were too dangerous to travel. Fortune was on his side, things could not have turned out better, whilst visiting the elf, one of the elf's spies had entered with information some of which the vermin human did not want to share, but after a little persuasion (a grin if one would call it that crept upon its face at the thought) he learned the whereabouts of the ones he wanted and had been tracking them for three days.

Believing the Elves by now should have captured and killed the captain and the pirates with that victory and the victory of killing those that were before him he knew he would be greatly rewarded. So now after he had sent his men out to surround them he crept silently towards the small camp. Through the trees he could see the girl, she was dangerous and not like any normal being he had come across, she had a power that the Greys themselves would be interested in. he had sent word over a radio at Hastings a message for one of the twelve giving them information about the girl and what she could do, but now he thought it best to kill her and let the Greys experiment with her body, it would be too much of a risk to take her alive. The grotesque Orcus being took a poison dart from the belt it wore around its waist and with its clubbed disfigured fingers he placed the dart in the barrel of a plastic looking gun. "Today they would all die," he thought. At that moment a gunshot went off, thinking fast as to not give his target time to find cover Imrarge fired the dart. He missed; he had hit the dark one instead.

The captain rushed around barking orders at his men to prepare the ship for departure, Bullet was doing the same, ordering the great gates to be opened and advising people to leave and run to the hills. Two pirates used great whips to strike the Ogres who in response began to turn the great cogs that opened the gates. It seemed like pandemonium when Blackheart stepped out from his sleeping shack having just given two of his whores a good seeing to. He grabbed his horn and blew it. The sound echoed throughout the cove shocking everyone to stop in his or her tracks. There was silence as the people looked up the rocky steps that lead to where the giant pirate stood.

"What the fuck is going on here?" The angry look upon Blackhearts face showed he was in no mood to be played with.

"Its Nape, he is a traitor working with Purroc the captain is certain he will bring the Elfin army here you must leave Tony we all must?"

"Leave, Leave." Blackheart stood high above everyone

else and roared with laughter, he laughed as though he was possessed with madness.

"No one is going anywhere, Men!"

Bullet stood back as Tony Blackhearts men and half of his own crew turned their guns on them all. The captains' men and the few remaining pirates that were loyal to Bullet hole reacted by drawing and raising their own weapons.

"Don't be foolish you are out Numbered you really are stupid sometimes Paul did you know that?" Blackheart smirked.

"I knew it" Kir whispered to Navi "Never trust pirates, look they can't even trust themselves."

"What Ye be thinking Tony hav ye lost ya mind" The captain could not believe his old friend had turned guns on him, many of times the captain had helped Blackheart and showing him nothing but respect and friendship.

"I am sorry Gill and of course Bullet hole here, but I have known about Nape for some time, it's a fact that we share the money he gets from the Elves for being their spy and in turn I give him names and other useful information so I know for a fact that he would never give this place up to the Elves there is too much profit for us both, right now Nape is telling Purroc where you captain can be found, so we must make sure you reach that place by the time they turn up looking for you, we don't want Nape to disappoint." The evilest grin spread wide across his face expressing how little he cared about their lives.

"But why?" Bullet shouted holding his rifle firm itching to raise it and take a shot.

"The captain has the best ship the world has ever seen, with it we could sail the deadly waters and travel the Americas we would be sea gods in his ship but Unfortunately I knew you would not go along with it, so I am afraid Bullet when they find the captain your body will be next to him."

"Ye know what ye yellow bellied poor excuse for a pirate, before I die I will be killin ya first, and that my friend" the captain smiled "That is a promise Cannons!"

The large cannon guns on the captains ship turned and bullet raised his gun ready to shoot the Giant where he stood but before anyone even fired a shot, the harbour bells began to ring, it was a sound that had never been heard since the Pirates made home here but every pirate civilian prostitute or traveller knew what they meant. The bells stopped and in its silence someone shouted, "It's the Elves, the Elves have found us."

"Wouldn't give us up you're a foolish Pirate Tony and you will keep until another time." Bullet turned to his crew "All who is not with me get the fuck of my ship" No one moved "So are you with me men" he shouted and the crew roared in reply "Then get that fucking Anchor up were leaving."

The people rushed around gathering their things some rushed out the back exit not knowing they were headed straight towards the Elfin soldiers, others jumped into the water and started swimming through the gate, the Elves were here and no one would be spared.

"Get the cannons out, arm the Machine guns stop them from entering our home, and you." Tony bellowed to his own crew as he boarded his own ship "get the anchor up."

The Captain was already aboard his ship and sailing slowly towards the gate. Kir and Navi watched from the stern as the Elfin army swarmed the Lair like ants to sugar, they were everywhere the pirates that had not boarded any ship fired there machine guns and killed many but they still kept coming Hundreds of them firing arrows and shooting human made gun's. There was no mercy not even for the children or the women, anyone associated with pirates were to die by the order of Ecitsujni himself.

The captain did not see how the Ogres got free but they

were now picking up boulders and throwing them at his ship missing but not by far causing big waves to rock them side to side like a rocking horse.

"Cannon guns to starboard" his voice echoed over the radio to the radio tech in the war room who in turn repeated his message to those that controlled the guns.

The great Guns rotated and faced the giant creatures. "Fire at will" was the order and they did, one of the Ogres moved quick jumping across to where the people that had held him captive for so long ran around arming themselves trying to fight off the Elves, he stomped on them and crushed them like they were little insects. The other was not so quick taking a blast from the captain's guns he was buried by falling rock that came away from one of the walls that surround the cove. Stopping the ogre was all they needed to slip through the gates safely leaving the once Pirate cove behind in disarray and certain destruction.

Behind HMS Daring sailed Bullet on his ship the Argol and following tightly behind came the Sharron a few other ships followed and many small fishing boats all in single file they sailed along the narrow passage way while those that did not anchor away quick enough were killed and their ships and boats set on fire. This was the end of all their years of piracy, most wondered where they would go what place could they now call home, as they sailed they watched the flames and the black smoke raise high into the sky letting them all know that there is no place on earth where they would be safe from those that ruled. The ships drifted out along the Narrow way to reach the Open Sea, calling an all stop to the engine room the captain was a little surprised to find a heavily armed ship blocking the path at the end of the Narrow way Purroc was not stupid he did not intend to let anyone escape.

"Full speed ahead and load Torpedo bay one and two" The captain ordered as the ship moved forward once again.

13

The Lady in the Woods

Katie was crying as she dragged Xela through the dirt into the trees away from the gunfire. She did not know if he was dead or alive but she had to get him away from this, she tugged and pulled at his heavy body moving him a little at a time as she slipped and crawled through the mud dragging using every muscle in her arms and legs. She could hear them they were also amongst the trees; she cried and tugged at Xela working herself up into a frenzy she did not look behind as she tugged at the only other person she had connected with in her entire life other than her mother and Clare. She would not let them get him too. If she had taken the time to look behind it may have made little difference, the dark made it very hard for anyone to see the drop that waited. She pulled and pulled having no idea where she was dragging him or where they could hide until danger had passed, when at last she used her last surge of energy pulling Xela she went over the edge, as she fell she grabbed onto Xela's arm his weight holding her for only a moment before the weight of Katie took over dragging Xela down into the darkness with her.

The young girl opened her eyes; at first her vision was blurred but soon adjusted to the bright sunlight that shone down on her. For awhile she laid there wondering where she was or how she had got there, when at last she did lift her head to look around it all came back to her in a rush of memories accompanied by a sharp pain in her frontal lobe. She took the time to make sense of what had happen by going through the events that had led her to this point, it had been night she remembered, and we were attacked by creatures hiding in the trees her mind began to race, and Xela was hit by something, oh gosh Xela. It came back quickly that she had fell from high up, dragging Xela with her.

She rose to her feet, now she could feel the aches and pains all over her body, her arms and legs were badly bruised she remembered they had dropped and must of fell on some kind of slope she had tumbled hitting rocks and bushes until she lost consciousness she believed because from then on she remembered nothing but waking up only moments ago. She ignored her pains; Xela had fell also he had to be around here somewhere she thought. It only took a moment before she found him not far from where she had found herself, he was camouflaged by a bush and that was why she did not see him immediately, at first she was terrified that he was dead, panicking she laid her head on his chest and felt his chest raise slightly a little

Pleased with herself she smiled as she heard his heart beat, he was alive her prayers had been answered, she shook him but he did not wake, something was wrong now she shook him wildly but still there was no response, she finally resorted to slapping him but this did no good also, Xela was not well she knew this and now she wondered if he would ever wake up, having no idea what to do she shed a tear and curled up next to him falling into an uneasy sleep.

It was hours later when Katie woke surprised that none of the others had come looking for them, it only occurred to her a little later of the possibility that none of them survived last night's attack, she did not want to think of it but if it were true she would have to face the fact that they were alone and it was up to her to get Xela some help. Xela still had not opened his eyes since the fall, he was breathing but his heart beat was faint, She checked him over to see if he had been injured during his fall and found a dart still stuck in his back, she removed it and tucked it away in the pocket of her hooded cloak, if she found someone who knew medicine it might be helpful to them to know what had caused it.

She then decided to find her way back up to where they had camped before the attack believing and hoping that the Orcus where long gone, looking up to where they had fell from she realised immediately that it was too steep for her to climb she had to find another way up, leaving Xela wrapped up in his long coat she wondered for a minute if she should remove it because the weather had become warm, but more eager to get help she left him and continued to walk around until she found a slope that led upwards that was not so steep.

It took the brown haired girl a short time to find the area where the battle had taken place, she moved quietly in fear that the creatures may still be nearby, but as she moved through the grounds that had been her camp the night before all she found were bodies upon bodies of Orcus. The stench was unbearable the sun burned down on the dead flesh while insects took their fill, puddles of blood and a few decapitated limbs roasting in the heat filled the air with a scent that would attract wild animals for miles. She hated it but she found herself turning over the carcasses of these creatures as she went through the camp making sure they had not fell on one of her companions. She was pleased but puzzled that none of her group had been amongst the fallen, where were they?

Katie turned over one more body and found herself staring at the corpse, death was a strange thing, she had seen it before her mother, when one of the farm animals back at the shallows had died it had made her wonder then, but in beings it was different somehow, she thought on her mother's eyes as the life drained away from her how the coldness appeared in them and her mother became still, and the others her friends she had laid amongst their still bloodied bodies, the images were so clear in her mind she would never forget them. The thought of her own death had not scared her, but staring at this thing, this being that was of the same breed as those that hurt her friends and killed her mother that had the audacity to seek and attack them while they slept, it made her glad that it was dead and its comrades beside it, she hoped that in death that these creatures would never find peace but find themselves in eternal torment because they deserved nothing less. She spat on the creatures face and turned to walk away, but her thoughts had built up an overwhelming feeling of anger, a fury at what these things had put her though, a fire burned deep within her and she need to put it out. Turning back she rushed to the corpse she had spat on and began kicking it she kicked frantically and when her legs became tired she dropped to her knees in the mud and began beating upon the creatures face with her hands curled up into a fist she thumped as though she was beating a heavy drum hitting as hard as she could while she wept. "Why" she shouted "Why" the Orcus face began to bleed and blood covered her fists and splattered up her arms she hit and hit until her arms was so tired she picked up a rock and smashed at its face until it caved in causing her garments to be blood stained. She slumped down in the mud in the middle of many other Orcus corpses, crying. It was the ugliest thing she had ever done, and it had not quenched her anger and hatred towards the Orcus. She knew now that she would never get over what they had done to her and she would never rest until every last one of them were dead. It was the sound of the horse that made her look up from where she sat.

"Distant" She screamed with excitement, picking herself up she ran over the bodies like stepping stones until she reached the horse.

"Distant you came back to me I should of known you would" at that moment nothing could have cheered her up more with the exception of Xela being well. The captain's horse that had been entrusted to her had returned, and with distant they might have a chance of making it to where there were people or a doctor of some kind to help Xela, she took the horse by the reins and headed back to where she had left the dark-skinned man.

People mingled in and out of shops and along the high streets chatting and smiling, tables and chairs were outside coffee shops so passerby's could sit and drink coffee whilst smoking their cigarettes in the sun before continuing whatever else they had planned for the day, it was summer, men wore long shorts and tight vest or t-shirts or bare back to show off their bodies to entice the pretty ladies whilst keeping their cool, girls and women strutted around in tight short skirts and skimpy tops, some wore clothing that resembled a Bikini and wore sandals upon their feet as if they were taking a trip to the beach.

The town centre market stalls sold fruit and veg and cheep swim suits, sunglasses anything that one would want at a cheap price in the hot weather giving the market traders a great chance of capitalising also on the wondrous summer heat. There were tall buildings and small ones some grand and some not but all the building were intact, none destroyed or crumbling from old age. Many cars, Bmw's Corsa's, Mondeo's Mercedes models of all kinds drove along a road named Princess street, it was familiar this place, it was right— it was reality, this was how things was meant to be.

He walked past two police officers in dark blue uniforms with white collar shirts they peered as he walked by but continued in their stride as they walked their route with promises to protect and serve, taking his attention away from the uniformed men, he stopped in his tracks when he stood before the building with the giant yellow M sign. He knew this meant food and entered the premises without a second thought. Children, young people and families sat at tables eating burgers and fries provide by the employees of the establishment.

"Hey Alex" The girl on the other side of the counter called him by this name as though she had known him. Alex she had said he excepted it as his own with no quarrels as she babbled on about how she had just got the job working there and it had been a long time since she had seen him. While she chatted he reached into his pocket and found coins, which he offered her for the burger he had asked for.

"Its Okay." she told him "It's on the house it's been good to see you again take care of yourself ok and say hi to the others for me. Okay. NEXT!"

Alex if that was really his name took the burger and waved the girl goodbye, he stopped a moment to examine the coins that was in his right hand, there was a ladies head on the coins he remembered her Queen Elizabeth, that was her name, he walked to the door and exited the fast food restaurant stepping outside his heart began to race, he was no longer in the high street it was as if he stepped through the door straight into a car, a car that was moving and to his surprise he was driving the vehicle really fast, looking in his rear view mirror he could see that he was being pursued by two black tinted windowed Bmw X5's he had no idea of where he was all he could tell that he was on a lonely country road with nothing in sight but fields and meadows. One of the cars pursuing him moved alongside him, shifting his attention back to the road ahead of him he realised there was a third car waiting, within moments he was surrounded and with the car in front controlling the speed he soon had no choice and was forced to slow down then eventually stop.

Men in black suits and dark glasses surrounded his car, guns unholstered, ordering him to exit the car. He was confused not knowing how he had got from the car to being strapped down on a table with wires prodding in and out of him, he struggled to break free trying to scream or shout for help but nothing would come out but a mumble, it was as if he had been gagged. A woman enters the room and began to shake him.

"Xela! Wake up!" She shouted "Xela wake up!"

He thought he was already awake but found that his eyes had been closed forcing them now to work he fought the weight that had seemed to be keeping his eyes closed, a drowsiness everything was spinning he knew he had to open his eyes and then he found the strength lifting his eyelids slowly a bright light shone upon him taking a moment to focus he found before him a young pretty face.

"Xela I knew you would wake up"

Katie hugged him; squeezing so tight that for a moment he found it hard to breathe.

Upon his awakening Xela had known he was not well something was wrong with him and he was not sure he was getting any better. Katie had helped him up from the ground and moved him where he could sit up against a rock, it had been a struggle for him to move even with the young girls help, he could not remember a time when he had ever felt so much pain, his legs felt bruised from the ankles upwards, and there was a swelling under his right eye, it seemed as though he had been through the wars and this time actually felt it.

"What happened to me, and where are the others?"

Katie sat beside him.

"You were hit by some kind of dart, I think it is poison, if you did not move in the way it would have been me sick instead of you, I don't know where the others are we fell from up there" She pointed "I woke up about two hours ago and went in search of them they were nowhere to be found."

"It looks like we have little luck these days, you and I." He winced as he spoke she could see he was far from a great recovery.

"We have a little I guess, I found distant she will carry us as long as it takes."

"Carry us where, to France."

"We must get you some help we have to go east"

"What's in the east?"

"Xela I trust you with my life, now it's your turn to trust me"

"But… " it had become a struggle to breath with every word he spoke, the pain in his ribs was excruciating but he continued.

"But if the others… . Survived they… would be going west to… "

"I know but we have time to get you some help"

"Katie… even if my companions did not… make it… " He took a deep breath "On my life I will go to Paris… and save the little men or die trying."

"I know Xela I know but you would do no one any good in this condition, we can spend some time to get you some help and I promise we will get to Paris before the flying ship arrives."

Xela gave in knowing that she was trying to help she seemed certain that they would find someone that could help him and he knew she could not live with herself if she did not try.

After a short rest and retrieving what little food was left

at the camp, Katie helped Xela into the saddle and then Mounted distant herself, sitting in front of him she allowed Xela to hold her waist while he slumped over her back laying his head on her shoulder, taking the reins they moved at a trot headed east. She had no idea where they were going her only hope was a dream of a girl that she had never met.

"We must go back for them"

"He is dead probably the girl too" Zepol answered Vlad.

"We have seen Xela's ability there is no way..."

"I told you I saw him get hit before the battle really started in the confusion the girl dragged him into the tree's at least ten Orcus followed I tried to help but got cut off they overwhelmed me Heffer saw it too"

"He is right" Heffer spoke up "there is no hope for the girl with the dark one down or dead they were both surely killed and we still have many of them tracking us turning back now would be suicide"

"I hate to say it Vlad but my men are right we would not stand a chance with Heffer's leg and your shoulder and Leron gone off to who knows where our only hope is to push onwards."

Vlad new the truth was in Knarf's words, he had taken a bullet to his left shoulder and though he had wrapped it tight the bleeding would not stop, and the wound to Heffer's leg was not good for anyone. Two horses is all they had and the Orcus were closing in, it had been a good battle they had taken out over half the Orcus that had attacked them but now they were out of ammo, Knarf had a few rounds left in his hand gun and there were two clips in the saddle bag for Zepol's weapon. Leron had left them promising that he would catch them up and that was over four hours ago, so turning back now would certainly be the end of them all and he knew it. It was his mission and his choice bearing in mind that his whole race, his own people's future, not just one but also thousands of his kin's lives were at stake.

"You are right we must make it to Paris no matter what it takes we shall move as quick as we can and make distance between us and our pursuers, please someone wrap the bullet wound up tight on your friends leg or else he will bleed out before we reach."

Knarf did what was asked and fixed up Heffer's leg as best he could, after drinking some water from their canteens they mounted the horses two to a saddle and rode as fast as the horses could carry them west to the French borders.

^
‑

It was on the fifth day since the battle on the dusty hill that a small shed of hope came along. The last few days had been tough; though Xela was awake his condition seemed to be worsening. He spent most of the time shivering with cold sweats, and when they stopped for rest and a little food he had found it hard to keep anything down, Katie soon realised that food only sent him in fits of convulsions only ending with vomit of the recently digested, the young girl decided to only give him water and watched over him closely while he slept, his health seemed to border on the line of life and death.

Sometimes he would stop shivering and moaning and laid still, so still that Katie felt the worse checking for a pulse or a heartbeat, more than often there was neither and she found herself continually weeping besides the still presumably dead Xela, but her flooded eyes found joy every time he woke from death shivering and moaning once again. It was sad to see him suffer, but she did not want to be alone she didn't want to lose another it was almost impossible for her to think what she would do if he did die, she was not sure if she could or even would go on, he was the only thing that was driving her, the hope of saving him like he had many times before saved her, the hope that something might go right for a change the belief that they both could make it through all this. But he was strong she could see this no other being she knew could fight to stay alive like she had watched this man do, it was as if death himself kept stealing him away but a great fight was happening between them and somehow he always found away to escape, inside she applauded his bravado but worried extensively after all her mother had told her that no one could escape death forever.

By the second night she had no food left and she helped her sick companion to drink the last drop of water from her canteen. They had crossed over the dry lands and now they had entered a land of trees, where there were trees Katie knew there was often water. Getting Xela into the saddle had become hard, often he did not want to get up or move anywhere, he kept telling her to leave him to die peacefully, but she nagged and would not let him rest until he struggled to his feet, words like "the only peace you will have is when you are on that horse and in that saddle" Showed Xela a strength in this young girl that he had not seen before and knowing her words to be true he lent on her and used what little strength he had left to get on Distant and continue their journey.

It had become obvious to them both that the maze of trees they had entered was much more than woodlands. The trees went on and on showing them only a little sunlight. It was hard to be sure if they were travelling east. So Katie started to climb a tree every morning to watch the sunrise making certain of their eastward heading. It was the first time she had did this when she realised the vastness of the trees they had entered, as far as her eyes could see there were rows and rows of trees they had entered a forest, giving her hope that this was where she was meant to be. They pushed on always moving and resting little. On the fifth day after starving for two nights she ate some form of berries she had pulled from a tree which had made her ill causing her to vomit it had made her a little pleased that she had tried them first she could not imagine what those vile berries would of done to Xela in his current condition, but both of them still gasping for just a drop of water, so desperate they had resorted to chewing leaves for their juices but this too made Katie sick and made Xela maybe a little worse. But drained and feeling ill from last night's leaves she climbed the early morning tree as she usually did to find directions, but almost fell backwards when she noticed smoke rising above the trees about a mile west of their position.

"People, Xela someone that might help us we must be quick" She began to help him into the saddle.

He had spoken very little these past few days making Katie feel as though she was all alone but it was understandable it seemed to hurt him each time he spoke, his mouth had become very dry and his lips had began too chap he had whispered to her before that his throat had swelled making it even more difficult for him to breath, but that day he spoke to her whispering in her ear after he was in the saddle clasping her waist holding on as distant cantered navigating her way through the trees.

"They... may... be people... . who could hurt ... us.. be ... careful." Taking pauses between almost each word to catch his breath as he weased the words from his mouth.

It had dashed Katie's hopes only a little, he was right there maybe dangers so she would be careful.

It did not take too long before they reached the clearing amongst the trees where Kate had seen the smoke. She had expected to find a camp fire with maybe a few people sitting around cooking their early morning meal before moving on to their desired destination. But what she found was far beyond her expectations; she would have never imagined a place like this. Not here, not this deep in the wild midst of a dark forest. Standing before them was a large building made in the old ways, grand in appearance its walls were built with stone bricks, ten wondrous large windows two at the very peak, four along the middle and four on the ground level with each pane made up of crisscross glass sat in perfect arrangement in the face of the building.

Above the arched bronze decorated oak wooden front doors set in stone and colourfully painted was an ancient coat of arms. The same copy could be seen above the balcony and top windows carved into the building with words written under it in a language Katie did not understand. The coats of arms reminded her of some of the stories Navi used to tell about the time before the old ways, with Knights in silver armour and great kings such as Arthur and his round table when honour and justice was the dreams and desires of most men. The clearing in the Forrest had created enough space for whomever lived here to have and to tend the most beautiful garden Katie could ever of hoped to ever be in. with flowers of all kinds and colours perfectly placed in an arrangement of patterns with four flower beds at every corner of the garden, the green well cut lawn oozed with the fresh smell of morning dew. To the right of them just through the open gate a little tiny pretty house stood on a pole with nuts hanging from some kind of weaved nets. The Dover girl watched in amusement as little birds flew in and out of it pecking at nuts as though it were really their own home.

A group of white doves sat atop of the grand house staring down at the newcomers as if they were the guardians of this realm and Katie and Xela had been recognised as trespassers. At the centre of the Garden in all its beauty and stature with a carving of what seemed like a cherub was a fountain. On seeing it Katie did not stop to admire the art that someone had carved from stone probably many many years ago, or to glance in awe as the water trickled down over stone steps like a small miniature waterfall, nor did she stop to even consider if the water was fit to drink. She rode across the grass with no care of the damage she was doing to the lawn, dismounting at the fountain she drank her fill then putting her head under the water she splashed about giggling almost like a farm pig finishing its slop and rolling around in mud. It was then that she felt a little selfish for not considering Xela first, filling her canteen then dragging Xela from the saddle she laid him on the grass and gave him water allowing him only to take small sips.

"You are here oh goodie"

Startled by the strange voice Katie pulled out the hand gun she had taken from Xela in case of trouble.

"Oh put that thing away silly girl you will have no use for that here" The dark frizzy haired women stood fearless of the gun and the girl before her.

"Who are you?" Katie still held the gun pointing it at the strange lady not forgetting Xela's words of warning.

"No my dear that's the question I should be asking you but as I already know the answer there is no point in asking." The strange women looked to the garden noticing the horse hooves.

"Oh no what have you done" ignoring Katie and her gun she passed by them and stood ranting and raving about her grass.

"There is a path! There is a path! Could you not have just rode along the path? Look how you have ruined it; you see you have ruined it."

"I... I'm... sorry" Katie did not know what to say, clearly this women was mad or slightly unhinged. "We were thirsty we just needed water I didn't think..."

"That's the problem with you youngsters these days

you just don't think. Bess! Bess!" The unsettled women shouted towards the house.

There were others here Katie felt momentarily frightened an unsure of what she should do, wondering how many people would come out of those front doors armed and ready to hurt those who had damaged the mad women's garden. She held her gun firm which startled the young blond haired girl that came from the front of the house she stopped in her tracks on seeing the two visitors and Katie's drawn weapon.

"Don't worry about her she won't use it, come hither Bess oh I wish you would stop dithering around. My daughter Bess" She half whispered to Katie. "Very good looking don't you think she's a very good girl never runs around the Forrest pointing guns at mothers and their daughters" She said with a disapproving glare making Katie feel a little ashamed.

"Bess my dear help Katie move the dark one to the guest room I will be along shortly to see if there is anything I can do for him."

"You can heal" All Katie's hopes seem to have come along in one moment.

"I can, but those I cannot heal I can help them to pass painlessly, but my dear your friend seems past my help on both accounts but I must have a thorough examination to be sure, now put that gun away and help Bess I must tend the garden I can't bear to see it this way."

Katie tried to say more but the mad women ignored her and continued to rant and mumble to herself about the destruction of her garden. Still cautious of these people the Dover girl did as she was told putting the gun in her pocket she helped the blond girl get Xela onto his feet and into the house.

As they passed through the doors they stepped into a great hall that was beautifully decorated with furniture and paintings made in a fashion that the Dover girl had never seen before, great oil paintings of landscapes and portraits of people wearing unfamiliar clothing with large thrill collars fixed like an old fashion dog collar around their necks, she took note of the date written on one of the paintings next to a signature at the bottom it read 1818, these were paintings from the ancients, from a time long forgotten by most men, well decorated ordainments of forest animals sat on the mantel piece of the great fire place that cracked and popped as the logs burned and the flames rose heating the large black iron pot that had been hooked on an iron rod which seemed to be fixed firmly into the walls of the fire place. As she looked up she was overwhelmed by the feeling of being in the belly of the beast, or in this case a great dragon. The design of the ceiling interior which rose high above their heads was made in such a manner that the support beams made from stone arched in such a way that one could only describe them as a giant spine and rib cage.

"Its amazing, your home I mean."

"Yes, mum always said that this place was once a great king's hunting lodge after it was a monastery. Our family lived in Butley Priory— that's the name of our home, when it was in Melton England."

"It was in England?"

"Yes my great great great or something or other grand parents had it taken down brick by brick rebuilt it here in the middle of nowhere and our family have lived here ever since."

They did not cross the hall as the stairs where to the left of it, moving up the long grand stairway they headed towards what Bess called the west wing, helping Xela was still a hard task even though Katie had help, both girls were relieved when they finally reached the guest room and laid him on the bed, they undressed him both feeling a bit bashful, but more concerned with the many scars they had uncovered, his entire muscular body seemed to be riddled with old scars.

"Your friend has been through the wars."

Katie did not know what to say surprised and shocked by what she was seeing she did not answer but stared at Xela's body, it was as if someone wondered how many times they could cut into him with a very sharp objected without killing him, she could not nor did she want to imagine how much suffering this poor man had been through only to wake up in a world he did not understand. The girls tucked him in bed wiping his brow with a cold damp cloth and waited for Bess's mother.

After some moments of silence holding back the tears trying not to show how upset she was by her friends' scars, Katie made conversation.

"What's your mother's name?"

"Francis, Francis Yllehs,"

"Is it just you and her here, I mean don't you have any brothers or sisters or a father?"

"No not anymore... there was Georgiana, my sister."

"You have a sister where is she?"

"Well she's... "

"She is not here anymore" Francis interrupted as she entered the room peering at Bess in an angry manner.

"Go get some boiling water and my medicines and I will speak to you later" She barked.

"Yes mother" Bess left the room like a scorned child.

"We lost Georgiana a long time ago and it hurts me to even hear her name, Bess knows better than to speak of her"

"I'm sorry" She paused not knowing what to say to a mother who had lost her child, she understood a little having lost herself but not to speak a loved one's name was a strange rule.

"It was not Bess's fault I asks too many questions I

always have, my mother... my mum use to tell me that."

"Well no more question then young Katie, let's see how bad your friend is."

"That's the second time you called me by my name how do you know it?"

"I told you, this is my part of the forest, here I know everything, in fact I was expecting you yesterday but they say better late than never."

Taking her attention away from the Dover girl and tending to Xela Francis said no more leaving Katie dumbfounded by what the half crazed woman had said. Bess soon returned and following her mother's commands insisted that Katie went with her. She took her to a room not far from Xela, Fresh clothes were on the bedside, and at the centre of the room a tub filled with water and sweet smelly foamy bubbles.

"Please bathe, I have given you my riding clothes I am sure they will fit we appear to be the same size."

"But Xela I don't really want to leave him"

"Mother is good at what she does clean up have a little something to eat and then we will check on him." Bess turned to leave the room.

"Bess?"

"Yes" the blond girl answered.

"Thank you; you are good people your mother and you."

The girl looked almost ashamed and turned hurriedly leaving the room making Katie wonder what she had said wrong.

^
—

Yatnahc sat firmly on the shoulders of the great beast with Light digging her claws into the tough scaly skin being assured that she was not hurting the creature. She had never imagined that in her entire life time she would experience what she was feeling now, being so high above everything made the world seem so small, landscape rushed by as the air pushed past them like one giant invisible wave threatening with every moment that if she let go then it would take her with it to a place of no return. They were fortunate to befriend Drawoh that was what he called himself. It had been the mountain tribe that had led them together; they had thought she was a warrior goddess sent to save them, at her feet on bended knees the tribal king spoke to her in his tongue.

" Zaman boyunca biz seni bekledik."

"Maya" Yatnahc called. The girl approaches making the monk feel uncomfortable when she reached her with a bowed head.

"What's going on what is he saying?"

"He say a long time waiting us you" The tribe women spoke with a trebly voice seeming a little frightened to get to close or even meet eyes with Yatnahc, which was strange as it was only the day before when they sat as friends on a rock and watched the black craft floating.

"Waiting for me, why?"

Maya asked the king and began to translate as he spoke.

"For as long we here live our people cursed, many warriors die to rid land of horribleness, you understand?"

The monk nodded and Maya continued.

"For many years warriors practise. Men and women, we learn to fight in the sacrifice that keeps horribleness from the village."

"What Horribleness?"

"Those who see it never come again. once warriors leave day after day we were once a great people thousands be here, now we are few every four moons warriors leaves now to fight and die, it is said on wall of tomb that a day comes when Goddess Safire mistress of elements will walk amongst the Yarazk and stop beast and end curse our punishment for stealing Mountain."

Yatnahc stood silently thinking and trying to understand fully what she had been told before speaking.

"And you think I am the Goddess?"

"You have power like no mortal you command the elements you will for us destroy monster?"

"Monster?"

"Yes great demon punish us for stealing mountain, our king begs forgiveness for the manner this night you were treated."

"Tell him all is forgiven but I am no goddess."

The young girl conveyed the message and the king answered.

"He says he does not believe, he has seen your might, and ask for you climb rock and defeat demon."

"What rock?"

Maya pointed up towards the peak.

"It is cold dangerous to climb but there is where demon sleeps."

"Tell your king for the burial of my friend and nursing me back to health I will go to the peak to investigate."

On hearing her answer all the people of the village cheered and rejoiced, she had made no promises but already she was treated as though she was already a heroin of the people. The following night a celebration took place, drums played men and women danced, Light was revered as a spirit cat and was fed cooked wild boar and lambs meat. It was good for her to eat cooked food it reminded her of the luxuries she had missed when spending time with the old man and she wondered when they would meet up again.

The following morning gifts were bestowed upon them, a Sheepskin hooded coat had been made and offered to Yatnahc by a young pretty lady.

"Seni ölümcül doruk so_u_undan korumak"

"She says for protect you from deadly cold of peak." Maya translated.

Two Iron forearm clasps wonderfully pattern with the symbol of the eagle were presented by a young boy that the young Monk believed was the king son.

"He says to protect you from the demons bite"

And finally the king himself presented her with a great spear.

"To pierce the demons heart" Maya told her.

It was a surprise to both the Cat and the Monk when two men came forward carrying armour that appeared to be made of steel.

"This is for Spirit to protect it during many battles it may have."

The men were frightened to approach, but did so cautiously so Light let them attach the armour, the metal was surprisingly un-heavy but further more it made her look more menacing than she did before, if people were not frightened of her before they would most definitely be now the armour covered all of her back and her under belly a separate steel head piece was attached which covered her neck and part of her head slits were made so that her ears could slip through comfortably covering only the side and top of her head. eye slots were also made leaving her jaw totally free from armour or any restrictions, the armour itself was forged with ancient symbols engraved all over it Yatnahc was told that these symbols would ward off evil spirits. Having the ability to disguise anything that she touches Light choose to make the armour black for now feeling pleased with the gift she had been given. Four men were to accompany them and by the worried looks on their families faces and the long tearful goodbyes it was obvious that none of them expected to ever return.

They left the village with the brightness of the early morning sunrise making herself and her amour invisible light tracked on a head of the others in case they stumbled on anymore unwanted surprises. It had not been long before they reached the base of their expected steep climb and began their ascent. Their journey was tougher then Yatnahc had expected, the higher they went the colder it became. The air had thinned making it hard for any of them to breath it had been five hours since they had left the village and the only one that seemed little affected by the climb was Light. She had found pathways going upwards as though they were steps carved and made precisely for her paws and nothing bigger, the Monk could see how comfortable the cat was in the mountains and envied her a little. She was a mountain girl herself but had never climbed so high that she almost reached the clouds. One of the warriors that accompanied them had already turned back he had not come as prepared as the others a sheepskin coat with no underlining clothing which seemed to do little for those that did have it had caused him to become very ill, now another was affected wrapped tightly in layers and layers of material more than Yatnahc and the others it still had not been enough for him, their clothing was no longer enough to keep the freezing cold chills that crept into every inch of their bodies at bay.

The mountain coldness had affected the poor man's mind he began to speak frantically saying words the Monk girl did not understand, even his fellow warrior their guild to their destination seemed confused by what he was saying, but before anyone could do anything he threw himself off the mountain as he fell echoing for what seemed like eternity was a shrilly laughter of a half crazed man, she had heard of this before, the lack of oxygen at this height could sometimes make one hallucinate and imagine things that are not really there, Yatnahc only hoped that his delusion was of something pleasant before his final end. Their guide said a few words that she guessed was a prayer and then continued trekking. It had become obvious that he had been up here before when they prepared to ascend the monk noticed while he wrapped his hands in the protective material they were all given that many of his finger tips were missing she assumed that this was down to frostbite from the time he came here before, but the scars he had on his whole right arm and the right side of his face explained nothing at all about where they were headed they seemed to be burns and up here there was no heat.

Six hours and finally they reached the mouth of a cave there was still a lot more climbing to do to reach the peek but it appeared that was not where they were going. Yatnahc began to enter the cave but the burnt face guide stopped her with fear in his eyes and motioned that they should not go and immediately he began to setup camp. It seemed silly to sit outside the mouth of a cave when they could get a little protection from the cold inside. But it was the Yarazk Mountain and it was their way so she complied. For the next two hours they drank soup to warm their bones and rested the guild had intended to build their strength up make them ready for what laid ahead and when he felt that Yatnahc was ready he motioned for them to enter the cave, he and the other would not be coming with them it was here she knew they would find the demon, looking back at the two unwilling men Light understood that this was the place and immediately made herself unseen and scouted a little ahead once again.

The deeper they moved inside unexpectedly the more warmer it became thirty minutes in and the cave only seemed to get bigger. It became so warm that Yatnahc had taken off all her warm clothing and left them behind. It was as though a great furnace was burning somewhere deep in this cave giving warmth to the inside of the mountain. It was not long after when the sound began, it could have been mistaken for a thunderstorm that could turn itself off and on every two minutes sending echoing vibrations throughout the entire network of caves, It was only then she wondered what she had let herself get into. She was not invincible as she sometimes like to believe this thing had been killing villagers for years and they had no hope in stopping it so little that they send men up to be sacrificed to stop this beast from returning and killing them all, what made her think that she could make a difference, what made her think that she could defeat whatever it was, she had her own mission, she had to survive because what she carried could hold the fate of the world, she now began to realize how stupid she had been, like her master had said she was always to rash to fast to dive in without considering her actions first. He had warned her before she left that this was her weakness this is why he trusted her with this mission because he believed she would learn to notice her action and consider first before acting. How wrong he had been, though she had been taught to help others and to always show kindness her master had expressed and even more so before she left that she must always consider the greater good, and right now for her to get to the black Forrest was the only important thing because it is for the greater good.

"Cat" She whispered loudly.

She had decided to go back but not to return to the village, they would simply go around it and climb down the other side of the mountain and continue to Germany.

"Cat" She called again then hearing the paw steps before the cat appeared before her.

"We are leaving this place come." She would prove that she was worthy of this mission the Abbot had given her. She turned to leave when a great roar entered her head, she screamed out loud holding her ears as if to stop the sound as she fell to her knees, but covering her ears did nothing, she looked at the cat who seemed unbothered by the sound but was looking at her as though it was confused at why Yatnahc was screaming. Still on her knees images entered her mind as if someone was showing her photographs. The pictures were clear they were memories but they were not her own, great battles flashed in her head, human Orcus and Elfin bodies riddled the battle field, man and elf standing and fighting side by side, great war flying crafts shooting and destroying each other great beast with wings casting fire from their breaths, Ogres stomping and killing all in their path. These were memories from the time before, from the wars that had left the world the way it was now, these were not her thoughts but the thoughts of something old something older than she could imagine and it was communicating with her, the images changed and the pain and roar left her head, they had become warm inviting, drawing her in asking her to come closer.

She did not fear or felt threatened, getting up off her knees she began to walk deeper into the caves as though she were sleep walking confused and worried Light followed her closely knowing something was not right with the monk. They walked deeper and deeper turning right and left through the riddle of caves as if the monk knew exactly where she was going until they came to a cavern and before them stood a great beast, Yatnahc did not fear or step back at all in fright but light roared and moved to attack and protect her friend.

"No Cat he won't harm us."

Light stopped still unsure that the creature would not attack she stayed on guard.

"Who, what are you, why do you harm the people of the mountains?" Yatnahc shouted unafraid.

The answer came back in images, the creature was in her head this is how it communicated and she now understood this. There was no voice as such, but just pictures which somehow made up for words and though some things were hard to understand she grasped the true meaning of what she was being told. He told her his story. Many years ago after the war when his brothers and sisters were killed and his whole race were nearly wiped out of existence, people of the lands below had forgotten what his kind had done how they had sacrificed themselves to defend the land of men and died for their ancestors. No one wanted him around he was seen as a beast, once there had been a time when men would see his kind and offer food and cattle in remembrance of what he and his kind had done for them, but soon no one remembered what he was or what his kind had done living so long made it easy for man to forget, the days had turned dark and man had turned him away forcing him to steal cattle and soon declared him a beast a monster that must be destroyed.

The Elves knew what he was they had never forgotten, they seek to capture him to use his strength for their own purposes. But he had decided he no longer wanted to be part of the land of men and Elves and Greys, he wanted to be left alone. He should have slept for another thousand years but he needed enough food to sustain him he would have to eat regularly for three hundred years before he could hibernate. So he came here to this mountain where the mountain goats flourished and wild pigs ran free, there was enough food to sustain him for generations and no being to interfere with his way of life. That was until they came, the humans from the lands below, taking his goats and calling them their own hunting and catching wild pigs making it hard for him to hunt his own food. Once again he was forced to steal, so at night he would go to the village and steal goats and pigs and he did this often, until one day someone had seen him and it was there the war began between the villagers and himself. At first they had sent large groups to hunt him and they had found where he slept here in this cave and in their attempt to kill him he instead killed them. Their bodies were nutritious and sustained him for a much longer time than ten pigs or goats could.

There was an energy that burned within man that filled his appetite. but before he could get hungry again they sent more men to him and he ate them, until soon there was no need for him to go down the mountain and steal, time after time men would come to him and he ate them, there was no guilt about what he had done, these people meant to harm and kill him so in defence he made them his food. But these days they send men sparingly so at night he once again has started to steal the goat, he had served men during the war and bared no hatred towards them, but here on his own he was willing to do whatever it could do to survive, knowing it was a great possibility that he was the last of his kind.

She had asked him why he had not attacked them and why he chose to speak to her and he revealed that not anyone could speak with his kind, only the special few could interlink with his mind, it had been over a hundred years since he last could speak with a human and he was surprised that a mind such as hers still existed in the world of man. It expressed its name to be Drawoh the last black dragon, they were the biggest and most feared of his breed, they could breathe fire with pinpoint accuracy and spit balls of fire like rockets. She told him of her mission or more like he took it from her mind and he understood he knew the world was once again in danger and without a second thought he offered to help expressing he had nothing better to do anyway and now holding on to his neck looking to her right at his wide wing span while light dug her claws in as deep as she could into the thick scaly leathery skin of Drawoh the Monk and the Cat were now flying on route to Germany to the black Forrest, both hoping their journeys would end there.

∧
—

The long mahogany wonderful varnished dining table gleamed in the candle light letting all who sat at it know it was a well polished and taken care of piece of furniture. Three tall silver candlestick holders each with four extensions that curved upwards made perfectly to hold the extra four candles that accompanied the one at its centre sat in a row along the middle length of the table illuminating the room. The great fireplace gave off a warm cosy heat and nothing could be heard but the crackling of the burning wood and the clink of knife and fork against beautifully decorated blue and white china plates.

Three unique females sat silently eating the meal Bess had prepared for them, Katie had been a little disappointed when she realised there was no meat, Francis was a vegetarian, but the second course as Bess's mother had called it was excellently made, roast potatoes with lettuce cheese and small crispy fried bread like things which Bess had called croutons and quiche, all made up for the absence of meat. No one spoke so Katie felt as though she had done something wrong when she broke the silence.

"Thank you for the meal and your kindness but I would like to go up and see Xela now" she had not seen him all day and the thought of him being upstairs alone while they ate made her feel uncomfortable. She moved to get up from the table.

"Katie"

The young girl turn and faced Francis.

"Yes"

"Please sit down I have something to tell you."

The tone of her voice implied that what she would say would not be to Katie's liking this made her feel a little worried. She sat back down.

"What is it?" not certain she wanted to know.

"It's about your friend, Xela"

The Dover girl sat silently already fighting back the tears as if she knew what Francis would say.

"There is nothing I can do for him."

She stood up almost angry.

"Well then I thank you for trying but I shall now have to take him to someone who can help him." She had not realised that her tears had escaped and were now running down her cheeks.

"Please" Francis got up from the table and took her by the hand affectionately.

"Get off me!" she snapped as she pushed her away. "We will leave, we will find help and he will not die!" she shouted, "He will not die! Do you hear me?"

"Yes we do" Bess moved closer wanting to hug her but held back.

"I, we did not survive a Orcus attack, and travelled all this way across lands and wastelands and through forest for him to die, why huh you tell me why!"

No one replied or even spoke both Francis and daughter just stared at her sympathetically.

"Why, why would God do this, why would fate put so much death in my life so much pain." She was crying so hard she barley could see, her tone had changed from anger to sorrow as she slumped down on the window bench. Both Bess and Francis knew this was the time to approach her and they did both hugging her as they sat either side of the young girl.

"My mother died in my arms you know, and then I watched my friends die and when there was no hope when I too wanted to die, then came Xela, the dark one, a stranger to me but still he protected me and saved me so many times" She wept.

"And just this once, just once I believed I could make a difference and help him, save him like he had saved me, it was more than my life he saved, he saved me in so many ways most would not understand, If he had not moved in the way that dart would have hit me instead, and that would be me laying upstairs now, waiting to die, it should have been me." She sobbed.

"Dart, my dear can you remember if it had a strong odour of any sort."

Katie thought it an odd question.

"You can smell it yourself I still have it."

"Where?"

Katie pulled it from her pocket, realising that she was silly not to have given it to Francis before. The not so crazy women as she had once thought took the dart and sniffed it and then smiled, making Katie think for a moment that maybe she was crazy with moments of normality.

"Roselwheel impossible" She leapt up half crazed.

"What is it?"

"Well I could not save your friend because I did not know what had poisoned him, now I do though I can't believe it myself."

"Why?" Katie was intrigued.

"Its Roselwheel one of the most deadliest poisons known to exists, and there is not one being known to ever survive longer than five minutes with just a drop of this in his system, not without the antidote, my dear your friend is truly special, we might save him yet." And she rushed off upstairs to mix her potions.

"There is hope Katie." Bess told her while she still held her tight.

It had been four days since Xela received the antidote and Francis could not believe how quick his recovery had been, everything about this man was remarkable though he kept insisting that he had not recovered and was weak, he was still strong enough to carry a log twice his body weight, making Francis wonder if he felt he was still weak how much stronger he would be, she knew there was nothing normal about this man. Xela cut down trees and carried large logs for firewood and made sure the fireplace was always burning he also fixed things around the house while Katie cooked and cleaned the both helped out as much as they could as payment for the help the two ladies had given them.

The dread-haired man had been in a place like this before, it was an old building, he knew the house was way before his era it was still stuck in its past a world and time much closer to him than this world and time could ever be. He liked it here and found that the more time they spent in the house the more comfortable they became, it was important for them to leave soon but it would be hard, already the Priory had become like their home. Every evening after food Francis and Bess would play the grand piano in the lounge and sing for them, their voices so calming and alluring making their bodies feel so relaxed making them forget all their problems and stress's and taking away the urgency to leave, filling their minds with imagery of peace and harmony and each night they slept and woke the following day with less desire to leave.

Xela and Katie sat on the garden beach early one morning watching the birds and enjoying the bright sun shining morning.

"You know we must leave today." Xela seemed sad to even of mentioned it.

"Yes I know you are right we must but where are we going?" She was hoping Xela would remind her.

"Have you forgotten? We have to go to… " he paused "To… to the place you know."

"You don't remember do you?"

"No I don't, don't you think that's strange?"

"Who cares we're happy here why do we have to leave?"

"I don't know but I'm sure it's important"

"It can't be that important if we can't remember don't worry yourself." Katie tickled him and ran, Xela got up and chased her through the gardens knowing he was way faster than her he let her think she could get away before he caught her.

"I'm not ticklish" She laughed

"We'll soon see" And he tickled her while she kicked and laughed.

Up peering through a window from a room on the second floor of the house Francis stood with her daughter Bess.

"It appears that are guests don't want to leave."

"I don't like it mother we shouldn't be doing this." Bess snapped and left the room feeling angry.

Already they had been at the house for over a week with all desires or thoughts of leaving long forgotten. Both of them rose early every morning doing the chores before breakfast and then they spent the rest of the afternoon playing games, they felt like they were little children once again with no worries or responsibilities running around the grounds of the priory like it was a playground. Every day they would make a new game to play and today it was hide and seek. Katie loved this game she was very good at finding small place to hide in, she had done this a lot at another place, a place so far away in her mind she cared not to remember. It was while she was playing this game hiding in the study that she discovered a secret. She had tried to hide in the small fireplace in the study by trying to climb a small way up the chimney. She knew Francis would not be happy seeing how messy the dress was she had made her but did not care much, she had never felt comfortable in dress's they made it harder for her to climb trees or run fast but every time she put on her old garments Francis gave her a disapproving look, so she wore them only to please their hostess.

While she attempted to climb she lost her footing and fell, causing soot to cover her making her yellow flower patterned dress almost look black, leaning against the wall in the fireplace to get herself back on her feet she found that one of the bricks pushed inwards and across the room at that precise moment a deep creaking sound caught her attention, wiping the soot from her eyes she noticed the bookshelf had moved. Katie's curiosity took over staggering out of the soot filled corner she went over to investigate. There was a dark room behind the shelf and hanging on the wall beyond the entrance was a torch she quickly went back into the study and took the matches that were in the desk draw returning to the secret room she set the torch alight before removing it from the wall, when she did take the torch from its place the bookshelf closed behind her. She was not afraid of being in dark small places she had spent most of her life somewhere dark, not quite remembering where she felt comfortable and excited in places such as this, Holding the fire lit torch in front of her to light up the way she could see stone steps that went down under the earth, but leading upwards were wooden steps she decided on going up and moved quietly upwards until she reached the landing.

There was only one way to go the path led along a narrow corridor with doors on each side, pulling aside the cobwebs she moved to the first door and enter the room. In the room was a chair and a table against the far wall of the room she brushed of some of the dust and sat down wondering what purpose this dusty old room could have served, she wonder if Francis and Bess knew about this place, it was clear no one had entered this room for years as it was cobweb and spider infested. It was then she noticed the little wooden handle on the wall right near where she sat, being curious she pulled it making it slide along revealing a hole in the wall, she peered through it to find that on the other side was her room "oh my gosh spy rooms" she thought now excited she was eager to learn what other rooms she could spy on, it would be fun to spy on Xela in his room she could mess with his mind for weeks she almost laughed to herself, she had spied on people in the shallows, "The shallows."

She was distracted for a moment the shallows was a place she had known she almost clasped to the memory but being too excited about her discovery she let the thought go eager to enter the next room, leaving the room she walked along the narrow corridor once again until she heard voices, entering the third door on the left she found herself in a room with a window, and on the other side of the window was Francis's room. Bess was there talking with her mother while her mother was staring in the window, at first Katie thought that Francis could see her but then she realised that she had paid no attention to her for some reason she could not see her through the window, it took her only a moment to realise and remember that where Bess's mother was staring from their point of view was a mirror. "Clever" she thought, she played spy and stood listening to their conversation.

"… You know why?" Francis was checking her hair in the mirror.

"She wouldn't want this you know that mother they are good people."

"It hurts me as much as it does you but it's the only way we will get Georgiana back"

"I won't trick them anymore, that girl has been through enough she has lost her mother mum! How could we give her to those… those things?"

How had she forgotten, a tears escaped her eyes rolling down her cheeks as her memories came flooding back to her as she sat solemnly listening to the two people she had thought of as friends. How had she forgotten, the shallows her home and her mother, oh her poor mother, she was feeling the pain of her mother's death all over again as if it had just happened, the Orcus had killed her and had chased them, and the mission Xela's promise to save the little men, she felt ashamed and disgusted at herself and at those that had made her forget, what had these people done to her. She sat still in shock not able to move listening as they continued speaking.

"Maybe the dark one can fight them you have seen his strength."

"Don't be stupid mother no one can fight them, do you really think that even if we do this they will let Jana go, do you even think she is still alive, wake up Mum those things only know death, I am going to tell them!"

"No! You will not child."

"I am grown now mother."

"Maybe so but I am still your mother and you will do as you are told, don't you think I would know it if any of you died, my own daughters, I would know it inside and I tell you your sister is still alive."

Bess knew her mother was angry and her anger made her scared, but she stood strong.

"I will still tell them and there is nothing you can do." She turned to leave the room.

"No Bess you are right, I just… " Francis slumped down on her bed and began crying."

It had been a long time since Bess had seen tears in her mother's eyes and it moved her.

"Mother I know I miss her too." Bess sat besides Francis cuddling her.

"I would do anything to get her back and I would do the same for you Bess you know that right."

"I know mum I know, but the Majestic are evil… "

That was all Katie heard as she rushed back down the steps into the study. The Twelve, they planned to give them to the twelve, she could not believe it. She closed the book shelf and found a brush to sweep up the sooty mess she had made in the study not forgetting to brush her feet off so not to leave a trail. She rushed to her room and undressed washing herself quickly in a basin of water she cleaned away the soot, instead of putting on another dress she grabbed her old clothes and put them on. The pants were so comfortable she had missed them. Packing a bag with things she thought they would need she left her room and rushed down the stairs.

"Katie!"

She turned and saw Bess and her mother on the stairs behind her.

"What are you doing?"

"Leaving XELA!" She shouted.

"What's going on?" Xela entered from outside.

"Ask them it appears they have plans for us."

"She heard us mother" Bess whispered.

"Katie we were now coming to tell you I swear." Francis pleaded.

"Tell her what?" Xela demanded now standing in front of Katie in protective mode.

"They have been doing something to us Xela, making us forget things."

"Forget what?" Xela could see how worried Katie looked.

"Forget my mother, the shallows, your friends Leron, Vlad, they made you forget that you have to save the dwarves."

"Le who, what are you speaking about?"

"Think, think hard try and remember Leron and the dwarf Vlad, your friends think."

Xela's eyes widened images flashed before his eyes, the chamber he had woken from, the people that had died at the elf station in Ipswich the fights and the adventures he and his friends had incurred, "Leron" he whispered to himself, his expressions changed from confusion to anger with the realisation of what Katie was telling him as his memories came flooding back.

"How, why and what did you do to us?" Fury flamed in his voice as well as Xela's eyes.

"I'm sorry" Francis cried. "My daughter… " tears poured and Francis sobbed uncontrollably. Bess spoke for her.

"My sister was taken six months back by the faceless ones we had long thought her dead until mother was contacted by them."

"How do you mean contacted?"

"We have a radio, and they told us that Georgiana will be returned to us if we kept you here until they could return."

"And how exactly did you keep us here."

"We are sirens."

"Siren?" Katie had never heard of such a thing.

"Sirens are females, who could bemuse men by their voices at sea and made their ships crash into the rocks, but Katie is no man and we are not at sea." Xela explained

"They are ancient tales Xela some parts are true. Our ancient ancestors did this most likely but we have a stronger power than the tales tell, we can control people male and female with our song only for a short time but our strongest strength is to make one temporarily lose their memories and that is why we sang to you each night so you would not remember."

" we … feel ashamed" Francis interrupted still crying "Bess did not want to do this but it was my daughter I would have done almost anything to get her back."

"But why us what is it they want?" Xela had calmed on listening to their explanation understanding what a mother would do for her own child.

"It is the girl, its Katie they want, I don't know why but I hope we can make it up to you but Katie is right you should leave as soon as possible I don't think it will take them many days longer to arri… "

Bess stopped speaking and everyone went silent, they had all felt it at the same time, it was the presence of darkness, so much evil had arrived in one place and fear struck them all. Outside not even the smallest creature could be heard all finding the smallest deepest place they could hide in, it was as if a thick large dark cloud had covered the land pouring fear into the hearts and souls of every living thing.

"It's too late they are here, I'm sorry, I'm sorry I'm sorry… " Francis said over and over again crying frantically at the fate she had bestowed upon her two guests.

"Xela come with me." Katie ran into the study with Xela trailing behind, she opened the secret room.

"I don't know where it leads but we must go down."

Lighting the torch they headed beneath the priory as the bookshelf closed behind them.

14

The Importance of the Heart

It had been two days since the large legion of soldiers had arrived at Regor's garrison in Paris. Knowing so many had come made him feel uneasy, the Garrison was only small he had only five hundred soldiers under his command and though his garrison was too small to be called a station there was room for many more, though he rather there was not. This was the place unruly soldiers or Elfin politicians were sent, Elves that did not care to much about ruling and controlling races that were not even their own kind. This place was meant to be a punishment a way for Maxius to keep opinions he did not like from the populous, so here is where they were sent to govern, a city surrounded by toxic and flammable gasses, a place where beings were always uncertain when they would have to run for shelter in case of a fire storm, a place where beings including Elves could get caught unaware and die and often did.

No one wanted to be here— Regor and his men made it their home, a place where they were not bothered by the politics of the world their home where no one bothered them, the Elves knew a long time ago that they did not rule here, the resistance did and Regor made sure he did nothing to antagonise them, the last commander before him tried to bring them down and the whole garrison was wiped out none left alive. It was not that he was afraid but more because he and his men understood why the resistance fought, they no longer wanted to be treated as second class beings and wanted lands of their own without being governed by a race that cared little for them, and the Elves here in Paris understood this because they themselves would fight like they did if the situation was reversed. He and his men liked a simple life a life where he felt the resistance and he had an understanding, one where they just left each other alone, and now he felt that life here was in jeopardy.

The door knocked and without waiting for an answer Anairda Grip entered his office. Every time they met he found that he could not help but admire her strength and beauty, she too was not pleased with the amount of men she travelled with, she had told him it was by the order of Maxius that these Elves accompanied her on their peace mission and she could not refuse. "Peace" He thought "does she really believe peace is what Maxius intends."

"Yes Anairda what can I do for you today?"

"I have come to let you know we have received a message from the resistance, they agreed to meet with us at ... On the morrow at first light."

"First light but this is the time the Greys craft will arrive for the prisoners."

"I am not here for your ship or your prisoners that business is your affair, to be honest I will be glad to leave this garrison just to be away from that... that thing that travels with those Orcus, he is dark and it makes this whole place stink of him, it makes me wonder what our world has come to when we have to do dealings with such beings."

"Careful my lady such talk will get you sent to places such as this." Regor grinned cheekily.

"An elf's tongue should never be silenced." She replied

"Anyway that thing will be gone with the ship we all feel the darkness that it brings and we will all feel a little relieved when they are gone." The garrison commander had returned to the original subject knowing the dangers of the conversation they could have had.

"You are welcome to join us at the meet as you are master here you must have some connection with these people."

"No I will stay well clear of you and the Faceless one on the morrow your meeting place is but fifteen minutes away from where the Craft lands and I smell trouble brewing."

"Trouble?"

"Anairda I have heard tales of you, it is said amongst the people that you and Lrac are of good souls so I tell you this, be careful on the maine and not just because of the resistance."

"What do you mean?"

"I have said too much already and there is worse places I could be sent than here, I hope your mission goes well, but for now I have work to do." He rose from his chair and shook her hand while he kissed her on both cheeks.

"Mother nature go with you," He said before he left his own office leaving Anairda to think on the meaning of his words.

They moved swiftly down the cobbled steps with nothing but the smallest light of the burning torch to guild them. Reaching the bottom they found themselves in a narrow passageway, the walls were damp and Katie's hand slid across the moss as she felt the stone wall for support as her feet kept slipping on the damp wet floor. The darkness the evil was all around them even here deep below the priory the presence of those things those creatures wriggled fear in the hearts of them both.

Xela's heart pounded at an incredible rate it was as if the darkness could find what frightened you most and play on it, and right now Xela found he was scared not for himself but for Katie, they had bonded more during their journey and now he felt as if she was a part of him and he would be damned if he would let any harm come to her. Katie's worry was for Francis and Bess, although they had done wrong they were still good people and she hoped that no harm would come to them if they found out that they let them escape.

They continued to move along the passageway until they came to a room or an opening of sorts, it was a wide open space which made Katie gasp when seeing the skeletons that were laid on stone beds that was chiselled into the wall. Xela took the torch from her to look around the room, there were skeletons everywhere and at its centre was a large silver box on a stone table, placing the torch nearer he read the words inscribed on what he now realised was a silver coffin.

Here Lays Michael de la Pole third Earl of Suffolk 1394-1415 died at the battle of Agincourt for king and country.

" These were the catacombs of the old monastery, it appeared that Francis's ancestors were sticklers for detail and had the catacombs brought here too as it would have been in England." Xela whispered.

"This must be the coffin of someone important they must have disturbed their graves and brought them here, my mother told me it was not good to disturb the dead."

"She was right, come this way." Xela took her hand and led the way, they entered yet again more tunnels, turning right and left and found more steps that lead downwards, it was not long before they heard the chilling screeching voices in the dark echoing from way behind.

"They have entered the tunnels Xela we must find a

way out."

She was terrified and she did not care to let Xela know it, the stories and rumours she had heard of those creatures had put fear in her since she was little. These were the demons that would eat your soul and now they were after her. Francis had said Katie, they wanted Katie why? She was nothing but a young girl, she now longed for home, for the shallows and for her mother, just for a moment she wished she was somewhere where she could feel safe.

They kept moving not really knowing where they were headed, Xela could see she was tired but he knew they had to keep moving. He was not well himself and felt the power of these things around him, he did not know who or what these things were but knew it would take all his strength to stand and fight and strength is one thing he did not have the best thing for now was to get Katie to safety.

They rushed along more passageways until they finally found steps heading upwards, both relieved they moved as quick as they could up the mossy stone steps, in her haste Katie slipped but Xela caught her saving her from tumbling down to the bottom. They climbed the steps for what seemed like an eternity, neither of them had realised how far they had come below the earth or how long they had been navigating their way through the catacombs but they had been moving for some while and now the dark presence felt stronger, they were closer to them now maybe gaining on them through the tunnels, Katie's heart began to beat with incredible speed as fear spread through every inch of her body like a plague gradually making her unable to move.

"I can't move my... legs, there too tired... those things, they will get me won't they Xela." She said sitting on the steps.

The dark skinned man could see that she was shivering and though it was cold here he knew it was the fear that had made her shiver so.

"No they won't come on look ahead I see the top it must be a trap door or something, just a little further and we will be free of this place."

"Free, where can we go where they won't find us?"

"I don't know but we will not see and wait to find out what these things want from you now come on."

His encouragements made her see hope and he was right, the torch lit up the way showing the end of the steps. Forcing herself back onto her feet she continued to climb the steps while Xela held her hand firmly until at last they reached the top and the trap door. Pushing it up slowly and peeking through he was pleased to find that the maze of tunnels below had led them to the stables, after helping Katie up he climbed up himself. The horses were spooked, they did not act wildly it was the opposite they seemed to be silent and had moved in the furthest corners of their stalls.

Katie did not think twice, opening the stall and saddling up she mounted distant while Xela mounted one of the other horses that Francis and Bess had in their stables both horses were uneasy they too had felt the dark presence that had fallen over the priory and was eager to escape, and without waiting for their riders to open the stable doors they galloped through them like crazy horse's galloping as fast as they could in a direction away from the darkness hoping to escape its presence.

The horses headed into the deepness of the forest; it was night— and they had spent almost a whole day below the priory. After shouting to Katie to keep her head down in case she was hit by a branch, Xela put his down also as though he slept knowing the horses would navigate the trees in the dark until they felt safe. As the horses raced Katie closed her eyes almost feeling the pacing heart of her steed as the wind rushed passed them and the leaves rustled she could not help but feel that they were being chased.

Four men two to each horse rode slowly through the dust roads of Paris leaving the toxic gases that surrounds the city behind them, they had been riding at full pace all through the night trying to keep some distance between them and their pursuers after learning that they should always keep moving. A few nights back they had setup camp and rested not knowing how close the Orcus were behind them, and soon enough they caught up nearly killing them while they slept. They had battled and fought that night killing many and leaving them with no ammunition at all, the possibility of more than fifteen to twenty Orcus still alive chasing them were slim but they all knew with no weapons it would be silly for them to stand and fight, so they moved on escaping into the night and now if they needed to sleep they did so on horseback while the horses trotted.

It had been a relief for them to see the big white windmill type fans that rotated so fast and swift. Heffer had heard of this and explained how his father had told him that the Elves had built these fans as tall as three buildings to keep the gases away and make passage for travellers to Paris, they had planned to make Paris a great city like the silver city London, but most of its population were dead or gone and no one wanted to be in a city surrounded by toxic fumes so they gave up on the idea and built little more than just these fans. There were two rows of the great wind machines that made a pathway that went on for miles blowing the gases away from either side making it safe for them to enter the city. No one knew what weapon had caused the toxic fumes because no one had been able to travel to the centre of the gases and survive, so it was just a hope that one day the gases would just die out, but it had been this way for years and it seemed as though the gases came from the ground itself and it would never stop.

They knew that Paris was only miles away and rode all night exhausting the horses until at last they had reached the city. The building's were crumbling and falling apart, at first they only saw rubble, and as they moved on eyes and faces began to peer through windows of old ancient ruins, the horses were breathing heavy so Vlad suggested that they should dismount and walk all except Heffer who was still injured.

"What if we need to ride fast?" Zepol said a little worried about the people that were now appearing.

"Well we won't be taking these horses; to gallop now would kill them." Vlad had thought this was obvious to all of them.

"But what about..."

"Don't worry Heffer we all see them, it's either they kill us or they don't there is nothing we can do about either just keep moving."

They kept walking, Paris was a large city but the captain had told them that no one lived on the outer edge people only lived at the city centre and the rest of the streets of Paris were always bare. So Vlad or the others had not expected to meet anyone so soon still being so close to the gassy borders.

As they walked more and more people made themselves visible coming out from frail old buildings and walking along roof tops men and women and children all disfigured and scared with what look like boils on their faces all dirty and rough looking wearing rags for clothes most looking half starved all gathered in the streets behind following them as the four men moved on trying not to stare, Knarf had made a point of holding his machine gun out in front of him letting the people see that they were armed hoping they would not test them as all their guns were empty. They kept moving until they came to a posse of people in front of them, now they were surrounded on all sides, A tall black haired one eyed boiled face man wearing torn trousers and what looked like an old blanket for a shirt stood in front of everyone else and address them.

"Où allez-vous?"

"I don't understand" Knarf said as it dawned on him that neither Zepol nor Heffer spoke French, he looked to Vlad.

"Don't ask me I don't speak French."

"He says Err... where do you go" A small bald headed man almost dwarfish in size with no boils on his face unlike the rest and better dressed than most stood in clean black trousers and a brown sheepskin jacket next to the one eyed man.

"Tell him we are headed to the centre" Vlad answered the man who was only a little taller than himself.

"A dwarf huh, plenty of err... how you say money for you guys no?"

"I would like to see someone try." Vlad stood stone faced putting his hand on the hilt of his hand gun as if he was ready to pull it from its holster.

"Look err... no need for trouble, you give us horse and weapon, then you go huh."

"Tell your boss we would sooner die." Knarf was quick to answer,

"No Knarf don't worry calm down I have this." Vlad patted Knarf's back before facing the small man.

"Anyway what he said."

"You are funny little man but it is not this man you err should worry." The bald head looked to the tall one eyed man who they had all assumed was the leader of these people.

"I rule here, and you could not err... how you say kill all of us with your guns huh, so you will die I can make money with err... dead dwarf body."

"Be careful, you might be mistaken for one yourself."

Zepol snapped.

He had not known Vlad for long but this adventure had brought them all close together and without the dwarf they would not have made it this far let alone out of the shallows, so now Vlad had become like family and for a small man himself to insult Vlad's height was unacceptable.

The small man gave Zepol a look that would kill if it were possible before barking something to his people.

"On va les butter!!!"

It was unclear what was said but their only guess was he had ordered his people to attack them. The people closed in with clubs and stick some pushing their children ahead of them to use for protection against retaliation; Vlad turned his gun around ready to use the butt as a club, Heffer still in pain climbed down from his horse.

"What about the children?" Zepol shouted to Knarf.

"This is war every child is an enemy soldier, fight or die!" Knarf shouted readying himself.

Just as it seemed they would all now fight until they died, gun shots began to fire all around them.

"Resistance!" someone screamed and the people disbursed running as if for their lives to whatever hole they had climbed out from.

"You are lucky this time little man." The bald headed man said before he ran off into the crowd and disappeared like the rest of them a short moment later the streets were bare leaving the dwarf and his three friends standing in the streets surrounded by over twenty men in green uniforms. Looking up they noticed there were uniformed men also on the roof tops all fully armed pointing their weapons at them.

"Who are you?" Vlad shouted out.

Not one of them moved or made a sound, there was silence for awhile until they heard the sound of an engine coming from behind them turning to look they were all surprised at the green metal vehicle with a large machine gun at the top It was an ACV an armoured combat vehicle Knarf and his men had seen these vehicles on old movies back at the shallows but they believed that all war vehicles had been destroyed to see one in real life was surreal.

"It's ok buoys dem mun garn." A tall slender dark skin man dressed in the same green combat uniform like the rest stepped out from around the back of the ACV; these were soldiers Vlad had fought beside enough uniform men during the war to recognise a real soldier when he saw one.

"Who are you?"

"Me my dwarf friend, we is da resistance, the last mun dat fight oppression in dese dark land, me name is Aubrey but my men just call me Pops."

"Why Pops?" Zepol seemed curious.

"Dem call me dis because when me see da enemy me just pop off dem head." He laughed as he showed them the sniper rifle he was carrying over his shoulder.

"Come now your mun der need sum looking too, my buoys will tek care of dem horses, come jump in."

He walked to the back of the AVC, they did not know if these men could be trusted but they knew for now they were better off with them so with no hesitation they climbed into the back of the almost tank looking armoured vehicle, and after shouting to his men to cover their track Pops climbed in and the driver drove off to who knows where.

Katie finally fell asleep resting her head on Xela's shoulders, the camp fire burned dimly as the first touch of daylight crept up slowly from the east, the forest was still dim, but Xela could still see the horses by the stream where he had left them, the horses had moved like they were possessed almost exhausting themselves before they would slow down, the water from the steam would rehydrate them so they could continue to wherever they were going. Those things had terrified Katie and Xela knew this was the reason she found it hard to sleep, she had begged him to promise that he would not let them take her and he did, only then did she calm and finally found some rest, now as daylight came he too also began to drift off falling into a deep sleep.

The beach was beautiful, the sun shone brightly as the gulls circled the air looking for their morning catch, the waves rolled back and forth across the sea creeping somewhat on to the beach before rolling back as if retreating from the dry warm sand. Few people sat out in the sun getting tanned or eating ice cream, it was a perfect day and Alex walked hand in hand with Suzanna his girlfriend, she had long dark brown hair that reached passed her shoulders, her body and her beauty was eye pleasing to all who saw her in her red and yellow bikini. He notice he was wearing his long black shorts and a thin almost see through short sleeve button shirt that was open exposing his chest, he could not remember putting them on, in fact he could not remember even coming to the beach, he looked to Suzanna

"How did we get here?"

"I don't know" she replied "but chase me" and she began to run giggling as she moved. For a moment he forgot all his questions and enjoyed the sun and the environment, he began to chase her laughing also as he left footprints in the sand, he finally caught up to her and they fell on the beach in each other's arms, after a moments glare they kissed, and while they kissed a dark cloud blocked out the sun and a terrible feeling came over him, Alex looked up seeing that darkness was all around him, he looked back at Suzanna who was underneath him still on the beech but only she was not Suzanna she was someone else someone he had never seen but yet she seemed familiar, she was beautiful and alluring her skin was a strange colour it seemed as though it was green, and her hair was as gold as the sun it was then he realised that she was naked and he was on top of her getting up quick he apologized. She was not bashful but stared at him as though she knew him.

"Run, Xela, Run"

"Xela who...?"

"No time get up and run, Run RUUUUUUUN!"

Xela awoke panicking, his heart beating so fast he was surprised he could gather his senses after such a strange dream, but it was not the dream that had scared him, he could feel it, the dark presence, they had caught up to them. Without thinking he got to his feet grabbing Katie and putting her over his shoulder he ran.

Katie woke instantly scared and terrified, she was on Xela's shoulder and he was running moving so fast even a horse would have trouble keeping up with him, she was not sure what was going on until she looked and saw what was behind them. Three dark black long coated white masked things were chasing them, their mask had no mouth, just eye slits and what peered through them send chills through every fibre of her body, deep red eyes almost as though a fire burned within them peering at her eagerly, they were gaining on them she had never thought it possible that anyone could move as fast a Xela.

"They are gaining!" She let Xela know.

Then the voices came, screaming screeching through both their minds like a blacksmith grinding metal or sharpening his tools on a spinning grinder.

"Give us the giiiirl and you may paaaass." They hissed

Xela looked a head though it was dawn the day was still dim but he could see that seven more of the things stood waiting before them,

Katie was screaming, "don't let them get me please don't leave me."

She was hysterical, and he understood how frightened she was. He stopped running knowing now that they were surrounded; taking Katie from his shoulders he put her down and held her face.

"I told you" he said as a tear rolled down his face. "I would never leave you."

Then he kissed her gently on the lips as though he was saying goodbye before shouting at her to run. She watched as he moved fast attacking the things that had come for her fighting with every inch of strength he had left, he was amazing for a moment she fought he would win, but the creatures were just as fast as him surrounding him on all sides.

"Run" he shouted, it was the last words she heard from him, as she turned to move a grey thin hand grabbed her wrist and then covered her mouth, she was scared and her heart began beating more fast and stronger than what it was already she looked to her chest and a strange light was glowing beneath her clothing, it was like the time on the ship, but before anything could happen the creature knocked her unconscious.

Leron had been tracking a trail he believed to be Xela's and felt now that he was close, he had no horse and was on foot, but it had taken days to find the trail that had led him to where he was now. He had believed what Knarf's men had said but he had fought Xela, and had seen some of the amazing things he could do, the belief that he was dead, would not sink in until he had seen it for himself. He had doubled back leaving Vlad to go on to Paris without him, giving them sometime he killed a few Orcus in their sleep and alerted the rest to his presence hoping they would all follow him, their leader was not as stupid as he had hoped and had sent only seven of his men to pursue him while they continued his hunt for Vlad and the others.

Leron ended the seven Orcus lives quickly feeling a sorrow that the world had come to such a place that he was forced to kill in order to survive, it was these times he longed for the voices and thoughts of his people. When he finally found the trail it took two weeks before he came to the wondrous home in the forest, it was there he spoke with a lady and her daughter who had told him of the horrid events that took place and the escape of his friends the night before, the faceless ones had come for the girl, and now Leron moved swiftly not stopping for breath moving his legs as fast as he could, he was close he could feel the darkness of the twelve all around, his only hope is that he was not too late.

Xela had fought the toughest fight he could remember; he was not well and felt he still was not at full strength but these creatures, these beings were fast, at first in his attack he felt like he had surprised them, that they had not expected such speed and power from him, so now they did not fight so carelessly and as he tired he found that he was now on the defensive surprising himself that he could defend against such speed by so many, he knew now that this was the end for him, the possibility of him surviving this was very unlikely his only constellation was that Katie ... he looked around and found that Katie was still standing there. "Run!" he shouted before he took a blow to the head. He flew backwards hitting the ground hard, dazed and blurred vision he could just make out the shapes of the dark things as they closed in around him, their boney fingers appeared to have changed shape all now extending fingers as they changed into long sharp knives, one struck him across his chest ripping through his Mac his own blood soaked his clothes, once again he felt the pain in his head as they spoke to him.

"Yoooou should of given uuuus heeeer" they hissed and screeched, raising their long arms he knew they were about to stab him to death, he laid back with no energy even to resist them, thoughts wondering to another time and another place, one where he had a girlfriend a home and probably a normal life in a normal world, he wonder now if such a life ever existed or was it a world he had created in his mind, his head was thudding but he fought to keep his eyes open, he wanted his killers to see his eyes and know that he did not fear them. Closing around they prepare to strike, but just as they leaned in, something large with very sharp teeth leaped onto one of them, now there were more creatures. Creatures were attacking the creatures, he almost laughed, he could not make out what they were, but he hoped Katie was safe,

"Protect Katie Lord if there is one thing you do I pray you protect her" they were the last words he whispered before one of the dark creatures returned and jabbed its knife type fingers into his stomach twisting them a little, it stared at him and he looked the thing in its red fiery eyes then he went limp and the faceless thing pulled it bloody hands out from his stomach changing its knives back to bony long grey fingers and turned to attack the things that were now attacking them.

The Wolves had been amongst the forest beyond their own borders for almost a week now living off the land they hunted as a pack, the great bird always watching out for them circling up above, they had seen some strange things during their travels the forest had changed, it was no longer a safe place for even their kind, ogres had torn up trees as if searching for something while killing animals not even to eat, leaving trails of carcasses behind their path. They had tracked one a few days back it had not been hard to find the clumsy creature, its prints were clearly marked in the forest earth and it stench drifting on the morning breeze filling their sensitive noses.

When they had caught up to the thing they position themselves in front of it, giving it warning to turn back to where ever it had come from, the ogre not intimidated at all attacked ferociously, the wolves in turn retaliated each sinking their mighty teeth into its limbs as it roared and swung them around, but they refused to let go, the mighty Eagle flew down digging its claws into its face and pecking out one of its eyes. It was blinded and the largest wolf of them all leaped up hitting the beast in its chest making it topple over. It was down and now the wolves were all ripping and biting away at its throat, blood oozed until the ogre did not move anymore. The pack had a code that they must always eat what they kill, the ogre had now become there feast as they tore away at it flesh with their sharp teeth and blood covered mouths, the eagle too flew down and took its fill. To peering eyes these wolves were no ordinary creatures it was unheard of for a pack to even consider taking down an ogre.

Now as dawn fell upon them, darkness had filled the forest, an evil that had stirred the bones of each and every one of them as they rested. The largest of the wolves stood on a rock and Howled loud as if in warning to those that threaten their way of being, the others got up from there rest and they all ran moving with such speed swiftly and silently, they headed towards what had caused the darkness, they were the protectors of this forest now and they feared nothing.

Yatnahc could sense that something was up with the cat, though she clung firmly to Drawoh she roared out as if eager to be grounded, it was then the mighty flying beast showed her images explaining that the cat sensed something up a head as it did to, but it was not long before Yatnahc sensed it herself, she knew what it was, she had encountered something similar before, but it had not been so strong. As they flew the scenery became dull, there were no clouds and the sun had risen but now everything around them was dull as if they had entered some type of dream. Looking down below as she had thought nine of the twelve was in conflict with what looked like wolves below.

"Fly low." She sent the imagery to Drawoh having gotten used communicating with the dragon.

Drawoh flew low into a clearing nearby slowing its speed, while the cat and Yatnahc leapt from its back The monk landed and rolled back up onto her feet and began to run, the cat already way ahead of her.

The seven wolves had reached the dark figures in the process of killing a being, they had leapt catching the things by surprise ripping and clawing at the creatures, the dark beings hands were like knives swiping and kicking at the wolves trying to break free, the lead wolf looked to his left seeing one of his pack having its heart ripped out of its chest. The creature held the heart in its grey hands almost bemused at how it was still beating.

The mighty wolf in rage attacked knocking the thing to the ground. With one motion of its hand and invisible force knocked the wolf flying against a tree, hurt and bruised after a wimp the animal came back to its feet howling, the five other wolves retreated from those they were attacking and formed beside their leader, the dark creatures formed also extending their hands using the art to hurt the wolves, but together these doglike creatures were strong focusing their minds, the invisible force pushed at them but they held it back as they had created a protective force around themselves, concentrating hard each animal knew that their force field was weakening and they could not hold out much longer, they watched in horror as one of the creatures returned to the injured man and put its sharp knifed fingers through his chest, just then out of nowhere came a being tall and slender almost elflike, moving with speed using his staff he tripped one and began to fight them soon finding he was on the defensive, the creatures attack on the wolves had stopped freeing the wolves once again to attack, as they fought trees around them fell as two Ogres of great size stepped into view wielding clubs they swiped low knocking three of the wolves back one was left unconscious while the other two regained their footing and ignoring their pain ran forward to attack the ogres.

Leron was now under serious attack four of them fought him trying to use the art to gain an advantage, he did not wield the power to move objects with his mind he had been a poor student at these lessons but he had learned to use his staff to defend against such attacks but now he was overwhelmed, so it was a relief to him when someone had used the art against them, two of the dark creatures were hoisted up into the air as if they flew pushed beyond the grounds of the battle, looking to his left, a young light skinned girl almost Asian looking stood wielding a sword with a large panther at her side.

"Thank you." He shouted.

"You're welcome" She replied.

Then before his eyes the cat vanished. The large bird had kept the Ogres occupied while the wolves attacked by flying about their heads and scratching at them, while they took slow clumsy swings at him missing every time, the wolves tore away at the ankles making one topple over, but just as they thought they had a chance of winning this battle, at least five more Ogre rushed in knocking trees down and trying to crush the wolves with their big feet. They were done for, it was over, the dark nine creatures formed together in front of the ogres while the injured and battered wolves formed in front of the strange man and girl that appeared, the Cat made itself visible and stood also beside the wolves.

"Weeee have what weeeee came for a bonus too seeeee yooou all die" The words screeched through their heads.

The dark creatures moved in with the ogres behind them, when a great roar came from the skies, looking up all except for Yatnahc and the cat were surprised, casting a shadow now on them all with its great wing span was a dragon, swooping down in attack form fire roared from its mouth burning up the ground towards the faceless ones and their minions, within an instant just as they appeared the dark ones were gone and their dark presence with them leaving the Ogres behind to be obliterated by the great fire of the dragon. The battle was over, but they knew it would not be so easy if they ever faced them again, the dark creatures had been caught by surprise and all knew the power the twelve held, but it was the dragon that seemed to have scared them making them disappear to who knows where. Leron rushed to Xela kneeling beside him, he could not believe it but Xela was dead.

^
—

Villacoublay was what appeared to be an abandon airbase, the old rusty sign with the words, Armée de l'Air which meant Army of the air was all that was left above the surface to remind those who ventured that way of the valour of those men that fought to protect the city of Paris over a hundred years ago to no avail. The large gate was open and great signs riddle the fence with warning of mine fields and poisonous gasses beyond that point, the only sign of life came after driving some distance to the only remaining hanger left on the airfield. The large hanger door opened and one soldier stood armed as the ACV drove slowly in.

After speaking with the driver the soldier spoke into a radio he carried and the hanger doors closed behind them remotely. The door was impressive but the hanger was empty and Vlad began to wonder what they were doing here. But before he could ask the question the Vehicle began to sink or rather go down, it took a moment for the dwarf and his companions to realise they were going under the ground in some kind of lift. After a few moments they arrived at an underground facility, seven armed soldiers awaited them as their escort when they left the vehicle. There were men everywhere training in the art of war. Great aircraft simulators were operational and had become part of their training.

"Pops how many men do you have here?" Knarf was impressed at the training of these men.

"We have two thousand men here all trained in the art of war."

"Two thousand?" Vlad was surprised.

"Yes this place is bigger than you think; this underground facility goes on for miles, there is ample space to hold much more."

They walked on down a corridor and turned right into a doorway. To find a little man seated at a desk. Immediately the little man rushed from his seat and grabbed Vlad and hugged him.

"Welcome brother welcome."

He was a dwarf, but Vlad did not recognise him, but he was pleased to see one of his kin.

"I am Suinuj of the house of Hurdin; it is good to see my own kind after so long."

"I am Vladlin of the house of Bowin I do not recognise you brother how is it that you came to be here?"

Suinuj seemed puzzled for a short time before he spoke again.

"Bowin you say, are you from the house of Korin the great."

"He was my father"

"Valdarrior be praised you are from across the sea?"

"Are you not?" Vlad was confused

"No my brother we I mean my people have survived

since the war in Italy we did not know many of you survived over there our colony is about three hundred strong, but we live in fear you know how it is the Elfin bastards trying to catch and kill us at every turn, but we survived huh brother ha ha they can never keep us down." Suinuj laughed loudly and Vlad laughed also.

"We did not know that others had survived, this will be great news back home that we have pure blood brethren on another continent we must find a way we could communicate with each other when I return home."

"Come let's eat and talk I feel we have a lot to learn from each other."

Suinuj led the way down the corridor to what they called the mess hall there they would eat good food and tell each other of their adventures and what had brought them all here to the once famous city of Paris.

∧
‒

He sat up, sweating, not knowing where he was or how he had gotten there; he asked himself the question, was he dead? He was sure he was, putting his hands on his stomach he looked down at his belly and found no wound or even a scar, "it was a dream" he told himself. Looking around the room he was in he was disappointed that Katie was not with him, moving from the bed he warmed his hand by the fire burning in the centre of the room, the smoke whirled up and out through a hole in the roof, he felt like he was in some kind of wooden made tepee, not thinking to put on the rest of his clothes that someone had removed and left by the bed on seeing the entrance to his room he was eager to leave and find out where he was even if that meant leaving in his underwear, but before he reached the doorway someone came in.

"Good, I see you are on your feet"

"What's going on I thought..."

"Yes we all thought you were dead my friend but my

cousins have ways that my people do not."

"Leron how did you find me and where are we and Katie is she o..."

"All will be explained put your clothes on there is a lot to be discussed this night and there are those who would speak with you."

Xela clothed himself curious about what had happen since his almost passing, Leron would only answer little about what had happened while he was dressing, explaining that his cousins whoever they were had brought him back from the brink of death with the permission of nature herself, not quite understanding what he meant he excepted that in this time it seemed as if anything was possible, but he had noticed that every time he asked of Katie Xela moved the subject onto something else. They left Xela's accommodation as they walked the dark-skinned man looked back at his abode to find that it was in the base of a tree the doorway sealed up as though it was never there making it look no less ordinary than any other, as they walked many people clothed in an assortment of dark colours left trees similar to the one he found himself in, they found themselves walking amongst the crowd of people all curious about them both looking at them eagerly.

"Leron where are we?" he found he had asked Leron this question more than once and talking to the Fairrien made it easier for him to ignore the stares he was getting from the people of the village, camp or wherever he was.

"We are still in the forest in the Village of the Nemlaer, they look at us strange because it is unheard of for any being to be here that is not Nemlaer, it has never before been allowed but their king has allowed it and my cousins agreed."

"And Katie?"

"We are almost at the meet; all your questions will be answered."

They walked with the crowd until they came to two throne like wooden carved Seats, it was as if the earth herself had created these chairs as roots extended from the seats along the ground a short way and then into the earth. Two figures sat in the seats, one male and the other female, Xela could not help but stare at the female, her skin was green and her hair was almost golden, and the clothing she wore left little to the imagination, a green glittery fabric type gown opened down the centre of her body and what could be described as her underwear was showing, not that it made much difference because if one looked close enough they would notice the clothing was actually see through. But it was not her next to nakedness that had made him stare, he had seen a girl similar in his dream in the forest and he had thought it his imagination that had created such a being, but when five beautiful breath taken being's of the same complexion and race came from the trees behind them and stood at either side of the throne like chairs, Xela found he could not take his eyes of one girl in particular, and she too stared at him. It was the girl, the one that told him to run in the dream.

"You may all sit" The Tanned skin man said that sat on the throne.

"Where on the floor" He whispered to Leron?

"No look behind you."

Xela watched as a tree stump grew from the ground before his eyes to make a seat, the overwhelming feeling that he was still in a dream had returned, seating himself he listened to what was about to be said. The man besides the green skin ladies rose from his chair and addressed the people.

"I see strange looks upon the face of my people I hear whispers of concern that strangers are amongst us." he looked too xela "but there is reason for concern, not that these men are here but because the danger our goddess

Luceria warned us about is upon us, one of our guest's is cousin to the nymphs and is of Fairrien blood he has more right to be here than us so please show our guests respect, now we may discuss what has happened, Ola you have the floor." He then seated himself.

A man seated not far from Xela stood up, Leron whispered that he had been the one that helped save them.

"As you asked I left with seven of my pack to look for the girl and find out what has been happening beyond our part of the forest. We travelled for days in Wolf form and Asher accompanied us, as bird clan leader he chose to come himself rather than send another and we owe and show him much respect for his eyes and help on this venture, he circled high above and reported to us of the destruction he could see to the forest from the skies, we then tracked Ogres some bigger than they once were, there are many in the forest now, they are killing animals and destroying trees for no reason other than what we feel there masters had asked of them."

"And what do you think there purpose is?" someone asked from the back

"I cannot really say with any true conviction, but I would guess they are clearing a path claiming all the forest but what belongs to us so maybe if they could breech our lands we would be surrounded on all sides, these are strange day's people, one day ago we came across ten of the twelve in our forest together."

There were gasp of surprise and murmurs amongst the men that sat at this council.

"Why are they surprised" Xela whispered.

"Because it is unheard of that more than two has ever been seen together" Leron replied.

Ola continued.

"We failed in our mission and we did not save the girl."

Xela mind was racing, what girl? He waited to hear

more.

"They had taken the girl before we arrived but we have brought back those that travelled with her and the dark one."

All looked to the two strange men that had a seat at the front of the council meeting, but Xela was now on his feet.

"What!" He almost shouted.

"They have Katie and you all failed to tell me", he looked to Leron with disgust. "We must go after her now; they came for her and no one else"

"Please be seated." The throne man stood.

"I don't know you" Xela was angry now his friend was in danger and he had broken his promise, he had told her he would never leave her and here these people sat talking nonsense while she was with those... those things he did not dare to think what they had done with her. "Who are you to tell me to sit" He was shouting and Leron put his arm on his shoulder to calm him but he pushed his hand away.

"I am Werdna King of the Nemlaer and we have come here to discuss what we should do about your friend."

"I don't care what you discuss show me the way out of here I will find her myself you ff..." he wanted to swear but he could not "you people have no idea" he turned to walk away before he said something he may later regret when she called him he had heard her voice in the shallows and she had shown herself in his dream and now he knew it was her.

"Xela" he stopped in his tracks and she spoke, her voice like music on the wind, almost dreamy her words were sincere and reached places that other peoples words could not.

"It was me that brought you to Katie do you remember?"

He nodded but found he could not speak.

"I also called her here to this forest and I told her to

bring you, there is something in you a power that must not fall into their hands but Katie's power could doom us all we will not allow them to leave with her, sit please let us discuss how we will catch up to them and bring her back."

Her voice had calmed him almost immediately he had seen the truth to her words and found that he had already seated himself, it was then the women on the carved throne like chair spoke.

"I am Isnat Queen of the Nymphs and mother to these girls you see beside us we are first cousins to the Fairriens and we must tell you the importance of your friend, Lucy show him."

The short golden haired girl walked over to Xela carrying a scroll of some sort as she came close from the earth before him a small table grew and was formed, he again wondered how these things were possible but now his attention was more on the girl before him.

"This scroll is from a collection of scroll once put together by a human a famous philosopher named Nodrog Niarlum, he was the only human that had travelled to our lands since before the war he was like no other, before he disappeared a hundred and fifty years ago he split his scrolls up and sent them to the leaders of every race, some for the humans some for us some for the Fairriens the maids Elves and dwarves, his scrolls contained a Prophesy by a famous man from many years before even you lived Michel de Nostradamus have you heard of him?"

"Yes he could see the future he predicted many things that happened before and in my time."

"Then you know we take his words seriously, this man had written scrolls that no one found but Nodrog he had called them the secret scrolls, and in his works Michel had seen the war from the Greys, he had predicted that man would lose, but also he talked of a time when the whole world would be no longer habitable for any being but the

Greys all will die." Lucy then opened the scroll, "this is only one scroll of the few we have, thanks to shaolin we now have the human scrolls", she looked over to the oriental girl whom Xela had only just now noticed sitting a few seats to his left.

"Read here" she pointed and Xela read.

...The heart will bring either doom or peace to the world the power it holds is beyond any other being but coquille, if a Grey hand holds the power then the Earth will be lost... it then went on

About how darkness will fall upon the earth and how all beings must join with the Concha to save all, but Xela did not understand what all this meant.

"Don't you see Xela Katie is the heart with her the Greys could use her power to breach the Fairrien forests and our own and destroy even the maids kingdoms below the seas, if this happen then all is lost."

15

The Battle of Eifel

Imrarge was a determined beast; to be defeated was not acceptable to him these being's had proved themselves skilful in the art of killing leaving him with only twenty Orcus, a hundred men he had come across the seas with, one hundred was more than enough to kill a small group of being's, but they had out smarted him at every turn, he had thought that killing the girl would make things easier but he had missed but still he had hit a target one was lost to them and the girl was nowhere to be found, he had reported the strangeness of the young human to the twelve, she was their problem now but these few that eluded him this small band of being's was no normal group. They had entered Paris there was no doubt in his mind why they had come here travelling with a dwarf, he almost laughed to himself they would be fools if they thought they could rescue the small group of dwarves that he already knew was here in Paris waiting for the Grey flying ship, though he despised Elves he respected their speed and power as a disciplined warrior race, without the girl and the dark one they would not stand a chance. He moved on with his few men, he would go to the garrison and wait, for he knew it would not be long before they made an attempt at a rescue.

It had been grave news to hear the miss -adventures of

Vlad and his captured Conrad's, Suinuj understood the dangers and the importance of retrieving his men before the arrival of the Grey's ship, he had been well informed and knew that it was on the morrow that the craft would arrive.

"You do know Vlad that if we cannot save them we have to kill them."

A sad expression fell upon the taller dwarfs face.

"I have thought this too and I know that it has to be done."

"I have heard strange things about those who have been in the presence of those things, it is said they can reach into a beings mind and see his soul, they will extract the information from your men and your great city that you have told me about will be at war, we have been preparing for a battle already my friends so you arrived at a good time this fight may be the distraction you need"

"How so?" Knarf said who had sat silently with the others at the table eating a well deserved meal listening but letting the two dwarves get acquainted.

"Well a small army has arrived at the Elfin camp in the city they have come to discuss peace terms with us huh." Suinuj laughed and the men in the mess hall who sat with them laughed also.

"Peace terms?" Heffer had never heard anything like it.

"Yes they think we are stupid we know they come to fight us, so we will have a meeting with them on the morrow and let them make the first move but my friends ha ha we will be well prepared." His bold colourful laughter and his cheeky smile was enough to make him liked.

The new comers sat and ate their food and conversed, their words becoming part of the cacophony of many voices that flowed all around the mess hall, Knarf was thinking on the size of the place, before they ate they were given a short tour, the airbase armoury was filled with weapons of all types ranging from M4's much like his own weapon to rocket launchers and claymores, The dwarf was of high rank here while showing them the underground facility filled with well taken care of Aircrafts of the likes he had only heard in stories of old, Suinuj explained that he was the colonel and had spent plenty of time with the Italian forces back in the war, he had learnt much about their weaponry and had trained most of the men here how to be soldiers, neither himself or many of the men had actually flown any of the aircrafts, though many have been trained in the simulators, only one man takes a craft out for flying, and he takes only the best simulator pilots out with him so they can experience the real G-force and handle the craft themselves, and that was Andre Sllim the founder of this place, he knew that if all pilots regularly flew the Greys would know they had crafts and they were not prepared yet to take on a whole army.

There were only men posted at Villacoublay most had families back at the city centre, from the age of sixteen families would send their sons here, these men were known as the last resistant fighters and their fathers and their fathers father had fought oppression from the Elves and Greys and most thought it was their duty to continue the fight. Suinuj had explained a lot, the working and the ins and outs of this place was genius, these were truly the last freedom fighters.

Silence fell upon the mess hall, every soldier stopped eating and rose to his feet at full attention, Vlad Knarf Heffer and Zepol stood to full attention not really knowing why.

"General in the mess hall!" someone shouted.

As Andre Sllim walked in, he was of average height and overly muscular but he was not a pale skinned human though his skin colour was light not dark like Pops, he wore a uniform dark green in colour much similar to the one Knarf had from his father which he had left back at the shallows and probably would never be found again, medals of honour hanged from the left breast of his jacket, medals he had inherited.

"At ease men" He said calmly and the men sat back at their tables and continued to eat and chat filling the mess hall once again with their voices.

"Arh err Pops I have not err seen you for a few days."

"Yeah mun me been patrolling de eastside wid me men, and brought back sum guest."

"Yes I have err heard, nice to meet you gentlemen, I am Andre." He addressed the newcomers and then sat at the table, he was French though his accent was strong his English was good. They sat and ate discussing the plans of tomorrow, all knowing it would be a bloody affair.

Xela walked amongst the trees thinking over the things he had learned and heard at the meeting of the Nemlaer, it was late Leron had retired to the tree home that was prepared for him and most of the Village had gone to sleep. The Nymph named Lucy had told him Katie was the heart referred to in the scrolls that were collected by a Man named Nodrog who had understood the secret encryptions written in the works of Michel Nostradamus and translated them, he had at first been reluctant to believe it, but then she had told him of Katie's bloodline and who her mother and father was , it was a strange world these days and he had no reason not to believe what he was told, but now he wondered if they meant harm to her, he had gone to visit Leron where he slept but did not enter for he had heard voices, it was Werdna Taylor the Nemlaer king.

"Leron it is your duty, not just to your people but to the world."

"I was sent to stay with the dwarf and warn my cousins and make alliances with those I can for the upcoming war, my people have known the change in the earth for a while now this is my duty, I don't know what it is you are asking of me."

"Yes you do, all I am telling you is that the girl must not board the Greys' ship by any means necessary you must stop this if she does we are all doomed."

"You should be telling Xela this"

"He only thinks he can save her what if he can't he could not or would not think of any other possib..."

Xela had walked away then not wanting to know what else would be said the thought that he could not save Katie had not and did not enter his mind he would save her, it was a promise to himself and no one was going to hurt her he would make sure of that. They were all to leave at first light, the monk girl had spoken with him asking if she and the cat could accompany him, he agreed he liked the cat and the cat seemed to like him, where ever he went she seemed to follow him and he knew she was following him now though he could not see her he could sense her, he smiled to himself feeling like he had some kind of guardian.

He had been walking sometime now beyond the Nemlaer village when he came across a Nymph, it was Luceria she was sitting beside a great oak tree, it was dark and with no light his eyes glowed like a cat caught in the headlights, he had no problems seeing in the dark. since he had been healed by these people, he had never felt this strong or well since he had been poisoned by the dart even after Francis had healed him certain abilities had never returned until now the Nymphs were truly great healers.

"How did you find this place?" Lucy's voice was calming melting away all other thoughts that was in Xela's mind.

"I...dont know I was just walking." He felt as though he had done something wrong.

"This is a sacred place, you know not even the Nemlaer could find this place and they live beside our lands, you truly are special."She turned and faced the tree as if their conversation was finished.

"It was you, wasn't it?" Xela was nervous, he did not know if it was because she was half naked or because he was mesmerized by her beauty but he felt as though he was acting like a shy school boy.

She turned to face him.

"In my dream, you warned me to run."

"Yes, we have the ability to enter ones dreams, who was the girl in your dream you seemed fond of her?"

"I don't know I... I don't remember much about before ..." he trailed off.

"It does not matter I have been watching you for awhile you are truly remarkable Xela or should I call you Alex."

She laughed and giggled childishly then she placed her hand on the oak becoming serious once again. Xela wondered for a moment if she was slightly unhinged or if it was the way of her people.

"Can you not hear him, come feel?"

He walked to the oak and placed his hand on the tree also.

"Do you feel it?"

He was surprised that he did feel something, it was as if the tree had a pulse every moment he touched it he could feel it, stronger and stronger the pulse became.

"He is Deidtahtlla, the only Male Nymph ever born, it was a miracle that our Ancient grandmother almost two thousand years ago bore a male child before she returned to the earth, it had never been heard of before so he was deemed special a saviour of our people or even the world. When he grew from a root to a man he..."

"A root" Xela said confused?

"Yes did you not know we are of the earth, we are the closest beings to Mother Nature, we are her first children."

"Okay" Xela was still unsure of what she was talking

about but he let her continue.

"Well he grew to a man and was expected to pick one of the Nemlaer's women or a nymph to mate with but instead he left our forest and our realm and went out into the world and took a worldly women it was a shame and also against our laws, so our people went out and retrieved him and he was imprisoned in tree form until his spirit will be called back to the earth, but to this day he is the oldest and wisest of us all, mother nature converse with him all the time so his wisdom and words are always revered."

"The tree speaks?"

"Yes but only Nymph can hear him; I am surprised that you can feel his pulse."

"I never told you I could"

"I know but I can feel it flow through your veins like you are one with him, you only found this place because he wanted you too"

"What do you mean?"

"You don't know a lot do you, let me explain something's about my people and the Nemlaer, come sit with me."

Xela sat beside Lucy and she began telling him about the rituals of her people, he learned about the Nemlaer that became changelings, it had been eight of the Nemlaer that had saved him from the faceless ones they had lost a comrade during the battle he had learned that much at the meeting earlier, there had been a sorrow amongst the people and with his heart ripped from his body there was nothing the Nymph could do for him, there would be a ritual in the morning before they were to leave, the Nemlaer's fallen comrade would return to the earth. But Luceria continued telling Xela that his bloodline was different and she had suspected something and the Oak tree knew the truth of things but was not ready to reveal it.

"But all truths eventually reveal themselves."

She kissed Xela firmly on the lips then leapt up and skipped and danced away.

"I will see you in the morning" She giggled as she vanished into the trees.

He had learned a lot and whilst feeling very drawn to the strange Nymph girl, his thoughts were now on tomorrow and saving Katie.

The following morning all came out to the ceremony, Leron had never realised that so many Nemlaer lived in this one village, for as far as he could look back and all around there were people, there had to be over a thousand at the gathering all carrying cups with wine in them. Ola and his pack had prepared the body of their fallen comrade Divad, his body had remained in wolf form, on passing he would normally return to human form but this only happened with the last beat of his heart, but as his heart was taken he remained as a wolf. Divad was placed on a bed of leafs on a wooden table made from a log, the crowd was silent and Ola stood before the gathering holding his cup.

"Divad was of my wolf clan, and for you who did not know him, he was the bravest of us all." He paused a moment "he was wise beyond his years and I found he sometimes kept me inline" Ola's eyes became teary.

"No Nemlaer could ever replace him but he died fighting to protect the rest of us and our home. These are dark days my people and I fear more of us will pass before the dark is done, but we must SOLDEIR ON! As Divad did and FIGHT LIES and RECTIFY the TRUTH... TO DIVAD!"

Ola raised his cup and for as far as one's eyes could see all the villagers raised theirs and knocked back the wine from their cups it was then the song came, a melody so sweet and pure flowing all around as the Nymphs all dressed in see through white gowns with Isnat at the head of them, (Xela had not realised there had been so many of them,) walking in unison in an arrow shape formation came over four hundred of them, the trees themselves seem to part and made the clearing in the forest even bigger for all the Nymphs to fit in. As they sang leafs swirled around everyone's head as though there was a breeze but there was not one. The leafs swirled around until they gathered themselves around Divad spinning so fast that one could no longer see the body, the song of the Nymphs became stronger and louder pitchers reaching levels that Xela did not think was possible until at last they were silent, the leafs fluttered around only a little more before resting on and around the now human form of Divad. He was a long dark haired man with what appeared to be a wolfish beard upon his chin, Isnat spoke.

"As human he began" her voice almost sang. "And as a hero he will return to our gracious mother."

It was then roots raised up from the ground wrapping themselves around him pulling the table and Divad down into the ground, all stood and watched, tears rolling down faces as they said their goodbyes, and Divad and the log table was pulled entirely under the earth, there was silence again. For a long moment there was nothing whispered or even said until at last the earth began to shake as though there was an earthquake, Xela was a little worried but no one else seemed to be, so he stood his ground and watched as a carved monument raised out of the ground in the same spot where the earth had swallowed Divad, it was a remarkable piece of art, if one looked from one side they would see a Wolf but if one looked from the other side they would see a perfect carving of Divad crouched down naked on all fours. But to look head on at the creation you would see a monument with an half wolf half man face, it was remarkable.

"This monument is a gift from Mother Earth, so we may never forget our fallen companion and for us to know his soul has become part of the earth."

The people cheered and drums began to play, what was once a quiet almost eerie moment had become a party where the Nemlaer now rejoiced that their friend was now in a great place.

"It's time to go my friend" Leron was beside Xela "The dragon awaits us."

The monk who Xela now knew as Yatnahc came over.

"He will leave us in Paris he has some..."

"I know he told me." Xela answered.

"You can hear him?" Yatnahc was surprised.

"Yes don't ask me how, let's go."

They began to walk to where they knew Drawoh waited, as they got closer Luceria stepped out from the trees.

"I am coming with you."

"No you can't" Xela knew from what she had told him the night before that they were not allowed to interfere with the world of beings.

"It is my fault that Katie came this way therefore I am partly responsible for her capture, I am coming with you and I won't take no for an answer."

Xela looked to the monk and Leron who seemed to have no complaint.

"Okay, lets go."

They reached Drawoh who had what one could call a great metal carriage of sorts fastened to his back and the cat already sitting inside.

"I asked the elements and they made it for us so we may fly safe." Lucy said.

Wondering what other powers this girl possessed Xela climbed the ladder that was at Drawoh's side and so did the others seating themselves in the carriage. The great dragon wings began to flap causing a mini windstorm to blow through the villagers and their party, all now looked up to see the dragon fluttering its wings before it turned and flew off towards the west.

Werdna Taylor watched.

"Do not let them leave with the girl" He said silently as if Leron could hear his words.

"And may Mother Nature be with you."

He pulled his great fur about him and returned to his queen.

∧
—

The battle had been fierce; cannons fired across the waters obliterating the small boats that were exiting the narrow water way, the sea rocked the ships back and forth as though it was in a rage, angry that all these beings dared to ride her waves. The only consolation was that the Elfin ships were not equipped as the Daring or the Sharron or even the Argol, these Elfin ships were cargo ships, made from wood and quickly armed only for this day. It had been no problem getting past the ship that had blocked their path of escape, two torpedoes from the Daring quickly cut through their bowels exploding and sinking the ship in a blaze of fire almost immediately, "such ships were never made for battle" the captain had thought, sailing swiftly through the Narrow way out.

Out into the sea they had found that their fight had not been over, a small armada of Elfin cargo ships all armed with cannons awaited, they were not dumb and they were not willing to let them escape so easily, the ships had formed an half circle blocking off their escape they were surrounded but the captain was going to go down fighting, bullet had spoken with him over the radio explaining that they would now have to work with blackheart if they had any chance of surviving this, knowing the situation the captain agreed and the three ship's positioned themselves in a triangle shape protecting what was left of the small fishing boats at their centre. It had been fifteen minutes since that battle had commenced, breaking formation they had already sunk five of the ships but now all three of them were taking heavy damage they sailed now all taking their own target as the cannons fired hitting the waters and hitting them, they had left the small boats to fend for themselves the Elfin ships had concentrated their attack on them, now the boats may have a chance of escape, but the three captains had the overwhelming feeling that it would be here they would die.

—

Tsicar was a pale skinned red eyed elf, he believed in the rule of Maxius much like most of the men that he had been sent here with, but his mission here today was not the same as his commanders, but his orders had come directly from Maxius himself. He had once been a palace guard always grateful to be so near to his king, he had done work, secret work for his king before with the help of Elpoep the Orcus guard of Maxius personal chambers.

Some years back they had been asked to dispose of a family, one that spoke out against his king, at first he had thought it wrong being bold he explained to the king that no elf should ever harm another elf that was the law that was their way the Elfin way. But Maxius had explained that a new day was coming and showed him that he was now the Law revealing to him a power that was not light but dark, Flames burned in his hands but yet Maxius was not burned, and then the flames rose to a great fire engulfing his entire body and when the flames went out the king was left unharmed. The powers of nature had left most of them it was no longer easy for any elf to command the elements only a few still had the gift but none had displayed such strength.

"This is the power we will all have, we need not nature's permission to wield such strength, we will all be like Nature ourselves if we change our laws to what I believe in, do you want this power?"

He tempted him and seeing it he knew he wanted it, he had carried out his mission that night setting the family's home on fire while they slept trapping them in so they could not escape they were burned alive. The next morning he woke and found that his vision was sharper and his eyes had become as red as blood, Maxius had told him that this was a step on the right path and when the new day arrived he would wield a power such as his. Since then he never questioned anything his Lord asked of him, he had become part of the Legion like he was told, over half the men were red eyed and were also loyal and under strict orders from the king, but now he would do his part.

He climbed the steps of the old cathedral building, though the building was crumbling and he had to be careful where he stepped encase he fell, he was still surprised that that the Notre Dam church still stood after so many years. When he reached the top he took out the human made weapon that he was given, putting all its parts together and loading the rifle he took a moment finding his target as the one he was looking for stood so very far away, he would have to calculate for the wind but he had practised and he had hit a target this far away before, he waited now it was not time yet, he had to make sure that it was at the right moment.

The plan had been set, Andre now stood face to face with the Elfin woman, who had said she came for peace, they had agreed to meet at this place, it was known as the Invalides Church, a place that did not look much like a church any longer, all that stood was the pillars that had once held this place together, steps led them to its centre he had come from the north and she the south, and now they stood in the middle of the ruins' with nothing but a monument between them, the monument was at the centre of this place covered in filth it was still apparent that it was made from something red and its base was made from a green type granite. It was here the stories said that an emperor was buried, this place was known as the Tomb of Napoleon and if an emperor was buried here then it seem fit that Elfin occupation in Paris would end here, he smiled at the thought.

He stood now before her and her two companions, looking behind them some way he could clearly see around three hundred Elves, armed with laser weapons they had acquired from the Greys, some had human weapons which the Elves also seem to stock pile and right at the back were the Archers, they always had archers he thought to himself, most people fear an Elfin arrow more than a bullet they flew as fast and instead of killing you out right most found they suffered much before they died.

"Give me a bullet any day" he thought, but he himself had not come alone, on his right stood Pops and on his left was Lewis, he had let Suinuj join Vlad and his group though Andre had five hundred men in clear sight some way behind them showing the Elves that they too were well armed and prepared for whichever way this day would end, he had thought it best that Suinuj went with Vlad not wanting to antagonise these Elves by approaching them with a dwarf all knew the hatred they had for them he would give them no excuse to attack, if they were truly here for peace then he would hear them out, Vlad had sixty men he had gone to where the Alien craft would land if everything went to plan then they may just have a chance.

Vlad had found his way to the roof of one of the buildings not far away from the place they called the Eiffel, It was known that once a great Tower stood here but the war had brought it destruction like most of the city of Paris, all that remained of the once great Tower was four iron legs that reached the height of a tall human, it appeared that something had ripped up the top of the famous landmark and discarded it out of plain sight, the Greys had weapons that probably took the thing to space, Vlad wondered. Andre had allowed sixty men to go with them and now all laid in wait, waiting for the go ahead waiting for the flying ship to arrive and the Orcus to make their move, he knew it would not be long now, looking through the lens of his sniper rifle he could see one of his given men up on one of the buildings across the way, he had sent fifteen of the men on other buildings to help pick off as many as they could when the fighting began, he focused again on the task at hand, things must not go wrong as this would be their only chance.

Lrac was a Legend amongst his people, he was known as the most fierce fighter of all their kingdom, he had led armies into battle time and time again during the wars for King Lithor and had won many victories, when his king died he continued to do his duty for his king and once friend Maxius, they had been close once they were childhood friends, but things had changed he detected a long time ago that Maxius no longer liked him and he wonder if the king thought he wanted to rule. It was Lrac and his army that won the final battle between the humans and the Greys, at the time America had already fallen leaving over half the country desolate and inhabitable, it was mostly the humans themselves that had caused this by using Nuclear weapons on their own lands trying to wipe out the millions of Orcus and drones that had been taking over the country one state at a time.

It was England where the humans made their last stand and it was Lrac and his men that brought down their defences at the Battle of London, it was here they had taken all their best technology and weapons of war and half made force fields protecting them from attacks from the sky, the city could have been under siege for years, but Lrac had gotten through and once that happened the Orcus invaded killing like wild beast. They were filthy creatures with no emotion not even flinching when they killed defenceless women and children London had been won but yet the killing went on for days. They hunted humans as though it was a sport making Lrac wonder why Elves had business with such beings. It wasn't until a week had passed that the Greys gave permission for the Elves to police the city giving them command over the Orcus, he had made sure certain laws were put in place and enforced and allowed the surviving human to stay and live in peace, his people saw him as merciful and his battle and fair play spread throughout the Elfin kingdom, rumours had then started, people whispered saying that after Lithors death he should have been king, and questioned where Maxius was during the fighting but all knew he stayed home, but Lrac would never want the throne, he was a warrior and his mission in life was to protect his people and his world.

He had thought it strange that Maxius would not allow him to bring more than twenty of his own trusted men, Elves he had fought with during the war, being limited he took only the best on this venture fearing that the humans could not be trusted on this peace mission, so now he stood on the right side of Anairda with Anaird on her left facing the leader of the resistance, the man had just introduced himself when Lrac felt a pain in his back that went through to his chest something splattered a little on his face and on to the man named Andre it was blood, feeling his chest and looking to his bloody hands he realised he had been shot from behind, he collapsed and Anairda caught him.

The Alien craft was hovering coming down to land where the Eiffel tower once stood, it was always a site to see whenever their crafts landed here. Suinuj had watched from afar in the past but never before had he been so close to one as he was today, he marvelled at the sight, unlike the

Aeroplanes back at the base their crafts engines were almost silent only making a wisp as quiet as a strong breeze, it was almost a circle shape disc, though its shape was slightly oblong, an amber light could be seen pulsating from underneath as it came lower and lower, he was ready for them.

The Orcus came across the square walking in a two line formation with the dwarfin prisoners hands bound at their centre, in front was one of the twelve wearing a hooded cloak, he had heard that two of the Twelve were masters to the others and that these masters were distinct because they wore cloaks with hood such as this one, the others did not, they wore long dark Macs, showing their bald pale head with the mask with no face that made one not want to reveal what was behind it. He hoped this was not a master as these beings were the most dangerous of them all. The dark sensation of the creature's presence had made him a little worried hoping that it did not put fear into the hearts of his men. It would not be long now before the prisoners would board the craft just as he thought this he heard the weapons fire in the distance, Andre and the resistance were now at war and he wonder if there would still be a resistance before this day was over, Readying himself he gave the order and his men began firing at the Orcus.

He had found his target and taken his shot, He watched through the lens of his weapon as Lrac fell into Anairda's arms, he would have taken another shot to make sure of the job, but she had moved him to cover too quick, his mission was complete Lrac was dead and his master would be pleased, all who threatened the new way that was to come must perish and the red eye Elves that had come on this venture understood this and now they were doing their part, it was a pity that Anairda too would now die after all she was very attractive, Maxius may have given her too him when the new day arrived.

"Hmm it's a shame" He said out loud as he dismantled his weapon throwing its parts in at different angles into the river. He then left the Church he would not join the battle between elf and elf and man, it was not his duty he would return home and let his king know the good news.

⁁
—

They had been moving running fast for a day and a night nonstop needing no rest or food these being were abnormal, they had sustained only minor injuries during their fight but it had not bothered them much they were modified to tolerate such things, to be able to take damage and continue. All traces of their former lives had been eradicated, wiped out from their memories all they knew now was to serve their masters and there was nothing they would not do for them. Their movement was almost dreamy, trees whizzed past them making one believe that these beings were actually floating running on air their feet not touching the ground. One of the masked creatures held the girl firmly over its shoulder, it had drugged her and she would not wake before the mission was completed. They had now passed the great wind machines

"It would not be long now" One of the things thought, they moved on swiftly and as they moved a darkness began to fall over the city of Paris.

Laser fire and bullets were flying all over the Invalides, the group of six were pinned down, it had not been the humans that had caused this it was Anairda's own men, Lrac had been shot in the back she had seen this herself and now ten of his own men were trying to make it to the tomb. The redeye had turned crazy, killing their brothers as if they were an enemy race, she had never thought such a thing possible that she would see the day when an elf other than Maxius would intentionally hurt another elf, The white-eye Elves that had travelled here with them were now dead, she had seen them run to her and were lasered down shot in the back and arrowed as if they were vermin, she was still in a state of shock and there was nothing she could do to help Lrac's men who now fought for their lives to escape they were the only white eye left and Anairda wondered if the red meant to kill all white eyes.

"It err seems that your king does not err like you, come you will be safe with us."

They had ducked down behind the red monument that was now taking heavy fire; Anaird was firing arrows back feeling disgusted at himself every time he killed one of his brethren. The two humans Andre had brought were also firing killing his brothers his people making him want to turn his arrows on them for doing such a thing in his presence, but they now fought beside him making him confused at what exactly was going on, he no longer knew who the enemy was, Anairda was still holding Lrac who was bleeding uncontrollably.

"Let me up I will fight" he insisted but it was a bad wound and she held him not allowing him to move.

"If we retreat we will be shot down" She addressed the human.

"My men will buy us some time."

The strange French man pulled out a flare gun and fired it behind him over his men's heads who had found cover. It was a signal and moments later a human vehicle with a large cannon gun rolled from amongst the nearby buildings into the clearing it was a tank, she had not seen one since the war believing that the Greys had destroyed nearly if not all of the human's war machines. The tank rolled forward and fired into the Elfin horde killing a few, the redeye now spanned out finding good cover giving Anairda and the group time to retreat to the human defences, Lrac's men followed losing only two along the way they were now at war and the Elves would not leave so easily.

It did not take long for the Orcus to form up a circle in their defence, during the confusion one of the dwarves broke free and ran off towards one of the old derelict buildings only three Orcus pursued him while the other stood to defend themselves.

"Hey Knarf," Vlad said.

"I hear ya" A voice came back over the small communication radio that was given out amongst the men so they could keep in contact.

"I got an escapee your side two blocks north take three and go hunting my friend."

"Got it"

"And be careful he has three unfriendly's in pursuit."

"Copy"

Vlad took this to mean he understood and hope they would find him, a bound dwarf against three Orcus was not a fair fight, he continued firing his rifle the Orcus and their master must know by now that they were surrounded. The snipers were finding their targets and were picking them off one by one from a distance, while the ground troops fired repeatedly making sure they avoided the captured dwarves while they keep as safe as they could behind the cover of the rubble of buildings that were all around. The Orcus fought back firing and hitting a few of Suinuj's men, then the dark faceless being that travelled with them invoked a power causing a small energy field to form somewhat around them giving the Orcus a little cover from their attack. The snipers above still found and hit their targets, but the group of Orcus and their master began to move steadily towards the now landed Craft.

It was as they moved that Vlad noticed two of the

snipers leaping from the rooftops where they were placed, hitting the ground with a thud. At first he had thought they were suicide nuts, but he watched the faceless being motion with its right hand, while he concentrated his left to holding the force field it had created— more to protect its self than the Orcus. Another sniper was lifted off the ground and thrown off the roof, he had no idea these creatures could do such a thing from such a great distance, down below the Orcus were nearing the ship, and the voice of his father played in his mind reminding him of what he should do if he could not save them.

    Suinuj realising the Orcus had almost reached the craft ordered his men to move out to cut them off, leading the way he rushed out with his men in toe from their cover and blocked the road. Firing their laser bolt weapons the Orcus were now killing his men with more ease, the once hundred Orcus had now diminished to around thirty, but in clear open combat they were masters at their trade and their trade was killing, without breaking a stride they marched forward taking multiple bullets they continued the faceless beings energy field providing enough cover making it hard for his men to find headshots, they came at them fearless breaking the human line of defence, they no longer needed weapons this close they preferred to snap Suinuj's men's necks like they were snapping twigs, but Suinuj was strong and fast, firing his weapon with one hand he removed his blade from his waist with the other whilst leaping into the air he pierced two Orcus through the centre of their heads before he landed, now he was in his element, close combat was how he liked it, up and personal against these things, these destroyers of lands he would make them pay as best he could.

    The battle was bloody and though the snipers still left upon the roof tops helped, the dwarf had already lost most of his men, but the Orcus could not handle him, and the dark creature was too busy shielding itself from the bullets that was still being fired at it, so while Suinuj fought he broke the bonds of the captured prisoners who in turn joined the battle, with the dwarfs free he thought for a moment that they had a chance, that was until the day turned to night as what appeared to be a very dark cloud fell over them all and its presence brought fear and Suinuj's remaining men ran and before he knew it Suinuj was running too, he looked around the dwarves were running with him, when he looked back he realised they still held firm to one dwarf, and one was all they needed.

^
—

Two tanks now rolled forward and the army of soldiers spread out pushing forward behind the tanks firing at the enemy. Four of the white eye moved forwards to join the humans.

"Elswye, horcory swylesia!" Anairda ordered, she had told them to stop, "We will kill no more brothers today."

Eleven elf's and four humans watched as the human army forced the Elves to retreat.

"Where will they go" Andre asked?

"Back to the Elfin garrison Regor will not be pleased." Anairda said not paying much attention to the Andre she was still worried about Lrac.

"Then we shall lay siege; no offence, me lady, but your people here today killed many good men. I will not sleep until your people leave my city."

Anairda understood but for now she did not care, first she will help Lrac back to health and then she would see what could be done about her king Maxius.

"Come I have my men take you somewhere you will err...be safe" Andre understood that none of this was their doing, he had thought it naive of the lady to believe Maxius would really agree to peace between them and the elf nation, and now for once an elf might see their king for what he really was, an evil power crazy elf. The white eye came to help Lrac on his feet when they all looked up and saw the dark cloud that was coming and already they could feel its evil.

    Xela was desperate he had left the others behind running while he ran as fast as he could with Leron only a short way behind. The dragon had set them down somewhere in Paris and flown off on his own mission leaving Yatnahc and Xela with images letting them know that he would one day return with help when the time was right, not really thinking on what he meant Xela concentrated on saving Katie, the darkness was near and he followed it like a lion to the scent of blood, he navigated the streets astonished at how this once great city had become nothing but rubble. He had been here once, he could vaguely remember, it was a city of lights and wonder and this is what war had turned it too.

    He moved fast still knowing that he was gaining on his prey, he could feel them they were close, the evilness spread all around like a plague, not bringing fear but anger, he was angry that they had took her from him making him leave her causing him to break his promise, he ran now along a straight path crossing one of the few remaining bridges that still stood he glanced at the river as he passed not even considering too much the blackness of it, there was nothing but death and sickness in its waters, it was toxic waste that had made it what it was and any being would be a fool to even touch it.

    The darkness was all around, it appeared to be almost night, he heard someone calling from behind, it was Leron, with no time to stop his eyes adjusted for the dark and he kept moving on, it wasn't long before he saw them, walking bold now toward a large oblong disc that sat where the

Eiffel tower once stood, the Eiffel Tower he remembered this, there were men running and Dwarves, "dwarves" they had to be Vlad's guys, but the faceless things were using their energy walking and throwing the running men through the air without getting close or even laying a finger on them, they thought together they were invincible, but Xela was angry and would soon find out how invincible they really were.

It was too late for the masked being that trailed behind the rest of them, it had not senses nor heard Xela's presence or footsteps behind him, this was unnatural as they were tuned into most things, but Xela was now fuming an energy that they could not detect, an energy that was fuelled by his rage, the creature did not think it was possible that it could feel so much pain as the blow from the dark strange man sent it flying, still in pain it tried to regain its thinking to muster up enough energy to control its fall, but by the time it could it was already too late, it fell into the poison river, a fire lit up its body as it made contact with the dark liquid substance it wriggled in the river of flames trying to swim free and then the scream came, so loud it was that it reached into the souls of every living being within five miles, echoing also in Xela's head he ignored it, he would not be deterred pushing past the scream that would cause any normal human too much pain he moved forwards ready to deal with the rest.

Knarf had taken Heffer Zepol and a young man named Nicolas, he was French and spoke English the best he could, they had moved away from the battle and spread themselves out evenly so still insight of each other as they moved silently through the wreck and rubble of the buildings, the gun fire could be heard but now they moved away through one building into the next, three Orcus were out here somewhere and an escape dwarf was hiding also. It was Heffer that had heard movement to the left outside the building they had entered, he raised his fist, and the other three stopped, using hand signals he let the others know to follow him.

Moving outside and still away from the battle they all found cover behind rubble and Knarf stood on the corner of a building they had blocked off the narrow road, and the three Orcus were moving slowly and quietly with their back towards them in search of the Dwarf, Knarf signalled and they all fired immediately killing the three Orcus before they had a chance to turn, bullets passed through their skulls and they dropped in the narrow street staining it with their blood. The four men moved out, the dwarf was here somewhere as the Orcus were in pursuit of him, walking forward passed the bodies of the Orcus they soon found him the dwarf hands still bound and muscle tissue wasted away, he had been tortured underfed and beaten badly, the small man was exhausted and had curled up at the end of the street with no energy to push on further. Knarf broke his bonds, and pulled out his canteen offering him water.

"Have no fear friend I am Knarf we are here to help, we have been sent by your fellow brother Vlad."

The dwarf could barely speak being out of breath but his face lit up upon hearing Vlad's name.

"He... he came for us...I... knew he would, thank you friend... I am Mada and forever... in your debt."

The four men moved to help the dwarf on his feet when gun shots went off hitting Nicolas in his back, Nicolas dropped and the other three men moved to cover around the corner at the end of the street where they had found Mada, dragging Nicolas with them, Vlad took a peak, there were about fifteen of them maybe more, but he noticed the one with the horned helmet as it took cover and sent its men forward, they had tracked them here across lands to France, and now was the time for it all to end, Zepol threw a smoke grenade filling the street with smoke, while Heffer and Knarf began shooting giving cover fire so Zepol could make it across the street opposite Knarf and the others, this was a good place to pin them down and pick them off one by one.

They shot from both positions through the smoke as Orcus shapes immerged, multiple rounds were fired from both sides but it was the Orcus that were moving forward in the open and it was them that took the heavy casualties, one by one they dropped some died instantly receiving the bullet to the head while others took multiple gun rounds to the body eventually slowing them until they dropped and bled out, Zepol took a shot to the shoulder stopping him momentarily, he ripped a piece of clothing and stuffed it firmly down his jacket to slow the bleeding, the streets then went quiet, the Orcus that were left had taken cover behind rubble and neither side were firing. "There could be no more than five or six of them left" the thought crossed Knarf's mind, it was then Nicolas began coughing and trying to sit up, the boy was not dead, Vlad tended to him while Heffer kept an eye out, pulling of his jacket there was no wound, the kid had been smart he had taken a flap jacket, bulletproof but not entirely laser proof, if these Orcus had lasers they would of burned through the jacket into his back leaving him to die slowly without help, the only real wound were the bruises to his back and a bullet wound that seemed to have gone right through his arm, Knarf tied it up the best he could, then signalled to Zepol.

The man across the street watched as his commander took a grenade and attached a wire to the pin using duck tape he firmly fixed the grenade to the wall on the corner and finding a stick he dug it into the earth attaching the wire to it, it was a trap what was known as a trip wire, Knarf then told Heffer to take Nicolas and the dwarf to the far wall of the building behind them and find cover and they did.

Zepol knew what to do, he pulled the pin from a grenade he was holding and threw it out to where the Orcus were and then ran, he headed back towards Knarf and the Orcus began firing, the grenade landed and exploded giving Zepol time to reach the other side, they did not know if they had hit any but now they retreated and the Orcus knew they were on the run, moving forward they did not think to look to the ground as they reached the corner, all five of them were bunched up as the first Orcus tripped the wired, the explosion had knocked them flying, while bringing part of the building down on top of them.

It was over, the Orcus that had tracked and killed Xela were dead, the small battered group pulled themselves up from there hiding places and slowly began to return to where they had left their men in battle, but on reaching the corner, bricks from the rubble flew up.

The horned Orcus grabbed Knarf smashing him into the ground with its mighty strength, Zepol Heffer and Nicolas unloaded their guns into the creature, while Knarf battered climbed to his feet unsheathing his knife, he swiped slitting the creatures throat as blood rushed from its neck onto Knarf, the creature fell forward onto him knocking their leader to the ground, they all moved to push the great weight of the tall beast off Knarf when the scream came, it was so loud they all thought they were sure to die, covering their ears they fell to their knees, what on Gods earth could have caused such a sound were the thoughts of most of them as they curled up like small children on the ground.

Vlad watched as the men ran, the darkness was all around but his scope on his rifle was equipped with some kind of night vision, he could clearly see that they still held one of his men, it was Vali, ten Orcus had survived their attack and remained and now eleven of the dark faceless creatures had joined them, he could not believe his eyes one of them was carrying Katie, so he was surprised and also a little relieved when Xela appeared out of nowhere knocking one of those things so high that it disappeared from his vision.

A short while after that the scream began he covered his ears, but it did no good, he curled up now in a ball on the roof; the pain was unbearable, the pitch was so high his eardrums began to bleed he almost laughed at the thought that this was going to be the way that he died and just as he thought it the sound stopped.

He clambered back to his feet picking up his rifle he looked through the scope, there was no sound anywhere not even the sound of the breeze passed his ears, or the screaming men that were down below holding their ears as they got back to their feet to run, it was then he knew he was now deaf, four of the faceless ones held Xela in his tracks using all their energy to freeze him while the others began to board the ship, it was too late for Vali he knew what he had to do, finding his target he was about to shoot when he was hit on the head, surprised he looked up and saw Leron .

Leron had been trying to keep up with Xela but the man was fast and would not slow down however loud he shouted at him, he arrived only seconds behind just in time to see a flying member of the twelve head into the river, he had intended to help Xela but after the scream the others were alerted to his presence and four of them used their power to hold Xela at bay, he could see behind the four that the others were still headed to the ship but there was no way pass the four creatures without having to fight them and there would be no time to save the girl, it was then he caught a glimpse of someone on one of the roof tops he knew who it was, words flooded his mind making him realise what was at stake here, he ran now a tears rolling as he moved fast climbing the steps faster than any normal being could, he did not want to do what had to be done but there was no other way, he would hate himself forever and he would never be forgiven nor did he expect it, he reached the top and found Vlad, shouting at him the stubborn dwarf did not respond not until he hit him on the head.

"Leron, where did you come from?"

"Listen you must do as I..."

"Don't bother I can't hear you" the dwarf shouted as if he thought Leron couldn't hear him "I think I am deaf."

Leron thought quickly and wrote in the dirt on the roof, Vlad could not believe what he had read.

"Now" Leron shouted "Now."

The dwarf could not hear his words but understood what he meant, he now aimed with his weapon, not seeing clearly as tears flooded his eyes, he aimed at Vali, his brother in arms a dwarf he had taught to hunt who was like family to him he knew Vali would understand he knew this and then he shot the dwarf clean through the centre of his head and before he could reconsider his next action he aimed at Katie and pulled the trigger, it was then everything seemed slow, the bullet glided through the air piercing Katie's heart, penetrating her body like a dart to a beautiful red apple, the blood splattered on the creatures Mac that was holding her and Vlad dropped the gun and began to sob uncontrollably.

Leron tried to comfort the dwarf while he also shed tears, but below Xela had heard the shot and saw Katie as she died, the fury in him now was uncontrollable, he gained a strength that even the Twelve did not think was possible, he was walking fighting their energy pushing them backwards, they struggled with every fibre of their being to hold him but they could not, the others were already on the ship, but all could hear Xela cry, his voice echoed bouncing off nearby objects, it was a cry of anguish of anger of pain, the four had turned and began to move fast towards the ship and Xela now pursued them.

He grabbed one and the others turned to fight him, he was like a man possessed, they could not move as wild or as fast as this being, they could not believe this was the same man they thought they had killed back in the forest, this being was more powerful more dangerous and even more stronger.

He blocked their blows with ease; striking one he put his fist through its body and out its back pushing the thing to the ground. He had thought it would be dead but now it crawled toward the ship, it was not blood that had stained his hand it was a white substance and though it burned he could not feel the pain. He was overwhelmed by anger and spilling these things white poisonous burning blood was all he wanted no matter how much of it he burned himself with, it was a few moments after that he found himself hovering frozen high above the ground and above the buildings suspended in the air he watched as the four creatures retreated into the ship.

Looking below him he could see a small thin being naked with no genitals or chest of any kind its body was thin and one straight shape it had an overly large grey head with very big black eyes, so black and dark there was nothing but emptiness behind them, it stood with its grey body holding out one finger pointing at him, it was like hearing Drawoh, it showed pictures to his mind letting him know it was too late for all of them making him feel the emotion of despair the feeling it promised the whole world will feel soon, it dropped its finger letting Xela drop also from a great height, his body slammed into the earth causing the ground to crack, the creature returned to its ship certain that would be the last it would see of this being, Xela laid unable to move and watched as the craft lifted off and headed into the sky, they had taken Katie's body and he wouldn't even get to bury her, as the ship disappeared into the distance, the misty daylight returned once again, there was nothing now, nothing left for Xela to live for, he hoped no one would come and help him so he could just lay there and die.

16

The Parting

It had been two days since the battle at the tower, and Xela woke in a tent, they had fixed him up and Lucy was beside him, he woke but he was not pleased.
"Who did it?" He asked.
Lucy looked ashamed she knew what he meant but felt like she could not answer.
"Who Fucking did it?"
"He had too he has never forgiven himself"
Lucy tried to explain, but Xela was already out of his bed and walking through the camp, there were men everywhere soldiers fully armed a few tanks rolled along he felt like he was walking amongst soldiers from the British army or something,
"Where the hell are we?"
Lucy had followed him.
"We are still in Paris, the soldiers here are laying siege to the Elfin station they are planning to claim back Paris"
"Lucy please tell me who did it?" he asked her calmly
And she thought he was sincere.
"It was the dwarf Vladlin Bowen" she said sorrowfully.
Xela turned from calm to mad shouting as he moved through the camp.
"VLADLIN! WHERE ARE YOU VLADLIN

BOWEN"

His voice bellowed and it caused a stir amongst the men, "VLAD WHERE ARE YOU!"

Vlad came through the crowd with Leron beside him and a few others, teary eyed the Dwarf looked sorrowful.

"Tears won't save you."

Vlad did not try to defend himself; he took the powerful blow from his once friend that sent him flying back through the camp knocking over many soldiers as he went.

"I will kill you," Xela cried tears rolling down his face.

If it was not for Leron and the others who held him he did not know what he would have done.

"Why" he cried "why"

"It was me my friend"

Xela looked to Leron slowly with shock and hatred in his eyes, making the Fairrien release him and face him.

"What do you mean?"

"I told him to do it, Xela we could not save her if they would have taken her alive you know what it meant you know what would have happened to us all."

"Well I don't care about you all, you're fucked up all of you" he talked to the whole crowd that surrounded him.

"This world this fucking world has gone to shits, and now you all want to fight, fight for what there nothing left but crap, and you think it's good huh," The crowd was silent and Vlad had gotten up and limped over to where Xela was shouting.

"Good, good to kill an innocent girl, a girl who wanted nothing but a normal life, to save all your own arses, well fuck you, that one girl is worth a thousand of anyone of you."

Xela pushed through the crowd.

"Xela" It was Vlad and Xela turned to face him the dwarf was injured bad from his blow and tears of sorrow flooded his eyes as he held out his bag that he had always carried.

"It is yours, papers I found when we found you are in it, I am sorry my friend I will never forgive myself for what I done."

Xela walked over to the dwarf and took the bag

"Good because I will never forgive you either, just pray we never see each other again" and then he turned and walked from the camp.

"Where will you go?" He heard Leron shouting at him as he walked off in the distance carrying his gun and his new bag over his shoulder he whispered under his breath as he limped battered and bruised.

"Anywhere away from you"

Lucy followed and Yatnahc watched as Xela walked off with the Nymph trailing behind, the cat faced her as if to say good bye then turned and followed after the dark man, it was as if she had come here for him and where he went she would now follow, she waved good bye and hoped one day they would meet again, she watched as the cat became invisible and disappeared as the dark man and the Nymph disappeared into the distance, now they had their own battle to win, they would take back Paris and with the help of a few Elves this could be the beginning of a new age.

It had been six months now since he had been in this place and he spent most of his time studying and keeping news of what was going on in the outside world, his mentor had taught him well and he had never forgotten the day when he changed his point of view about things, but who would have guessed that he would be standing here now amongst the council a respected being in their community, he had read secret scrolls and learned things, and now news had come to him of strange goings on in the outside world, so he had took his idea to Gustavius and his mentor agreed, but now he wondered if the council trusted him enough to take on such a plan.

"Eed Resarf" it was King Alex that spoke.

"Your idea is sound but I do not think we are ready as a nation or even ready to let you leave this place."

"My lord, I have read the sacred scrolls and have heard the news of the top world. The times are drawing close, already they have been able to destroy some of the maids kingdoms and now they attack the Thetford's, the home of the Fairriens, there is no such power that can do these things accept that which was written in the scrolls, these are the times and as the only elf here I swore an allegiance too you and the dwarfin kingdom and that is a trust I would never break."

"You have become wise Eed, and we will now deliberate, and if we find in favour of you, then you will have your army and the dwarf Nation will go to war."

THE END

A special thank to Joanna Bustos who without her help and input the journey would never find its end.